For Deborah —
With Warmest wishes,
Geri Fitzgerald Board
2007

The Bed She Was Born In

Jeri Fitzgerald Board

Parkway Publishers, Inc.
Boone, North Carolina

available from:
Parkway Publishers, Inc.
Post Office Box 3678
Boone, North Carolina 28607
www.parkwaypublishers.com
Tel/Fax: (828) 265-3993

Library of Congress Cataloging-in-Publication Data

Board, Jeri Fitzgerald.
The bed she was born in / Jeri Fitzgerald Board.
    p. cm.
ISBN 1-933251-22-0
1. Women--Southern States--Fiction. 2. Southern
States--Fiction. 3. Domestic fiction. I. Title.
PS3602.O16B43 2006
813'.6--dc22

2005026909

Book design by Aaron Burleson, spokesmedia
Cover and author photos courtesy of Chris Bartol
Cover photo: Fitzgerald Family Reunion, Johnston County, NC, 1914

For my parents, Suzette and Alton,
who kept the stories alive; and for
Warren, who gave me the freedom.

This book would not have been possible without the
following: the exceptional editing skills of my mother,
Suzette, known affectionately by family and friends
as "The Word Merchant"; the excellent manuscript
preparation skills of Carol Oakley and Emmy Gainey;
and the kind support of friends Georgann Eubanks,
Clyde Edgerton, Lee Smith, Jack Roper,
Dorothy Spruill Redford, Hepsi Roskelly,
and Mary Ellis Gibson.

The author would like to express her heartfelt appre-
ciation to Les Stobbe, agent; Allison Matlack, editor;
Aaron Burleson, designer; and Rao Aluri, owner of
Parkway Publishers, Inc. Thanks for believing
in me and in the women of

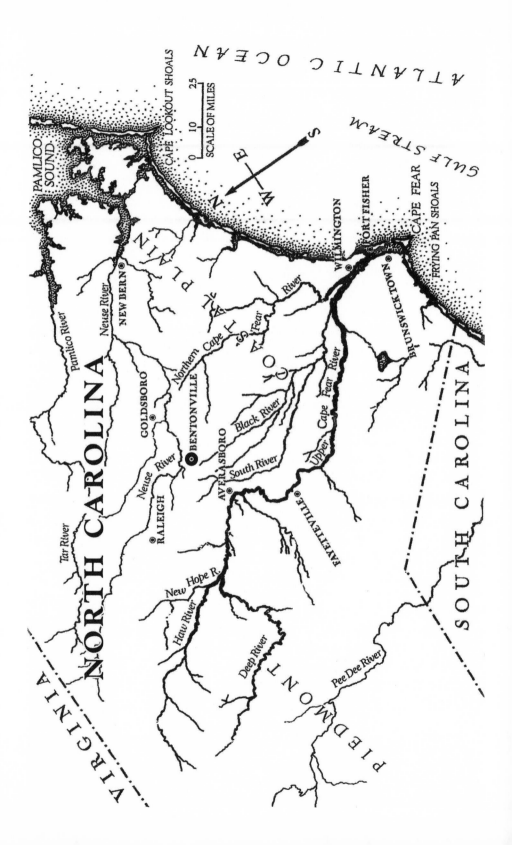

Baker is a mythical place somewhere in eastern North Carolina. The characters in this novel, with the exception of Miss Gertrude Weil of Goldsboro, are fictitious, and any resemblance to any real person is coincidental. Miss Weil was a highly-respected social and political activist who led the fight for woman's suffrage in North Carolina. While Miss Weil's philosophy and sentiment are portrayed with authenticity in Part IV of this book, the wording used therein was created entirely by the author.

The Families of Sand Hill Farm

The Sanders

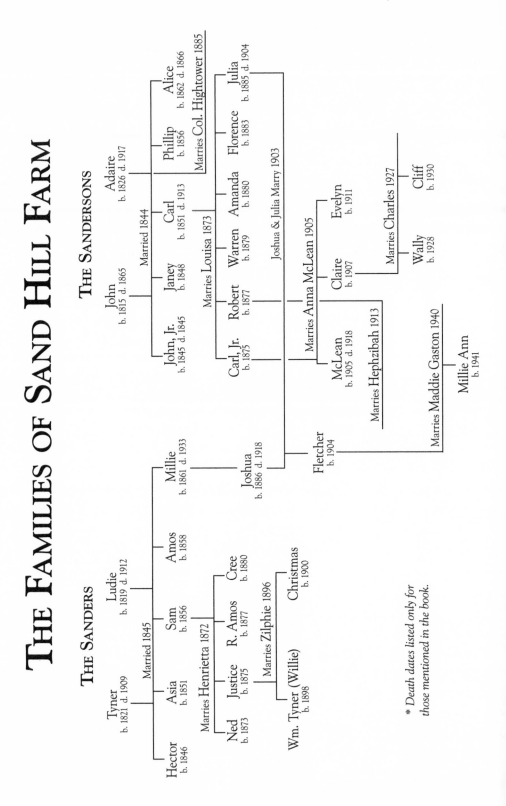

The Sandersons

*Death dates listed only for those mentioned in the book.

CONTENTS

Prologue

November 8, 1941

"You sure you want to do this today, Miss Anna?" Fletcher asks as he pushes against a small planked door. "This attic ain't seen no light for many a year. Don't look like there's nothing up here now but a old rocking chair and that trunk yonder." He steals a glance at his life-long employer. Still as tall and straight as ever, he thinks. And strong, too, even if all that coal-black hair done gone white. She gotta be closing on sixty.

Anna pauses to look around at the low-beamed room with its sooty chimney and water-stained walls. "I want this old house to be cleaned out and ready when you and your bride and stepson, and that beautiful little Millie Ann, move in next week."

Fletcher grins. "Your namesake is beautiful, ain't she? Just wish Mama could have seen her." He lets out a sigh. "Everything is gonna be fine, Miss Anna. Maddie and me mighty lucky. Guess Old Mr. Carl be turning in his grave knowing we was moving in here."

Fletcher pulls the dusty rocker from the corner, draws a bandana from his hip pocket, and dusts the seat. "You sit right here and I'll drag this old trunk over close by so you don't have to stand and bend over it. Don't want you to get too tired."

"Don't worry about old Mr. Carl, Fletcher," Anna says, picturing the florid face of her father-in-law. "He couldn't care less about any of us who are still here."

Fletcher goes to the room's only window and looks out through the squares of wavy glass. "Never been in this attic before, Miss Anna. Didn't know you could see the burying ground from up here. Old Mr. Carl's been out there nigh on to thirty years. I was just a little shaver, but I'll never forget the day he was buried. Some crowd." He turns from the window. "They're all out there now. Mama, Grandma Ludie, Papa Tyner, Miss Adaire. All gone to glory."

1

Anna sits down in the rocker and rests her head on its dusty pillow. "I know they don't miss us, but I sure do miss them. Especially your mother, Fletcher. I miss Millie every single day."

"She's up there with Saint Peter. I guess all those ugly scars is gone now 'cause they ain't supposed to be no scars on folk what gets to Heaven. And you know my mama went straight to Heaven." Fletcher crosses to where Anna sits in the rocker. "You sure you'll be all right? I don't like leaving you up here alone. It's starting to rain again."

"I'll be fine," Anna says, waving a hand at him. "You just run along to your work."

"Yessum. Better go see 'bout them boys that's loading the cotton bales down at the barn." Fletcher starts toward the attic door. "Be back to check on you in a little while." As he clumps down the steps, Anna scoots the rocker closer to the trunk. I've never been up here either, she says to herself. Wonder what I'll find.

She struggles to open the heavy lid of the trunk and the odor of stale lavender drifts up to her. Adaire, she thinks. That's what she always smelled like. Lavender. Anna peers into the trunk, where layers of ancient tissue are tucked carefully around its contents like a shroud. She gathers the graying paper into a bundle and throws it to the floor sending clouds of dust into the air around her. She sneezes once, twice, and turns back to the trunk.

Lengths of heavy dark wool, scattered with dry mouse droppings, are folded on top. When she runs her finger along the lapel of what appears to be a jacket, a silverfish darts across its collar. "Oh, my," Anna whispers, "a uniform. Perhaps it was Colonel Hightower's." Dragging the dirty jacket from the trunk, she settles it across her lap and looks closely. No, she thinks, this one is black, not blue. It probably was not his. But whose? She turns the collar toward the window, and a bit of dull light strikes the embroidered name band inside. "John Sanderson," she reads aloud. "Adaire's first husband. My husband's grandfather. This uniform belonged to him." Beneath the jacket, she finds a pair of moth-eaten black trousers rolled into a ball. As she takes them out, a tattered dress of pink muslin unfurls across her lap and its voluminous skirt settles over her knees. Holding the dress by its lace-trimmed shoulders, she finds the bodice and skirt dotted with brown spots. Oh, God, she shudders, casting the ruined finery aside. *Blood.*

The trunk contains little else. A filthy baby blanket of faded yellow yarn, a moldy buggy robe, the threadbare remains of what must have been the bodice of an elegant satin wedding gown. Anna removes these items and piles them near the attic door.

On the floor of the trunk, she sees a Bible. She picks it up, push-es her glasses back against her nose, and goes to the window to read the faded inscription on its cover, *Adaire Morgan Sanderson*. Sifting through the much-read pages, she finds a folded piece of yellowed news-paper. She slowly opens the dusty packet to reveal the front page of the *News Argus* dated April 10, 1865. Bold headlines jump from the page. LEE SURRENDERS TO GRANT AT APPOMATTOX. Well, that's something I didn't expect to find, but I'm not surprised that Adaire kept it. I'll have to give that to Carl. My, but he loved to tell the story of how his Granny Adaire defended Sand Hill against the Yankees. She refolds the brittle paper and puts it in her apron pocket. She continues to sift through the pages of the Bible and near the back discovers a thin lav-ender ribbon serving as a marker. When she turns to the marked page, she gasps, startled by a photograph she finds there. That's the same photograph I accidentally found in Adaire's drawer, she remembers, when I moved here to Sand Hill after Carl and I were married. Let's see . . . that was the summer of 1905. Yes, this is the picture of the family Adaire told me she had made in 1900, the anniversary photograph. Anna stares at the picture, studying the faces of her once-handsome husband, Carl, his parents and siblings, and his grandmother and her husband, the Colonel. And she is struck again, as she was when she first saw the photograph so many years before, by the haunting image of her husband's sister, Julia. Beautiful Julia, whose long silvery hair spills over her proud shoulders. Julia, looking boldly at the camera as if she dared it to capture her loveliness.

Anna lifts the photograph and finds a folded piece of grayed sta-tionery beneath it. Someone must have read this a lot, she thinks, as she carefully unfolds the thin paper. The ink is faded, the handwriting small and difficult to read, but the writer's name stands out on the page like a trademark. "Ah, ha," she whispers.

September 5, 1902

Dear Granny Adaire,

I know you are mad at me, and hurt, because I ran away and mar-ried Joshua. You are the only one I know who will understand. Sand

Hill has been my home for so long, Granny, and you and Millie have both been like a mother to me. I love you both very much and I will miss you.

You will find this letter that I am going to hide in the bottom of your sewing basket and you will know that even as I planned to leave and marry the man I love, I was thinking of you. You once told me how your friends shunned you when you married Colonel Hightower, how they would not speak to you or invite you into their homes anymore because you married a Yankee. Well, I must be like you, Granny, because I love Joshua like you must have loved the Colonel. If you still love the Colonel that way, then you will understand why I cannot live without Joshua. We have loved each other all our lives and we will go on loving each other in a place where we are safe. I hope you can find it in your heart to forgive me, Granny.

> Your devoted granddaughter,
> Julia

Anna's hands shake as she refolds the letter and puts it, along with the photograph, back in the Bible. She cups the book in both hands and leans back into the rocker. At last, she thinks, I have found the missing piece at last. Now I have something Julia wrote that I can show her son. And a picture of her, too, that I can put with Joshua's letters to his mother along with that photograph she had of him . . . the one she gave me for safe-keeping. Oh, Millie, I wish you were here to help me explain this . . . to say the right things to Fletcher and Maddie. I just don't know how to tell them...or exactly what to tell them about the mother and father he never knew. And their families . . . all the Sandersons, and the Sanders, who lived and died here. All the love and hate and passion and regret stored up on this old farm and buried in that cemetery out there. And here I sit in the rocker Granny Adaire sat in so often with that sewing basket . . . the one Julia hid her letter in . . . on her lap. And I can see Ludie standing just outside Granny's bedroom door with a tray in her hands . . . can see her just as clear as if it were yesterday. What secrets you have kept these many years, old house. And I . . . who am I in this place? A mere interloper . . . one who came and lived here a few short months . . . just another pair of hands gathering apples and pears in the orchard, sugaring the hams while Millie and Ludie made the sausage, threading needles, and cutting and arranging bouquets with Adaire. I was so young then . . . so unaware of what lay before me. Just another wide-eyed, hopeful bride trying to help her new husband find his dream. Those days went by so fast. Life came into this house and, just as quickly, went out of it. My boy was born here and he's buried here. And, one day, I'll join him and all the others out in your burying ground.

Clutching Adaire's Bible in her hand, Anna leaves the rocker and goes to the window. Through rain-spattered panes, she looks down the walk in front of the house, and her eyes follow the muddy path to the cemetery. Decaying fields of brown cotton stalks, once laden with leaves bright green, and bolls snowy white, surround its black wrought-iron fence. Granite gravestones and rotted wooden markers glisten with wet, their carvings obscured in the weak November light. Before long, I'll be out there, Anna thinks. And my old bones will leach into your soil and I'll become a part of you, too.

PART I: 1865-1866

CHAPTER 1:
COW A HARD THING TO HIDE

Sand Hill Farm
March 16, 1865

Adaire Sanderson gazes through a window at the heavy mist that blankets her barren fields. Haven't had a spring this wet in years, she thinks, hugging herself into the loose black frock she's worn for days. We can't plant corn now. The seeds will drown.

The thought of fresh corn, of golden roasting ears, steamy hot and gleaming with melted butter, makes Adaire's empty stomach growl. "Oh, God," she whispers, "when will this devilish rain end? Would you have us starve?" A shudder courses through her body with the power of poison, reminding her that her cornmeal barrel will soon be empty, her only cow might suddenly go dry, and Confederate deserters, deadly as a pack of wolves, could be hiding in the woods hoping for just the right moment to steal what little she has.

From a distance, Adaire hears someone calling her name. She can't see the small brown boy, but she knows from the urgency in his voice that she must hurry. Jerking open the drawer of a dresser, she hunts among ragged pieces of underwear until her fingers find cold steel. She removes the Colt .44 from its soft burrow and hastens out of the room.

The heavy front door, swollen with damp, clings to its facings as she wrestles its tarnished knob. It flies open, and she stumbles across the threshold to find Sam. "Rider coming yonder, Missus," he blurts, pointing toward the field that forms a boundary along the west side of her house. "Look like young Master Newton."

Adaire can't make out the rider's face through the gloom, just the outline of a scrawny mule kicking up clods of wet earth. She slides the long-barreled pistol into her pocket as he approaches. Thank God it's someone we know, she says to herself while Tom Newton hauls on the reins of his hungry beast.

"Miz Sanderson, howdy!" A stream of water trickles from the brim of the boy's hat as he nods toward the small, dark-haired woman. "My pa sent me to tell you that Sherman's Army is moving out of Fayetteville. Uncle Ned rode up this morning to warn us 'cause he heard the Yanks are headed up here to Goldsboro to try to stop General Lee's supply train. My pa says for you to pack up your folks and come over to our place now. You ain't got no menfolks no more, Miz Adaire. If them Yanks show up tomorrow and meet our boys that's camped at Bentonville, it could get right hot around here."

He waits for her to respond, his freckled face bright with excitement. But Adaire stands rigid as a statue before him, her eyes fixed on the sagging barn beyond her house. He watches as she clasps both hands together beneath her chin, making him think she might begin to pray. But she doesn't, and he goes on.

"Well, I gotta get. Gotta go on over to Mr. Rose's place and tell his folks, too. You want me to tell my daddy you'll be coming today, ma'am?"

"No, Tommy." Adaire shakes her head. "Thank you for riding over here to warn us. No, we won't be coming, son. But please tell your daddy I appreciate his hospitality." She glances at the barn again, back at the house, and then somewhere beyond. "I can't leave Sand Hill."

"I don't blame you none, ma'am. I just come from the Harpers'. Old Mrs. Harper said she wasn't leaving even if Sherman himself showed up. Hope you've got a gun. Uncle Ned says them Yanks tore up Fayetteville for a fare-ye-well. Stole all the food and horses they could find. Cows and mules, too. Even burned down the courthouse and lots of the homes in town. Folks are living in brush tents out in the woods." He touches the brim of his wet hat and slaps the reins across the mule's sweaty neck. "I gotta get," he yells, and a moment later, he's making tracks across another field.

Adaire turns to find her former slaves, Ludie and Tyner, and their daughter, Asia, huddled together, Tyner in front, the women behind. "Miz Adaire," Tyner begins, his otherwise smooth forehead bunched and wrinkled, "we ain't got much left, but we don't want them Yankees to get it. What about our children? What about our hogs and Sadie?"

Without answering, Adaire starts back up the porch steps, black brows knit tightly over her steel blue eyes. You'd think giving a husband was enough, but no. Now they want our food, our stock, and God knows what else. And here I am with eleven hungry mouths to feed.

At the war's onset in the spring of '61, Adaire had begged her husband, John, to remain at home and tend the farm. He stayed through the harvest that year, but he grew restless during the winter months and soon joined the ranks of his old friend, Colonel "Bald Dick" Ewell, in Richmond. He had left her with instructions for overseeing the field-workers, the livestock, the outbuildings, and the account books. Adaire had always looked after the household—the food, the furnishings, the children and their clothing, and the never-ending tasks required to keep it running. The first two years after John went away, there had been plenty to eat, good crops of cotton and corn, and a half dozen Negroes to work the fields. Things became more difficult as word spread of the Emancipation Proclamation. All of the formerly enslaved, save Tyner and his family, had run away. The past year had been the worst. John Sanderson had been killed at Fort Fisher in January, and Adaire, with Tyner's help, had driven a mule and wagon to Wilmington to fetch his remains.

The widow looks across a muddy yard to the cedar where her husband's body is buried and beyond his fresh grave to the stubbly remains of last year's vegetable garden. Calluses have hardened like leathery pebbles on the palms of her hands, testimony to the hours she and Ludie spent hoeing the garden in the hot June sun; hours that became miserable in August when they spent weeks bent over rows of field peas; hours that stretched into a muggy, wet September as she and the rest of the family worked day and night tearing rough husks from five acres of hard corn, grinding it by hand, praying they would have enough to keep them alive in the winter ahead.

"Why can't you just leave us alone?" she asks aloud, turning south as if to face the approaching Union Army. She sighs and turns back to see three puzzled brown faces, three motionless bodies ready to do her bidding. They're waiting for me to tell them what to do, she thinks, but what can I tell them? How can we defend ourselves against an army? She rubs a knuckle across pursed lips, her eyes on the thin brown woman who is her mainstay. "If they come here, they'll take everything. The cow, the hogs, the mules, everything. Oh, Ludie, what are we going to do?"

Ludie, who is tall and long-limbed with skin the color of nutmeg, never hurries, never wears a headrag, and never looks down when Adaire speaks to her. She was in the room when Adaire was born. "Don't know, Missus," she answers. "Cow a hard thing to hide. Ain't like we could pack them animals in a trunk. They needs room."

Ludie works her jaw for a moment, lifting her chin to spit a stream of tobacco juice into a mud hole near her feet. "What about that lean-to down on the creek? The one Tyner fix up for Mistuh John's fishing trips?"

The fish camp. It might work, Adaire thinks. At least it's far enough away to be safe and big enough to keep the rain out. Tyner and the boys could stay there for a couple of days. "It'll have to do. The boys can camp there and take the stock with them. You'd better fry some cornbread for them, Ludie. How much side meat do we have?"

"Piece 'bout the size of my fist, not much more."

"Well, fry that, too. And send Sam and Amos to the root cellar to bring everything out. There isn't much left."

Ludie calls to her sons, nine-year-old Sam and seven-year-old Amos, and gives them instructions on what to do with the few fruits and vegetables in the cellar.

Adaire looks at Ludie's daughter, a spindly girl of thirteen, whose head is wrapped in a ragged dresser scarf. "Asia, get some flour sacks and pack the silver bowls and plates in the dining room. Get the flatware out of the drawer and wrap it, too." She turns back to Asia's father. "Tyner, go to the barn and tell Carl and Phillip to come to the house right away. You'd better call the hogs and pen them up. Try to find all the shoats. They're probably in the woods behind the barn, and bring Jupiter and the wagon up here. And don't waste any time." She grabs at her damp skirts, hurrying into the house, where she finds her newly married daughter, Janey, crocheting a baby bootie. She pauses for a moment, her eyes fixed on the tiny oblong of pale yellow yarn. Five pink toes, she thinks, will soon find their way into that bootie and my daughter will know exactly how I felt when I kissed her little feet and guided them into the booties I made for her before she was born. Life goes on in spite of war, in spite of hate, in spite of hungry armies and starving animals. Let her have her baby, Lord, and let me be there to help her, to feed her and care for her, as Ludie always cared for me.

Adaire clears her throat and gently rests a hand on Janey's shoulder. "It looks like we may have some unexpected company, honey," she says. "I've sent for your brothers. Tom Newton just rode over to tell me that Sherman's army is moving this way."

The ball of yellow thread falls from Janey's lap and rolls silently across the wide plank floor. "Oh, no. Not Sherman. I thought he was somewhere west of here, Mama, near Raleigh." Janey's dark eyes search her mother's face. "That's what Mr. Cole told us. Why would Sherman come here?"

"I don't know, child. Why did Hannibal cross the Alps? All I know is we've got only one cow and two sorry mules left to keep this place going. We've got to try to save the hogs or we'll have nothing to eat." She pauses as heavy footsteps sound outside the door. "Come on, Janey. The boys are coming in. We need to make some plans."

Inside the cool, dim light of the hallway, Adaire looks at each of her children. They're too young for all this, she thinks. Janey, only seventeen and pregnant, with a husband fighting somewhere in Virginia. She's a spirited thing, but so unpredictable. And Carl . . . taller than I am, and so hardheaded. Only fourteen, but begging me to let him join the army now that his father's dead. Thank God for Phillip. He's a bit small for twelve, but still affectionate and obedient. And Alice, my darling baby . . . so much like her father, even at three. They're a good-looking lot, strong and healthy despite the pitiful diet we've had the last couple of years. I don't want to frighten them too badly.

"Mr. Newton sent Tommy over to tell me that the Yankees may be headed to Goldsboro. He thinks Sherman's army might pass through this area sometime tomorrow. Even if his troops don't come this way, his scouts will be looking for food for miles around. Your pa was always afraid this would happen. When he came home last spring, he gave me two ten-dollar gold pieces that he hid in the barn loft before he joined up. Your father was always prepared for the unexpected, Lord bless him. He told me to save the money in case we got into real trouble. Well, I guess this might be it. Remember when that pack of thieves came by here in October? The Commissary? And they took our chickens and turkeys and half of our hogs. Remember?" Carl nods as his mother continues. "They even had the nerve to take two quilts Ludie had airing on the porch. Well, I expect a horde of army troops, even our boys, would take everything we've got. Which is precious little, but it's still ours, isn't it? We're not the first people this has ever happened to, and we won't be the first who ever tried to save themselves." Adaire pauses to look at her sons. They're too young to do this, she thinks, too young to have to face this kind of responsibility. Carl's not even shaving yet. She closes her eyes, steeling herself for the task. Either they go and take what's left of the stock, or all of us will be lost. "I want you boys to take one of the mules, the hogs, and Bunchy and Sadie down to the fish camp."

"Ma, that place is all growed over now," Carl protests, recalling the lean-to of rough-hewn logs that John and Tyner built for John's fishing expeditions with his sons. The two men and their boys had spent perhaps a dozen nights in the crude shelter before John left for the war.

"I hope it is grown over. The more grown over, the better, Carl. Go to the barn and find those big pieces of canvas your daddy kept to cover the cotton wagons. You'll have to rig some kind of shelter down on the creek for the animals."

"What about Star, Mama? You want us to take her, don't you?" asks Phillip, referring to Adaire's favorite, a black mare with a tiny white star on her left flank.

"No, I'll keep her here, son. I want you to take Bunchy instead."

"But, Ma, if some soldiers come, you know they'll take Star. Aren't you and Janey and Alice coming with us?"

"Janey can't spend the night out in the damp, honey. And Alice is too little. You boys have got to do this. Go upstairs and get your warm clothes and the quilts from your beds and what's left of your socks and underdrawers. There won't be any heat down there because you can't have a fire. Ludie is cooking some food. I'm sending Tyner with you."

Asia enters the hallway from the dining room, a loaded flour sack in each hand. "The silver packed, Miz Adaire," the brown girl says, handing the heavy sacks to her mistress.

"Thank you, Asia. Go help the boys get some warm clothing bundled together. Put it in their pillow slips. Carl, you better hurry. It'll take a while to unload the wagon and get the animals settled."

As the boys and Asia start up the stairs, Janey takes Alice in her arms. "Now, Mama, what can I do? Want me to help Ludie with the cooking? Is there something I can gather up for the boys?"

Adaire takes in her daughter's shapely body, noting the swelling breasts, the rising waistline, the creamy complexion, the mouth full and inviting like a ripe plum. If your father could see you now, she thinks, how happy he would be to know a grandchild is on the way. Just wish you were further along so it would be more obvious. "Janey, honey," she says, her eyes on her daughter's small belly, "we've got to find a way to make you look . . . look more pregnant."

Pink creeps across Janey's young face. "Mama, I'm surprised at you! What a silly thing to say. I can't make myself look . . . look more . . . you know. Only God does that."

"Well, you're going to have to get real big, real fast or hide somewhere so the soldiers won't see you. There's no telling what they'll do if they see you like you are, but I doubt any man would bother a pregnant woman. At least, not one he knew was pregnant, and I want them to know you are. It's safer that way." Adaire chews at her lower lip. "Go get your oldest hoopskirt and take out the hoops. Cut the material into strips about three inches wide. Save the hoops. We may need them. Take Alice with you, and keep her occupied for a while so I can help Tyner and the boys get off. I'll be out in the cabin. Bring the strips to me when you finish."

"But, Mama, do I have to tear up my hoopskirt? I don't have but one left, and I'm saving it for when Edward gets home. I wouldn't want him to see me without my hoops. Can't we tear up feed sacks or something?"

"No. I'll need all the sacks to pack things in. Go on, honey. We've got a lot to do or we'll starve to death, if the Yankees don't burn us out first. Do you want your baby to starve?" Adaire's look silences Janey. "And put your jewelry on my dresser."

Leaving Janey in the hall, Adaire hurries out the back door, across the dogtrot, and into the log cabin that is home for Ludie and Tyner. Inside, the odors of corn pone, side meat, and woodsmoke fill the airless room. On a pallet in the corner, Ludie's five-year-old daughter, Millie, plays with a yellow-striped kitten. Adaire watches as Ludie bends before the blazing hearth to drop spoonfuls of wet cornmeal into a hot skillet, and her mind drifts back to the first night she spent at Sand Hill Farm.

At eighteen, she had come with her new husband to a fifteen-hundred acre parcel of some of the finest land a hawk ever flew over. Work had begun on their new home, but it was far from complete when the newlyweds arrived after a month-long honeymoon in Kentucky and Virginia. Several yards behind the raw frame of their new house was an old two-room log cabin that smelled distinctly of the cedar shavings that covered its dirt floor. It was here that John Sanderson had brought his bride. The main room had been spacious, warm, and dry, with a clumsy stone fireplace, several pieces of furniture made by John's slave, Tyner, and two windows. Above it was a loft for storing seed, food staples, and tools. The second room was an attached shed with a tin roof. John and Adaire spent the first six months of their married life in the cabin where Adaire gave birth prematurely to their first child, John Sanderson, Jr., who died two weeks later.

Ludie, who had come with Adaire from her home in Kentucky, slept in the shed. Tyner and his two younger brothers, Ben and Grady, who had been born on the farm, worked the fields with five other male slaves. They bunked in a storehouse behind the barn and ate Ludie's cooking around the storehouse door or out in the fields. Ludie, who was a good cook, had been trained as a lady's maid. She excelled at dressmaking, embroidery, and quilting. As a child growing up in the big house in Kentucky, she had slept on a rug beside Adaire's bed and had eaten the same food the white family ate. Adaire's father, Phillip Winfield Morgan, a state senator, was an aloof and soft-spoken gentleman who was widowed when Adaire was born. Order in his household was kept by Ludie's mother, Pearlene. At Phillip Morgan's death, Pearlene and the other house servants were freed by his will, but Ludie became the property of Adaire at birth and has lived with her mistress for thirty-eight years.

The house John Sanderson built for his bride stands at the top of a knoll which overlooks large fields on three sides. When John's father bought the property fifty years earlier, folks called it Sanderson's Hill, which eventually became Sand Hill—a misnomer since its soil is a black loam. The house is of a simple design with generous covered porches, front and rear. Its interior contains a parlor, a dining room, and two bedrooms downstairs and one upstairs, all furnished with pieces Adaire had shipped from her home in Kentucky. The center hall serves as the family gathering place, as well as an informal dining room most of the year. Although rarely used now, the parlor contains a rosewood settee, two side chairs, and Adaire's piano—a Knabe grand—the only touch of elegance in a house where no Chinese porcelains, no Turkish carpets, nor oil portraits exist. Compared to the dwellings of most downeast farmers in the mid-nineteenth century, the house seems palatial, and Adaire, with Ludie's help, had made it warm and inviting. In the years before the war, visitors slept in its soft featherbeds, relaxed in cool breezes on its wide front porch, and relished Ludie's wonderful dishes in the spacious dining room.

Lately, many foodstuffs have disappeared and Adaire's larder has dwindled. The cabin hearth that once held steaming pots of fresh vegetables and dutch ovens bursting with spoon bread, spits of venison, and wild turkey is now host to an occasional skillet of fried chicken and, more often, a few slices of rancid bacon.

Small rations of hog meat and a variety of dried fruits and vegetables from the cellar round out this meager diet. Fortunately, the chickens lay plenty of eggs and Sadie is generous with her milk. Tyner spends hours in the woods setting traps for rabbit, squirrel, and possum; he keeps trotlines in the creek and often brings home a mess of fish. Occasionally, he is lucky enough to catch a sunning turtle, and the family enjoys one of their favorite treats, cooter pie.

Adaire pauses to take a quick inventory of foodstuffs in the cabin. A peck of dried peas and a small jar of gray salt sit on the table; several clumps of dried peppers and sage hang from the rafters. A half-empty barrel of cornmeal stands in the corner beside a demijohn of sorghum. Precious little, she thinks, as she steps out of the doorway to find Tyner waiting with the wagon. "I done got all the hawgs penned up," he announces. "What you want me to do now, Miz Adaire?"

"You'll have to go with the boys down to the fish camp. Put the shoats in some croaker sacks, and get Carl to help you tie the sows' feet and drag them up on the back of the wagon. Let the boars go. You won't have enough room to take them with you, and they'll be safer in the woods. Get the ham from the smokehouse and wrap it up good. And fill the front of the wagon with sacks of corn. And, Tyner, take Jupiter with you, but leave Shadrack here. I may need a mule. I'll look after her and Star while you're gone. And don't forget Sadie and Bunchy. Clean out the cribs in their stalls, and don't leave any feed in the barn that we won't need. I'm sure Red will follow you all down to the camp. You'll need to tie him up because the Yankees might shoot him if they come around here in the night and he starts barking. I don't want them to kill John's dog."

Tyner is thoughtful, scratching a spot above his ear. "Miz Adaire, we gotta keep them shoats and sows down at that camp else they gonna run off in the woods."

He's right, Adaire thinks. "You'll have to fashion some kind of stockade, Tyner. Cut some big branches and make a circle off one end of the shed. The boys will help you. If the armies are foraging the woods for food, they'll be sure to hear a bunch of squealing pigs and that'll be the end of our meat. Understand?"

"Yessum, I understand. Ludie gonna stay here?"

"All us womenfolk and the children will have to stay, Tyner. Why, with these little girls and Miss Janey's condition, we'd be fools to try to stay out overnight in the damp. Tyner, you know you and Ludie are free to go anytime. I don't want you to, Lord knows, but I can't keep you from it."

Tyner's eyes shift quickly to the ground. "We ain't going nowhere, Miz Adaire. We could of gone off when our boy, Hector, left a while back, but Ludie . . . she didn't want to. At least we got food and a dry place to sleep. That's more than lots of folk has got these days. Missus, if this war ever finish up, I'd relish a talk with you about working a bit of land here now that Mr. Lincoln done say we is free."

"Tyner, when this hellish war finally ends, if we can get back on our feet again, you know I'll do right by you and Ludie. I don't know what I would have done without you. Especially since Mr. Sanderson's passing." Now I've said too much, she thinks. He knows that I know we've lost the war. She turns abruptly from the brown man and steps back inside the cabin where Ludie is packing a large basket.

"Got enough here for about two days, I reckon, Miz Adaire. I hear you telling Tyner he'd be going, too. You planning on sending them apples and such the boys drug out'n the cellar?"

"Yes, and everything else we can get on that wagon."

Janey enters the cabin with Alice on her hip and strips of white cotton folded over her arm. She puts the little girl down on the quilt with Millie and thrusts the material at her mother. "Mama, I did what you told me, but I don't see how this is going to help. If you wrap all these strips around my waist, I still won't look very big. I tore up my last hoops for nothing."

Adaire tucks a dishrag around three baked sweet potatoes, puts them in the basket, and takes the material from her daughter. "Ludie,

I want to fix something to make Janey look really big. Like her baby is coming soon. I need to hide some things. Have you got some meal sacks?"

"Yessum, I got three or four." Ludie's eyes travel over Janey's middle, to the strips Adaire's holding, and back to the girl's waist. Ain't gonna have no baby of no size, no how, she thinks, too puny. Take a lot of mess to fill her out, she's such a scrawny thing. Meal sacks ain't gonna change it.

Adaire drags the heavy basket of food across the table. "After the boys and Tyner leave for the camp, bring what you've got to the house, Ludie. We'll try to figure this thing out. Bring your young'uns, too. You can stay up in the boys' room tonight. If an army is coming this way, either ours or theirs, I want you to be safe. I want all of us to be as safe as we can under the circumstances."

Adaire walks toward the corner where Millie and Alice are playing. "Come on, let's go outside and help the boys load the wagon or they'll never get to the creek."

Sam and Amos are standing in the yard beside the four feed sacks they have filled with wrinkled fruits and vegetables from the root cellar.

"You boys haul one of those sacks of apples over to the back door of the house," Adaire orders. "We'll have to have something to eat here. As soon as you finish, take the others to the barn and help your daddy load the wagon."

* * * * *

Carl and Phillip climb up to the wagon seat while Tyner checks the bridle and reins on Jupiter. Sadie gives a mournful low and tries to jerk her broad, black head away from the rear of the wagon as Bunchy, a high-spirited bay, prances beside her. Adaire leans over the side of the wagon to check the burlap sacks that hold seventeen baby pigs. Just behind the seat, two hog-tied sows snuffle and grunt. She turns to Tyner, a question in her eyes.

"Don't fret, Missus. I got a bucket for to milk Sadie. Got some cups and such for drinking and what we don't drink, we give to the hogs. Wish we could take some chickens."

"Well, you can't. They'd just fly off and come back here to roost." Adaire looks at Carl. "Did you get the silver, son?"

"Yes, Ma. We're all packed up. Don't worry about us. We'll be all right. And if them Yanks show up at our camp, we'll chop their heads off." From beneath the wagon seat, he raises an ax and, waving it above Jupiter's rear, shouts, "Yee hah!"

"Now don't do anything foolish, young man. And remember, no fires. You got some blankets and warm clothes for tonight, didn't you?"

Carl slams a muddy boot against the front of the wagon. "We're not babies, Mama. Quit worrying. You act like we're gonna set up house-keeping and live down there. We'll be back in a couple of days."

"You're not to leave that place for any reason until I send Sam down there to tell you to come home." Adaire takes hold of Carl's arm and feels it stiffen beneath her grasp. "The Yankees may stay out on the Goldsboro road and never come anywhere near this place or they might head straight for the river. Just be careful and, above all, be quiet. You've got a lot to do, so you'd better get going. It looks like it's going to rain again."

"Bye, Ma." Phillip leans around his big brother and begins to wave, obviously pleased that he is going down to the camp. "Bye, Janey. Bye, Alice. Bye, Ludie."

Tyner picks up Millie and hugs her to his chest. Then he grabs both his young sons with one arm and gives them a squeeze. "Don't worry, Miz Adaire, I'm gonna look after your boys," he promises. He jumps on the back of the wagon as it moves slowly down the path be-side the barn. As it begins to disappear into the mist at the edge of the woods, Red crawls out from under the house, nose to the ground, and lopes after it.

* * * * *

Caught between waking and sleeping, Adaire wrestles with the unknown, wrapping herself like a mummy in the fancy coverlet she crocheted as a bride. She kicks the heavy covering aside and stretches her legs across the bed she was born in, the bed her mother died in the following day, the bed she brought from Kentucky to share with John.

Ludie opens the bedroom door, bringing in a plate of corn cakes and sorghum. "Brought you some breakfast," she says, carefully noting the frown on Adaire's face.

"No, thank you, Ludie. I'm not hungry. Take those to your boys. I need to get dressed. Is it raining?"

"Tryin' to spit a little."

Adaire sits up and swings her legs over the side of the bed. "Bring me some petticoats and camisoles instead, Ludie."

Ludie goes to Adaire's dresser, opens the top drawer, and pulls out an assortment of underwear, holding up each piece to inspect it for holes and tears. She helps her mistress remove a faded nightgown and watches as Adaire puts on three camisoles, three pairs of pantalets, and two threadbare petticoats. "Lordy, Miz Adaire, how come you puttin' all that mess on?"

"So the Yankees won't get it. You remember that letter we got from Cousin Hettie in Savannah last January? Remember old Doc Haynes brought it to us?" Ludie nods and Adaire continues. "Well, Hettie said the Yankees took everything they had. Remember? Clothes, food, shoes, horses, even their china. And they set fire to the barns and the smokehouses and dragged her beautiful piano out in the yard and played it while they burned everything. You remember that letter, don't you, Ludie?"

"Yessum, I sure do. And I remember how upset you was, it comin' right on the heels of Mistuh John's passing."

"I still have that letter and I've heard plenty about the Yankees and what they do. We're going to try to be ready for any thieving devils who show up here." Adaire grabs her hairbrush and hands it to Ludie. "Nothing fancy, just get it off my neck, please."

Ludie brushes Adaire's dark hair in long strokes, parts it in the middle, and plaits each side, exposing the gray that sweeps like dove's wings above her mistress's ears. She winds the plaits into large circles and pins them on the back of Adaire's head. Then she helps her mistress into a worn black skirt and a yellow-and-black-striped shirtwaist.

"Better get me the jacket, too, Ludie," Adaire says.

"Miz Adaire, you gonna burn up. It's muggy outside. Too warm for that jacket."

"I'm going to wear it. If the Yankees come here, I don't think they'll have the nerve to ask me to take my clothes off." Adaire jerks the faded lapels together as she stomps across the room to her dresser. She studies the pile of jewelry Janey has left there—two pairs of earbobs, a gold chain, a collar pin set with sapphires, and the pair of gold cuff links her daughter had given her husband, Edward, as a wedding gift. She opens the top drawer and takes out her own jewelry box.

As she lifts its lid, light falls on a small gold locket. Pulling it from the box, she caresses its contours, feeling the warmth of the gold and the raised settings that hold tiny pearls and diamonds. Memories flood her mind. I can see John kneeling beside the bed where I struggled through a merciless day and night to give him his first son. Can see his eyes as fresh and green as new leaves on an apple tree. And almost feel my fingers run through his hair . . . so thick and blond. The eyes, the hair, the man I fell in love with a year before when we met at that reception in Washington City. We waltzed several times . . . he was such a graceful dancer. And then we fled from the old lady gossips to a little alcove where we talked for hours. John C. Calhoun had just been appointed Secretary of State. Of course, I had to voice my doubts about the senator's ability to deal with the moneyed interests of the North, but John Sanderson seemed to appreciate my candor. So unusual. And I remember his smile as I told him my thoughts, how he nodded at my observations. Then he stayed an extra week in town so that he could spend time with me, so he could tell me of the life he hoped to carve out of the forests in the Carolina lowlands, of the house he hoped to build, the family he hoped to raise. And, lo and behold, he went right to Father and asked for my hand. That took a lot of courage . . . more than I realized at the time because we had known each other only two weeks. But we knew we loved each other. And I was so consumed with that overpowering feeling that nothing else would do. I wonder what we would have done if Father had said no. But he didn't. Our wedding that Christmas was beautiful, even if I was a little nervous. Thank God Ludie came with me to North Carolina. I would have been useless without her . . . and lonely. This was the most desolate place. I hardly knew what to do when I realized in those first few months of marriage that my life would be changed forever and that it was up to me to make it better. Lord knows I tried to do right by my husband, by my children, by my obligations to Ludie and Tyner. And I want to do right by them now. We've worked so hard to make a life here. How can it all end like this? With John dead? And our home, this hard-earned land, threatened by a mob of plundering, lawless strangers?

Adaire takes the locket, earbobs, and broaches from her jewelry box and puts them in her skirt pocket. As the clock on the mantle strikes eight, she goes to the bed and draws the pistol from under a pillow, checks the chamber, and slips it into her other pocket. Sitting down on a rocker, she begins fastening up her last pair of high button shoes. Suddenly, she looks up, the shoe hook gripped tightly in her hand. "Did you hear something, Ludie?" she asks, her eyes on the hallway door. "Where are the children?"

"They in the dining room with Miz Janey. She telling them a story."

"Where's Asia?"

"Out to the barn feeding Star and that old mule."

Adaire sits motionless, her head cocked to one side. "Listen," she whispers.

From a distance comes the sound of creaking wagon wheels and the jingle of harness. Adaire straightens her skirts and rises from the chair. "If that's a bunch of Sherman's devils, I'm going out on the porch to meet them before they break down the door."

"Miz Adaire, you can't do that." Ludie moves quickly toward the door, spreading her hands to block Adaire's passage. "You know they got guns."

Adaire crosses to the front window and pulls back the shabby curtain. She sees two wagons carrying several soldiers in dark blue uniforms coming up the path. Ahead of them, another soldier rides on horseback. "Just as I thought," she says, balling her fists. "Well, they're not going to take everything we've worked for." She jerks the curtain back and pushes Ludie aside. "Keep the children in the dining room and keep them quiet."

Putting a hand over her hammering heart, she tiptoes across the hall and leans against the closed front door. She can hear the soldiers talking and laughing and wonders what they will do. Search her? Tie her up? Shoot her? She grabs the brass doorknob and flings the heavy door open, straightens her shoulders, and steps onto the porch. Her hands go to her skirt and she flinches, a quick, almost imperceptible jerk. Oh, no. The jewelry. How could I have been so stupid? Why didn't I just send it to the creek with the boys? She looks around for a hiding place and sees nothing but rocking chairs. Walking to the edge of the porch, she kneels down and pretends to button her shoe while she throws the jewelry into the leafy branches of an old boxwood. She looks up in time to see a mud-spattered officer coming up the walk. He touches the brim of his hat.

"Good morning, madam. I'm Lieutenant Charles Montrose, 9th Ohio. We're here to collect food and supplies for our army. Are you alone?"

Adaire rises slowly. She stares at the lieutenant, her eyes dark with fear, and presses her hand against the contours of the gun in her pocket as the officer turns back to the group of men who have accompanied him.

"Richardson, you and Hartwell come with me. Jones, you and Williams go check the barn and the other buildings we saw on the way in. Come back to the house and report to me right away."

He starts up the steps with the two privates close behind. "I'm sorry, madam, but we must make a search." He walks quickly across the porch and into the open door.

Inside the house is still; not a sound is heard. The lieutenant pauses and looks up the stairs. "Hartwell," he calls, "check the second floor. Richardson, you and I can look around down here." He opens the door to the parlor and, with the trained eye of a scavenger, surveys the room. "We can use this rug, Richardson. Roll it up. And get that shawl over there on the divan." Richardson, a skinny man with a wispy beard, moves toward the center of the room where he stumbles over the quilt frame that stands in front of the hearth. He grabs it with both hands and thrusts it aside before he begins rolling up a hand-hooked rug made by John Sanderson's mother.

Adaire follows the lieutenant from the parlor to her bedroom and watches as he strips her bed of its quilt, marriage coverlet, and feather bolster. He crosses the room to the dresser where Janey's jewelry sparkles in the dull light.

He picks up a cuff link. "Nice," he says, twirling it in his fingers. "I think I can use these." Scooping up the rest of Janey's finery, he stuffs them into his jacket pocket. "Fold up the bedclothes, Richardson, and be sure to go through all the drawers in this chest." He looks carefully around the room and his eyes stop at the trunk Adaire took on a tour of Europe with her father. "And check this trunk," he orders.

Adaire holds her breath. Several old ball gowns, her wedding gown, and a christening dress are stored in the trunk, but beneath them are two of her husband's uniforms from military school, his saber, gloves, and hats. Years ago, she had sprinkled them with lavender, wrapped them in old bedsheets, and put them away. They are for her boys.

She watches in silence as the private opens the trunk and begins rifling its contents, throwing out Carl's christening gown and two of the ball dresses before he finds an old petit point pillow Adaire's mother made. He stands with it under his arm. "Not much here, Lieutenant. Mostly fancy ladies' stuff. Found a pillow I can use."

"Well, don't forget those bedclothes over there, Richardson. And be sure to get the featherbed out of that cradle." The officer points to a little cradle under the window. "That'll make a nice pillow. And get the cradle. Kindling is hard to come by in this damp."

Adaire takes a quick breath. They're going to steal the bed all of my babies slept in. The one thing their father made for them . . . ready now for his first grandchild. She steps in front of the lieutenant, her eyes bright, her voice like granite. "Damn your nasty thieving souls for stealing my babies' bed. I hope you burn in Hell . . . all of you."

A smirk settles on the lieutenant's young face. "So the lady does have a voice. For a while, I thought you were a dummy. Well, well." Chuckling, he walks across the hall and opens the door to the dining room.

Inside, Janey sits at the head of the table attired in a generous sack dress, her hands folded across an enormous "belly" made of hidden bags of vegetable and cotton seed, packets of paring knives, buttons, flint rocks, a ball of twine, the ten-dollar gold pieces, and several pounds of seed corn. In the other chairs are Sam, Amos, and Asia, who holds Millie. Ludie stands beside the fireplace with Alice in her arms. As he takes in the scene, the lieutenant starts to laugh. "So this is where your little band is hiding. I knew this place couldn't be deserted. Come on in here, Richardson."

The private comes in, with Adaire close on his heels, as the lieutenant continues. "Here's something I'll bet you've never seen before. A bunch of little niggers sitting with their white folks at the dining room table." He throws back his head and begins to laugh. "Yes, sir, wait 'til the captain hears about this! Damndest thing I ever saw. Guess we'll see this kind of thing all the time after the war's over." He looks around at Adaire. "You ready for that, lady? You gonna feed your niggers off that fine china you got hidden from us white boys?" Out of corner of her eye, Adaire sees Ludie stiffen. She feels her own face grow hot, but remains quiet. Just take what you want and leave us, she prays.

"Lieutenant!" a voice calls from the yard. "Lieutenant, you better come quick. We've found us a prize."

The lieutenant and private drop their bundles and run into the hall. From the window, Adaire watches them sprint across the back yard toward the barn. My boy was right, she thinks, as she gathers up her skirts. Men who'll burn a baby's bed for firewood won't hesitate to steal a horse. Especially a horse like Star.

She hurries after them, slipping in and out of muddy ruts across the yard, and pausing just inside the barn doors to let her eyes adjust to the dim light. The soldiers are lined up on the wall beside the glistening, black animal.

"Ain't she a beaut?" the sergeant asks his comrades as he strokes the mare's arched neck. "What a piece of horseflesh. How old do you think she is, Lieutenant?"

"Oh, four or five years, maybe." The lieutenant steps into the stall and runs his hand down Star's side. "She's mighty fine. 'Bout as fine as I've ever seen. These Rebs really know their horseflesh, don't they?" He steps out of the stall and looks over the tack hanging on the wall. "Get a bridle on her, Sergeant. Can't pass this one up."

Adaire pulls the revolver from her skirt pocket and clasps it with both hands. Holding it close and just below her breasts, she steps in front of the men. "Don't touch that horse," she says through clenched teeth.

The sergeant smiles. "Now, lady. Don't do nothing foolish."

"Leave my horse alone," Adaire warns, her eyes trained on his blue-clad chest.

The lieutenant takes a step toward her. "Lady, put that gun away. It's bigger than you are. You might hurt yourself."

Gripping the gun tighter, Adaire points it directly at the lieutenant's face. "You'll take that horse over my dead body, Lieutenant. And yours. I raised that filly from a colt and raised her mama before her. That filly was her last foal, and I intend to keep her."

"Is that right? You seem to know a lot about horses for somebody way out here in the Carolina sticks. And a woman to boot."

"I come from Kentucky, and we set a great store by our horses. And she's one horse you're not taking."

"Well, now," the lieutenant drawls. He crosses his arms and leans back against the barn wall. "So you're from Kentucky. I was born there. Where 'bouts you from?"

I wonder if other folks have gone through this, Adaire thinks. Have they made polite conversation with these rascals? Does talking make stealing easier? "Up near Lexington," she answers.

"Is that a fact? Well, I was raised about thirty miles south of Lexington. My folks owned a farm, but my daddy sold it and we moved to Ohio. My old man got a job with the railroad. I sure did miss Kentucky. Why'd you leave?"

"This is my husband's home."

"So you came here when you married?"

"Yes."

The lieutenant moves closer to Adaire, looks at her for a moment, and steps out of the horse's stall. She follows, the gun still cocked, as he checks the other stalls on his way out. Near the barn door, he stops to point at a milking stool leaning cock-eyed against the rough-hewn wall. "Where's your cow?"

Tiny beads of sweat gather on Adaire's forehead just below her hairline. "Uh," she stammers, "she died . . . hollow horn got her."

Stepping directly in front of the pointed gun, the lieutenant grabs Adaire's wrist. "I think you're lying, lady," he says, as his eyes narrow to slits. "You realize I could burn this barn down over your head, don't you?"

Adaire winces, pulling on her arm. But the man from Ohio won't let go.

"Only reason I haven't given the boys permission to torch this place is 'cause you're from Kentucky. You know that, don't you, lady?" He jerks his head toward the opposite stall where Shadrack, the aged gray mule, is standing. "Sergeant," he calls, "let's be sure to take this mule when we go." He turns back to Adaire. "What have you got to eat? And don't poor mouth about how you don't have anything. Nobody sitting in your dining room just now has missed a meal as far as I can see."

"Some cornmeal, a few apples and potatoes . . . some chickens."

"Fine. Get busy." He motions to the men under his command. "Come on, boys. This lady's gonna feed us a good meal before we take everything she's got."

* * * * *

By mid-afternoon, the farm is quiet. The soldiers have had a bel-lyful of fried chicken, cornbread, and stewed apples prepared by Ludie and Asia and served in the dining room. Adaire set the table with her best china and old pieces of tin flatware, and said a silent prayer thank-ing God that the silver was elsewhere. After the "guests" had eaten, she and the rest of the family gnawed the boney chicken wings and backs Ludie saved for them. Now, Janey and the little girls are having a nap, Ludie and Asia are washing dishes, and Sam and Amos are sitting out-side the cabin door listening to the blue-clad soldiers who are lounging on the floor of the dogtrot.

"You know these Reb boys can't last much longer," observes a pri-vate. "They ain't got nothing to eat and we keep hearing about how low they are on ammunition."

"Yep, but they've stuck like glue," says another. "Don't see how they've lasted this long."

"The captain says it'll be over soon," adds the lieutenant. "He says General Sherman is gonna burn down everything in the whole state of North Carolina if that's what it takes to get the Rebs to give in."

"Yeah, but them Rebs sure do stick," adds the private. "Just like glue."

From the other side of the woods, they hear the boom of a cannon.

"Here we go again, boys," says the sergeant. "Guess we'd better get on back to camp, Lieutenant."

"All right. You got those wagons loaded, don't you?"

"Yes, sir. We got all the bedclothes we could find, some quilts, lots of socks and underwear that was all rolled up together like some-body was going on a trip. Williams rigged up a coop for the chick-ens. Smokehouse was empty, but we got the butter and milk from the springhouse. They got a cow or two somewheres, but we couldn't find 'em. We pulled up all the fencing behind the barn for firewood."

"Good. I want you and Richardson to stay here for a couple of days until this thing blows over. Stand guard at night and keep the riff-raff away. I'm not one to give quarter to the enemy, but I'm a bit worried about these women. Especially that young one who's gonna drop a little Reb bastard any day now. She sorta favors my sister."

He walks over to the back door and knocks. After a moment, Adaire opens it. "You'd better stay real close, lady, and keep the children inside. Sounds like the boys are starting target practice. It could get dangerous here even if the fighting is a couple of miles away. I'm leaving Hartwell and Richardson to keep an eye out. They'll be outside your doors all night and all day tomorrow, unless the Rebs make a run for it and we have to go after them. After it's over, I'm gonna come back and get that filly." He turns back to the blue-clad boys. "Let's go, men. We're needed for bigger stuff now."

* * * * *

Adaire, Ludie, Janey, and Asia huddle around a circle of lamplight, trying to focus on the quilt they're patching. A constant barrage of cannon blasts keeps their already frayed nerves on edge. On the now bare floor, Amos and Sam play soldier with toy rifles they have fashioned from small hickory limbs. Alice and Millie sleep peacefully together on a pallet of feed sacks.

Just before midnight, the cannons fall silent, and after a moment the group hears a knock on the front door. Adaire rises from her sewing and opens it to Sergeant Hartwell. "That's probably the end of it for tonight," he announces. "You better get some sleep. They'll be back at it before daybreak." He touches the brim of his cap with his finger and nods. Adaire nods, too. "Good night, Sergeant," she says without thinking.

"Sure do seem quiet now, don't it?" asks Ludie. "Sound like the fighting was down 'round the Cole place. Maybe off the road what goes to Goldsboro."

"I wonder if the Coles are there?" Janey asks, struggling to get out of a chair. "Think they stayed, Mama?"

"I suppose. Mrs. Cole isn't able to travel. Remember how sick she was all this past winter?" Adaire turns the heavy brass key in the lock of the door and starts toward her bedroom, talking as she goes. "Mr. Cole told me she was practically bedridden when he was here last week. God help them." She turns back to the others. "Do you all realize we have not had evening devotionals for almost a week? We can't seem to hold on to anything these days . . . not even our faith." She looks up at the ceiling. "Lord, we promise to do better just as soon as we can get our boys back here safely. Just help us get through whatever is coming tomorrow. Amen."

Ludie murmurs "Amen" and looks at Adaire. "Want I should brush your hair?"

"No. I'll do it, Ludie. You take this lamp and go on up to bed. I'm sure tomorrow will be just as trying as today's been." Adaire turns from her bedroom door and watches as Janey leads Alice into her room for the night. "Good night, honey," she calls. "You were a real trooper to-day, hauling around all those things. I know you're exhausted."

"I'll be glad to get this contraption off, but it worked, didn't it? Try not to worry too much about Carl and Phillip, Mama. I'm sure they're fine."

Adaire enters her dark bedroom and begins to take the pins from her hair. As it falls about her shoulders, she picks up a brush and with quick, jerky motions, plaits it, tying the ends with twine. She slams the hairbrush on the dresser. I wonder how my boys are faring? And my neighbors? How are they? They're probably scared and worried like me. They're afraid a husband or a son or another brother was killed today. And, like me, they're wondering if this Hell will ever end.

Pausing beside a window, she stares out at the moonless night as tears well in her eyes. "Oh, God," she sighs, "if only I could run away." She sobs, just once, but her throat still burns as she wipes at her eyes. No, she shakes her head, you can't leave the place where your children were born and your husband and baby son are buried. This is your home, Adaire.

"I won't leave you," she whispers as she looks out across the fog-shrouded yard where her children, and Ludie's, ran and played, tramp-ing their very souls into the rich, black earth.

* * * * *

As gray light begins to creep into her room, Adaire stirs, listening to a tapping noise from the outside wall. After a few moments, she real-izes that it's coming from the window. It's just a branch, she reassures herself, but the sound becomes louder, more insistent. She slides out of bed and tiptoes across the bare floor to the window.

Kneeling by the sill, she pulls back the curtain to find Tyner staring up at her. Slowly, and without a sound, she raises the window. "Tyner," she whispers, "what are you doing here? The soldiers might see you."

"They sleeping on the back porch. You all right, Missus? Did they hurt you? My children all right?"

"We're fine. No, they didn't hurt us, but they took almost all our food and most of our clothes. What are you doing here? I told you I'd send for you when it was safe."

"Master Carl's gone, Miz Adaire. He snuck off in the night."

He got his wish, Adaire thinks. Now he'll join the army and be killed. Like father, like son. "Oh, Lord, Tyner. I don't think I can take anymore such news."

"Yessum. He took Mistuh John's squirrel gun with him. I look up and down the creek bank, but I don't find him. What you want I should do now?"

"Nothing, Tyner. You did the right thing. But you'll have to go back and stay with Phillip. Are the animals all right?"

"Yessum."

"Did you walk?"

"No'm, I rode Bunchy. She out behind the barn."

"Have you fed her?"

"Yessum."

"Tyner, I want you to get Star and take her back to the camp. Leave Bunchy behind the barn. You better hurry."

"Yessum."

"And, Tyner, stay with Phillip and watch out for him until I send Sam for you."

"I take care of Master Phillip. Don't you worry," says Tyner. He slips away from the window and moves like a ghost along the side of the house. Adaire watches him steal across the front yard, then drop to a crouch as he heads down the path to the barn.

She closes the window, sits down on her old trunk, and absentmindedly runs her hand along its smooth pine surface. I was afraid this would happen . . . one night away from me and he's gone. Now what? He could be miles away, and even if I knew where to look, they'd never let a woman near the fighting. I've heard of women who take secret messages behind the lines. Don't be an idiot, Adaire, you'd only make a fool of yourself. You don't have any secret messages. She taps nervously on the lid of the trunk, her eyes fixed on the dark window where Tyner appeared moments before. There's bound to be some way to find him if I can only get around the fighting. But how? I'll never be able to find him crawling around in these woods in the dark unless I can. . . . She jumps up from the top of the trunk and lifts its heavy lid. Those old uniforms, she remembers. Maybe I could wear one of those. And I'll ride Bunchy like I'm in the cavalry. She pulls at a plait, her mind busy with the idea of a disguise. I'll have to hide my hair, have to wear one of John's old hats. From a distance, his old black uniform might look like the dark blue ones those Yankee soldiers were wearing. And if I stay on Bunchy, maybe I can get away with it.

Upstairs, she finds Ludie and her children huddled on the floor in Phillip and Carl's bedroom. As soon as Adaire crosses the threshold, Ludie sits up. "What's wrong, Miz Adaire? Why ain't you sleeping?"

"Ludie, I need you to come downstairs and help me for a few minutes. I don't want to wake Janey or the children."

Ludie tiptoes out of the room and follows Adaire down the stairs. As soon as they enter the bedroom, Adaire lights the lamp and whispers, "Tyner was just here." Ludie's eyes widen as Adaire continues. "He's fine. I've sent him back to the creek. He came to tell me Carl has run away. I've got to try to find him, Ludie. Tyner rode Bunchy up here, so I'm going to take her and look for Carl."

"Miz Adaire, ain't that a mite foolish? Them armies all 'round here and you a woman with no one to go with you?"

"I have to do this, Ludie. If I can just find him, I can convince him to come home with me. Otherwise, he may be blown to bits. You wouldn't want Sam or Amos out there, would you?"

Ludie squares her shoulders. "What you want me to do?"

"Remember those old uniforms of Mister John's? The black one with the gold braid in my trunk here? I'm going to put it on and hide my hair under his old hat. Will you put my hair up?"

"You gonna go now? It ain't even light."

"The darker, the better. Tyner says those two Yankee boys who are supposed to be guarding us are asleep on the back porch. Maybe I can get away before they wake up. Help me get my nightgown off, Ludie."

As soon as Ludie finishes pinning up Adaire's hair, she goes to the fireplace and rubs her hands against its blackened walls. Adaire sits on her rocker, stuffing the long legs of her husband's old uniform into his old black riding boots. She has covered her striped shirt with his black wool cape that bears the insignia of a second lieutenant. Ludie kneels before Adaire and says, "Hold still." She rubs the soot from her hands onto Adaire's cheeks, chin, and upper lip.

"Keep your collar up and your head down and you might pass iffen you stays in the woods."

Adaire grabs both of Ludie's smudged hands and looks into her companion's brown eyes. "Oh, Ludie, I feel terrible leaving you and Janey all alone with these children. But I don't know what else to do. Try not to worry about me. I'm going over to the Harpers'. Now, you go fix those soldiers some breakfast. Ask them to come into the cabin to eat it. I'll wait here until you send Asia to tell me it's safe for me to sneak out to the barn."

As she sits down on the side of the bed to put on John's musty hat and stiff gloves, Adaire thinks about all the peaceful Sunday mornings her family enjoyed before the war. This Sunday will be different. No happy well-dressed children will sit at our table. No father will listen patiently to their chatter. Ludie's biscuits and hot cakes will not be wolfed down by two growing boys. No coffee on the sideboard. No Sunday clothes, and nowhere to wear them. I miss the services at our little church at Bentonville . . . miss our friends there.

Asia tiptoes in to hand Adaire a bundle wrapped in the tatters of an apron. "It's pone and side meat. Mama say for you to eat it 'fore you goes."

Adaire stuffs the food into a pocket and blows out the lamp. "Go on back to the cabin. Keep my room door closed all day, Asia. If they ask for me, tell them I'm not well."

Adaire approaches the front door and is overcome with a sense of dread. She takes a deep breath and opens it slowly. Then she slides through, dragging the long cape behind her. After pausing to look left and right, she carefully makes her way down the steps and through the mud to the barn, where Bunchy is saddled and waiting.

* * * * *

The woods are damp from recent rains, and Bunchy's hooves sink deep in the soft, wet ground. Adaire chooses a trail she and John rode often in the early days of their marriage, one that eventually takes her along the northern boundary of her farm, outside the village of Bentonville. Just as a thin crescent of weak light begins to spread beneath gray clouds, she notices several columns of smoke in the distance. She dismounts, ties Bunchy to a branch, and walks to the edge of the woods to get a better view of a pasture filled with rows of ragged tents. Soon, she is close enough to see groups of Confederate soldiers eating breakfast around small fires. Despite their bare feet and threadbare uniforms, they are laughing and talking as they pass around what appears to be pieces of blackened corn pone. Behind them, several wagons loaded with shovels, picks, and axes are mired in mud. A muleskinner stands nearby feeding a team of the most pathetic mules Adaire has ever seen. She pinches her nose and covers her mouth to stifle the odors of urine and unwashed bodies, then stands on tiptoe for a moment to study the ragged group. Too old, she thinks, mistaking the war-weary young skeletons for middle-aged men.

Adaire retreats again to the safety of the forest, maneuvering Bunchy through the thick underbrush dotted with huge pines, their needles bright green and bristling with the sharp smell of new sap. How quiet it is, she thinks. I haven't seen a single bird, or rabbit, or squirrel. They must know that it isn't safe for them here. It isn't for me, either. She looks cautiously over her shoulder and moves deeper through clumps of brambles, skirting the field of a neighbor's farm in hopes of reaching the Harper home before noon.

Dim light reaches the treetops and the blast of a nearby cannon and several rounds of rifle-shot break the still air. A moment later, the ground begins to shake as a sound like an oncoming freight train rumbles through the trees. Bunchy rears, then bolts while Adaire saws on the reins in an effort to control her. Ahead, thick columns of smoke rise like ghostly pillars, and Bunchy breaks into a run. Adaire jerks on the reins and pulls to the right, almost throwing herself over the animal's neck. To her relief, Bunchy slows to a trot and Adaire begins to talk to her. "Whoa, Bunch, whoa now, girl," she says, rubbing Bunchy's neck and pulling gently on the reins. As soon as she can safely dismount, she leads Bunchy back to the woods and ties her to a redbud.

She crouches near the trunk of a large oak and looks around. After a moment's hesitation, she inches toward an open field. From a distance of perhaps a quarter of a mile, she sees rows of heavy cannons mounted along each side of a pasture. In front of the cannons are earthen trenches filled with hundreds of guns that burst with deadly fire just as Adaire steps from the shelter of the trees. She watches, mesmerized, as cannon blasts send tons of mud and dozens of helpless men into the air. A bugle sounds and hordes of soldiers in blue arise from nowhere and charge across the field. A mass of ragged Confederates burst from the woods to challenge them. At the same moment, a Union cavalry officer hollers an order that calls hundreds of mounted soldiers into a stampede of yelling and gleaming bayonets. The din of the confrontation becomes so great so quickly that Adaire is caught off guard. As bullets whiz madly about her, she runs back into the woods, stumbling over the long black cape as she goes. Unhitching the frightened Bunchy, she urges the mare away from the scream of rifle balls. All around her, men are shouting at each other, their crude obscenities muffled in the smoldering air, and Adaire realizes her predicament as their voices come closer.

She spots a massive bramble and leads Bunchy toward it while the frightened animal snorts and flings its head about. Summoning all the strength she has, Adaire pulls Bunchy's head down, forcing her into the thicket as bullets zing over their heads, popping newly budded leaves off the trees with the sound of reeds snapping on a riverbank. Strips of bark fly around them as minie balls tear at the trunks of oak and pine.

Beneath the dripping branches, Adaire huddles near the ground, watching as a Confederate soldier stumbles, then falls, and a patch of red spreads across his neck. A group of blue coats emerges from the woods, and she is surprised to see one stop near the fallen Rebel and begin kicking him in the head. An old man dressed in butternut rushes toward the northern soldier, shoots him in the chest, then clubs him in the head with the butt of his musket. "You Lincoln-loving son-of-bitch, I'll show you!" he shouts as he stands over his victim, his foot planted on the boy's blood-covered torso. He bites the end off a paper cartridge and stuffs powder into his musket barrel, then raises the gun to hurry after his comrades. "No-good damn sons-of-bitches," he shouts in a voice reminiscent of Adaire's Kentucky hills.

The ground continues to shake from the constant barrage of cannon, while smoke descends over the area in thick, dark clouds. Hellfire and brimstone, Adaire thinks. Now I know what it will be like. Hunkering down in the mud, she rubs Bunchy's forelegs with hands that tremble. Her stomach churns and knots as a strong smell fills her nostrils. Reminds me of a hog-killing, she thinks, and she looks down to see rivulets of blood, thick with gore, coursing in the mud around her.

"God, help me," she cries. Tears fill her eyes and she begins to pray as she has never prayed before.

* * * * *

Adaire has no idea how long she has been in the bramble, but the rain has stopped and a pale sun is high in the clearing sky when she crawls out to stretch her stiffened joints and aching back. Cannons continue to roar somewhere in the distance as she leads Bunchy out of the thicket and into an opening where she steps over the bloody stump of a gray-clad arm. Nearby, a horse lies helpless, its chest heaving, both its hind legs missing. Bunchy begins a frantic dance at the site of the dying animal and her nostrils flare with the powerful stench of its blood.

All around Adaire are dead and dying men. One Confederate soldier's face is completely blown away; on another, the head is missing. A young boy lies sprawled before her, his lower jaw and right shoulder gaping holes. A Union officer is flattened against a poplar, his hands around a mass of bloody entrails that were once his stomach. Fallen blossoms from budding dogwoods lie scattered on dozens of mutilated corpses as the sweet, clinging odor of death overpowers the perfume of spring.

If I can just get away from here, Adaire thinks, drawing the blood-stained tail of John's cape out of the mud. If I can just get away from this God-forsaken place, I'll be all right. But I need some water . . . so foolish not to have brought some. I'll go up by the old Smithfield Road and stop at Mr. Brown's well before I start home.

She is dismayed to find that the old road to Smithfield is being used by Confederate troops, so she turns to a well-worn hunting trail she and John sometimes used on trips to the Harpers', one that will take her by the artesian well on Mr. Brown's farm.

As she nears the well-known spring, she hears the sound of voices, so she dismounts and slips behind a chinaberry tree. Peering from her cover, she's astonished to see dozens of soldiers from both armies crowded around a makeshift platform filling buckets and canteens. A white flag flies over their heads. Several soldiers are huddled on the ground playing cards; others are having idle conversations. This can't be happening, Adaire thinks. An hour ago they were hell-bent on killing each other, and now they're laughing and talking as if they were at a church picnic.

"Madam!"

Adaire's heart skips a beat. "Damn," she mutters, "I should have stayed away from here." She turns around to find a tall man with a bushy blond beard wearing a Federal uniform adorned with the chevrons of a colonel.

"Madam, I cannot imagine what you are doing here," he begins, "especially in that ridiculous get-up. But I suggest you vacate the area immediately or I shall have you arrested. Who are you?"

"Adaire Sanderson," she answers. "Mrs. John Sanderson. I live about a mile and a half east of here." She notices the gleam of wax on the officer's trimmed mustache, the mutton-chop sideburns that bush along his cheeks, the medals and campaign ribbons that cover one side of his spotless tunic.

"What do you think you're doing?" the Colonel asks, his deep blue eyes staring at her as if he were trying to get inside. "Don't you realize how dangerous this place is?"

"My son has run away and I'm trying to find him. He's fourteen and has begged to join the Army ever since his father was killed at Fort Fisher. I don't want to lose him, too."

"I have a fourteen-year-old boy myself." The Colonel's voice softens. "And I wouldn't want him to be in the middle of this hell. I suggest you go home now, Mrs. Sanderson. You won't be able to find your boy. Do you realize that we have more than sixty-thousand troops here? I'll give you an escort to see you safely home."

"That won't be necessary, Colonel. I'm not going home. I'm on my way to the Harper farm. My boy may be there. It's only a half mile, or so, south of here."

"As well I know, madam. The Harper home is in the hands of our army. We've converted it to a field hospital." The Colonel studies the woman before him—the sharp eyes, the determined mouth, the unlikely outfit. "But maybe that's not such a bad idea."

He turns and motions to a young man who detaches himself from the group at the well and starts toward the Colonel at a trot. "Yes, sir, Colonel Hightower," he says, his young face as serious as he can make it.

"Lieutenant, this is Mrs. Sanderson. She's offered to help out at our hospital down at the Harper place. See that she gets there safely." The Colonel removes a handkerchief from inside his tunic and hands it to Adaire. "I can see you've had a rough morning. Is there anything else I can do for you?"

Adaire throws the Colonel's handkerchief to the ground. "I came here to get water just like you did, and I don't intend to help out at your field hospital or any other hospital. I'm no nurse, and even if I were, I wouldn't help in a Yankee hospital!"

"You have no choice, madam. You'll help your friends, the Harpers, at their home, or I shall have you arrested and sent to the Federal Garrison at Goldsboro. Do you have any idea what becomes of spies?" The Colonel pauses. "Now, take my advice and follow the lieutenant out of here."

* * * * *

The Harper house is a two-story Greek revival shaded in summer by huge poplars and willow oaks that are just beginning to green. Adaire and her escort cross a large pasture where dozens of goats are huddled near an army wagon. Beneath its wheels, chickens peck in the rain-soaked soil. As she nears the back of her friend's house, Adaire pulls her horse to a stop as a long, low whistle plays on the lieutenant's thin lips. On the ground lie hundreds of dying soldiers. A few are on blankets, some on mounds of straw, but most are wallowing in mud.

"Let's dismount," suggests the lieutenant. "I wouldn't want my horse to step on one of these poor men. We'd better get our mounts out of the way of those wagons yonder."

A sour taste fills Adaire's mouth as wagons of wounded cross the yard, where the sweet smell of fresh blood hangs in the air. She is startled to see pairs of Negro orderlies in Union Army jackets push through the crowd bearing mud-caked men on stretchers. The wounded beg for water, cry for their mothers, and scream in animal-like sounds that float above the pasture. Adaire spots a young boy whose right arm is missing; a bloody stump signifies its recent amputation. She stares helplessly, her mind elsewhere. *Oh, Carl, your arms are so long and lean and strong. I wonder what I'd do if you came home without an arm. Or worse, with* both arms gone. Suppose you never come home? A shudder jerks her back to reality, and she hurries to catch up with the lieutenant.

The front porch of the Harper home has been made into an operating station, its wide door removed and placed across two casks to serve as an operating table. Blood-stained straw covers the floor. In one corner, an elegant mahogany table holds gruesome saws, hatchets, and knives, all coated with smears of drying blood. As Adaire approaches the front steps, a lanky red-haired man in a blood-soaked apron emerges from the entrance, followed by a tall, grim-faced woman dressed in green-and-yellow plaid. Splotches of blood streak the woman's bodice and dot the skirt of her dress where shreds of pink flesh cling to its filthy hem.

"Thank God, you're here!" the woman cries, crushing both of Adaire's hands. "I've been praying all morning that some of my neighbors would come. You're just in time to assist me with a really bad case." She leads Adaire across the yard toward a handsome soldier lying under an elm tree.

"Give me a hand," she commands. As she grabs the man under his right arm and lifts his torso, he starts to scream. "No! No! Please, lady!" Adaire stares down at his mangled leg and her arms remain limp at her sides.

"Got hit by a cannon blast. Tore his foot off," Mrs. Harper explains. This can't be happening, Adaire thinks. Why, she's never done anything more taxing than quilt. I've never seen her hands dirty. Now they're caked with dried blood and she's hauling a man around as if he were a sack of corn shucks.

"Come on, Adaire. Grab the other arm. We'll holler for someone to help us get him up the steps."

The soldier moans as the women drag him across the yard, pulling him in and out among dozens of prostrate men. "There simply aren't enough orderlies to take care of all these poor boys," says Mrs. Harper. "We have to move quickly or he'll bleed to death."

They finally reach the steps where two colored men in blue uniforms run down to meet them. They take the soldier from the women, place him on a stretcher, and hurry up the stairs to where a surgeon is waiting. As the doctor begins to probe the wound, the soldier struggles to sit up. "Leave me alone, you bastard," he cries, striking the doctor.

"Where's the chloroform?" the surgeon roars. Mrs. Harper rushes up the steps, grabs a bottle from her mahogany table, and begins to soak a linen napkin with clear liquid. As soon as she holds it near the wounded man's face, he falls back on the table and the doctor begins to cut away the blackened flesh around the wound.

"Bring that large knife from the fire, Sergeant," he orders. "We'll have to cauterize this one." He holds the searing knife against the man's leg, and the raw skin sizzles like sausage in a skillet. At the smell of burning flesh, Adaire fears she will vomit. She turns from the table to take in gulps of fresh air. Mrs. Harper grabs her by the arm and pulls her into the house. "Come on, honey. I know you must be burning up in that wool cape. Let's get you into something more comfortable."

As they enter the hall, Adaire sees another man at work, his hands and lower arms coated with bright, fresh blood. The soiled green sash of a Union Army Surgeon is knotted at his waist. A large medicine chest of half-filled bottles stands just inside the parlor door, and buckets of bloody water line the wall near the fireplace. Mrs. Harper's yellow, watered-silk draperies are spotted with blood, as is the damask settee where three men are slumped together, their arms outstretched, their eyes covered with bandages. "It's the same all over the house," Mrs. Harper explains. "Blood, blood, and more blood. Everything is ruined. But we can't think about that, can we? We've got all these poor soldiers to think about." *Yankee* soldiers, Adaire thinks, surprised at Mrs. Harper's compassion for the enemy, surprised at the woman who has always given outspoken support to the Confederate cause. As they start up the stairs, Mrs. Harper turns to Adaire once more. "I know you're wondering why we're helping the Federals, Adaire. The colonel who is in charge, Colonel Hightower, promised me he would find out where Mr. Harper is being held prisoner if we would cooperate. I had no choice, don't you see?"

She continues up the stairs, pausing on the landing. "The surgeons made us move all of our personal effects from the bedrooms so they could use them as wards. So we put our things in the trunk closet. It's the only place we can call our own and it's crowded. Old Mrs. Harper's in there, Adaire. She just sits in there and refuses to come out. She tried to shoot one of the Yankee officers yesterday. Don't be surprised if she doesn't speak to you. She won't talk, and she won't eat. She just sits at the window, watching the battlefield."

Mrs. Harper opens the door to a small closet-like room and ushers Adaire in. "Mother Harper, look who's come to see us. Adaire Sanderson's come to pay us a call."

The old lady sits in her night clothes and mob cap near a small window. She does not move, nor speak, nor change her expression, but continues to stare out the window as Adaire removes her cape, her gun, her pants. She rolls the gun inside the cape and pushes the bundle out of sight, while young Mrs. Harper opens one of the trunks and takes out a pink muslin dress festooned with Irish lace. As soon as she has it on, Adaire turns to her friend. "The reason I came over, Mrs. Harper, is to look for my boy, Carl. He ran off during the night."

"Oh, my dear, how dreadful. Do you suppose he's joined the Army?"

"I certainly hope not. But he wanted to. I came over here to find out if Lee might have seen him last night."

"Lee's out at the barn. Come with me."

They leave old Mrs. Harper sitting in her rocker and start down the hall. Adaire feels a tug on her skirt and turns to see an old man, his left arm bandaged, his left hand gone. "Ma'am," he croaks, "may I bother you for a drink of water?" Lice crawl over his greasy hair and down his putty-colored uniform. "I'll see that you get some," Adaire promises. Beside the man are two young boys, their arms draped about each other like brothers in a photograph. One is dead.

Adaire finds Mrs. Harper talking to a large colored man whom she knows as the Harper butler, Gabe. Gabe is shaking his head.

"No'm, I ain't seen Master Sanderson, Missus," he says. "Master Lee? He be out to the field by the big barn where they's burying them poor soldiers."

"Go get him, Gabe. We'll meet you in the backyard. Come along, Adaire," says Mrs. Harper. "We need to give these poor boys some water." She leads Adaire out back to the watering trough and begins to fill two buckets. Adaire sees Mrs. Harper's personal maid, Annie, and her cook moving among the soldiers, putting damp rags on their foreheads. She takes the bucket and gourd dipper from Mrs. Harper.

"Just try to get a little in the ones that aren't unconscious," her friend instructs. "It'll be hard. Just do the best you can, honey."

"What about those men upstairs?" Adaire asks.

"I'll send Annie to take care of them. Here comes Lee."

Like the other residents of the Harper place, her son's clothes are covered with bloody stains and streaked with mud. Adaire watches the heavyset boy as he picks his way among the wounded as if he were marching in a band. "Did you want me, Mama?"

"Son, have you seen Carl Sanderson?"

"Yes, ma'am." He turns to look at Adaire. "He came here last night, Mrs. Sanderson. A little after midnight. I was in the barn tending the soldiers. He talked a lot about his father and about how bad he felt running out on you and the family. I think he thought he was deserting you. He wanted me to go with him to join General Hampton's outfit. But I told him I couldn't. I promised Mama I wouldn't after we found out that Papa was taken prisoner."

"Where did he go, son?"

"I guess he went on down to Mr. Cole's place. That's where a lot of General Hampton's boys were camped. At least, that's what I heard from the Yanks in the barn. He stayed here about an hour. Had a musket with him. That's all I know, Mrs. Sanderson."

"Thank you, Lee." Adaire nods, grateful that someone knew Carl's whereabouts last night. "I know your mother is mighty glad to have you here."

Mrs. Harper puts a hand on her son's shoulder. "Run along now, honey, and take care of the soldiers," she says just as Annie comes around the house and hollers, "Miz Harper, the doctor need you. He say come right away."

Both women hurry to the front of the house where they find two soldiers holding down a young boy who has been shot in the upper thigh. "You sons of bitches, let me go!" the wounded man yells from a swollen mouth covered with sores. He starts to kick with his good leg while the soldiers try to keep him still. "You're not going to cut off my leg, damn you. Let me go!" After striking one of the soldiers, he loses his balance and falls back on the table. Adaire hears a chopping sound and turns to see a surgeon on the porch hacking off another soldier's fingers with a hatchet. He throws the severed digits into a bloody pile of arms and legs behind him and bellows, "Nurse!" Mrs. Harper takes the stairs two at a time. "Where have you been?" the doctor demands. "Can't you see we need you? Get the chloroform ready. We're going to look for the bullets in that boy's thigh." He looks down the stairs where he sees Adaire. "Get up here," he yells.

Adaire starts up the steps, but the doctor stops her midway. "Get some hot water and clean bandages." She stands on the steps not knowing which way to turn. She has no idea where to look for bandages.

"In the dining room, honey," calls Mrs. Harper. "Annie will help you."

After a few minutes, Adaire returns to the porch with a bucket of steaming water and a basket of freshly rolled bandages that look remarkably like pieces of her own camisoles and petticoats.

"Here, woman! Get that water over here!" the doctor commands while Mrs. Harper holds a handkerchief over the boy's face. The doctor begins to cut away the stiff, soiled material around the wound.

"Now, lady," the doctor says looking at Adaire, "this ain't gonna be no cake cutting. I want you to staunch the blood so I can see to poke around in there. I think this boy has two minies in him. Grab a couple of rolls." He points to the basket and Adaire takes out several bandages and waits for the doctor to tell her what to do.

"What the hell, lady! Get over here," he bellows. Adaire moves closer, looking down at the boy's fuzz-covered cheeks as the doctor beings to probe. "Now, lady, now! Stick the bandage in that hole!"

The tips of Adaire's fingers push against bone as the bandage fills with blood. "Do it again," the doctor orders. Poking in a fresh wad, she watches as the blood soaks the cloth and runs across her fingers. The doctor moves against her side and begins lifting the flesh around the bone in an effort to locate the ball, while drops of perspiration fall from his brow onto the boy's pale leg. "Yes, yes," he whispers, "there's one." He pulls out the tiny missile with its razor-sharp edges dripping blood.

"Let's try again, lady. You're doing a good job. Now push that wad of bandage in there real tight and we'll get us another one."

The boy begins to moan and Adaire, without knowing it, whispers, "Carl." As the doctor pushes an instrument deep into the wound, blood spurts over his shirt and spatters the lacey bodice of Adaire's borrowed finery. After a few seconds, he pulls out the second ball. "Stop that blood, lady!" he yells. "Press, press!" Adaire presses with all her strength until her hands are washed with the blood of her enemy.

She stands at the table assisting the doctor for hours that pass like sap oozing from a pine. Her shoulders and arms ache from holding the delirious men . . . all of whom have Carl's face . . . until Mrs. Harper can sedate them. Her legs and back feel as if she has spent the day chopping cotton.

She has learned to close her eyes when horribly gruesome sights become too much for her, has adjusted to the sound of a never-ending cannon blast, to the pitiful moans of the dying, the screams of the living, and to cursing, the likes of which she has never heard. With her help, the doctor has amputated nine limbs and removed dozens of minie balls. Late in the afternoon, Adaire had stood helplessly at his side while he stitched up the lower torso of a yellow-haired boy brought to the table with his intestines bulging out. Another Carl. She had wept quietly, knowing he would not live through the night.

At dusk, two large covered wagons, their sides laden with skillets and stew pots, arrive at the front of the house. Several grizzled men jump from the wagon seats and unload sacks of white flour and beans, pork shoulders, and gallon tins of sugar and coffee . . . more food than Adaire has seen at one time in over a year. Two of the men build fires in the front yard, while others come from around the side of the house bringing dozens of freshly plucked chickens. As the cook slices the hams, the sweet scent reaches Adaire and she realizes she has not eaten all day. Annie appears bearing a tray of Mrs. Harper's Haviland cups filled with fresh coffee. Adaire sits down on the porch steps to sip the wonderful nectar as the chuckwagon team works in the midst of chaos.

After a while, the cook yells to Mrs. Harper, "Hey, lady, we got some broth ready if you want to try to feed some of these poor devils." Adaire rises to help her friend.

Meanwhile, Gabe and Lee bring the Harper's dining room table to the front yard and Gabe sets it with a white linen cloth, china, and silver. Adaire, Lee, and Mrs. Harper join the surgeons at the table, where they consume a filling meal. Darkness descends, but is hardly noticeable as the blasts from the cannon keep the sky ablaze with a deadly glare.

Light rain begins to spatter the table and Mrs. Harper excuses herself. She spoons up a plate of leftovers, saying, "I must see about my mother-in-law. She hasn't eaten a thing for three days. Mrs. Sanderson, please join us when you are ready to retire."

Adaire has not thought about spending the night at the Harper's, but she knows it is much too late to start for home, and too late to look for Carl, so she bids the men a good evening.

The house and grounds are quiet now, except for the soft patter of rain and the sound of metal scraping against mud where the freed men continue to bury the dead in the field near the barn. Adaire picks her way down the crowded hall and trudges up the stairs.

She knocks quietly on the trunk room door, then opens it. As her eyes adjust to the darkness, she hears material rustling and sees Mrs. Harper putting a piece of cloth over her mother-in-law's face, carefully adjusting the length of material so that its sides are even. "I was afraid this would happen," her friend says. "She's never gotten over old Mr. Harper's death, and what with her only son taken prisoner. . . . You know she came here as a girl not long after the Revolution. Met old Mr. Harper at a wedding in Goldsboro." She pats the dead woman's white head. "She was a good woman. May she rest in peace." She hands Adaire an embroidered baby pillow. "I'm afraid the floor will have to do, Adaire. At least it has a rug on it." Adaire drops to the floor with the pillow, realizing that she has never slept in a room with a corpse. She considers this for a moment before her eyes close.

CHAPTER 2:
A LETTER FROM ADAIRE
TO HER COUSIN

Sand Hill Farm
September 12, 1865

Dear Cousin Hettie,

I pray my letter finds you well. It seems that good health is all we can ask these days. We were astounded and shattered by the news that the entire South will now exist under the military rule of the Union Army. Why, Hettie, must this most terrible burden be borne on the heels of all our recent burdens? What can the leaders of this newly re-united country be thinking? That we Southerners will rise up again to burn and pillage their houses and farms as they have ours? For God's sake, we are on our knees. Can they not see that? Must they take all our possessions, our beloved sons and husbands, our guns, our rights, the very ground we stand on? When will this horror end? In spite of the hardships we must endure, life goes on, and I have some good news to share with you, even in these difficult times.

Janey, with help from Ludie, delivered a small, but healthy baby girl on August 20. She is truly a beauty, with Janey's blue eyes and her father's golden curls. I am so sorry to report that we lost Edward. He was taken prisoner near Richmond in March and died shortly thereafter in a camp in New York. A Union officer was kind enough to write to Janey and to send her the chevrons and buttons from Edward's uniform (I suppose not much else was left). I was afraid Janey might buckle under so great a burden, but she held up well for the sake of the baby, whom she has named Margaret Adaire for the two grandmothers.

I'm sure you are aware that a battle was fought right here. Hettie, it was too horrible to describe. I pray that I shall never see such destruction again as long as I live. We had been warned that Sherman's

Army might come our way, so I sent Carl and Phillip to John's fish camp on the creek with Tyner. They took the only cow we had left and some hogs and a wagon loaded with food, clothing, and quilts. A troop of Yankee soldiers came to the farm looking for food and took most of my chickens. They tore up all our pasture fences and hauled the wood off on wagons. But you folks in Savannah know all about what they did, don't you? Carl ran away from the fish camp the night the battle started. (After John's death, he begged to join the Army, but I wouldn't let him.) I went out to look for him the next day, but without success. What I did find was absolute Hell on Earth in the form of a Union field hospital. Never have I dreamed of such horrors, such suffering, such agony. And so many men died here. We have heard reports of more than four thousand. I never found Carl, but I was told that he had gone down to the Coles' to join up. You remember the Coles, don't you? They were at Janey's wedding. Sherman used their house as his headquarters, and it was completely demolished during the battle. The Coles have moved to Smithfield to live with his brother.

Carl was brought home at the end of April across the saddle of a lovely young man, a Major Warren McLean, who was on his way home to Wilmington. My boy was plagued with the ague, Hettie. He had a high fever and a terrible cough and suffered from constant chills. Of course, he was covered with lice and couldn't keep any food down. Ludie made teas and poultices, but he didn't improve, so I went into Goldsboro to get a doctor. Old Doc Haynes was killed in the war, and the only doctor in town was a Yankee. I was so desperate, I never gave it a second thought. A Union officer whom I met during the battle, a Colonel Hightower, saw me and took me to the house where the doctor is living (the townhouse of the Cosgroves, who fled to England in 1861). The doctor came back to the farm with me and diagnosed Carl's illness as pneumonia. He gave Carl large doses of quinine and the fever went away in a couple of days. I am thanking our Lord every day for restoring my son's health. As soon as he was able, Carl told us of his "great adventure" soldiering. He joined up with General Johnston and went with his army all the way to Orange County (west of Raleigh) to a farm where Johnston surrendered to Sherman. We had heard that General Lee had had to surrender in Virginia. A messenger from Mitchner's Station came by here to tell us three days after it happened. But we had no notion of where Johnston or Sherman were or what had happened, until Carl was brought home.

There has been a steady stream of poor ragged boys passing here all summer. I feel so sorry for them and try to feed as many as I can. We caught one pitiful wraith stealing eggs from the henhouse, so I had Ludie cook them for him, and I sat down at the table while he ate. He was on his way to Georgia, barefooted, of course, and had not had anything to eat for two days. I asked him how he intended to walk all the way to Georgia without shoes and with nothing to eat, and he looked me in the eye and said, "Lady, the miles that's ahead of me ain't nothin' compared to them I traveled for the last three years." That broke my heart.

Hundreds of Negroes have come here, too. Most are ragged and starving (just like the soldiers) and utterly helpless. They are headed to Goldsboro, where the Federals will feed them twice a day and give them shelter (old army tents). At night, they play banjos and fiddles and dance around their campfires singing about the "jubilee." I wonder how they will stay alive this winter—and afterwards. I am fortunate to have Tyner and Ludie with me. Our field workers, including their oldest boy, Hector, and Tyner's two brothers, ran off. Ludie rec'd a letter in July informing us that Hector fled to Brunswick, where he joined the Union army. He is living in Boston and working on the docks there and learning to read and write (there's a new day coming, Hettie). His teacher wrote the letter for him, but he signed it himself. Janey spent a lot of time this summer teaching Ludie and Tyner how to read and write, and both are proving to be good scholars. Ludie is very quick with her sums, and Tyner loves poetry. They told me recently that they intend to shorten their name to Sanders.

Janey has been tutoring Phillip in Latin, mathematics, and grammar. I always admired the way her father insisted that she be tutored right along with Carl. Not many of our Southern gentlemen would have agreed to such a radical notion. Janey wants to open a school for the children on neighboring farms. Now that all our young men are gone, I suppose we women will continue to bear these heavy loads. It seems inconceivable that women will become tutors or school masters (mistresses?), but I suppose it may be the only way our children can learn their lessons.

Speaking of new jobs, I never thought I would be digging bullets out of tree trunks to feed my family, but Tyner and Ludie and I have been doing just that. I know this must seem strange, but Colonel Hightower (I mentioned him earlier) told me that the Federals in Goldsboro would pay for used lead from battle sites. We collected a half-dozen baskets full and divided the money. Had the Federals placed a premium on human bones, we would be rich as Croesus, we found so many. At first it upset me, but soon it became commonplace to discover a skull or two beneath the trees where we were digging.

There has been a great demand for dressmakers by the Yankee women who are living here. Of course, they are the only ones who can afford to hire someone to make their clothes. They have a tendency to dress quite lavishly even in the daytime—especially the officer's wives. You've never seen such furbelows and swags. All braided and whorled, too. Ludie has been sewing for several of them, including the Colonel's wife. I'm sure you recall what a fine seamstress Ludie is. (Remember my beautiful satin wedding dress?) She is making enough money to buy cloth to make clothes for her family.

Tyner and Ludie and I have a contract to work the farm on shares this year. As soon as we learned of the surrender, they asked me to talk with them about "a settlement on the work to be done." Tyner told me they wanted 25 percent of the profits. I'm sure that astonishment showed plainly on my face because Ludie immediately said that 5 percent per family member seemed fair since all of them would work, including their baby, Millie. I found the whole conversation off-putting. I was so upset that I went into the house to think it over. That night, I went out to the cabin to remind them that I owned the land and that I, not they, had to pay taxes on it, but they stuck to 25%. Ludie is the smartest darky I've ever seen, and I just don't believe, like I once did, that Negroes are as inferior as we thought. It took three days of conversation before we finally settled on 18 percent.

The Baker family is erecting a store up on the Old Smithfield road about a mile and a half from here. It seems that some of Sherman's men went to the Baker farm before the battle and torched the house of one of the brothers and then went on over to the other brother's house and began putting the torches under it. Well, Sherman came along, and in a conversation with the owner, he learned that Mr. Baker was a Mason, so Sherman ordered that the torches be removed and that his army move out of the area. It seems that he is a Mason, too. I heard that Mr. Baker used his Mason connections to borrow money from the Yankees in Goldsboro to build the store. It will be nice not to have to go so far to buy sugar and coffee—provided we can scrape up the money.

Carl is leaving Saturday for the Hillsborough Academy. I sold my mother's blue sprigged china (service for twelve) and a silver plate to a Yankee storekeeper in Goldsboro to pay for his tuition and train ticket. I refuse to send my boys to a military school, Hettie, even though many people say it's the best education a boy can get. I have given this decision much thought. In fact, it has been heavy on my mind since our travail last March. War is just too awful to contemplate, and I don't want my boys to grow up to be warriors. Goldsboro is full of dozens of helpless, maimed men who sit around on old ammunition boxes complaining about the Yankee soldiers everywhere.

I am sending along some paper and hope that you will be able to write to us soon. Colonel Hightower was kind enough to give me a whole sheaf and a bottle of ink. We have been without both all summer. Isn't it strange how we take so many things for granted until we no longer have them? Then they become the most unattainable luxuries. I want to share this luxury with those I love.

> I pray that you are safe and well and remain
> Your devoted cousin,
> Adaire

P.S.—We have not had a church since the battle. The Yankees burned ours over near Bentonville. Tyner made every one of its oak pews and he just cried like a baby when I told him. I did, too. Why would anyone burn a church? What harm can churches do? Some of the biggest, most elaborate churches I've ever seen are in the North. I wonder how their parishioners would feel if someone burned their houses of worship?

Ludie and Tyner want to build a church on the farm for the negroes, but I can't think about that until our own church is rebuilt.

CHAPTER 3:
BEAVER DAM

February 5, 1866

Ludie pours a cup of coffee and sets it on the table between Adaire and Colonel Hightower. "Cream, sir?" she asks, offering the pitcher.

The Colonel nods. "Thank you, Ludie. It sure is a pleasure to come in from the cold to a warm fire and some friendly hospitality."

"Well, you're to thank for whatever we have in the way of company fare," Adaire says. "If it weren't for you, I doubt we'd have any coffee. You really are too kind, sir, to bring us all these fine luxuries." She eyes the knapsack at the Colonel's feet and wonders about its contents. Since the end of the war, the Colonel has visited Sand Hill about once a month, bringing hard-to-get items such as sugar, white flour, spices, and needles and thread.

"Did you have a good Christmas?" the Colonel asks between sips of coffee.

"Well, we had enough to eat and managed to stay warm," Adaire replies. "Gifts were scarce this year. Mostly whatever we could make from scraps. I took apart an old hooked rug I had in the attic and knit caps and scarves for all the children. Tyner carved some little wooden dolls for Alice and Millie and a bow and set of arrows for each of his boys. We killed one of the shoats a couple of days before, and it was wonderful to have fresh pork. Thank goodness our sage bushes weren't destroyed. I want to be sure you leave here today with some of Ludie's fine sausage, Colonel."

"Why, thank you. I shall look on it as a gift from the gods." The Colonel turns to smile at Ludie, then looks back at Adaire. "You mentioned that Janey is away visiting Edward's sister and her husband. Where do they live?"

"Fayetteville. Janey left last Wednesday with Margaret Adaire and will be home sometime tomorrow." Adaire picks up a plate of Ludie's molasses cookies. "Won't you have another cake, Colonel?"

"No, no, thank you, Mrs. Sanderson. I just stopped by to see how all of you are faring in the cold. It's hard to believe that it's been almost a year since we met, isn't it?" He pauses and looks across the room to the mantle where a tintype of John Sanderson is displayed among several Confederate relics. "I'll never forget seeing you sneaking around in your husband's uniform, with that big cape dragging behind you like a train." He chuckles quietly to himself and then looks at Adaire, his face flushed with embarrassment. "Forgive me, Mrs. Sanderson, I know you think me an awful bore. I come here and enjoy your home and company and then laugh about one of the most dreadful days in your life." He moves closer to Adaire, his blue eyes filled with wonder. "You will never know how much I admired your courage."

Adaire puts her empty cup on the table. "I did what any other Southern mother would have done, given the circumstances. But it is hard to believe it was just a year ago. Well, almost a year. It seems as if that happened in another lifetime. And the sad thing was, I never found Carl."

"And how is the young scamp? Have you heard from him lately?"

"Yes, indeed. Bless his heart, he is good about writing. But I think he's miserably homesick. When he left here after Christmas, he almost cried. He says he's learning a lot at the Academy, but the professors are very strict. He's made several new friends, so it isn't all bad. He told Ludie he wished he could take her back with him because the food is pretty awful. They have oatmeal every morning and sop bread in gravy for supper nearly every night."

The Colonel brushes a napkin across his bushy mustache. "I had to endure some of that when I was a boy in Ohio. I suppose every young man who leaves home to get an education really misses the comforts and niceties he always took for granted."

"It's about time my boy appreciated something. Until Major McLean brought him home at the end of the war, he'd probably never had an appreciative thought in his life."

"How is the major?"

"From what we know, I would say he's doing well. We had a card at Christmas. He's working in his father's livery stables in Wilmington. Carl hopes to get down there to visit him when this term's over. Speaking of Christmas, how was your trip to Ohio? Is your family well?"

"Yes, but my father is beginning to suffer a bit from gout, and mother seems to be losing her hearing. We had a nice visit with my brother and his wife, though. You know, that's where my son, Stephen, spends his holidays from school. They're childless, so they really enjoy having him for a few days."

The Colonel and Adaire pause in their conversation as the back-door slams shut. Heavy footsteps in the hallway precede a knock on the parlor door.

"Come in," Adaire calls.

Tyner steps into the room dressed in a shabby brown coat, obviously dyed to conceal its original dark blue, and a multi-colored cap and scarf. He nods to Adaire.

"Afternoon, ma'am. Afternoon, Colonel," he says, removing his cap and rubbing his hands together. "Mighty cold, ain't it?"

"Yes, it surely is, Tyner," the Colonel agrees. "About as cold as it gets around here, I suppose. Nothing compared to Ohio this time of the year. Mrs. Sanderson tells me you and Phillip were out hunting. Have any luck?"

"Yes, sir. Sure did. Got a half-dozen rabbits. That Red, he a fine hunting dog. Just as good with rabbits as he is with coons."

"Did you see any deer, Tyner?" the Colonel asks.

"No, sir. Not a one. Seen a few tracks where they been to the creek to drink. 'Spect they's all hunkered down in the brush somewheres trying to stay warm. Seen lots of beaver, though. They busy building on they dam. Got it all fixed up. Guess they laying stuff on 'cause of the weather."

"Since this is my first Carolina winter, you'll need to educate me about what to expect. Do you think it might actually snow?"

"Yes, sir, I sure do." Tyner puts his cap on and heads to the door. "Well, I gotta get back out to the cabin. Oh, I almost forgot why I come in here." He looks over at Ludie. "Ben's come back."

"What? Ben . . . here?" Adaire stammers.

"Yessum, he's back, Miz Adaire. Brought his wife with him. They out in the cabin almost froze to death. Asia's getting them some vittles."

Adaire turns to the Colonel. "Ben is Tyner's baby brother," she explains. "He and Tyner's other brother, Grady, left here a couple of years ago. Ran away one night. We haven't heard from them since. Where have they been, Tyner?"

"Ben been with the Federals in Newberne. He say Grady gone up north. Ben work for the Yankees for the last year in they camp."

"Is that right?" The Colonel rises from the dainty chair that's barely broad enough to hold him. "I'd like to talk to your brother, if I may. You say he's in the cabin?"

"Yes, sir. I'm sure he'd be happy to 'commodate you, sir."

The Colonel bows to Adaire. "Won't you join us, Mrs. Sanderson?"

"By all means." Adaire stands and pulls a shawl around her shoulders. "If Ben's brought a bride, I want to meet her. Come on, Ludie. We'd better go make sure they get enough to eat."

* * * * *

Ben is seated at the plank table, his thick arms wrapped around a bowl of peas, one hand busy with a spoon, the other with a piece of corn bread. Beside him is a small young woman the color of cane syrup. At the end of the table, Millie and Alice pretend to play with their Christmas dolls, while they steal glances at the two strangers. Sam and Amos are huddled in a corner, giggling and pointing, their faces full of mischief. Asia ladles more peas into Ben's bowl while Ludie pours buttermilk for her brother-in-law.

Ben gets to his feet when he sees Adaire. "How do, ma'am," he says as if he has never been away.

"Hello, Ben," Adaire nods. "Who's your friend?"

Ben turns to the girl on the bench and takes her by the arm. She stands, but does not look up.

"This my wife, Letha," he answers.

Adaire looks quickly at the girl, at her patched jacket and thin calico skirt, at the shabby Army boots that have chafed her bare ankles.

"Welcome to Sand Hill, Letha," she says. "This is Colonel Hightower. He's a friend of the family who dropped by for a visit. You and Ben get back to your meal. I know you're hungry. The Colonel wants to ask you a few questions, Ben."

Ludie brings a plate of ash cakes from the fire and rubs off their black coating with a damp rag before she sets them on the table.

"Ain't no need to be afraid," she whispers to Letha. "The Colonel and Miz Adaire is good peoples." She pulls a side of bacon from a hook in the rafters and turns to Asia, who is standing near her parents' bed. "Run get me some fresh milk," she orders, "and take these little girls with you." She nods in the direction of Millie and Alice and gives a sharp look to her boys.

"Be sure to put on coats and caps," Adaire warns as the little girls hurry after Millie's big sister, who takes their wraps from pegs on the wall near the door.

Ludie begins frying thick slices of bacon while the Colonel lights his pipe. He stands in front of the hearth, drawing on it as Ben and Letha sop their peas with bits of ash cake.

"Tyner says you were with the Union Army in Newberne, Ben. How did you come to be way out there?"

Ben crams the last bite of food in his mouth and drags the tail of his frayed shirt-sleeve across his lips.

"Well, me and my brother, Grady, stay on Mistuh Sanderson's place and we hear that we is free and run off one night about two year ago. Stayed out in the woods for a long time. Mostly 'round Neuse Islands and back in there. Trap us some possum and catch a few fish. Mostly live on that. Possum and fish. 'Course in the summer we gots wild grapes, persimmons, briar berries and such. Summer weren't too bad but when winter come on, we decides to go on over to Goldsboro 'cause we hope we can find us some food and somewheres warm to stay. We was powerful hungry sometimes out in them woods. So we went on over to Goldsboro and hid out on some them farms west of the railroad for a couple months last winter. Mostly we stay in old falling-down barns at night and hide out in the woods in the daytime. One day we sees this group a Federals coming along, so we starts following 'em, but we's real careful and stay off'n the road. And one them officers, he holler out, 'We knows you is back there following us. Come on out. We ain't gonna hurt you none.' Well, me and Grady like most colored folk here 'bouts. We scared of army mens. So we just hunkers down in some bushes. Little while later that same Yankee, he say, 'You is free. Don't be 'fraid. Come on out.'

"Well, me and Grady knows we's free. We just ain't sure what it mean. Mistuh John done and told us we's free way back. That's when we left Sand Hill. Anyways, Grady and me step out'n the brush and all them Yankees commence to hollering and clapping they hands. They give us some bread so tough we hardly able to chaw it. Then they stops in this grove of poplars and sets up they camp. Me and Grady starts helping 'em build they fires and tote water, just anything they needs 'cause we so hungry. And they give us food, and a heap of it. I 'member how good that plate of food was. The best taters and salt beef I ever et. Then they says, 'We's on our way back to Camp Pierson. Y'all want to come and work for us?' Well, me and Grady ain't never heard of that place but we go 'cause we knows that way we can eat. So we stays with them soldiers and marches along with them about four, maybe five, days and then we comes to they camp. Rows and rows of tents all set out near the river. And big cook pots bubblin' everywhere. Soldiers setting outside the tents playing cards and all. Never had seen nothing like that before. No, sir. And off yonder, over this little ridge, you can see Newberne. 'Course I never did go down there 'cause I was afraid some-body," he says, pausing to look at Tyner, "I was afraid they might shoot me. Me and Grady got us some reg'lar work driving wagons, hauling supplies in from the river and taking 'em round to the diff'rent places for the soldiers. And us got paid, too. Then the war over and most the soldiers go on back north where they come from. Grady and me still working, but one day the major say they don't need us no more. Grady figures he gonna go up north with this soldier he knowed. But I thinks I come on back 'cause I miss my folks. I knowed Tyner and Ludie still here with you," he says, looking at Adaire. "Hopes you don't mind, Miz Adaire. This place my home."

Adaire nods. "What are your plans, Ben?"

"Ain't got none, missus. Me and Letha was hoping somebody might use good hard working peoples like us on they farm. 'Course we know white folk having some hard times. Seem like nobody we knows got nothing much now."

Adaire leaves Ludie's rocker and sits down on the bench across from the young brown woman who has, up to this point, said nothing.

"You're right, Ben," she agrees. "Everybody we know is having a right rough go of it. Tyner and I have worked out a contract based on shares. There's no money, so I can't pay. All I've got is empty fields. We could use some help. But before we talk about that, I want to know your wife better. Where's she from?"

"She come from over 'round Trenton." Ben grins as his chest swells. "Met her in the camp last year."

"Well, why don't you let her tell us," Adaire suggests, looking at

Letha. "Were you born in Trenton?"

Letha brings her thin arms closer to her body and pulls herself up straight. Before she speaks, she licks her top lip, and with eyes that are as soft and innocent as a child's, she looks over at her husband.

"Me and my mama live out on this big old farm called Briarcrest when I was little. Don't 'member exactly where that was. Belong to old man Jasper and his missus. My mama was they washerwoman. They won't too bad. Old missus, she give Mama a extra ration a cornmeal or side meat sometime. Old Mistuh Jasper won't around much, but one day he call me and Mama to the big house and he trade us for a mule and wagon. And that's how we come to belong to old Missus Pollock what own a big place near Trenton. She a widow. Her husband a preacher, but he die 'fore we been there more'n a week. Just up and fall out one day on the porch. Eyes roll back in his head and he making this funny noise in his throat. Real scary." Letha shivers at the memory and rubs her hands over the goose bumps on her crossed arms.

"We stays there with Missus Pollock nigh on to eight year. One day we seen all this dust a rising down the road and this little gal run up a'hollering that the Yankees was coming. I was fourteen year at the time. Everybody come from the fields and the barns and all and stand 'round in the yard while the Federals is marching up the road. We seen 'em for a long ways. And this soldier boss come right up to the porch where the missus standing and tell her they gonna camp there and for her to get some grub together to feed 'em. Well, my mama grab me by the collar and drag me to the cabin so fast my feets fly out from unner me. And she takes a big old knife and cuts every braid off'n my head. Law, that was awful. Then she tell me to take off my frock and she give me a pair trousers she grab off'n a bush on the way to the quarters. She take a sack and tear it up and wrap it all round my chest to make me flat. Then she put a old shirt on me and pull a cap down on my head and say, 'You keeps your mouth shut, gal, and do what I tells you. Now walk like this.' Then she commence to hobbling like she got a busted leg and she say, 'Them Yankees might hurt you do they know you is a woman.'

"Well, the Yankees goes out to the hog parlor and shoots three or four Missus Pollack's big old boar hogs and they scrapes 'em and digs 'em a trench to roast 'em in. And they drags everything out the smokehouse, too. They goes in the big house and hauls out all the feather beds and pillows and bedclothes and start rippin 'em up. Feathers flying every which way. They carries on most the night singing and dancing with one another, sashaying 'round and drinking Missus Pollock's fancy stuff off'n the sideboard. And they calls us to come and dance for 'em. Some the little 'uns start doing the buck and them Yanks start throwing money at 'em. And old missus, she come out and run them young'uns off with a broom and she say to them Yankees, 'Ain't you cause a heap of mis'ry already? You done took everything we gots. Now you making fun of us. Ain't you got no decency? Leave my little chillun alone!' And the man what rode his horse up to the porch, he say, 'They ain't yours no more, lady. They is free.' And old missus, she say, 'Fine with me. You take care of 'em!'"

"Next day, them Yankees packs up everything they can carry off with 'em. All the furniture, the tools out'n the sheds, the clothes, the milk cows and chickens, just everything. And the boss man, he come over to Mama and he say, 'How come you still here? You knows you is free?'"

"And Mama say, 'Yes, sir, we knows, but we ain't got nowhere to go.' Then the bossman say, 'You can come with us. We need a good washerwoman. And your boy,' he look over at me then, 'he can feed the mules and horses and haul water for us.' Well, the missus just cry and cry. 'Don't leave me, Nancy,' she say. That's Mama. But Mama don't pay no mind. She just put our mess in a sack and off us goes with them Yankees."

Adaire pinches off a bite of ash cake from the plate on the table. "Weren't you afraid," she asks, "going off with an army?"

"Yessum. We sure was. But my mama a big woman, and she don't take much off nobody. She told me to stay right with her. And I did."

"Where did the Federals take you?"

"Well, we camp in the woods two, maybe three nights. Everywhere we go, more and more folk joins up with us. 'Bout a hundred or more. They just come out'n the woods and all. And the Yanks feeds 'em and gives 'em something to wear. Finally, we get to Camp Pierson. Me and Mama, we start washing the soldier's clothes and the Army pays us. Won't much but sure was nice to get a little coin for the work we done. Then Mama start making pies for the soldiers and the money pick up considerable. She make pies, lots of 'em, every week, and the soldiers line up for 'em. She hide the money she gets in her old shoes. Then one day, I sees Ben. 'Course he ain't got no idea I'm a gal 'cause I still be wearing my cap and them worn-out trousers. I fuss and fuss 'til I get Mama to let me put a frock on. And I makes sure he sees me in it." Letha begins to giggle, covering her mouth with her hand. "You shoulda seen his face when I done it. Plumb stupified, he was," she says, laughing.

Ben bows his head. After a moment, he looks up and smiles at Letha. "Then we start courting," he says. "Ever evening after supper, I take her out for a walk down to the river. One night we hear that the war be over, so I goes to the cap'm the next day and say me and Letha wants to marry. So he come that evening with the preacher, and we stand down by the river and he say a few words over us and reads from the Bible. When he done, Mama give everybody some her pie and the cap'm pass out the coffee. He want me to stay on and help look after the camp for a while, so I done it. But I got powerful lonesome for this place 'round Christmas time, and me and Letha know we want to come here after that." He looks at Adaire. "I'm a hard worker, Miz Adaire. You knows that. And Letha and me, we don't need much. We be willing to work for you if you give us somewheres to sleep and something to eat." He pauses to look at Tyner. "And a share of the crop at harvest time."

Adaire rises from her chair, pulling the shawl around her shoulders. "Lord knows Tyner can't do it all, and Ludie and I aren't much help with the plowing and neither is Phillip." She looks down at Ben. "I'll make you a deal. You and Letha help in the fields this spring and summer, and if we have a good crop of cotton and some decent corn, I'll furnish you a place to stay and food and . . . and seven percent of the profit from the crops. You can sleep in the shed. Letha can help Ludie and me with the cooking and housekeeping, too."

Ben looks at Letha and grins. "I told you Miz Adaire be fair," he whispers. Then he stands up, twisting a blue army cap in his hands as he faces Adaire. "That be fine. Me and Letha work hard, missus. You ain't gonna be sorry. We thanking the Lord Jesus you letting us stay."

The door to the cabin opens with a rush of cold air, and Asia steps in, bringing a bucket of fresh milk.

"Where them little girls?" Ludie asks, taking the bucket from her daughter.

"They out in the barn playing with the kittens," Asia replies. "Sam and Amos running 'round in the orchard, hitting each other with sticks."

"They need to come in," Adaire says. "It's too cold for anyone to be out very long. Run back and get them, Asia."

"I've got to be going," Colonel Hightower announces as he empties the bowl of his pipe into the fire. "It'll be dark before I get back to Goldsboro." He steps to the table and offers his hand to Ben. "I want to wish you luck, Ben. Mrs. Sanderson will treat you fairly, you know. You and your wife can have a good life here."

"Yes, sir. I knows, sir," Ben replies as he shakes the Colonel's hand.

The Colonel turns to Adaire. "Let me know if I can do anything to help. Won't be long before you'll start plowing."

"Just a few more weeks," Adaire answers. "Maybe we'll be able to get back on our feet this year. Sure hope the weather will cooperate. Now that we've got some extra help, things should improve." She looks at Letha once more. "Ludie will give you some quilts, and Tyner can help Ben bring in some pine straw for a bed. You'd better open the door to the shed," she says, pointing to the narrow plank door at the back of the cabin, "or you'll freeze in there tonight." Dragging her heavy skirts across the hard dirt floor, she opens the cabin door to find Asia running toward her.

"Alice ain't in the barn," the brown girl says. "I can't find her, Miz Adaire. Millie say she seen Red and run out after him."

Adaire and the Colonel cross the yard to the barn, where they find Millie sitting on a pile of straw playing with her doll. They check the stalls that house Jupiter, Star, and Sadie, and near the back wall, they find Phillip currying Bunchy. "Have you seen Alice?" Adaire asks.

"Yessum. I told Asia I saw her just a few minutes ago. She's around here somewhere, Mama." He drops the currycomb, takes a cap from his pocket, and begins to button the jacket he's wearing. "Come on, I'll help you find her." He pulls the cap over his long, dark hair. "How far away can a four-year-old get?"

Adaire turns to Asia. "Take Millie to the cabin and tell Tyner and Ben to come help us look for Alice."

Colonel Hightower heads for the hog pen calling Alice, his booming voice resonating among the naked trees. Adaire hurries to look under the front porch steps, one of Alice's favorite places to play. Phillip crosses the yard to the orchard, and Tyner and Ben open the smokehouse and cellar doors. Ludie comes across the dogtrot to the back of the big house where she meets Adaire, and the two continue their search inside.

As the weak, winter daylight begins to fade, the Colonel gathers the group together outside the cabin. "She must have followed the dog into the woods. Tyner, get a mount and bring my horse. We'll go look for her. Phillip, you ride into Goldsboro and tell Mrs. Hightower what's happened. Tell her I may not be home for a while. And stay there with her. Otherwise, she'll be afraid with all the bummers looting everywhere. Besides, it's too cold to be out on the road late at night."

"Take Bunchy and go on, son," Adaire says. "We'll find Alice." The Colonel turns to Ben. "You stay here in case she shows up and you have to come find us in the woods. There isn't much light left, so we'd better get going," he says, as Tyner emerges from the barn leading the Colonel's piebald stallion and Jupiter at a trot.

The Colonel pulls on a pair of gold leather gloves, then rests a hand on Adaire's shoulder. "Don't worry, Mrs. Sanderson, we'll find her. Go inside and try to stay busy. You've been through worse things than this."

A gust of frigid air stings Adaire's face as she watches the two men mount. "I just hope you find her before it's too late," she whispers.

* * * * *

Ludie stirs, eyes full of sleep. The faint jangle of harness reaches her ears. She sits up and looks across the bedroom, where Adaire is sleeping in a chair, head thrown back and mouth open. Without making a sound, Ludie rises from her pallet and tiptoes out of the room. She opens the back door with the stealth of a seasoned burglar and steps into six inches of fresh snow. The crisp, cold air makes her eyes water, and she stands for a moment, shading them against the glare of the pristine barnyard, until she discovers a set of tracks she follows to the open door of the barn. She steps inside, where Tyner and Colonel Hightower are tethering their animals. Clouds of steam float above their faces, and the heads of the beasts as the men remove their saddles and place them on rests in a stall where a ragged, rolled-up quilt is lying on a mound of straw. Colonel Hightower looks over his shoulder at Ludie. "Where's Mrs. Sanderson?" he asks, his face pink with cold.

"Still asleep. She was up most the night pacing the floor. Finally dozed off 'bout an hour ago. Did you find Miss Alice?"

"Yes, we found her," the Colonel assures, "but I think it would be best if you didn't wake Mrs. Sanderson just yet."

Tyner pulls the bridle from Jupiter's head and hangs it on a peg in the stall. "She dead," he whispers. His eyes fill with water. "She fell," he mumbles, "into . . . into the beaver dam."

"She froze to death," the Colonel explains. "At least, that's what it looks like. We found her footprints early this morning up along the north end of the creek. They circled back, and that's when we found the dog's tracks, too. He was under some brush outside the fish camp when we got there, but he kept going over to the beaver dam and whining. Alice must have fallen down in there sometime after it snowed and couldn't get out. Her skirts were up around her chest and frozen stiff." He jerks his head toward the bundle near his feet. "I think it would be best if Mrs. Sanderson didn't see her for a while. I hope we can thaw the body a bit first. You see, her little arms. . . ."

He stops as Adaire steps into the doorway. "Where's Alice?" she asks, her voice barely audible. Tyner slinks to the far end of the stall as the Colonel takes a step toward Adaire.

"Well, where is she?" she asks again, her eyes moving from one corner of the barn to the other. The Colonel reaches out to take her arm, but she jerks away and moves into the stall. Suddenly, her blue eyes cloud and the corners of her mouth droop as she gropes for the dreaded words. "She's dead, isn't she? Isn't she?"

She steps back, trips on the rolled-up quilt, steadies herself, and turns to stare dolt-like at the bundle on the floor. Ludie straddles it and grabs her arm. "Come on, Miz Adaire," the brown woman says, but Adaire ignores her. Kneeling, she begins to claw at the quilt, her fingers curved like talons as she clutches at the faded images of Sun Bonnet Sue. The Colonel stoops beside her and gently removes the ragged covering from the child's small, stiff body.

Alice's tiny white hands are tangled together in her frozen curls. Her eyes, filled with the horror she must have suffered, blaze like emeralds. Shiny globs of saliva streak like icicles beneath her blue mouth.

"Oh, no," Adaire whispers, reaching to pull Alice's arms down. With a sob, she throws herself across the ghastly little corpse and digs frantically in her daughter's ice-caked ringlets. "Wake up, Alice," she cries. "Wake up, honey."

Ludie sinks to her knees and pulls Adaire's shaking hands from Alice's hair. "She gone home to Jesus," she says. "Some angel done flew down here and took our little Alice off to Heaven. Ain't no need for you to fret no more, Miz Adaire. Lord done took her home."

* * * * *

Two snowy days pass before a grave can be dug, its black mouth a stark contrast to the white that surrounds it. The Coles, the Browns, the Cosgroves, and Mrs. Harper are huddled with Adaire, Janey, and Phillip on one side of the pit while Colonel Hightower, Ludie, Tyner, and their children, and Ben and Letha stand on the other. The neighbors stare at the ground beneath them, avoiding the small pine box that is wrapped in pieces of white satin cut from Adaire's wedding gown. They steal glances at her, at her children, and at the imposing Yankee officer, while their minds travel back to other times, other funerals, other graves. They resent the Colonel's presence at so intimate a gathering, resent the resplendent blue uniform and satin-lined cape he wears, resent his relationship with John Sanderson's widow. But they keep their resentment to themselves, knowing Adaire might have lost Carl, too, had it not been for the Colonel.

"I am the Resurrection and the Life," Reverend Parker begins. "He that believeth in me, though he were dead, yet shall he live, and whosoever liveth and believeth in me shall never die."

Adaire's red-rimmed eyes wander to those who've come to share her grief. She studies the face of each friend and, in each, finds her own sorrow. There is not a mourner present who has not lost a husband, a son, a brother, she says to herself, and every woman here has suffered, as I am suffering, from the death of a child. She looks back at Reverend Parker and tries to concentrate on what he is saying.

"Blessed be God, even the Father of our Lord Jesus Christ, the Father of mercies, and the God of all comfort; who comforteth us in all our tribulation, that we may be able to comfort them which are in any trouble. . . . For as the sufferings of Christ abound in us, so our consolation also aboundeth by Christ."

The preacher's words fade again as Adaire turns toward the house, to the front porch where Alice played so often with Millie, fashioning clumsy beds of velvety moss for corn-shuck babies and rag dolls. The porch where Alice sat on Adaire's lap while they sang "Pop Goes the Weasel" and "Oh, Susanna," where Alice learned to count, and recite the alphabet, where cobwebs grew in corners while a mother and baby daughter waited for a soldier father who would never come home.

A sudden wind blows the brim of Adaire's black bonnet from her tired face. She turns back to see the Colonel and Phillip lowering the gleaming white box into a black hole next to her husband's grave.

"Mrs. Sanderson," Reverend Parker says, "would you care to say anything before the body of our precious Alice is committed to the earth?"

Adaire nods to Ludie who steps forward, lifts her face toward the gray sky, and begins to sing.

> Steal away,
> Steal away,
> Steal away to Jesus.
>
> Steal away,
> Steal away,
> Steal away home,
> I ain't got long to stay here.

Ludie's strong alto floats across the blanketed fields around the little cemetery, filling the air with a wrenching sadness that causes the other women to draw handkerchiefs from inside their sleeves.

> My Lawd, he calls me,
> He calls me by the thunder,
> The trumpet sounds within my soul.
> I ain't got long to stay here.

Reverend Parker kneels beside the grave and gathers a handful of damp, black soil. "Suffer little children, and forbid them not," he recites, "to come unto me: for of such is the kingdom of heaven." He drops the heavy clod.

Ludie puts a fist of cold earth into Adaire's gloved hand and takes her by the arm. "Come on, honey," she murmurs. "It's most over now." She leads Adaire to the edge of the hole, keeping a firm grip on her arm. After a moment, Adaire lets go of the mud and stares helplessly as it stains the virginal satin.

"Though I walk through the valley of the shadow of death, I will fear no evil, for thou art with me," Reverend Parker continues. "Thy rod and thy staff, they comfort me. . . ."

As the other mourners step to the edge of the grave and begin dropping their clods, Adaire slips away, eager to be done with the hollow sound of earth meeting eternity.

PART TWO: 1885-86

Polka-Dot Gal

CHAPTER 4:
UP JUMP THE DEVIL

April 8, 1885

I saw God before I saw Mama. Whirling in front of me like a ghost dancing. I reached out to touch Him, but He moved away. Then He spoke to me, His voice a whisper. You shall be my servant, Millie. I covered my eyes then, He scared me so. But He brushed my hands aside. Do good, He said, and good will live in your heart. Beware of the sign, child.

I felt this fluttering inside my chest. Then I was lifted up and all this light was around me. Mama found me sprawled under that old pecan tree with my arms spread out just like Jesus on the cross.

Next year, the bleeding came and I was so scared. Thought it was the sign 'cause I'd done something bad. All that warm red blood running out my private part to punish me. And I ran to the woods and got down on my knees and pray to the Lord to forgive me. Pray for Him to give me another chance to do good like He told me. And I try to hide it from Mama 'cause I know she gonna whup me for being bad. But she just laugh and give me some rags and show me what to do with them. And she told me I was a woman. No more tree climbing. No more running 'round the yard in summer without a blouse. No more mule racing with Sam.

The sign came two years later. Nothing was ever the same again. I was helping Mama make soap and fell against the lye hopper. Mama washed me over and over. Made a salve out'n chestnut leaves. Rubbed me with raw tater scrapings. Nothing helped. The right side my face, and down my neck and shoulder, got these blue-looking circles. Just sorta zigzag right down the side. Polka-dot gal, scar face. That's what folks call me. When I was little I thought I might want to be a school teacher, but after the lye hopper, I had to let go my dream. Now I'm grown, I teach Sunday School. Work with the little ones on their reading and writing. Study my Bible every night. Stay on this old farm with Mama and Daddy and help all I can to earn my keep. Plant crops, sweep floors, wash clothes, wait on the white folks.

We gonna have a wedding here in September for Miz Adaire and the Colonel and there's a whole lot of work to be done before. She up in Ohio visiting them folks of his'n. Got to get the big house whitewashed and some new frocks made for Miz Adaire and for Mama and me, too. Won't be 'til September, but Mama and me already planning for it. First thing we gotta do is finish planting the crops so they'll be lots of good things to eat. I see Daddy coming from the barn now. Got a hoe and a sack of seed. He'll be looking for me. Mama will, too.

Millie is jolted out of her reverie when she hears a door close and looks up to see Ludie coming across the dogtrot. She waves to her mother, then disappears into the cabin to fetch a bonnet to keep the sun from her scarred face. After tying its streamers beneath her chin, she pulls the long ends of the collar of the faded shirtwaist high around her neck. When she steps out of the cabin, Ludie and Tyner have put on broad-brimmed hats and started for the field with the goose-neck hoe, the sack of seed corn, and a bucket of water, a gourd dipper hanging at its side.

Millie catches up with her parents beside the creek, where Ludie is inspecting pieces of oak as Tyner throws them down from atop the five foot mound of next winter's firewood. "Wish I could find me a nice one," Millie hears her mother say.

"They all nice, woman," Tyner yells from his perch. "You just too fussy, that's all."

"It's gotta be straight, old man, and I don't see one be straight like I want."

"Try this one." Tyner throws another piece down. "Why you so fussy?"

"Gonna make Henrietta a egg basket," Ludie replies, referring to Sam's wife. "She done told me that old one what belonged to her granny is about wore out. Just gonna make a small one. She ain't got but a half dozen chickens. Don't need a big one."

Ludie picks up Tyner's last offering, runs her hand across the grooved bark, and tips the freshly cut end to her nose. "This one nice and straight and about the right size . . . maybe two and a half foot. Bit too green just yet, but it'll cure out." She walks away from the wood pile to lean the chosen piece against the base of a pine. "Now I know where it is, and I'll get it when we go home for dinner."

She and Millie start across the log bridge over the creek with Tyner close behind. "I'm gonna get me some grapevine," Ludie says, "and make a nice big basket to hold the cake bundles at Miz Adaire's wedding. I want that basket to be fancy. Gonna get me some reed off'n the creek bank and dye it a nice bright blue and work it in that grapevine so it look real party pretty. I promise Miss Janey I'd help her get everything ready when she and Mr. Henry come. They coming two or three days early so the Colonel can get to know his new son-in-law. Miz Adaire say Mr. Phillip probably won't be here, but Mr. Carl and all his fam'ly gonna be on hand. And all the neighbor folks, too. Be a big crowd, I 'spect."

Tyner frowns. "Um, um, um, woman. You got too many pots a'boiling. You don't watch it, you gonna burn yourself up doing all this wedding stuff. Better get Henrietta to come and help you."

Millie smiles, revealing her fine, white teeth. "You hush, Daddy," she giggles. "Cake bundlin' and that fancy stuff ain't none your affair. Us women gonna take care all the do-dahs."

A few minutes later, they reach an expanse of dark, rich soil where Tyner spent the last few weeks behind a stubborn Arkansas mule Adaire bought in Goldsboro. "Ain't this a pretty sight," he says, stepping into the field. "All laid out now in rows. Ready for us to put down the seeds and let the Lord do His work."

He points toward the nearest section. "Let's do these three rows first. Be 'bout dinner time when we finishes." He turns his hoe upside down and begins punching deep holes along a manure-laced crest of black dirt. Ludie follows with the burlap bag of seed corn across her shoulder, dropping several kernels in each cavity. Millie slides her foot across to close each opening, tamping lightly with her bare toes, before adding a gourdful of water.

As the warm sun rises higher, the three continue to plant, mindless of their rhythmic movement and comforted by its age-old ritual. Tyner talks about the weather, about Colonel Hightower being the new boss, and about the harness he's making. Ludie says little, her mind filled with the wedding dress she'll make for Adaire. Millie recites Bible verses in her head, preparing for the lesson she'll teach on Palm Sunday.

The morning wears on, the sun turns silver against a sapphire sky, and the spots on Millie's neck begin to burn. Pulling a rag from her pocket, she places it carefully across her right shoulder, up near her collar in an effort to shield the tortured scars from the heat. But it's no good. The pain is creeping up her neck now. She turns to her mother. "Mama, I don't feel so good. My head hurts. I think I better go lay down."

Ludie looks up. "You run along, honey. Your daddy and me be on in a bit."

Millie hangs the dipper on the side of the water bucket, sets it on the ground, and turns toward the path to the woods. As she reaches the edge of the field, Ludie calls to her.

"If it ain't a bother, get that piece of oak log and take it on with you. You know the one I mean?"

"Yessum." Millie nods, starting up the path that will take her back to the creek and through the woods that lie behind Adaire's barn.

* * * * *

I hear the call of a blue jay and the answer of its mate and look up hoping to see them. There on a high branch he sits, keeping watch while she carries food to their babies. I find a soft spot in the pine straw beneath their home and sit. My skin feels cool in the quiet shade of this big tree. The birds call to one another again. Their babies chirp, begging for more. I pull a piece of paper and an old pencil from my pocket and start to scribble.

> the voice of god comes down to me
> the dearest sweetest sound
> the song of larks the call of doves
> makes music all around

I read the verse over and over 'cause I like it. It's like one of the Psalms. Then I fold the paper and put it, and the pencil, back in my secret place and start walking toward the creek bank. I can see a wisp of smoke rising on the other side. Probably somebody fishing. I cross the log bridge, stop a moment, and look back at my tracks along the bank. Then I step into the shadows of the trees all full now with bright new leaves. Mama's piece of oak she done picked out for the basket is right where she left it. I pick it up.

"Whatcha doing, gal?"

I look up. See a white man with stringy yellow hair looks like fur on a wet dog. Got a straggly beard, all ratty with knots hanging down to his middle. Nasty lookin' devil.

"You jest stay right there," he says to me as he pulls a long, black pistol from inside the waistband of his dirty trousers. "Right purty little thing, ain't you?" Black teeth show between his lips. "And out here in the woods all by yourself, too. My, my, this is my lucky day." He waves the pistol around in the air. "Get over here."

My heart jumps. Feels like a little bolt of lightning rollin' over my chest and down my arms. Almost knocks me crazy. I still got Mama's log, but my hands is trembling so, I can't hardly hold it.

"Throw that down!" Spit flies out'n the devil's mouth. "Throw it over yonder." He points toward the creek with his pistol.

I hold the log tighter, watching as the mud from my fingertips smears along the grooves in the bark.

"Please, mister," I beg. But he don't hear. He grabs the log out'n my hands. It thumps when it hits the ground.

"Now, git over there near them hick'ry trees," the devil says, his voice kinda quiet. "Been a long time since I had me some good nigger pussy."

I begin to back away. "Please, sir. Please let me go."

"Shut up, gal," he whispers. "Take off your skirt." He points the barrel of the pistol right at my face, grabs the waistband of my skirt and jerks.

I start screaming then. "No! Let me go!" But he pulls harder. The skirt rips, falls 'round my feet. He starts laughing.

"Got some skinny legs, ain't you, gal?" He's looking at my legs, at my chest, my neck, my face. "God-aw-mighty! A freak! Whatever done got hold of you shore made a mess." He steps back and I jump over my skirt and turn to run. But he snatches me by the hair. "'Course it ain't gonna matter none to me," he says. "This ain't no social call. Jest gonna get me a little dark meat. Right, gal?"

Liquid fire runs down my legs. Little ants bite into my scalp. Pinpricks all over me and my hands so swoll, I know they gonna bust. "Help me, Jesus," I whisper.

The white devil starts laughing again. "Lay down in them leaves there," he says. He pushes the pistol right in my face and I see that little black hole staring at me. Then he knocks me on the shoulder so hard I fall flat of my back into them leaves all gray and brown and full of rot. Oh, Lord, I start to pray. You told me if I was good, I'd live with good and be your servant. Save me, Jesus.

The white devil unbuttons his nasty trousers and pulls out his shirttail. Holds the gun right under my chin. Lays down on top of me. Stink like a boar hog. "It ain't nothing you ain't never done before, gal. You little black whores like it, don't you?"

He draws the pistol back 'til it's right above my head. I scream and scream, but nothing comes out.

* * * * *

Ludie stops hoeing mid-row. She turns toward the woods, looking, listening. Dragging the hoe, she steps over the freshly planted mounds and begins walking toward the trees, the bag of seed corn on her shoulder.

When she reaches the creek, she sees the column of smoke rising over the far bank. Sidling up to the log bridge, she crosses it, scanning the bank as she goes, letting her eyes adjust to the glare of bright sunlight. When she steps off, she's surprised to find a piece of oak log on the path in front of her. She's near enough now to recognize it as the one she singled out for Henrietta's basket. The one she propped against the pine tree.

It ain't like Millie to forget. Wonder why she left it here? Ludie drops the hoe and picks up the log, sniffs it, and runs a finger along its rough bark. A noise distracts her, and she turns toward the woods, listening.

The sun is so bright it almost blinds her, but she moves toward the sound. She stops and peers into the shade of the trees. That's when she sees a black gun in a white hand, a spot of bluish skin, and yellow hair reflected in the sunlight.

She sees the filthy jacket, the flat pink buttocks above a pair of thin brown legs that are streaked with bright red. She takes a step, raises the oak log and swings with all her might, bringing it down on the man's skull. A stream of dark blood spatters along the bark. Ludie grips the log again, pulls it out of crushed bones, and throws it to the ground.

"Jesus, have mercy," she cries, falling to her knees. She tears at the worn blue material of the man's jacket. Her nails gouge flabby pink flesh as she pulls him off of Millie. She does not flinch when she sees the bruised pulp of her daughter's cheekbone or the blood pouring from her broken nose or even the bloody smears inside her thighs. All she sees is her baby. She lifts the thin battered body, ignoring Millie's mumbled protests, and carries her to the creek bank. With trembling fingers, Ludie removes her shirt and dips it in the cool water. Then she touches the bloody places on her child's face.

"Your mama's here, baby. You lie still now. Mama's here." Tears roll down Ludie's face as she presses the cool cloth against Millie's forehead. "I'm gonna get your daddy, honey. You gonna have to be real still while I get your daddy."

Millie tries to raise her head but falls back. "Ma," she whimpers, "that man. . . ."

"He ain't gonna hurt you now, honey. Ain't never gonna hurt nobody again. I done fix him good. Now you lie still." Ludie rises, her rounded shoulders and sagging breasts streaked with sweat, and starts across the log bridge.

As soon as she reaches the clearing, she begins to yell. "Millie hurt! A white man hurt our baby!" She turns back to the woods as soon as she sees Tyner. He hurries after her, dragging the hoe behind him.

They find their daughter exactly as Ludie left her, sprawled half-naked on the bank of the creek, her crushed, blood-stained body helpless in the heat of the sun. "Oh, Lord Jesus," Tyner whispers, shielding his eyes to get a better look. Ludie presses a fingertip into her husband's shoulder and points to the grove of trees. "Tyner, we got to get rid that devil what done this to our girl. He's over yonder."

"What you tellin' me, woman? The man what done this still here?"

"I mean he's dead and we got to get rid of him." Ludie pulls on Tyner's arm. "Come on. Help me."

"Dead? You tellin' me you kilt a white man? You musta lost your mind, woman. What make you do such a thing?" Tyner moves closer to the man, slowly taking in the bloody straw-colored head, the nakedness, the spattered oak log. "Lord, help us. You done and done it now." He shakes his head. "Let's just leave him here."

"Naw. Somebody sure to find him. And the first place they gonna come is the farm. We got to bury him."

Tyner begins to back away. "You crazy, Ludie. I ain't messing with no white man. The sheriff find me for sure. I ain't gonna do it."

"Then go get the mule and wagon. We got to have some way to get her home. Go on, old man, and get a quilt from the shed. She need looking after."

Tyner looks once more at the bloody rapist and sets off, making a wide circle to avoid coming near the crushed skull.

Ludie goes over to where Millie is lying. "Mama's gonna take you home, honey. Gonna take care of you." She picks up the hoe Tyner threw down and walks over to where the white man is lying. Lifting the tail of her skirt, she wipes the sweat from her face. She studies the ground, calculating her mission. It won't take much . . . just enough to slide him in and rake the dirt back over. Then cover him with limbs and brush. She begins to hoe, throwing up clumps of dirt the size of dinner plates. Soon a shallow trench emerges as, over and over, the blade finds its mark in the damp earth.

Ludie pauses to catch her breath. She looks over at the man, sees him try to raise his bloody head, watches as he falls back, burying his face in the pile of old leaves. She lets the hoe fall, kneels beside the man, and, grabbing his right shoulder, begins to pull. With a grunt, she rolls him over. His eyes open slowly, then flutter closed. Ludie picks up the oak log, and with a grunt, brings it down. Blood spatters in new places along the piece of wood, painting her naked breasts, arms, and shoulders. She drags the wood over the pale, crushed forehead, down the flattened nose, along a path of tiny red bubbles suspended in the man's matted beard. Raising the log again, she aims for the man's genitals, then strikes over and over until the stench of his bowels overtakes her. With arms that tremble, she throws the log into the wide end of the shallow trench and takes up the hoe once more.

CHAPTER 5:
A LETTER FROM ADAIRE
TO HER DAUGHTER

Sand Hill Farm
July 18, 1885

Mrs. Henry Blanchard
Fayetteville, North Carolina

My dearest Janey,

I trust you and Henry are well. I received your letter before my trip to Ohio to visit the Colonel and was so pleased to hear that Henry's new enterprise is going well and that Margaret Adaire has not suffered any complications. You must be filled with joy at the impending birth of your first grandchild. Remember how excited we all were when Margaret Adaire was born? It is hard to believe that she is all grown up and married and expecting her first, and that I'm to be a great-grandmother! I shall send up special prayers each day for her health and the baby's. Of course, I understand that you must be with Margaret for the birthing. The Colonel and I will miss having you with us at the wedding, but I promise to write afterwards and tell you everything that went on. We have set the date for September 18.

Ludie and I have been so busy planning and sewing. She is making a lovely taffeta gown with an elaborate bustle for me. I would call it lavender. The Colonel brought me a yard of Belgian lace from his last trip to New York. It's as wide as my hand, embroidered with tiny flowers and leaves in a pattern of wreaths. Ludie has fashioned the collar of the dress and the trim down the front using this beautiful lace. She even managed to trim my hat with the remnants. I shall be crocheting buttons for the next few weeks as we'll need sixteen for the bodice front.

My recent trip to visit with the Colonel's people was most interesting. I journeyed to Richmond on the first day, and the train ride was pleasant enough, as I sat with a lady from Smithfield who is Dorothy Cole's cousin. She was on her way to Washington City to visit her sister. We had a very nice conversation about all our mutual friends and acquaintances and shared our picnic baskets along the way. Even after twenty years, Richmond is still a sorry sight to behold. The old hotel there, the Marshall House, survived the war, but I could see repairs around the foundation and in the walls. It was clean and the service and food impeccable, but it isn't the same. My lord, what is?

The next day, I traveled from Richmond to Charleston, West Virginia. You will remember all the hullabaloo after the war started and the folks in the Western part of Virginia pulled out to form their own state. That has proved to be a tremendous misfortune because the folks there just cannot seem to get on their feet again. Almost every person I met on the streets was thin and hollow-eyed. They reminded me of the soldiers who stopped at the farm on their way home after the war. Remember the defeat in their faces? Well, that is how these folks look. My hotel room in Charleston was sparsely furnished with rickety, unsteady pieces and a chipped pitcher and bowl. Even the linen had holes in it. I got very little sleep due to a noisy mob in the barroom below. At breakfast I ordered scrambled eggs. They, too, were gray. Covered with a thin film of coal dust.

Tears came into my eyes as the train rolled into Kentucky. I loved seeing all the new colts frolicking in those glorious bluegrass meadows. Aunt Una and Uncle Jerome and cousin Grace met me at the station in Lexington. All are older, as I am, but their health appears to be good. We had a lovely week long visit and shared old stories about the war and our hardships. Lexington itself remains virtually unchanged. Our old homeplace in town is somewhat shabby now, but Jerome is doing well in his practice. Una hinted that money had been scarce for them for several years after the war, as it was for everyone, but they have done well because of recent bounteous crops of tobacco and Jerome's astute investments. I slept in my old room on the same bed I slept in as a girl. Even the draperies remain, as does the rag rug on which Ludie slept. I was plagued with memories of dear Mama and Papa. Jerome and I went to the cemetery to visit their graves the day before I left for Ohio.

When I finally arrived in Columbus, the Colonel and his brother and sister met me at the station and took me to the Columbus Hotel. I wish you could have seen its lobby. Huge panels, murals I would say, of Christopher Columbus and his three ships cover its walls. And above each one is a large cross like those we associate with the Medieval Period. I'm sure Columbus was a papist. After I had rested and bathed, we had a wonderful dinner of pheasant and champagne. During the meal, the Colonel went over to visit with the violinists who were playing. Then he returned to our table, got down on one knee in front of me, and sang, "Drink To Me Only With Thine Eyes." The dining room was full of people, and I was mortified. Everyone applauded and several of the men shouted bravos. Gladsden Hightower may be many things, but he is never dull. His brother and sister live in the old family homeplace now (I'm sure I've mentioned this to you before), which is on Broad Street in the heart of the city. It is three stories high and made of huge granite stones. The windows on the second, or main floor, rise almost to the 14' ceilings. The mantels in the drawing room and the library were purchased in Italy and shipped to Chicago, where Glad's father hired a barge to bring them to Columbus by river. Marble statues and oil paintings fill each room. There is a large lavatory on each of the upper floors with lovely porcelain basins and tubs, and the floors are made of tiles shipped from Greece. What luxury! With servants everywhere, I never lifted my hand to do one thing.

On Saturday evening of the first week I was there, Glad and his brother and sister invited thirty people for dancing and a midnight supper. The cream of Columbus society was present. I wore my dark-blue watered-silk; it seemed fine. After a busy week in Columbus, Glad and I traveled by train to a small town called Upper Sandusky. Isn't that a strange name? Glad has relatives there and an old army chum whom we visited for several days. I enjoyed the train ride through Ohio tremendously. You have never seen such farms, my dear. Huge, rolling acreage that goes on as far as the eye can see. All newly sown with wheat, barley, and oats. The barns are massive affairs of three stories with two or three gigantic silos on each end. I never dreamed that any farm could be prettier than Sand Hill, but now I am not so sure. While we were in Sandusky, Glad and I went to a tool manufacturer where Glad bought three planes for Tyner. Glad is very impressed with Tyner's talent with wood. I bought a cream-colored shirtwaist trimmed in cotton lace for Ludie.

All along our trip, I looked for tobacco and cotton, but Glad said they don't grow them up north because the soil isn't right. He says the demand for tobacco is growing by leaps and bounds and that we should be planting every available acre with it. Tyner and I decided we would plant three acres more than we did last year, but I have some concern. We will have to hire a half-dozen extra workers to get it out of the fields. The Colonel plans to be home from our wedding trip in time to go with Tyner to Wilson to sell our crop. Having Glad on the farm will surely lift some of the more oppressive burdens I have had to endure over the last few years. Tyner is busy with the cotton now, and two of Sam's boys are here (Ned and Justice) helping him and Ludie keep the fields clean. Henrietta will come later in the fall and bring their two youngest boys to help with the picking. Tyner says that unless we have several good rains this month, our yield will not be as high as last year's. The garden is coming off, so we have plenty of vegetables, and the orchard is full of tiny peaches and pears. I hope there will be enough peaches and apples for Ludie to make brandy. Glad says her brandy is, by far, the best he has ever had.

Greetings once more, dear Janey,

I apologize for this unexpected disruption. Carl dropped by yesterday afternoon as I was writing to you, so I had to leave my letter unfinished. His dry goods business in Baker is doing quite well, but he talks constantly of forming a banking enterprise there. He wants the Colonel to make an initial investment of $2,000, and he will have to raise an additional $3,000 through other investors. I want to give Carl my support, but I am hesitant to invest such a large amount. Baker is growing, having acquired a new livery stable and sawmill; however, I feel it is too small to support a bank. Carl and Louisa are looking forward to their new baby, which should arrive a few weeks before the wedding. Louisa has suffered some complications this time, and the doctor has told her that it would be best if she spent the next month in bed. If the baby is a girl, they have decided to name her Julia after Louisa's grandmother. All of the children are excited, especially Carl, Jr., who is hoping for another little brother. The children are growing like weeds, and the two oldest boys are helping on the farm as much as time permits. Carl, Jr. seems to have grown a foot this year, and Robert is not far behind. Warren is still too young to do much work, but he is so sweet and dear.

I fear Amanda got the short end of the stick when it comes to looks—or maybe her big brothers got all the beauty. It's too soon to tell with Florence, but she looks just like Robert did when he was a year old. Glad is crazy about "his grandchildren," and they seem to be quite fond of him. Louisa is making new frocks for the girls to wear to the wedding, and Carl says his oldest boys will have new suits of clothes for our "special occasion." I'm just sorry Phillip can't be with us.

Ludie has been hoarding pecans from last fall for the wedding cake, and I have ordered two pounds of Egyptian dates, a pound of citron, and white raisins from Mr. Weil's emporium in Goldsboro. Ludie will grind these and add them to its batter. We have decided to have fried chicken and ham biscuits. Glad has asked Ludie to make divinity, but we will have to wait and see how the weather is. All told, we will have about fifty guests. Oh, Janey, I must confess that I am a little excited and nervous. Such a foolish notion for an old lady like me.

I have one last piece of news that may seem rather baffling. It certainly has been for all of us here. Millie is expecting. I have seen her only once, and it was from a distance. She does not come into the house now. Ludie says the baby should be born sometime near the end of the year. She has been very quiet about it, so I have no notion of the circumstances or the man. I had no idea Millie had a suitor. Carl thinks I should ask Ludie about it, but I cannot. I wouldn't dream of questioning Ludie about it. It's interesting that two people can live together all their lives, like Ludie and I have, and know each other well, but Ludie knows me much better than I know her. And you know as well as I do, dear daughter, that Ludie tells you what she wants you to know and you can forget the rest. What she thinks is important to me, but I can't bring myself to ask her about Millie.

Please give my warmest wishes to Margaret Adaire and a fond greeting to Henry, as well. Take good care of our little girl and write to us as soon as the baby is born.

With fondest regards and much love
I remain,
Your mother

P.S.—An interesting encounter occurred as I arrived home at the train station in Goldsboro last week. Carl's old friend, Major McLean from Wilmington, and his wife and daughters were waiting for a train.

I finally met his bride, a lovely girl (very soft spoken and delicate in appearance) named Sarah. They have two beautiful little girls, Bethany, age seven, and Anna, age four. He has taken over his father's saddle and harness business and livery stables in Wilmington. We had a grand conversation relating all our news, and I invited them to the wedding. They seemed most enthusiastic at the prospect, and the major said he will bring along his fiddle. It will be nice to have them, as I know Glad and Carl will enjoy reminiscing with the Major about their war years, and I look forward to getting to know Mrs. McLean and those precious little girls. Bethany is tall and light-haired like her mother and very grown up. Anna is a cherub with huge black eyes and fat rosy cheeks and a head full of dark curls. She reminds me of darling Alice at that age. Remember how like an angel our dear Alice was? And gone to God all these long years. I am so thankful that you never suffered the loss of a child, dear Janey, for it is the saddest and most crushing loss a mother must endure. I shall pray for our sweet Margaret Adaire and hope that her confinement, and the birthing, go well.

CHAPTER 6:
MY FRIENDS THINK I'M A DISGRACE
September 15, 1885

Gladsden Hightower has never known how I hated him the day we met. How he made me feel like a fool in front of all those Yankee boys, ordering me around like I was one of his lackeys. Well, he'll never know. If it hadn't been for Glad and his doctor friend in Goldsboro, Carl would have died and we might have starved that next winter. Besides, what woman could resist all that beautiful white hair of his? And that soothing voice? And the beautiful presents he brings? How could any woman?

Adaire continues with her dusting on this fine September morning. She's taking particular care to see that everything is in order for her husband-to-be, who will arrive on the noon train tomorrow. She knows that Glad's presence at the farm will throw everyone into a stew. Tyner loves having another "family" man on the place and is eager to show the Colonel the results of a hard summer's work. Ludie is preparing some of the Colonel's favorite dishes and will spend all day tomorrow cooking peach pies and roasting a young pig for his homecoming dinner.

Adaire dresses the guest bed with her finest coverlet, smooths it with a loving caress, then makes her way to the log cabin to check on the cooking. As she crosses the dogtrot, she meets Ludie and Tyner, who point to two riders coming up the path beside the barn. She recognizes the older man, but has never seen his companion. Standing in the open passageway, the three wait until the men bring their horses to a stop. The older man tips his hat in Adaire's direction.

"Morning, Miz Sanderson. Nice day, ain't it?"

"Yes, it is, Sheriff Brown. What brings you out this way? Am I in trouble with the law?"

"Not that I know of, ma'am. This here is Mr. Pilkington. He's from up 'round Caswell County. Up Reidsville way." The stranger, who wears a leather vest and a broad-brimmed hat, nods toward Adaire as the sheriff introduces him.

"Mr. Pilkington is down this way looking for his brother-in-law. He thinks he might be 'round these parts 'cause he came down here last spring to work for an old army buddy in Goldsboro. They know he was here 'cause he wrote 'em a letter. But they ain't heard from him for several months now and the man's wife, Mr. Pilkington's sister, is real worried. Folks in Goldsboro remember seeing him back before Easter, but they say they ain't seen him since. We thought maybe some of you folks might of seen him 'cause we found his knapsack tangled in some brambles down on the creek bank 'bout a half mile from here."

"I haven't seen any strangers hereabouts, sheriff," Adaire responds. "But I was away on a trip from early April until late July."

"What about your niggers? Think they might of seen him?" The sheriff looks beyond Adaire to Ludie and Tyner.

"Have you seen a stranger, Tyner, down at the creek or around in our woods?" Adaire asks.

Tyner looks down, drags a bare foot along the weathered planks of the dogtrot, and shakes his head. "No'm," he answers in a small voice.

Adaire looks at Ludie, but Ludie does not reply. She shakes her head once, spits in the dust, and turns toward the log cabin.

"Sorry we can't help you, Sheriff," Adaire says. "Hope you find your brother-in-law, Mr. Pilkington. You might try down at the Rose farm. It backs up to the creek, too."

"Already been there, ma'am. One of Mr. Rose's hands saw a man camping on the creek. Said he saw him fishing a couple of times. Fit Mr. Pilkington's description, too. But that was all. Guess we'll go on into Baker and see if he's around there." The sheriff touches the brim of his hat. "Good day, Miz Sanderson, and good luck on your new marriage."

"Thank you, Sheriff Brown. We'll let you know if we hear anything. Goodbye, Mr. Pilkington, and good luck." The stranger nods and follows the sheriff out of the yard.

Adaire returns to the house, her mind immediately free of Sheriff Brown's questions. She begins to dust the frame of a large landscape oil by Frederick Church that Glad had shipped to the farm from his home in Columbus. It hangs over the parlor mantel, and its companion is now across the room above Glad's ornate roll-top desk. This room used to be so dull, Adaire thinks. But it's more graceful now with all this new furniture, all this rose-colored velvet. I don't miss that old black horsehair one bit. Why, I'm in here all the time now . . . playing the piano, reading . . . and staring at Glad's desk. Twenty years of widowhood and I'm going to live with a man again. And not just any man, either. A man who smokes smelly cigars. And drinks too much whiskey. And curses something awful. But he spoils me rotten and writes the most endearing love letters. I know my friends think I'm a disgrace . . . running up to Ohio without a chaperone and going off to White Sulpher Springs with Glad. But I don't care.

She moves to the mantel and picks up a daguerreotype of her late husband. I loved John Sanderson. Gave him the best years of my life. He was a good husband and a good father, but he's dead and I'm not. Let the ladies gossip. They have so little to brighten their lives, and I have everything.

She grabs John's picture and puts it in the piano bench.

* * * * *

That night, Ludie sits near the light of a fire, her knees wide apart, a dozen apples in her lap. Wooden trays of drying apple rings sit on the cabin shelves, table, benches, and along the window ledges. Over the next few days, trays of apples, covered with cheese cloth, will be set out of doors to allow the fruit to dry in the sun. Ludie will pack it in an airtight barrel that will be opened periodically throughout the winter months to make fried apple pies. Only the finest apples are dried. Those that come from the orchard bruised or brown with age are peeled, quartered, and layered in crocks with gallons of sugar. It will take three years to produce good results, but folks don't seem to mind the wait. Ludie's apple brandy is a coveted and rare treat, reserved for Christmas dinner and other special occasions. Adaire has already mentioned the brandy to Ludie, who has inspected their supply and chosen two crocks, one of apple, another of peach, for the wedding. No part of the apple Ludie is peeling is wasted, not even the core and skin. These will be hauled to the compost pile behind the barn where they will eventually be used as fertilizer in the vegetable garden.

Hauling out this garbage is Tyner's responsibility. As he lounges in a chair near the hearth, he watches Ludie toss the circular rings of skin into a waiting basket. He's not interested in apple leavings. It's time for bed. Millie, who tires easily these days, climbed the ladder to the loft an hour ago. Tyner wants to go to bed, too, but he has something on his mind. "How much longer you gonna mess with them apples?"

Ludie does not look up. "'Til I finish 'em."

"Ain't you ready for bed? You done wore yourself out this afternoon bustling 'round here. Where all them pies go?"

"Over to the pantry in the big house. I got to cook up a pot of succotash in the morning and make the Colonel some cabbage slaw." Ludie throws another core in the brimming basket.

"Be glad when this wedding mess is over. Then we can get back to the work to be done 'fore the cold set in. We ought to plan to leave here soon as the cotton be ginned."

Ludie cuts her eyes toward her husband. "What you mean?" she asks, her mouth pressed to a thin line.

"I mean find some other place where we can work on shares. Miz Adaire don't need us no more. She got money now. She can hire her some workers."

Deep creases form on Ludie's upper lip as she puckers to spit a long dark stream into the fire. "You crazy."

Tyner stands up. "They might come here. Might hang us."

"What you talking 'bout? Ain't nobody gonna hurt us." Ludie senses Tyner's fear and not for the first time. "Miz Adaire ain't gonna let nothing happen to us, old man. 'Sides, things'll be diff'rent when the Colonel live here with us."

"Miz Adaire and the Colonel can't fight the sheriff, old woman. He one the high ups in that White League. Them men come here in the middle of the night and drag us out'n this cabin and take the skin right off'n us before the Colonel even wake up."

"That White League mess is over, Tyner. Busted up years ago."

"Naw, it ain't. And it ain't never gonna be over."

Ludie picks up a paring knife and holds it out to her husband. "Help me with these last ones and we can get on to bed 'fore long. Ain't no need to worry on this, Tyner. Them men done gone. Besides, I ain't about to leave this farm. I know Miz Adaire all my life, and she been good to us. When she ain't got nothing but a peck of cornmeal and some side meat that first winter after the war, she fed us. Colonel bring her something nice, she share with us. Coffee, sugar, flour. Lots of folk was going hungry 'round here. Thank the Lord Miz Adaire willin' to let us stay. She could of took her boys and Miz Janey and gone on home to Kentuck when her baby girl died. But she didn't. We making a good living here now. So hush up and help me finish these apples."

Ludie's voice floats up to Millie, who lies on a corn-shuck mattress overhead, listening to her parents quarrel. As usual, Mama will have her way, she thinks. And Daddy's gonna be lookin' over his shoulder for the rest of his life 'cause he knows we gotta stay here. I done this. It's all my fault. Done got on the wrong side the Lord. Now He's punishing me with this swelling belly. I hate you! Hate you! I slam my fist right in that hateful belly, but it don't change nothing. We all stuck.

* * * * *

The day of the wedding dawns clear, and Adaire awakens to the sound of familiar voices outside her window as Ludie, Tyner, and their daughter-in-law, Henrietta, prepare for the festivities. Tyner has scrubbed the wash pot with corn shucks and sand, and lit a roaring fire of pine bark chips beneath it. Ludie cuts fist-sized chunks of fat bacon and throws them into the searing cauldron, while Tyner cleans and dresses the two dozen shad, bream, and bass he and the Colonel caught that morning. From the root cellar, he has brought a peck of potatoes and a half-peck of onions to be peeled, sliced, and layered, along with the fish, in the pot of hot fat. Fresh tomatoes, ground sage, and red pepper will be added to the concoction and it will simmer all morning. The wedding guests will not go hungry, for ten dozen biscuits are stored in tins in the dining room and two hams have been cut into biscuit-size pieces, wrapped in cheese cloth, and sent to the spring house. A dozen chickens have been plucked and quartered. Jars of pickles, jams, and jellies stand in rows along the sideboard in the dining room. Jugs of wine and brandy have been brought from the cellar.

Ludie is tired, having been up late the night before taking care of last-minute preparations. With Adaire's help, she has iced the three-tiered brandy-laced wedding cake. She secretly complied with an old custom by putting a small darning needle in the cake for blessedness, a penny for good fortune, and a tiny silver ring from Adaire's childhood for eternal faith. (She did not include the usual thimble among the cake's treasures, as it meant children to sew for.) Because the weather has been hot and dry, she was able to make a platter of divinity and dozens of buttermints to serve with the cake.

As they went about last night's chores, Ludie and Adaire were interrupted by the Colonel, who announced the arrival of Carl and Louisa and their children. Glad had insisted that Adaire join them in the parlor for a prenuptial toast and proceeded to open a crock of apple brandy to "have a wee sample and be sure it's fit for the guests." Carl and Louisa had come to present the bridal couple with a silver carving set. Afterward, the adults enjoyed a sip of brandy and talked about the time Carl and his friend, Major McLean, traveled together to Capitol Square in Richmond to witness the unveiling of the commemorative statue erected in honor of the men who died in service to the Confederacy. Then the conversation moved to the present, with Glad's news that a man from Durham named Duke had a patent on a cigarette-making machine that would cause the demand for good tobacco to triple. Glad told his future son-in-law that he and Adaire planned to plant twice as much tobacco on the farm next spring and that they would hire extra croppers to bring it in.

Carl brought up his desire to establish a bank in Baker and proceeded to persuade the Colonel to invest as soon as they could have the necessary papers drawn. Carl and the Colonel shook hands on the deal, and then Adaire went over to the piano, where she began banging out a jaunty "Camptown Races." All of the children, save two-week-old Julia, who slept in her basket, danced about the room, clapping and singing. As Carl and Louisa gathered their excited clan about them and prepared to leave, the Colonel put his hands on Adaire's thin shoulders and kissed the top of her silver-crowned head. The room became quiet as Adaire's children and grandchildren watched Granny and her lover. All were happy about the upcoming marriage, especially Louisa, who rushed over to throw her arms around the betrothed couple. "Oh, my dears," she exclaimed, her eyes brimming with tears, "what a grand life you shall have. We are so happy! So very happy for you both."

* * * * *

Louisa plays the wedding march as Adaire enters the parlor crowded with dozens of smiling faces. Glad wears a purple silk waistcoat embroidered with fleur-de-lis. He holds out his hand to the bride as she steps into the room. She pauses for a moment to look about her. She sees Carl's mustache twitch, a grin on the handsome face of Warren McLean, and the luminous dark eyes of his young daughter, Anna. Standing beside Glad, she tries to listen to Reverend Parker, saying "I do" and looking into Glad's eyes as he makes his vow to her.

Soon, she is lost in a maze of congratulations, damp kisses, warm hugs, the twang of the fiddle, and the shuffle of worn leather across the porch floor. She dances with Glad, then with Carl, with Mr. Cole, and then Carl, Jr. as Major McLean saws with his bow and Tyner picks his banjo on a round of lively tunes. "They Hung John Brown's Body to a Sour Apple Tree," "Sally Goodin," "Dixie," and "Pop Goes the Weasel" fill the air. Round and round the dancers go, ignoring the heat, as by-standers and chair-sitters clap and whistle.

Then the major steps forward and begins a fine rendition of "My Old Kentucky Home." Adaire and the Colonel waltz with a grace that surprises and delights their guests. Things slow down a bit after that, as the major and Tyner play a repertoire of ballads and husbands and wives sway across the porch floor. Adaire sees Carl and Louisa in one corner and Carl, Jr. and Bethany McLean in another. After several waltzes, she steps over to the Major and whispers, "I think it's time we cut the cake, or folks'll be mighty late getting home." Major McLean nods, bringing "Annie Laurie" to an end.

Hand in hand, Adaire and Glad lead the guests down the porch steps and into the grove of trees in the side yard where the cake is standing on one end of a long cloth-covered table. A silver punchbowl filled with frothy syllabub stands at the other. Ludie has wrapped the handle of the knife from the bridal couple's new carving set with ivy and white ribbon. Adaire picks it up and presses the point into the thick silvery icing of the cake's lower tier as Glad places his hand over hers.

They cut the first slice and discover Ludie's penny. As the guests clap, Carl, Jr. grabs the coin and holds it up for all to see. "You're gonna be rich, Granny!" he shouts, his blond mane flying. "Ain't that fine? You can put it in Papa's new bank." Mr. Cole slaps the Colonel on the back. "Where's the thimble, old man? You better watch out or you'll have a passel of young'uns round here. Where's the thimble?" Glad and the male guests roar with laughter as Adaire presses a handkerchief to her damp forehead. She hands the cake knife to Louisa and heads for the punchbowl at the other end of the table.

* * * * *

From my secret place up in the barn loft, I see everybody having a big time, but don't nobody see me. They sashshaying 'round on the porch, clapping and stomping while Daddy plays his banjo. I see the Colonel slip him some money when he thinks nobody looking. All them white folk eating Mama's cooking and talking to her like she one of 'em. And her hauling 'round that fancy punchbowl the Colonel done brought from his big house up north.

I hate that old Colonel. Always laughing so loud. Always bragging 'bout something he done. Ordering Mama and Daddy all the time. Do this, do that. And that stringy old wife he just got. How come she such a busy body, always sticking her nose in, wondering how Mama and Daddy gonna take care their no-good daughter? And what will Miz High-and-Mighty do if she ever finds out what really happened to that white devil? Will she have the sheriff come and take Mama off to jail?

I can't do nothing 'bout it. Can't do nothing but haul this hateful belly around and write these stupid poems. Been hiding this paper and pencil for the longest.

> heart of pain
> belly of hate
> punishment to bear
> cold hard looks
> the devil's eye
> no wedding dress to wear

I got to keep this put away where nobody won't see it but me. Gonna slip it back in my bodice 'fore somebody start calling me. I know I gotta go help Mama and Henrietta clean up after all them fancy folk. But I ain't wantin' to. Don't want nobody to see me. I know they gonna call me names. Polka-Dot Gal. Polka-Dot Baby. Gonna be all white and ugly like that devil-man.

Got to get goin' now. Mama's calling me. Move, feet. Move 'cross these old creaky floor boards. Gonna bend over my big belly so I can see down these stairs. Mighty steep, ain't they? Maybe Jesus'll give me wings and I'll just fly over 'em. He don't want no ugly polka-dot baby either. I'll hold out my arms and let Him take me on over.

CHAPTER 7:
THE MOON AND THE STARS
December 24, 1885

Thick clouds of steam rise above Ludie's head as she stirs a cauldron of grayish intestines beside the cabin door. At a makeshift table nearby, her daughter-in-law grinds scraps left from the butchering of a fat Berkshire boar. "We got right much here, Miz Ludie," Henrietta says. "You 'bout ready to start stuffing this mess in them casings?"

"Reckon so. Stand back. I'm gonna put this last batch up on the table."

With steady hands, Ludie lifts the intestines from the fiery pot and dumps them into a rough tin colander Tyner made early in their marriage. Henrietta thrusts her large hands into the slimy entrails, pulls out a long section, and begins cutting it into pieces. Ludie hauls the bucket of fresh ground meat to the table, opens a croker sack, draws out a handful of salt, and sprinkles it over the meat. Then she adds generous pinches of dried sage and red peppers and a lump of brown sugar.

"Lots of folk don't like sugar in they sausage," she says, crumbling it over the bucket, "but I says a bit of sugar don't hurt nothing. This one the nicest hogs we kilt over the last few years. 'Course we waited 'til the moon's full to be sure he was good and fat."

Henrietta cuts the last section of intestine and draws a ball of twine from her pocket. "And it sure helps to pen them hogs up and feed 'em lots of corn, don't it?"

"If you can afford to. Now, after the war, we ain't got enough corn to keep us folk alive. The pigs, what few was left, they just roam 'round in the woods, living off acorns and such. And they meat mighty stringy and strong tasting. Remember? Nice to have lots of good meat now. Still got room in the smokehouse for one more hog. Reckon as how we're gonna slaughter another after Christmas."

"I know you miss Millie helpin' you with all this," says Henrietta. "She seem kinda poorly these days. Look like to me if them sacks of feed and Miz Adaire's horse blankets hadn't been lying around under them rickety stairs in the barn, she might of really hurt herself . . . might of even kilt that poor baby. Wonder why she go way up there in the first place?" When Ludie does not answer, she stuffs a handful of ground meat into a casing, packing it tight. "Reckon the daddy of that chile know Millie feeling poorly? Reckon he gonna come 'round when it born?"

Ludie turns away from the table to look back at the closed cabin door. "He ain't never coming back," she whispers. "Don't let her hear you talking 'bout it."

"Oh, I ain't said a word to her, Miz Ludie." Henrietta shakes her big head. "She don't talk nohow these days. Don't even read no books no more, does she?"

"She's just tired. Goes to bed soon as supper's done. I been trying to make a few little sacks for the baby and knit some booties, but she ain't making nothin' for it."

"Do she want a boy or girl?"

"She don't care."

"Law, Miz Ludie, every woman say that. Now me, I got four big boys, and I want me a girl, but it sure don't look like I'm gonna get one. I need to go over yonder to the graveyard and clean 'round them places where my girls are. Reckon how many chillun buried over there?"

Ludie looks across the dogtrot to the clump of cedars on the other side of the white house where a lone marker stands as a memorial to John Sanderson. Below it are several small mounds of earth.

"Lemme think. There's Miz Adaire's first chile, John Sanderson, Jr., and then my boy, Clancy, what died before Millie come. And then Alice, Miz Adaire's little girl. Then your two baby girls what died. That makes five."

"Sure hopes they ain't no more. Hope Millie gonna do good when that baby come." Henrietta removes the last of the fresh meat from the bucket. "She gettin' mighty swoll. When does she 'spect it to come?"

"Most anytime now."

"What she gonna name it?"

"Ain't said." Ludie ties off the end of the filled casing and begins to pack the heavy ropes of sausage in the bucket. "Sam's daddy and me sure glad you all could come help us with this hog killin' and getting the scrap cotton out'n the fields. Them boys of yours is good help, even if they is young. They got strong backs. I know they having 'em a good time today a-chasing 'round in the woods."

She puts the heavy bucket in a wheelbarrow, lifts the handle on one side, and looks through naked oak branches toward the horizon where the thin winter light is fading. "This weather ain't gonna hold much longer. Let's get this on to the smokehouse. Light 'most gone, and them boys be home soon lookin' for they supper. Christmas come mighty early this year, didn't it?"

Henrietta takes the other handle and helps Ludie push the wheelbarrow beyond the cabin to a tiny clapboard building, its foundation of clumsily laid stone resting directly on the ground. "Fresh backbone and sweet taters gonna be good," Henrietta says as they approach the smokehouse. "I know them boys gonna bring home some squirrel and maybe some rabbit, too. They could eat a elephant, could they find one," she giggles. "You want me to cut a mess of collards 'fore it gets dark, Miz Ludie?"

"Be right nice. And, Henrietta, go on down to the root cellar and get a few onions and white taters. We gonna want to stew 'em with that backbone tonight. Gotta get a few extry eggs and some more fresh milk 'fore dark sets in. Miz Adaire left one her burnt sugar cakes for Christmas dinner tomorrow, and I'm gonna make some custard to go with it."

"When you think Miz Adaire and the Colonel come on back home? This gonna be another one them long trips?"

"I heard Miz Adaire say they gonna stay with the Colonel's son in Pittsburgh 'til after the new year. Then they going up to New York for a few days. Since young Mr. Carl went with them, they gotta get on back here 'fore too long on account of his schooling."

"Law, that boy sure spoilt, ain't he? Going off to a big city like that."

"Miz Louisa, she was some upset. She don't want her boy to be away at Christmas, but the Colonel say Carl, Jr. need to see something 'sides Sand Hill and Mr. Carl say he don't want his son to grow up not knowing nothin'. So Miz Louisa hush and Miz Adaire tell her not to worry. They gonna take good care of her boy. Young Mr. Carl the apple of his granny's eye. Her favorite gran'chile by far. She and the Colonel took him off to Goldsboro and got two new suits of clothes made for him. Too dandified, if you ask me, and riding mighty high. Them girls Mr. Carl and Miz Louisa has . . . they seem right nice. That second boy, Robert Lee, nice, too. But that Carl, Jr. . . . I just don't know 'bout him."

Ludie pushes the leather thong away from the catch on the smoke-house door, opens it, and peers inside for a moment before she turns back to Henrietta.

"Lord strike me dead for passing that last judgment on Miz Adaire's gran'chile. Just hope that boy don't break her heart." She steps over the threshold and sticks her head back out. "Hand me that bucket, honey, and come on in 'fore you freeze. They say it's a good sign to light your smokehouse fire on Christmas eve."

* * * * *

Slices of delicate pink ham, stewed squirrel swimming in gravy, a bowl of field peas, sweet potato pudding, white rice, and crocks of pickles crowd a pie tin brimming with biscuits on the cabin table laden for Christmas. The family bows for Tyner's blessing.

"Oh, Lord, we know we ain't worthy of this fine meal, but we thank you just the same. On this, your big day, we ask a special blessing on us what gathers here in your name. Help us to be good Christians and to raise these young folk up in the Christian way. Forgive us our many sins. Happy birthday, Lord Jesus."

Ludie sets a three-legged pot on the end of the table and begins to spoon steaming collards onto everyone's plate. When she finishes, she removes the empty pot from the table and holds up the spoon. "After dinner, I tell you boys a story 'bout this old spoon if you want to hear it," she says to her grandsons.

All four boys nod, their eyes big at the thought. It's the best they can do with their mouths full of Granny's Christmas treats.

Sam and Henrietta's oldest son, Justice, washes his down with a gulp of buttermilk and looks at Millie. "Aunt Millie say we gonna take turns reading from the Bible after dinner today. Gonna read 'bout when Jesus born."

"We'll see," says Sam. "You just mind your manners and bide your time, boy. We ain't even got to dessert yet." He jerks his thumb in the direction of a long wall shelf where his mother's baking has cooled for the past forty years. On it rests Adaire's cake, a bowl of egg custard, two pecan pies, and a plate of fried peach pies. A crock of apple brandy sits on one end. On the other is a cardboard box filled with carefully wrapped pralines and rolls of sugarcoated peach leather from his sister, Asia, and her blacksmith husband, who live in Charleston with their six children.

Henrietta, who is dressed in the gray wool skirt Sam gave her that morning, looks down the table to where Ludie is sitting. "I know there was something special 'bout that spoon 'cause you always so careful with it, Miz Ludie. Always rubbing it with a rag. And you kept it hanging on the hearth all the years Sam and me been married. I was hoping one day you'd tell us where it come from."

Ludie cups little Cree's chin. "Been waiting for these boys to get bigger so they 'preciates it. It's kinda like your granddaddy's banjo. Once you know where it come from, you know how to value it more."

Cree's eyes brighten as he claps his small hands. "Granddaddy gonna play the banjo after dinner?" He grins at Tyner, his tiny teeth shiny with collard grease.

"Don't know, chile." Tyner shakes his head. "It's mighty cole. Can't get much sound out'n that thing when the weather's like this. Gonna snow."

Smiles spread across the boys' faces. Snow means no work in the fields, rides on a makeshift sled hooked to the back of a wagon, and corn popped over the hearth. Snow means fun.

"How you know, Granddaddy?" asks Ned, wiping his hands on his shirtfront.

"You see them rabbits we kilt yesterday?" asks Tyner. Ned and Justice nod in reply. "Well, they got so much fur on they feet you cain't see they paws. That's a sure sign a big snow coming."

"You probably right, Granddaddy." Henrietta spoons another helping of sweet potato pudding on Sam's plate. "Seem like we got some mighty foggy mornings when we was tying that 'bacca this fall. Y'all remember?"

"Time to get out the quilt frame," Ludie adds. "Ain't nothing like a good snow to put you in the mood to sew a stitch or two. Me and Millie gonna make a new quilt for that bed Miz Adaire gave her. The Colonel done brought me all these fancy old vests of his. He says he don't wear 'em no more. And we got us a new border pattern call worm trail. Real pretty." She leaves her chair and begins to bring desserts to the table. "'Course, we got all that scrap cotton to clean and comb 'fore we can start on something nice."

Tyner reaches under the long shelf and pulls out the crock of brandy, pouring a cup for Sam and himself. "Weather like this, a man needs a good strong drink to keep him going." He lifts the cup to his mouth and winks at Sam, who begins to laugh. "Some fine ad-vice," his son replies as he raises the cup to his father.

"You men," grumbles Henrietta. "Always got some kinda excuse for drinking."

"Hush, woman. It's Christmas. You done got your gift, now we gonna have ours." Sam rears back in his chair and throws his booted feet into the seat his wife has vacated. He looks back at his father. "Did I tell you about them boys what work with me at the livery stable that's going to Texas?"

Tyner shakes his head. "Why they want to go way out there?"

"Gonna work on a cattle farm. Going to a place call Abilene."

"Why they want to do that?" Tyner wonders, finishing off his collards.

"They say they gonna make some money and then buy a place. All these cattle they raise gonna be sent back here to the east and to places up north 'cause folks here gonna eat cow meat."

"Why would somebody want to eat cow when they got hog?"

"Don't know, but that's what they say. And this man who be their boss, he sent 'em the money to ride the train all the way out there."

Henrietta puts a broad slice of pecan pie on her father-in-law's plate and spreads a spoonful of creamy egg custard over it. Tyner looks down at the pie and grins. "Don't know why a man would want to leave a place like this and go way 'cross the country where he ain't got no kin around to keep him happy."

Ludie sets the platter of peach pies on the table. "You just want somebody to wait on you, old man," she admonishes, nudging her husband. "Those traveling boys is too young to care 'bout their kin. Ain't nothing sacred to them. They just want that money. They come on back home after 'while. When y'all finish this sweet mess, your gran'pa will give out the gifts. Maybe you boys can sing for your old granny and read the verses on baby Jesus in the Bible. Then I'll tell you a story 'bout that old spoon."

* * * * *

Coached by Aunt Millie, Ned, Justice, and Ralph Amos make it
through the verses of Luke, Chapter Two. They read from the Bible
Adaire gave Ludie and Tyner after Janey taught them to read from it in
the years following the war. As soon as they finish, Henrietta leads the
group in "Joy to the World" and "Go Tell It On the Mountain." With
help from little Cree, Ludie passes out gifts wrapped in coarse brown
paper tied with tobacco twine. Each of the boys gets a new wool cap
and a pair of gloves from his parents. Henrietta gives Sam a pipe. Tyner
goes to the hearth, lifts down a basket, and gives a toy to each of his
grandsons. To Ned, he gives a hawk; for Justice, a fox; for Ralph Amos,
a squirrel; and for Cree, a rabbit. Each is carved in meticulous, life-like
detail. From behind the cupboard, Tyner draws a package and hands
it to Ludie. As the family looks on, she opens it with a slow, deliberate
patience that tries her audience. A smile breaks her face as she finally
holds up a piece of bright yellow calico for all to see.

Now it's her turn to surprise Tyner, and she does so with a small
but heavy package that contains the head of an ax. "Mighty fine,
mighty fine," Tyner says, running his thumb along its sharpened edge.
Ludie brings out a small egg basket with a red bow tied to its handle and
gives it to Henrietta. Then she hands her daughter a package wrapped
in sacking. Millie acts as if she's delighted with the beautiful lace collar
inside. "I know you been wanting something nice to wear to meeting
when you gets your figure back," Ludie says to her. "That's gonna look
nice on your blue dress, ain't it?"

"Yessum," Millie replies, not looking up. "Thank you, Mama. It's
mighty pretty."

Tyner pulls a long narrow box from under the bed and places it
in the middle of the cabin floor. "This box from your Uncle Hector
and Aunt Bernice in Bethlehem," he says to the boys. "Not the place
where baby Jesus was born, but a big city up north in a state called
Pennsylvania. Your Uncle Amos up there visting with Hector right
now." The boys begin to move close to the box, crawling across the rag
rug in front of the hearth. As soon as their grandfather lifts the lid,
they know their prayers have been answered. Their noses twitch, then
all four start to giggle, falling over one another like pups. Packed among

pinecones is a bag of peppermint sticks, one of horehound drops, and a dozen golden oranges. Tyner opens each candy sack, gives each of his grandsons a quick peek, and closes it again. "You can take some home with you," says Ludie. "No need to eat it now. Just make you sick after all that sweet mess you've had." Justice starts to protest, but feels Sam's eyes and hesitates. "Yessum," he says to his grandmother as Tyner draws a present wrapped in brown paper from the bottom of the box. "For Millie," he reads aloud and hands the package to his daughter.

I know it's a book. Hector always sends me books. I don't want to read a book, but everybody's watching me. Gotta open it. It's pretty. Red with gold letters. "*Treasure Island* by Robert Louis Stevenson," I whisper. Now Ned and Justice done run over here to peek over my shoulder. Them boys just can't wait for nothin'. "I promise not to read one word of it 'til you come again," I tell 'em. Might be a while since I got other fish to fry. Big fish. Mama got her eye on me now. She ready to open Miz Adaire's fancy presents, but I don't care.

She always save Miz Adaire's gifts 'til the last 'cause she thinks they special. She hands Sam a square wooden box with "Sam and Family" scrawled across it. She hands Daddy a box and me a package wrapped in blue paper. I don't want it, but I take it.

I watch Henrietta pull out a heavy white china cup from the box Sam has opened. Then he sets a matching saucer on the table. They got a box full of fancy china.

"Um, um. Ain't they the finest you ever did see?" Henrietta's smiling. Pretending she's drinking from one of the cups like one them fancy ladies. "Miz Adaire done fix us up. You boys have to be extry careful of these 'cause they break."

Sam says, "Mama, you tell Miz Adaire and the Colonel we thank them for these nice dishes. For you know it, Miz Henrietta gonna want a lace tablecloth."

Everybody laughin' now. Henrietta and Sam huggin' . . . all lovey-dovey.

Daddy pries the lid off'n his box. Pulls out these pieces of wood like you make furniture with. Pretty oak. Come from somewhere in Ohio.

"Look," he says, holding the planks up for all of us to see. "Ain't got none like these. Reckon as how I be makin' somebody a chest or a table before long. Millie sure need a chest, don't you, honey?" He looks over at me and Mama says, "Go on and open your gift, honey. See what Miz Adaire give you."

I pull the ribbon from 'round it and tear off the blue paper. Yellow baby blanket, all fancy with fringe. Look just like something that old woman would make. I hate it. Ain't never gonna put nothing 'round no baby what come from that devil man. I throw it to the floor. "Wish that old woman would leave me alone!" Start to get up, but it's hard to raise up out'n this old rocker now. Too big. I gotta get out of here 'fore I spoil things. "Y'all go on with your party. I need to lie down."

Cree begins to whimper as Millie crosses the room. When she slams the door to the shed, he crawls into his mother's lap. "What in the world?" asks Henrietta. "What's in that package?"

"It's a blanket for the baby. Miz Adaire showed it to me 'fore she left." Ludie goes to the hearth and removes the large wooden spoon she used at dinner. "You boys come on up here 'round the hearth now, and I tell you that story." She settles into the rocker Millie vacated with the wooden spoon lying across her apron-covered knees. The boys gather on the floor near her feet.

"Now, I want you to take a good look at this spoon and tell me what you see." She hands the spoon to Justice, who turns it over, studies the back, then hands it to Ned.

"Looks like some kinda boat carved on this handle," says Ned. "Like Grandaddy's boat he take us fishing in last summer."

Ralph Amos peers over his big brother's shoulder. "Looks like a moon to me." He points to the figures carved above the boat. "And them's stars 'round it."

Ludie reaches for the spoon. "That's right. It's a boat with a new moon and some stars." She sits back in the rocker and begins to rub the spoon's smooth, reddish bowl and long handle.

"This hung on the hearth of the cabin where my mama stayed when she was a little girl. She give it to me and tell me a story. Long time ago, there was this man and this woman what live on the big plantation belong to Mistuh Ludlow up in Buckham County, up in Virginny, way north of here. The man was called Easter because that's when he was born. At Easter time. And the woman be called Pricey 'cause Mistuh Ludlow say he pay so much for her."

"What you mean, Granny?" asks Ned. "Pay for her?"

"Well, back in them days, folk like us was bought by the white folk to do they work. That's over now. Like I say, the man be called Easter and the woman called Pricey and they live in Virginny, way up north of here. Anyways, Mistuh Ludlow raise all these horses, and Easter, he looks after them. Everyday he feeds them, gets them water, takes them out for they run, and then he combs them and makes they hides shine. And Pricey, she work in the big house for the white folk. She cooks in the kitchen. Not the head cook, just a reg'lar cook. Anyway, Mistuh Ludlow sell the plantation in Virginny and head out for Kentuck. It's a long way off, and they all be travling 'cross the mountains 'most a month. They go to Kentuck 'cause of the horses. Mistuh Ludlow, he want to have a big horse farm and he gonna make him some big money in Kentuck racin' them horses. When they finally get to the place they gonna live, they have to sleep under the wagons and cook outside everyday 'cause they ain't got nowhere to stay. Ain't nothing there but all these long white barns for the horses.

"First thing Mistuh Ludlow done was have his mens build him a house. It's a big house with lots of glass windows and a brick drive for the carriages, and it looks out over the river. Easter and Pricey and all the other folk what come from Virginny with Mistuh Ludlow, they build they own little cabins back behind the big house. All nice in a row. Easter got lots of horses to look after now 'cause Mistuh Ludlow raising them to sell. Well, Mistuh Ludlow get married and have these chillun. Three boys and a girl. And Easter and Pricey, they has them a girl, too. Her name was Pearlene. And one night Pearlene sleepin' on the pallet with her mama and daddy out in they little cabin and she hears feet shuffling 'round outside the door. And then her daddy gets up and opens it, and these folk Pearlene ain't never seen before come in the cabin. There's a passle of 'em. Five or six. They all ragged and got mud on their clothes and in their hair. And Pricey, she give them cornbread and buttermilk, and they eat it so fast. Ain't had nothin' for two days. Then they lie down on the floor and Easter cover them up with corn shucks."

Ludie pauses, takes aim, and spits in the fire. "The next morning, Pearlene go on up to the big house with her mama, Pricey, and help her clean the hearth in the kitchen and the stew pots and such. And then fix the biscuits and pies. After dinner, they go back to the cabin in the street and Pearlene's mama gets down on the floor and whisper to the folk in the corn shucks, and they stick their heads out and she give them the biscuit she brought from the big house in her pockets. Then she cover them up again. That night, everybody be sleepin'. Come a knock on the door and Easter opens it. And this white man come for them folk what was hiding in the shucks, and they leave with him in the middle of the night. Pearlene say this kinda thing happen 'bout once a month. Folk she ain't never seen before are in her house most the time hidin' down in the pile of shucks and then a white man come in the night and get 'em."

"Why they hide like that, Granny?" asks Justice.

"'Cause they scared, chile."

"Scared? Why?"

"'Cause they afraid they get caught and be sent back where they come from. See, they were trying to get to freedom."

"To freedom? What you mean? Ain't they got they own mule and wagon like us?"

"No, chile. Those folk ain't got nothin'. Hardly no clothes and nothin' to eat. They running way from they massa. Once they get out of Kentuck and get 'cross the river to Indianny, they be free. They ain't gonna work for no white massa no more. Ain't gonna be bought and sold no more neither."

"What happen to them people hiding in the shucks, Granny?" asks Ralph Amos.

"Well, after while, Pearlene's mama and daddy 'fraid they gonna get caught hiding them folk in the shucks. So they decides they gonna dig a tunnel under their cabin, one that goes on out to the river. They get some of the folk what live in the street to help them, and they start digging way late of a night, hauling out buckets of dirt and putting them in the hog pens. When the folk that be on the road to freedom come in the night, Pearlene's daddy take a light'erd knot and lead them crawling down through the tunnel and out to the woods near the riverbank. Some men in a boat be waiting and they tell the folks to lie down in the boat, and they covers them with croker sacks and row 'cross to the other side the river to freedom."

"Who was them men, Granny? Was they white men?" asks Ned.

"Pearlene didn't never go to Indianny, but her daddy, Easter, told her some white folk be living on the road to freedom. They got barns and stables and such where they can hide the folk that be runnin' and give them food and quilts and such to help keep them warm. She say it get mighty cold there come winter."

"Did it snow there, Granny?" Cree asks, his bright eyes dancing.

"Sure did."

"Did them folks pop popcorn like us, Granny?"

"No, they didn't have none, I don't reckon. Just had what other folk give 'em on the road. Most likely cornbread and fatback. One night, Pearlene in the cabin in the street. Her mama settin' by the hearth sewing, and her daddy smoking on his pipe. The door to the cabin fly open, and the overseer what work for Mistuh Ludlow standing there with the law. They call Easter out the cabin and ask him if he knows the man they got chained to the back of the wagon. Pearlene say her daddy knew him. He was one the white men what row folk 'cross the river. She say he always call her daddy friend and that he was a preacher. Pearlene's daddy don't say nothin'. The overseer hit him 'cross the shoulders with the whip, but he don't answer. Then the overseer and the law come in the cabin and start throwing things ever which way. They kicks all 'round in the corn shuck pile and tears up all the covers and the pallet. Then the overseer turns over the table and benches and grabs the rag rug from under there and points to the door of the tunnel. Then he starts laughing. 'Think you some smart nigger, don't you, boy?' he say. And he slap Pearlene's daddy 'cross the mouth, and then he ties him up. Then the law grab Pearlene's mama, and they take them out'n the cabin and up to the big house. Pearlene so scared she hide behind the cabin rest of the night.

"The next day the overseer take Easter down to the river and throw him in with his feet and hands tied. Some the folk in the street fetch his body out that night and bury him in the woods. Mistuh Ludlow tell Pricey it gonna break his heart but he gonna have to sell her, and the next week he take her to town and put her up on the block and sell her to a man from Tennessee.

"Then he gave her little girl, Pearlene, to his head cook to raise, and Pearlene stay in the kitchen and clean and cook for a long time, 'til she most a woman. And one night she be servin' in the dining room when Mistuh Ludlow having all this company and this man tell the massa he sure could use a good cook. His cook done and died and they need a cook bad. So Mistuh Ludlow sell Pearlene to that man. Sen'tor Morgan, Miz Adaire's daddy. And the next day, Pearlene tie her clothes up and get ready to go on home with the sen'tor. And the head cook brings her this spoon." Ludie rubs the handle of the spoon, pausing to let her fingertips caress the ridges on the outline of the boat. "And the cook say to Pearlene, 'I promise your mama you get this when you grown. She left it with me and told me to keep it safe. It's been behind the dough tray nigh on to eight or nine year.'

"And Pearlene took this spoon and look at the pictures on the handle and she knowed it to be the one her daddy, Easter, made for her mama when she was a little thing. And she put this spoon right in with her clothes and take it with her on down to the sen'tor's place. And she keep it all those years and give it to me when I leave with Miz Adaire to come down here to Carolina."

"And you knew that girl with the spoon, Granny?" asks Justice.

"She was my mama. Pearlene. You won't never see her 'cause she gone on to the other side. But maybe you gonna remember her name. Pearlene. She was the best cook in all of Kentuck." Ludie gets out of the rocker and hangs the spoon on the hearth. "She was a good woman," she says as she looks across the room to where Henrietta, Tyner, and Sam still sit at the table. "When I goes to join the Lord, I want Asia to have that spoon since she be the oldest girl. I told her that story long time ago 'fore she left here to go live in Charleston." She looks directly at Sam for a moment and says, "You see that your big sister gets that spoon, son." Sam nods and turns to Henrietta.

"Come on, woman. It's gettin' late and we got to get on home. You boys bring your extry clothes and them nice gifts and put them in that sack by the door. Better get you some hot stones. Gonna be mighty cole in that wagon."

Ludie takes the fire poker down and begins to drag several large, hot stones along the hearth. "You go on and hitch up the mule, son. Me and Henrietta will help the boys get ready."

Within minutes, the family is bundled in the wagon. Sam and Henrietta sit on the seat, their feet resting against warm stones wrapped in old sacks, their gifts carefully stored among the boys who are crouched down in the wagon bed, dreading the seven-mile ride to their home on the south side of Goldsboro. The youngsters wave to their grandparents, shouting goodbyes as the wagon rolls out of the farmyard and onto the path by the barn. They watch Ludie and Tyner hurry back inside the warm cabin, then quickly pull their new wool caps down against the wind.

* * * * *

Millie removes a handful of cotton from the waist-high basket sitting between her and her mother. She drops it into the apron spread across her knees and begins to rub the sides of her thighs.

"What's wrong, honey?" Ludie asks. "You hurtin'?"

"My back and legs killing me, Mama." Millie begins picking pieces of trash from the ragged cotton. "They been aching most the night. Did you ache, Mama?"

"Lord, yes, chile. Right at the end before each you chillun born, seem like I was hurtin' all the time."

Millie leans back in her chair, places her hands across her bulging belly, and absentmindedly stares at a fluttering cobweb near the ceiling. "Seems like Christmas was short this year, don't it?" she says, more a statement than a question. "Henrietta and them been gone a week now, and it seem like they left here yesterday. The days gettin' shorter."

"New Year's Eve always short, honey. Days seem shorter to you now 'cause you grown. The older you get, the faster they go. 'Specially days like this when there ain't much light. I cain't hardly believe it's gonna be 1886 tomorrow."

Millie throws the clean wad of cotton into a mound resting on a burlap sheet in the middle of the cabin floor. "Where's Daddy gone?"

"He's out hanging sacks over the backs of those poor mules and cows and putting old sheets over the railing in their stalls. Poor critters. He's afraid they're gonna freeze come night. You know the wind just tear through that old barn." Ludie rubs her cold hands together and brings them to her mouth for warmth. "My hands shrivlin' again. Better set that stew over the fire. Soon be time for supper."

As Millie pushes herself up out of the chair, a gush of warm water runs down her legs. She watches it puddle on the cabin floor, holding fast to the chair arm as her head begins to swim.

Ludie hurries to put an arm around her daughter and guide her to the bed. "Just lie down, honey," she says, raising Millie's swollen feet. "Your water done broke. Ain't nothin' to worry about. Just means the baby coming." Ludie begins to undress Millie, throwing her daughter's wet petticoat and stockings in a corner.

Ludie hobbles across the room to an old chest and bends to pull a quilt from its bottom drawer. "This the birthin' quilt," she says as she helps Millie roll onto the ragged, brown-stained patchwork. "This is the bed you was born in, right on this here quilt. You just lie still now, and I'll get your nightdress." Ludie fluffs the feather bolster and eases Millie back down. "The baby gonna do the work for the next little while. You just lie here and stay warm."

When she opens the cabin door, Ludie sees a thick snow falling. She calls to her husband, slams the door, and adds another log to the fire. Where can that old man be? Under my feet from mornin' 'til night most every day, and now, when I need him, he ain't nowhere to be found. She hears Tyner stomping his boots on the planking outside the door and looks up as he comes in.

"Ain't this something?" he says, a boyish grin on his face. "Look just like the Lord done threw down a big old bucket of dry hominy, don't it?"

Ludie moves a kettle of water over the fire. "Did you get them animals fixed?"

"They got somethin' to eat and all the sacks and covers I could find, but that wind whuppin' in and out that barn worse'n I ever did see." Tyner removes his hat and begins to unbutton his coat. "Coldest winter I can remember."

"Keep your coat on. Millie's water done broke. Go over yonder to the big house and look in the pantry in the dining room. There's a red can in there that's got catnips in it. Gonna make some tea for her. She gonna need it after while." Ludie nods in the direction of the bed, and Tyner goes over and takes his daughter's hand. "How you doing, honey?" he asks.

"Got a ache in my belly, Daddy, and my back hurts something awful."

"You just take it easy. Your mama right here with you." He squeezes Millie's small hand, puts it back under the cover, and starts for the door.

Ludie takes a wooden bowl to the cornmeal barrel in the corner. "I better fix us some extra pone to nibble on later. Look's like we're gonna be up a while."

"What you mean by *we*, woman? Ain't Henrietta coming?"

"Don't be a fool, Tyner. You know she can't get here in this weather. You and me gonna do this."

Tyner stands at the door, his hand on the latch. "What if they's a problem and the baby need help? What we gonna do?"

Ludie pulls a stack of clean flour sacks from a drawer and slams them down on the table. "You make me tired, Tyner. Act just like a young'un sometimes. I done brought a dozen or more babies into this world, and I aim to help my girl with this one. And you gonna help, too. You just do what I tell you and everything'll be all right. Now go get them catnips."

* * * * *

The fire is low, the night almost gone, when Ludie rouses Tyner from his pallet on the floor. "You better get up now, old man. I'm gonna need you in just a bit."

Tyner pulls himself up to the table and sits, rubbing his head, while Ludie pours a mug of strong coffee. He drinks it, making loud, slurping noises, and looks toward the bed, where Millie is moaning softly as she rolls from one hip to the other. "How come you have to get me up so soon? It ain't even light yet."

"You think a baby gonna wait 'cause it ain't light outside? She gonna have it soon. That baby been fighting her all night to get out. I can see the top of its head real good now. Better get the biting stick." Ludie opens the top drawer of the chest and digs around to find a finger-size piece of smooth hickory dented with teeth marks. She sets it on the table, along with a ball of twine and some scissors.

"Hand me them flour sacks," she says to Tyner. "And get up on the bed and hold her up so she can push."

Ludie throws the cover back, and Tyner reaches under his daughter's arms and drags her into a sitting position. Millie cries out and bites him on the hand.

Grabbing Millie's head, Ludie slides the hickory stick between her daughter's teeth. "Push," she orders, her face only inches away. "Bear down with your hips, chile. High time this young'un got born."

Millie grunts. Her face contorts as the baby's head emerges, then its shoulders. Ludie reaches for the bloody body and gently pulls its legs and feet out of Millie. "It's a boy," she shouts, lifting him for Tyner to see. "Look like he's all here. Sure did put up a good fight, didn't he? Reckon we ought to call him Joshua. What you think, old man?"

Ludie ignores Tyner's mumbled reply. She cuts the cord and wraps the baby in a piece of sacking. "Lord, you a ugly little white thing," she says, rubbing the slimy fluid from his wrinkled red face. She puts the bundle on the bed beside Millie and, cradling his fuzzy white head in her pink palm, guides his mouth toward her daughter's breast.

Millie pushes up on her elbows and tries to back away. "No, Mama," she whispers. "Get that devil child away from me." Her sweaty hands snatch the edge of the quilt, and she pulls at it in an effort to throw the baby off the bed.

"Stop it," Ludie hisses through clinched teeth as she grabs Millie's wrist. "This helpless thing is one God's creatures same as you and me, girl." Lifting the baby from the bed, she holds him against her breast. "Can't help who his daddy was anymore than any other baby can," she croons. "Didn't have nothin' to do with how he got here, neither." She runs her index finger along the baby's narrow forehead, pushing back damp strands of pale hair. "Might not look like it, but he got your blood and my blood in him, too." She smiles down at the squalling pink baby in her arms. "Don't you worry, Joshua," she says. "Your granny'll look after you."

PART THREE: 1904-05

What We Women Know

CHAPTER 8:
CAESAR'S SAFETY PINS

October 7, 1904

Anna McLean steps down from the train into bright afternoon sunlight and scans the lot of the Goldsboro depot in hopes of seeing her old school-friend, Olivia Andrews, among the dozens of buggies and wagons churning in the yard. A thin, well-dressed young man emerges from the crowd, pauses to slap the dust from his striped suit, and hurries toward her.

"Miss McLean?" He removes a gray fedora and smiles, revealing a tiny gap between his two front teeth. "I'm Robert Sanderson. Olivia asked me to come and fetch you from the train. She and Carl had to go to a birthday party. I hope you don't mind this inconvenience." He sprints up the platform, two steps at a time, and picks up Anna's bags. "If you'll just come with me, Miss McLean. I've got the buggy right here."

Anna takes up the long skirt of her burgundy traveling suit and follows him down the steps. "Thank you, Mr. . . . did you say Sanderson?"

"Yes, ma'am. Robert Sanderson. I'm Carl's brother."

Anna squints, placing a gloved hand above her eyes to get a closer look at the man who has come to meet her. It can't be, she says to herself. "You mean Olivia's Carl is Carl Sanderson?" she blurts. "Of the Sand Hill Farm Sandersons?"

"Yes, ma'am. That's us. Didn't you know?" Robert hands Anna into a handsome, but dusty black buggy, and slaps the reins across the back of a roan stallion. "Giddup, Caesar," he hollers above a clamor of screeching wheels and calling voices. They make their way out of the lot and into a bustling street where dozens of black men crack whips over the heads of mule teams hauling schooners of freshly ginned cotton.

"It's been a while since we've seen you," Robert says, turning to Anna. "We saw your parents back in '99 when they stopped at our farm on their way from Wilmington to Raleigh for your sister's wedding. You were in school in Raleigh then, weren't you?"

"Yes, I was at Peace Institute. That's where I met Olivia. But I never dreamed her Carl was Carl Sanderson. In her letters she always referred to him as just 'Carl,' or 'my beau, Carl.' I guess those things happen when you're away for a while. I must be terribly out of touch."

"Well, everyone is mighty anxious to see you. All we've talked about lately is the time your mamma and daddy brought you and your sister to visit when Granny married the Colonel back in '85. Do you remember that?"

"All I remember is a big cake. And a little baby in a basket."

"Hmm, that would have been Julia, I guess." Robert is quiet for a moment. "I was pretty small myself. Just seven. But I remember you had lots of black curls and big brown eyes." He glances at the tall, dark-eyed beauty beside him. "Still do, don't you? And you had on a pink dress and were dancing around on the porch."

"Oh, my. I'm sure I was some sight." Anna blushes, turning to give Robert a toothy grin. "Tell me about Olivia. She hinted in her last letter that something special might happen this weekend. Do you think she and Carl are going to announce their engagement, Robert?"

"That's the general consensus. Her parents are having a social tomorrow night in your honor. But I have the feeling we may have another reason to celebrate." He winks at Anna. "Olivia says you've been in Italy studying at an art academy for the past year. Did you like living in a foreign country?"

"Florence was wonderful. But please tell me more about Olivia and Carl before I see him. Olivia wrote that he runs the bank in Baker. Where's Baker?"

"A little town north of our farm. Daddy owns the bank, and Carl works there."

Anna nods. "Do you work there, too, Robert?"

"No, ma'am. I run the mercantile across the street."

"Your family have a lot of interests in Baker, don't they?"

"Yes, ma'am. My daddy built a hotel by the railroad tracks several years ago, and Carl and I live in it. But Carl won't live there much longer because he's building a house in Baker just around the corner from the bank."

"So he and Olivia will live in Baker. When will it be finished?"

"Not for a while yet. Sometime next year, probably. It's pretty fancy. Etched window panes and a big wrap-around porch with one of those French drive-through things with a cover."

"A porte cochere?"

"My French is pretty lousy. The house is a Colonial Revival . . . whatever that is. Anyway, Carl saw the plans for it in a magazine and sent off for 'em. Plans cost three dollars. And then he hired this outfit from Raleigh to build it. Almost six-thousand square feet, not counting the porch. Probably need a half a dozen lightning rods for it."

"My, that does sound fine. I suppose Olivia's already planning for the decorations and furniture."

"I suppose so. The only time I ever spend with her, Carl is along. She dotes on his every word, which at times can be considerable. It's probably a good thing that Olivia's a bit on the quiet side."

They make their way down the busy main street of town, pausing briefly to allow a young boy to herd a flock of geese across their path. Anna leans out of the buggy to get a better view of the buildings ahead. "Goldsboro is certainly thriving, isn't it? What's that big brick building?" She nods toward a three-story structure.

"That's the Messenger Opera House," Robert replies. "All kinds of concerts and plays are held there, and touring companies come several times a year."

"I had no idea Goldsboro had such a facility. I suppose the folks around here give it a lot of support."

"Yes, ma'am. They sure do. And there's a thespians' group here that really runs things. You know, stage productions and things like that."

"How grand. Thespians, too. This is certainly a pleasant surprise. Goldsboro has changed so much since I was here last."

Robert pulls at the reins, turning Caesar into the circular drive before a two-story house of dark orange stone. From its porch, Anna's school chum, Olivia Andrews, waves and then hurries down the steps.

"Anna McLean!" she shrieks, as her auburn curls bounce above her tiny shoulders. "You are surely a sight for sore eyes. Do get down from that buggy so I can give you a big hug." Robert watches from his seat as the women embrace, survey each other at arm's length, laugh, and embrace again.

"You look wonderful," Olivia reports to her old friend. "Aren't you happy to be home?"

"I've missed everyone tremendously," Anna gushes. She turns back to the buggy. "Here, Robert. Let me help with those bags."

"No, ma'am. You and Olivia have too much catching up to do. I'll handle these." He points at the house. "Here comes my relief now." Anna looks toward the door where a tall, broad-shouldered man is emerging. He steps off the porch into the sunlight and Anna gets a good look at his wavy blond hair, his long, well-defined nose, and his glistening moustache. Handsome, a very handsome man, she thinks as Olivia rushes toward him. "Carl, darling. This is my friend from school, Anna McLean. The girl from Wilmington I've told you so much about."

Carl takes in Anna's face, her hat, and the outfit she is wearing before bowing. "A pleasure to see you again, Miss McLean. The last time I saw you, you were dancing up a storm on the porch after my grandmother's wedding."

"This is a surprise, Mr. Sanderson." Anna laughs, extending her hand. "I had no idea Olivia's Carl was you."

He reaches for her hand, places it in the crook of his arm, and guides her up the steps. "And I wouldn't let her tell you. Come with me, Miss McLean. You must tell me all about things in Wilmington. How are the major and your lovely mother?" He opens the front door and pulls Anna close to his side. She looks up at him, intent on their conversation, but her reply is somehow lost as his deep green eyes meet hers. Why am I so nervous, she wonders. I know this man. Know his family. "They're fine," she manages finally. "Just fine, Mr. Sanderson."

* * * * *

That evening, Anna sits in the chair of honor at the right of Olivia's father, a skinny man with bulging eyes and big hands who has become rich in the commercial building business. He dominates the conversation among the small gathering at the dining table. All eyes and ears are turned in his direction. All voices are silent, save his.

"If we could keep the damn darkies in the fields and get rid of these crooked cotton merchants around here, we could get a decent price for our crop," he thunders. "And those sorry cotton agents down in Wilmington," he says, pausing to look at Anna, "beg pardon, Miss

McLean, but those no-good, thieving rascals are just itching to get their hands on our crop and then hold it in their warehouses 'til the price goes up. Same thing they did during the war. And what's anybody gonna do about it?"

"Nothing," says Carl in a quiet tone that seems a sharp contrast to his host's bellowing. "Nothing," he repeats. "Those agents are smart, Mr. Andrews. Foxes in hen houses. All they have to do is bide their time. Our brother, Warren . . . he was named for Miss McLean's father, the major. Anyway, he told me just last week that he's getting less now for our cotton than Granny Adaire did after the war. I'm afraid we're boring the ladies with all this talk about business. Maybe we should move the conversation to a more interesting subject." He looks across the table. "How is your sister, Miss McLean? Bethany, isn't it? I understand she married a man from Raleigh. Do they live there?"

Anna, who is relieved at being asked about her family, smiles at Carl. "Bethany married Mr. Bryson Pearce. He's the junior partner in a law firm there. They have a young son, Graham, and have recently moved into a new home around the corner from the governor's mansion. We had a letter from Bethany just last week telling us that they will be blessed with another child sometime late next spring. She's hoping for a little girl."

Mrs. Andrews, a heavyset woman with fading orange curls, leans forward and offers a plate to Anna. "Do have some more ham, honey. You've hardly eaten a thing. I was hoping you would tell us about your trip abroad. It isn't every day that a personal family friend crosses the Atlantic Ocean."

"Oh, Anna. Do tell," Olivia says, batting the pale lashes above her amber eyes.

"Did you go alone, Miss McLean?" asks Carl, his voice filled with implication.

"Oh, no. My parents would never allow that. I went with my roommate from the Peace Institute. A young lady from Salisbury. Holly Sprinkle."

"She was in some classes with me at school," adds Olivia. "Her father owns a big textile factory, and she thinks she's Mrs. Astor." She lowers her eyes for a moment and then gives Anna a sheepish grin. "Sorry."

Anna ignores Olivia's snippy remark and takes the conversation again. "Miss Sprinkle and I were accompanied by her aunt who acted as chaperone. We sailed last August from Baltimore on the *S.S. America*, one of the ships of the Cunard Line."

"Do tell them about Florence," Olivia interrupts. "Tell them about the villa you wrote about in your letters and about the Italians."

"Holly, uh, Miss Sprinkle and I lived with her father's cousin, a widow who married a Florentine. They have a lovely villa right in the heart of the city, and that's where we stayed for ten months while we studied at the Academe de Lorenzo."

"Why did you go to Florence to study, Miss Sanderson?" Carl wipes his moustache with the tip of his napkin. "Why not Paris or New York?"

"Oh, I don't know," Anna says, shrugging her shoulders. "Either of those other cities would have been wonderful, I'm sure. But I had a painting instructor at Peace who had studied at the Academe de Lorenzo, and he talked about it so much I just had to see for myself."

Carl nods. "How did you spend your days? Did you have classes every day?"

"No, only three days a week. Another day, I had music lessons, voice and viola. Whenever I was not in class or painting, I walked around the city. It's perfectly acceptable for a woman to walk the streets alone, provided she is a foreigner. Europeans think we Americans are barbaric, so they excuse our behavior if it seems inappropriate. Many mornings, I was up and out at dawn." She looks across the room to the sideboard where she focuses on the soft glow of a candle flame. "The morning sunlight creeping over ancient stones and settling like a veil on those old church spires . . . it's enchanting." Reluctantly, she turns back to her audience, casting in her mind for a subject of more general interest. "There are dozens of museums in Florence, filled with beautiful works. You could spend weeks just touring the buildings that contain famous paintings of madonnas, for instance."

Carl rises from his seat. "Papist art," he mutters as he heads to the sideboard where he fills two glasses with brandy.

"Yes," says Anna. "But many of the works depict scenes from the Bible, like the story of Ruth."

"I just love that story." Olivia looks over at Carl. "'Whither thou goest, I will go.' Don't you just love that story?" She touches his shoulder as she rises from her chair. "Excuse me. I need to call Delilah to start clearing these dishes. Please excuse me for a moment."

Robert accepts a glass of brandy from his brother. "Did you get to Rome, Miss McLean?" he asks, turning the stem of the balloon glass around in his fingers.

Anna nods. "Yes, for a brief holiday. The first place we visited was the Coliseum, and I just could not keep my mind on what the guide was telling us. I kept thinking about all the poor people who were persecuted and killed there. I enjoyed St. Peter's much more, especially the Sistine Chapel. Can you believe someone would lie on a scaffold eighty feet in the air to paint a ceiling? And when I saw the results, I was . . . well, I was just speechless."

Mrs. Andrews refills Anna's water glass. "I read somewhere that all the people in those paintings are naked."

"They are. It's as if they're in Heaven or the Garden of Eden. But many of the artworks are quite realistic. You should see Michelangelo's statue of David. Every tiny detail is just magnificent." Anna looks down at her hands and absentmindedly rubs the knuckle on her left index finger. "Even his toes are beautiful," she whispers. She looks up to find an expression on Carl's face that betrays his thoughts and quickly turns to her hostess. "Enough of my life in Italy. What can I do to help you get ready for the party tomorrow night?"

"Just be your charming self, my dear." Mrs. Andrews puts her napkin on the table and Robert jumps up to pull out her chair. "You young people go on in the parlor and amuse yourselves," she says. "Olivia told us you have a lovely voice, Anna. I'm sure Carl and Robert would like to hear you sing."

Olivia returns to the table and takes Carl's arm as Robert offers his to Anna. They cross the threshold into the large, gas-lit parlor where Olivia sits down at the piano.

"It's a bit late in the season for it, but I learned a new song; Anna may not have heard it yet." She removes a piece of music from a stack on the bench beside her and spreads it above the keyboard. "It's called 'In the Good Old Summertime.' Robert, you help me sing."

As Robert crosses to the piano, Anna follows him with her eyes and then turns to smile at Carl. He's watching me, she says to herself. He's watched me all night. Carl Sanderson, Jr. Who would have ever thought. . . .

119

Olivia's sweet voice fills the room, and Robert adds his strong baritone. Anna laughs at "tootsey-wootsey" and catches Carl looking at her again. "What an amusing little tune," she exclaims when Olivia brings the song to an end. "Thank you."

She looks up at Robert as he takes a seat beside her. "Do you play, Miss McLean?" he asks.

"Yes, but I fear I'm a bit rusty."

"Perhaps you'd favor us with a song," suggests Carl. "Olivia says you sing like a lark. Those were her exact words."

Anna feels the heat rising in her cheeks. "I fear Olivia exaggerates, Mr. Sanderson," she says, and turns away.

Olivia leaves the piano bench and goes to stand beside Carl's chair. "Do sing, Anna. You have such a lovely voice. Sing anything you like."

"I'm afraid I don't know anything new. I've been away so long."

"What do they sing in Italy?" asks Robert. "Sing one of their songs for us."

"All right." Anna gets up, but takes her time getting to the piano. "You must promise not to judge me too harshly. After all, it's been years since I've played."

She sits down on the bench and places her hands on the keyboard, her mind a blank. Oh, dear, she thinks. All I can think of are hymns. I surely don't want to sing a hymn at a dinner party. She looks up, her eyes fastened on the elaborate carvings in the walnut panel before her and strikes a few keys at random. C chord, then F, then G. That's better, she says to herself, turning back to her audience.

"Puccini is all the rage in Italy. His latest opera is *Tosca*, and this is one of the songs from it called, 'Vissi D'Arte.' That means love and beauty. Tosca is a young Italian woman who is in love with a painter. Unfortunately, their love is not to be. In this song, she is begging for his life."

Anna strikes a chord and begins to sing the mournful aria, and her mind drifts back to the evening when she first heard it at the Florence Opera House. Puccini cast a spell that evening, and her memory of his music, and her sympathy for the beautiful Tosca, emerges and fills the Andrew's parlor. As she brings the sad song to a close, she is consumed by the story of the doomed lovers and unaware that her audience sits in complete silence. After a moment, Robert rises from the settee. "Why, Miss McLean, that was breathtaking, utterly breathtaking." He begins to clap as Mrs. Andrews hurries into the room.

"Oh, my dear," the older woman cries, rushing to the piano, her hands clasped above her ample bosom. "I never dreamed such sounds could be heard this side of Heaven. What a gift you have. Do sing some more."

Anna pulls the piano lid over the keys. "Oh, no, not tonight. You'll forgive me, won't you? I'm a bit tired."

Carl looks at Anna, his green eyes dancing. "I haven't heard anything like that in years. Did you attend other operas in Italy, Miss McLean?"

"Yes, but only two, unfortunately. Are you an opera lover, Mr. Sanderson?"

"By all means. My grandmother Adaire and Colonel Hightower took me to New York when I was a youngster, and we went to the Metropolitan. It was brand new then. I get to New York about every other year and never miss an opportunity to enjoy one of its wonderful performances. As I recall, we saw *Tannhauser* that first time and. . . ."

He pauses when footsteps sound in the hall. The group turns as Delilah fills the doorway, a lantern in her hand. "'Scuse me, Mrs. Andrews. Sim at the back door. Says something wrong with Mr. Carl's horse. Wants him to come out to the barn right away."

Carl springs from his seat. "What on Earth?" he mumbles, crossing the room in two strides and taking the lantern from Delilah. "Come on, brother."

"Let's go, too, Anna," says Olivia, grabbing a shawl from one of the chairs and throwing it around her shoulders.

"You girls be careful out there." Mrs. Andrews follows Anna and Olivia down the hall. "You've got no business around a barn. You never know what animals might do. You never know. . . ." Her voice fades as the girls pass through the door and out into the cool, dark night.

The familiar smells of leather, hay, and fresh manure reach Anna's nose as she and Olivia enter the barn. A small circle of lantern light illuminates its lower end where Carl and Robert are conversing with the groom, Sim, and his son, Henry. The women move quietly across the straw-covered floor and stop just outside the stall where Carl is rubbing Caesar's well-muscled neck.

"You say you rubbed him down good this afternoon, Sim?" he asks, pressing his fingertips into the horse's shoulder.

"Yes, sir," Sim nods. "He seem fine when you get back from your ride. But tonight he wouldn't eat nothing. Then I notice he feel sweaty to the touch like he's sick or something."

"What about water?" Carl asks, looking around the stall.

"Right behind you, Mister Sanderson." Henry points to a bucket of water. "He won't drink nothing neither."

Carl drags a feed sack from a saddle rest nearby and rubs it over the horse's back and down his left front leg. "Come on, Caesar," he whispers. "What's gotten into you? You've never been sick before." He continues to rub the big animal's damp coat. "Find a blanket, Sim. Let's try to get him warm."

"May I take a look at him, Mr. Sanderson?" Anna waits for permission before getting any closer.

Carl turns, and Anna sees doubt on his face. Like most men she has encountered in her father's livery, he seems hesitant to allow her to enter a man's domain. But he moves away from Caesar and lifts his hand in an inviting, palm-up gesture.

Anna steps in front of the horse's head and reaches high to the broad, flat area between his eyes. She runs her fingers in a slow spider-walk down his forehead to the soft velvety pad above his nose. Then she places her fingers under his jaw, and finally rests her open hand just beneath the animal's left nostril.

"He is a bit warm," she says without looking at Carl. "May have a fever. There's some congestion, too. See this mucous?" A pool of grayish slime rests in the corner of Caesar's right eye. "Probably a case of la grippe."

"What should we do?" Carl asks.

"We'll try to steam him. Olivia, please go back to the house and ask Delilah for some large rags. Old sheets will do. And ask her to send me a bucket of lard and some big safety pins."

Anna looks at Carl. "I'll need some kerosene and turpentine. And a large bucket of coal and a dozen bricks." She looks across the barn, searching. "And a small piece of tin."

Carl dispatches Sim and Henry for the supplies and watches as Anna drags a rake into the stall and begins to clean out a corner. He pulls his coat off and removes a pair of jade cuff links. "Where did you learn so much about horses, Miss McLean?"

"From my father. You know he inherited his father's livery stables, and he loves horses. Knows everything there is to know about them. I've seen him steam a sick horse many times."

Olivia returns with large pieces of yellowed sheeting and Delilah, who is carrying a five-gallon bucket of lard. Without giving her Italian gown a thought, Anna takes the sheets from her friend and kneels down to spread them on the floor. She folds one piece of the soft material into a long rectangle; the other, into a triangle. Taking the bucket of lard from Delilah, she plunges her hand into the gooey yellow grease and smears it on the sheets in thick swathes. "Please mix about a cup of turpentine with just a little of the kerosene. About two tablespoons full," she says to Carl, as she rubs the lard onto the sheeting. As soon as he hands her the mixture, Anna starts to spread it on the lard and a sharp, pungent smell fills the stall. She stands up, bringing the largest piece of sheeting with her. "Caesar won't like this, but I don't think he'll have the power to do anything about it for a while. Help me get this around him, Mr. Sanderson."

They manage to wrap one piece of sheeting across the big horse's neck and another over his chest, pinning each snugly in place as the others look on. Carl hands Anna a feed sack, and she begins to clean her hands while she talks.

"You'll need to build a fire on that piece of tin and contain it in those bricks. Keep it going all night. As soon as it's hot, get that bucket of water over it. You want to keep a good bit of steam moving around this horse for several hours. Keep the water boiling. Is there a large piece of canvas about?"

Sim points to the end of the barn where a canvas is draped over an open buggy. Anna sees it and nods. "Spread that canvas over the top of the stall. The more you contain the steam, the better." She looks back at Carl. "Whatever happens, you must keep a close watch on that little fire because it must not go out. You'll want to move the other horses and the cows to the far end of the barn. They'll be frightened by the fire if they're too close."

Carl picks up a couple of bricks. "You all go on back to the house," he says to Olivia. "I'll be along in a little while. I want to help Sim and Henry get the animals moved so we can start this fire." He bends down to place several bricks on the square of tin. Olivia and Robert start toward the barn door as Anna wipes her hands once more. She soon follows, but a curious feeling passes over her and she turns to look back. Carl is standing in the circle of lantern light, his eyes fixed on her. He laughs. "I'll be damned," he says, just loud enough for her to hear.

* * * * *

Anna retreats to the safety of Mrs. Andrews's kitchen to escape the ongoing demands of would-be dance partners. For the past three hours, she's endured stories of gay war parties told by Mr. Andrews's business associates who ogle her bust, step on her feet, and tell her about the courageous feats they performed at Gettysburg or Bull Run, or some other place sacred to the heart of an old Confederate. She's waltzed with every eligible bachelor in Goldsboro, including a one-armed veteran of the Spanish-American War. Robert Sanderson has claimed her more than a half-dozen times, though he lacks the grace of his big brother, Carl, with whom she has danced only once.

She's tired. She sits down on a chair at the far end of the table, and after carefully spreading the short train of her grape-colored gown, she watches Delilah arrange punch cups on a silver tray. "Lord, men sure can drink, can't they?" the brown woman says. "Soon's I get one tray on the table, there's another that's ready to be washed. Don't know where they put it." She laughs, pushing her backside against the swinging door as she leaves the room. There is a swishing sound, and Olivia runs into the kitchen with Mrs. Andrews on her heels.

"It isn't going to happen, Mama!" she cries, her voice a shrill whisper. "He still hasn't asked me. He just told me he's going home tonight so he can take Granny Adaire to church in the morning."

Mrs. Andrews puts her arm around her daughter's shoulder. "It's all right, honey," she says, her tone hushed and even. "Maybe he's not ready yet."

"Not ready!" Olivia shrieks. "Mama, he's almost thirty years old!" She sinks into a chair near the door. "Just yesterday I saw the outline of a little box in his trouser pocket. I know it was a ring box."

They don't know I'm here, Anna thinks, rising from her seat. She clears her throat, and the women look toward the corner where she is standing. "I'm sorry, I didn't mean to intrude. Is something wrong?" she asks.

Olivia clasps her hands together so tightly that her small knuckles whiten. "Oh, Anna, I don't know," she sniffles. "I just don't understand. The last few times Carl and I have been together, all he's talked about is settling down in Baker and moving into that big house he's building. And he told me last weekend that he wants me to spend Thanksgiving with him and his folks at Sand Hill. Now he's acting like we're a couple of polite strangers at a funeral. Everyone's been talking for weeks about when he's going to ask me to marry him. Well, he's not." She jumps up and throws herself into her mother's arms. "It's all over," she cries. "It's time for everyone to go home anyway. They can just leave without me. That includes Carl!" She buries her tear-stained face in her mother's ample bosom.

Mrs. Andrews pulls a handkerchief from inside her glove and turns to Anna. "Honey, will you go out to the foyer and help Mr. Andrews bid our guests a good evening?"

Anna nods, tucks a stray wisp into her chignon, and passes through the swinging door into the dining room, where Robert is standing beside the punchbowl.

"Miss Anna, may I have one last dance?" he asks, taking her hand as the musicians begin "Fantasy Waltz," the traditional signal that a party is over. He moves her onto the floor. "I've had a lovely time with you this weekend, Miss Anna. Will you be coming to Goldsboro again?"

"I'm not sure," Anna begins, but she stops as Carl taps his younger brother's shoulder. "Time to go, old man," he says. "I'll finish out this dance with Miss McLean, if you don't mind. You'd better get Sim to harness up the buggy. Now that Caesar's all well, we can be on our way."

Robert looks as if he might protest Carl's intrusion. But he smiles at Anna again and says, "My pleasure, Miss McLean." He bows in her direction, gives his brother a piercing look, and walks away.

"I can never thank you enough for all you did last night for Caesar." Carl puts his arm around Anna's waist, pulling her into a close embrace. They begin to dance. "You are an amazing young woman, Miss McLean. Not many ladies would have the gumption to walk into a barn and tackle a big, sick animal."

"Beginner's luck, I assure you. I've never before attended a horse myself, but I've watched my father many times."

"Speaking of your father, I sometimes have to be in Wilmington on business. Especially in the fall. I'll be there week after next, as a matter of fact. Might I call on you and your family? I would so like to visit with your parents. And you, too, of course."

Anna hesitates. She looks into Carl's deep-set eyes, and an uneasy feeling gathers in the pit of her stomach. She manages to smile at him, then focuses her attention on the pearl stick-pin in his cravat. Don't stumble over your big feet, she says to herself. He's just trying to be nice. "I'm sure my folks would love to see you, Mr. Sanderson."

"Carl," he insists. "Please call me Carl. I'll be staying at the New Hanover House and will let you know when to expect me."

He pulls Anna closer. For a moment, they stand motionless while a dozen couples swirl around them. "Goodnight, Miss McLean," Carl says before kissing her gloved hand. "It has been more than a pleasure seeing you again. It has been a revelation."

CHAPTER 9:
A LETTER FROM ANNA
TO HER SISTER

Hotel Waldorf Astoria
New York, New York
May 6, 1905

Mrs. Bryson Pearce
No. 76 Bloodworth
Raleigh, North Carolina

My dear Bethany,

Isn't this stationery grand? Everything here is exquisite, the perfect setting for a honeymoon. Our suite is filled with Louis XIV furniture, white with gold trim. And the windows are hung with blue silk moiré. The carpets are so thick that I have managed to find a dozen excuses to go without my shoes. It's Heaven, sister!

How are you and little Emily getting along? I suppose Bryson is overjoyed at having a tiny replica of you. I do hope she is a good baby and that you are getting sufficient rest. I'm glad you got your little girl, and I can't wait to see her.

Carl is meeting with some banking friends this morning, as he has every morning since we arrived Monday. But I don't mind too much. It gives me time to get my clothes in order and have a leisurely bath before he returns for lunch.

As promised, I shall try to give you a brief account of our wedding. About eighty-five guests were present, and the weather was good. My gown was even lovelier than we anticipated because Millie, Granny Adaire's seamstress, made dozens of miniature rosettes for the bodice and sleeves and decorated each petal with tiny iridescent pearls. Carl gave me beautiful pearl-and-diamond earrings for a wedding present, which were just right with my gown. He arrived two days before the wedding, bringing Millie from the farm, and she brought along the finery. We had one final fitting, and she hemmed it the day before the wedding. What a Godsend she is, and so talented. Millie is somewhat like Mama . . . gentle and soft spoken and so patient. She is a lover of beauty—the natural kind—and her hands can do anything. She helped Mother put magnolia boughs on all the mantles and over the pictures in the parlor and dining room, and she fixed huge bouquets of peonies all over the house. Robert stood up with Carl, and Holly Sprinkle (Remember my roommate from Peace?) was Maid of Honor. Carl's younger sisters acted as attendants . . . Amanda in pale pink and Florence in rose. Both of their gowns looked lovely with Holly's pale lavender. Warren (Papa's namesake) and his wife, Patsy, were not able to come because she is expecting next month. I wish you could have seen Mama and Papa. They were so proud and happy. I believe Papa has a more distinguished look now that he has grayed; it's quite becoming.

The most handsome man present was the groom, of course. He cut quite a figure in his morning coat and striped trousers. All of his family were present, including Adaire and her Colonel. I wasn't a bit nervous, but I did worry a little about Carl's mother, Louisa, who cried throughout the ceremony like her heart was broken. She finally excused herself after we cut the wedding cake and went upstairs to lie down. I have never seen anyone so upset at a wedding.

Mother and Classie made a lovely cake, four tiers high and full of orange peel, white raisins, and currants. Granny Adaire brought several tins of buttermints that were made by Millie's mother, Ludie (I just love to sit with her when I'm at the farm and hear her fascinating stories). We had Parson's Punch and toasted pecans with our cake and mints, and Carl brought a crock of Ludie's peach brandy for the gentlemen. A large crowd came to the train station to see us off. Robert gave us a bottle of French champagne as a bon-voyage gift, which we drank that evening en route to New York. (Carl drank most of it.) Our compartment was quite comfortable, even the bed, which is not often the case.

I have adored every minute in New York. This city is full of life, so noisy and boisterous. Motorcars are everywhere. Their honking reminds me of Granny Adaire's geese. And they cough and spit and toss their riders about and send up clouds of greasy black smoke every minute. Needless to say, they frighten the horses (and me) something awful. Carl thinks they're wonderful and has talked with a dealer about ordering one, but I have told him I'll stick with Caesar and the buggy, thank you. He says I'm a foolish, old-fashioned coward, but I don't care. I'd much rather pair up with a lovely, living animal—something I can talk to, and pet.

Last evening, we had dinner with one of Carl's old friends from the University who lives with his wife and two young sons on Fifth Avenue—the most fashionable address in New York. Their house is four stories, made of brown stones, and has what Carl calls a mansard roof. All the servants (I saw four) were Irish with brogues so thick I could hardly understand a word they said (And northerners think we talk funny!). We saw *Julius Caesar* night before last at the Herald Square and had dinner afterwards at Delmonico's. I haven't seen women so dressed up since I went to the opera in Italy.

Carl and I had a grand time day before yesterday at Altman's (a huge emporium), where we bought yards and yards of bright yellow silk for draperies and a lovely French wallpaper with pale blue and yellow flowers for our bedroom in the new house. The people at the store have arranged for all our purchases to be sent to Baker by train, so they will arrive long before we do. Carl has ordered a sofa of light brown leather (I'd call it butternut) for his library, and we are going to look for dining-room furniture tomorrow. I am so glad he convinced me to register our silver and china patterns. We received seven place-settings of flatware, several serving pieces, and enough china to serve ten people. We also received a dozen silver bowls and platters, a set of ice cream spoons, a silver coffee service from Carl's parents, and all kinds of beautiful linen. Your lovely candlesticks will be wonderful on our dining-room mantle. Mama and Papa gave us two leather-bound volumes of the complete works of Shakespeare. One of the gifts I cherish most is a beautiful quilt Millie and Ludie made for us in the wedding-ring design. We are certainly fixed to move in as soon as the house is ready. Carl says it will be at least six months, so we hope to be living there before Christmas. In the meantime, we will stay with Granny Adaire and the Colonel at Sand Hill.

I do hope I can be a good wife and do the right things for Carl. He is anxious to entertain as soon as the house is finished and has already asked me about the possibility of having an open house on New Year's

Day for all the bank's clients. I am so lucky to have a husband like Carl. I've never known a man more generous. This morning, I found a little black box from Tiffany's inside my lingerie drawer. It held a precious little pin of diamonds and sapphires with tiny gold leaves forming a circle, and a gold cherub in the center. Carl loves to surprise me, and I love his surprises.

We are going riding in the park after lunch today, so I must close now and dress. Ladies ride astride here, just like gentlemen, and I find it most enjoyable. And Central Park is one of the most beautiful places I've ever seen and one of the most romantic. That may be because Carl's with me. Day before yesterday, when we were having a stroll there, we stopped under a big arched bridge, and with dozens of people passing overhead, Carl kissed me in broad daylight. I'm sure I blushed all the way to my hairline! I must confess that I find married life a lot of fun. At least, our honeymoon has been. Being with Carl in this busy place is so exciting. He knows all the best restaurants and how to get tickets to the most highly rated shows. I'm amazed at what he knows about music and art (he gives Granny Adaire credit for that) and his ability to deal with strangers. He's very enthusiastic about our future and my ability to entertain and help him attract new clients for the bank.

I would consider it a great favor if you would give me some advice on running a household. I'm afraid I'm not the best candidate, having never learned to cook or supervise help. Granny Adaire has built a new kitchen on the back of her house where the dogtrot was and has had a new woodstove put in. I suppose I will be expected to try my hand at cooking. Oh, Father! What a trial that will be. Not only for me, but for those poor souls who will *try* to eat what I *try* to prepare! Carl has asked Millie to come and live with us in Baker, but she has not said she will. I'll certainly need someone to help me in that big house and pray that Millie will come.

Unless some unforeseen circumstance arises, Carl and I will visit you and Bryson on our trip home, as planned. You can expect us on the 20th. I cannot wait to hold little Emily. Until then, take good care of yourself and your precious Emily, Graham and Bryson.

> Your loving sister,
> Anna
> (Mrs. Carl Winfield Sanderson, Jr.)

P.S.—I'm afraid I cannot help feeling some remorse about my friendship with Olivia Andrews. I fear she will never speak to me again. Robert says she is being courted by an old family friend from Goldsboro. I do hope she is happy with her new beau.

CHAPTER 10:
MIGHTY BAD SIGN

July 26, 1905

For Anna, Sand Hill is a welcome change from the excitement of her courtship, wedding festivities, and New York honeymoon. She has come to love the soft murmur of the sharecroppers' voices as they eat breakfast at dawn, the hum of July flies around the porch in the hot afternoon, the lonesome call of a whippoorwill as twilight wraps the farm in soft shadow.

She is surprised to find herself busy and content. She rises early to have breakfast with her husband in the dining room, where their morning conversation invariably centers on the construction of their house in Baker. With help from Millie, she is crocheting an elaborate tablecloth for the dining table she and Carl bought in New York. With Ludie, she is learning to prepare the dishes Carl loves, like planked shad, oyster fritters, scalloped tomatoes, and smothered quail . . . all made more difficult by the unpredictable nature of Adaire's new wood-stove. Millie is teaching her to make cakes, pies, and cobblers. She has learned to select the ripest melons from the garden, and to shell and cook butterbeans and peas. Each morning, she spends time with Adaire in the Colonel's rose garden, selecting a half-dozen blossoms for the dinner table. Persia, Queen Elizabeth, York, and Chaplin's Pink ensure variety, and Anna has learned to identify each one. She passes warm afternoons, an easel before her, transferring their beauty to canvas.

One hot afternoon, she forsakes her usual subject, and arranges in an old wooden bucket an armful of wild daisies. She puts it against the chimney of the log cabin and opens her easel a few feet away. After studying her palette, she dips a fine-tipped sable brush into a mound of oily brown paint and begins in the center of the canvas, making long, well-defined strokes. After a few moments, the outline of the bucket appears.

Millie stands at the back door of Adaire's new kitchen catching the breeze, her eyes on Anna. If only I could do that, she thinks. I'd be happy if I could draw a simple thing, like an apple or a pear. She steps into the yard to get a better look. "Oh, Miss Anna, that's so pretty. The Lord sure has seen fit to bless you, ain't He?"

"I suppose so. At least it's something I truly enjoy, Millie. I'm afraid I can't say the same for that battle I'm fighting with Granny's woodstove. Do you suppose I'll ever learn to cook?"

"You're doing just fine, Miss Anna. Why, I don't know when I've seen a nicer peach pie than the one you turned out last night."

Anna frowns. "You mean the one Ludie turned out, don't you?"

"Now, Miss Anna. Don't you go selling yourself short. You peeled them peaches and made that pie crust yourself."

"With Ludie standing over my shoulder telling me every move to make."

"Miss Anna, just about anybody can make a peach pie. But not many folks can do what you're doing." Millie continues to stare at the easel as Anna shades the outer edges of a daisy's petal. "I'd give anything to be able to paint a picture or just draw something with a pencil. You got the gift, you know."

Anna places the brush she is using in a Mason jar of turpentine and removes another from her paint box. She dabs at the bright yellow spot on her palette. "Millie, you have gifts. You sew beautifully, and you're a wonderful cook. Believe me, that's a gift. I'll bet you have other talents, too."

Millie takes a step toward Anna, lifts the dirty brush from the bottom of the turpentine jar, and swirls it around in the murky brown liquid. "I write poems," she whispers, her hand busy above the jar.

Anna holds her brush still for a moment and focuses on the flower she's painting. "Poems?"

"Yessum. They ain't much. Short little verses I make up as I go along." Millie reaches into a pocket and draws out a piece of paper. "I write at least one most every day, and I keep them in a box under my bed. I wrote one this morning." She hands the paper to Anna, who unfolds it and reads aloud.

> Great orange ball
> Rising in the mist
> New day is at hand
> Warm golden rays
> Fingers of the Lord

"Why, Millie, that's beautiful." Anna stares at the neat square-shaped letters that form the words of each line. "What a lovely verse."

"I ain't never let nobody read one my poems before, Miss Anna. Not even Mama. But I somehow know you won't tell." Millie smiles as she takes the paper from Anna, folds it, and puts it in her apron pocket again. "You won't tell, will you, Miss Anna?"

"No. Of course I won't, Millie. But why? You should do something with them . . . have them published or something."

"No, ma'am. I can't do that. Folks would make fun of me, a country gal. They'd laugh and call me names. Uppity or something like that."

Anna puts a hand on Millie's arm. "Well, I think you're very talented," she says as she catches a twinkle in the brown woman's eyes. "Please share your poems with me again."

"That's right nice of you. I will, Miss Anna." Millie drops her head for a moment. "I been meaning to ask you something. Are you happy living here at Sand Hill?"

Anna puts the small brush in the turpentine jar and reaches into her paint box. "Yes, I'm happy here, Millie. A woman is supposed to be happy with her husband and his folks. I do love it here. It's so quiet and peaceful."

"I know you must miss your ma and pa, and all the stuff that goes on in a big place like Wilmington."

"I do miss some things." Anna looks across the yard to where rows of cotton plants grow green and bushy in a nearby field. "I miss the way the moss hangs from the live oak trees along Market Street. And the breeze that blows in off the river all day. And fishing. When I was a girl, my sister and I went fishing almost every day in summer."

"I like to fish, too, Miss Anna. Maybe you'd like to go with me down to the creek one morning before it gets too hot."

"I'd love to, Millie. Are you sure I won't be a bother?"

"No, ma'am. Be nice to have your company. Daddy usually goes with me, but he's so busy right now with the crops. The creek got some nice bass and bream, and I'll teach you how to cook whatever we catch. Mr. Carl loves fresh fish outt'n the creek."

Anna laughs. "Just so I don't have to clean them."

"I'll take care of that for you," Millie says as she starts toward the house. "I got to go help Mama peel some potatoes for supper." She raises the hem of her skirt and pads across the dusty yard in her bare feet.

"Oh, I almost forgot. Miss Adaire wants you to come have tea with her. How she can drink that stuff in this heat, I don't know. Must be her age. They say old folk feels the cold much more than younger folk, but the heat don't bother them near as much." She stops and turns when she reaches the back door. "I'll tell her you're coming."

* * * * *

Anna finds Granny in her bedroom sitting before its empty hearth, an embroidery hoop in one hand, a needle poised in the other. She crosses the room and sits down opposite the old woman, who scowls at her, jabbing the needle into the air.

"Darn thing," Adaire mutters. "Can't see where to put the thread. Getting old is Hell, Anna. Don't let anybody ever tell you otherwise."

Anna takes the needle from Adaire and opens the spool chest sitting on the floor between them. "What color thread do you want, Granny?"

"Pink," Adaire snarls. "Pink! And then I want blue and yellow and three shades of green—dark, light, and in between." She thrusts a bony finger into the sewing box. "See that big pincushion in there, honey?" Anna leans over the box and nods. "Well, get it and take out that paper of needles. I'd appreciate it if you'd thread every one of 'em for me. At least I can still make out the colors." She sits back in the rocker, resting her head on an elaborate antimacassar, her eyes closed. "I understand Miss Andrews is going to marry that man from Goldsboro. The one in the furniture business."

Anna looks up. "Olivia?"

"Yes, honey . . . your friend, Olivia. I heard at church that she and her new beau, Mr. Hardy, are going to be married next month."

Anna pulls a rich peacock blue through the needle's eye. "I'm so glad, Granny. I know she must have hated me for taking Carl away from her. She loved him so much."

"Pshaw! He certainly didn't love her," Adaire snaps. "Never did fall in love with her. He just didn't. Don't you feel guilty, Anna. I expect Carl was mighty happy you came along and saved him from that little gold digger."

"Granny!"

"Well, it's the truth, and you might as well know it. Every time she looked at Carl, all she saw was the bank. Where's Millie? I thought she was going to bring us some tea."

"She is, Granny. She'll be here any minute," Anna replies, filling another needle with bright yellow thread. "I'll have you fixed up in no time. You're going to have so many pretty colors to choose from, you won't know where to start."

Adaire sighs. "Thank you, honey. That's so sweet of you. Lord, I can remember when we didn't have any colors. Hardly even had a needle. During the war, they were scarce as hen's teeth. Tyner carved a couple for me out of chicken bones. And there wasn't any thread to be had. I unraveled an old hooked rug we kept in the barn and used as a buggy robe just so we could sew some things together. And then the Yankees took everything. All our clothes. Our quilts. Our shoes. Even our underwear." She leans forward to inspect the pincushion that's filled with a dozen needles trailing bright colors. "That's fine, honey. You're an angel."

Millie pauses at the doorway and waits for Anna to motion her into the room. She sets a tray on the table beside Adaire and goes over to the old woman's bed to fluff the pillows. Anna pours a cup of strong black tea for Adaire and one for herself. From a Limoges pitcher, she adds thick cream to both cups and scans the plate of sweets Millie has brought. I'm going to be as big as a cow if I stay here much longer, she thinks, selecting a ginger cookie and waving to Millie, who tiptoes out of the room.

Adaire sips her tea and stares into the empty fireplace. After a few moments, she sets her cup on the tray. "Isn't that tea delicious? After the war, we lived off dried peas and cornbread and pickled herring. No tea. I never want to eat pickled herring again. It's a mighty sorry excuse for a meal. Ludie and Tyner and I spent days scouring the woods around here looking for uniforms and cook pots and blankets left by the armies. Anything we could find, we could use. We found two Yankee jackets and several pairs of breeches that Carl and Phillip wore for a couple of winters. Had to dye them brown, of course. Your father-in-law took two pairs of those trousers off to Hillsborough Academy when he went that fall. 'Course, we took the badges off the jackets. Didn't want anybody to think we were traitors. One jacket had belonged to a lieutenant and the other to a captain, and they fit the boys pretty well, considering. Kept them warm, even if they were enemy clothes." She picks up her tea cup again and points to a chest of drawers on the other side of the room. "Look in that chest yonder, honey. Look in the top right-hand drawer."

Anna leaves her chair and crosses to the dresser. She pulls the drawer open and finds a jumble of fancy cotton handkerchiefs, silk ribbons, and scarves.

"See that handkerchief in the back corner, the blue one," Adaire calls. "Take it out." Anna unfolds the cotton square and finds four gold chevrons inside.

"Those are Yankee badges, honey. I took them off those jackets. Don't know why I saved them all these years. Hail the conquering heroes. Heroes, my foot!"

Anna refolds the handkerchief and puts it in the back of the drawer where she found it. Beneath a roll of stockings, she sees the corner of a photograph. She pulls the picture out and finds the Sanderson family posed together on the steps of Adaire's front porch. In the center are Adaire and the Colonel, and to their left are Carl, Sr. and Louisa. Anna locates her husband and his brothers, Robert and Warren, standing behind them. On the bottom step are Carl's sisters, Amanda and Florence. To their left is a light-haired girl dressed in a lace-trimmed shirtwaist and plaid skirt. Anna turns toward Adaire. "When was this photograph taken, Granny?"

"Bring it over here, child. Lord knows I can't see it from here."

Anna crosses the room and hands the picture to Adaire. She waits for a response while the older woman adjusts her glasses. "Our fifteenth wedding anniversary. September 1900. That's Carl, Sr. and Louisa and all their children with us." She hands the picture to Anna. "Put it back in the drawer, honey."

"Who's this?" Anna asks, pointing to the blond girl in the plaid skirt.

"It's Julia. Carl's baby sister. She's dead."

Anna looks at the girl again, at the pale hair falling over her obviously proud shoulders, at the dark eyes focused directly on the camera. "I didn't know Carl had another sister. What happened to her, Granny?"

"She died." Adaire slides her swollen feet into a pair of worn slippers and, with some difficulty, stands. "I think I'd better rest. What are you surprising us with at supper, dear?"

Anna takes the old lady's arm and walks her slowly toward the bed. "Ludie is teaching me how to make a dumpling this afternoon."

"Fine, fine." Adaire lies down and spreads a shawl over her thin legs, smoothing it with knotty, arthritic hands. "You put that photograph away and run along now, honey. Let me rest. I wouldn't want to miss that dumpling."

* * * * *

As darkness settles over the farm, Anna slips on a satin nightgown, fastens the lacy collar around her throat, and begins to remove the hairpins from her chignon. From just outside the bedroom window, she can hear Carl and the Colonel as they share events of the day. It's their usual night time ritual, one that begins when they meet at the dinner table, continues over dessert, and leads them, ultimately, to the front porch. Tonight's conversation has centered on the new house: the problem of finding good, steady workers; of paying top dollar to artisans who will carve the elaborate moldings and finish the marble mantles; of hiring skilled craftsmen to hang the expensive wallpaper sent from Paris; and the bricklayers, who are designing walkways for the immense yard.

At Carl's request, Colonel Hightower is acting as agent to ensure not only the highest quality of workmanship, but also a reasonable building schedule. Carl insists that the house be completely finished by the first day of December.

Anna has visited the site at least once a week since returning from their honeymoon. Along with a dozen curious onlookers, she watched just the day before as a team of men and mules raised a pair of heavy Doric columns at the front entrance. Leaving a trail behind her in the sawdust, she then inspected each room. Entrance hall, drawing room, dining room, library, sitting room downstairs; four large bedrooms and two bathrooms upstairs, the first ever installed in Newlan County. Behind the house is a covered walkway that leads to a combination kitchen and maid's quarters.

Anna prays regularly that Millie will come to Baker to run the house and do the cooking. Tonight is no exception. She opens a tin of Lily salve and dabs at the red streak along the inside of her thumb. The huckleberry dumpling she prepared for supper was tasty, but she paid a price, as usual. She closes the tin and returns it to her drawer as Carl and the Colonel come down the hall. Soon the house will be still and she and Carl will talk and, perhaps, make love. She smiles at the thought, for Carl is a wonderful lover.

She is still smiling as he enters their room and throws his suit jacket on a chair near the bed. He pulls off his shoes and socks and walks over to the bed where his wife is reclining against a pile of pillows. Cupping her chin, he kisses her softly on her mouth. "Ready for bed, beautiful?"

"Just about." Anna watches as Carl strips off his shirt and collar and throws them on the floor. "But first I want to ask you something. Who's Julia?"

Carl steps out of his trousers. "My sister," he says, his voice suddenly quiet.

"What happened to her, Carl?"

"She died." Carl crosses the room to the washstand, sprinkles his toothbrush with powder, and with his back to his wife says, "Did you have a good day?"

"I've had a busy day, Carl. Cooking makes me nervous."

"You'll get the hang of it, honey. Your dumpling was very good. Very good indeed."

"Carl, I know I'll never be a good cook, not a good cook like Millie. But maybe I'll be good at something else."

Carl puts the toothbrush on the washstand and turns to his wife. "Why, honey, you're good at lots of things. You sing, you play the piano and the violin, you paint, you ride better than any woman I've ever known. And you're a wonderful hostess. People are at ease the minute they meet you. What else could you possibly want?"

"Well, something more domestic, perhaps."

"Like what?"

"Like being a mother. I want to be a good mother."

Carl comes to the side of the bed and rubs Anna's cheek. "When the time comes, you'll be a wonderful mother, honey."

"It may be sooner than you think," Anna says, smiling.

Carl's eyes widen in disbelief as he grabs Anna's hand. "Do you mean . . . do you mean I'm going to be a father?" he stammers.

"I think so," Anna says, grinning back at him. "Since this is my first time, I'm not positive, but I'm pretty sure. Oh, Carl, isn't it wonderful?"

Carl jumps up from the bed and lets out a yell. "I'm going to have a son. Oh, God, a son!" he bellows. "Carl Winfield Sanderson, the Third."

"Shush!" Anna warns, a finger over her smiling lips. "You'll have Granny and the Colonel in here. Sit down, honey. Don't be so loud."

"Can you believe it?" Carl asks as if he were addressing an audience. "I'm going to have a son." He sits down beside Anna, his face flushed with excitement.

"It might be a girl," she cautions. "But we don't care, do we?"

"No, it won't be. It's gonna be a boy. A big boy with yellow hair and green eyes just like his old man." Carl grins at Anna. "When?"

"I'm not sure. Sometime next winter, I suppose. Maybe early spring."

"We'll go to Goldsboro tomorrow afternoon and take you to see Doctor Cobb."

"Oh, Carl, I don't need to see a doctor just to have a baby. Women have babies every day." Anna begins to snuggle down under the sheet. "But I will need some new clothes."

"I want my son, and my wife, to have the very best care. Besides, I'll bet the doc can tell us when to expect our boy. That way, we'll have everything ready. I think I'll write Altman's and ask them to send me that big wooden rocking horse we saw in their toy department."

Anna giggles, putting her arms around her husband's neck. "You've got plenty of time for that. Come to bed, honey. Try to get some sleep."

"I'm too excited to sleep. I can't wait to tell Daddy and Mama they're gonna have a grandson. Just think, Anna, when I get old and feeble, there will be someone to take my place at the bank. Someone to carry on the Sanderson name after I'm gone. Thank you, Lord," Carl whispers. "And thank you, little mother," he says, looking at Anna. And to her surprise, he kisses her on the cheek.

* * * * *

Anna clears her breakfast dishes and puts them on the sideboard. She sits down at the table and pours herself another cup of coffee. I suppose I should talk with Millie about letting out the waist in some of my dresses. And I need to get some pretty yarn and start making baby blankets. I wonder what color Carl will want to paint the nursery? There's no need to even consider a name. Carl is set on Carl the Third. If it's a little girl, her name will be left completely to me. Maybe Julia would be nice. Maybe Carl would want to name our little girl after his dead sister. She sips her coffee and looks down at her middle. Oh, my, I am beginning to thicken a bit. As if to confirm her thoughts, she pats her stomach.

Millie tiptoes into the room. "Morning, Miss Anna. How you feeling?"

"Just fine, Millie. How are you?"

"Can't complain. Could be a lot worse, I suppose."

Anna sets her empty cup back in its saucer. "Millie," she says, "would you help me with something?"

Millie begins collecting dirty dishes from around the table and stacks them on a silver tray. "Yessum. Want to make you a new frock?"

"No." But it won't be long before I'll need some, she thinks. "Millie, yesterday when I was having tea with Granny, I found a picture in her dresser drawer. She said it was made on the fifteenth wedding anniversary of her marriage to Colonel Hightower. Have you ever seen it?"

Millie nods as she picks up the heavy tray. "She showed it to Mama and me right after she got it."

"There's a young girl in that picture. A pretty girl with blond hair." Anna watches as Millie's hands tighten around the handles of the tray. "Granny said she was Mr. Carl's sister, Julia.

Millie's shoulders droop suddenly as if the tray she's carrying is too heavy. "Ain't nobody allowed to speak of Miss Julia 'round here."

"But I don't understand. What happened to her?"

Millie straightens her shoulders and begins to back away. "Miss Adaire be some upset if she knows I told you, Miss Anna. I can't."

"I certainly don't intend to let anyone know I asked you about Julia. Won't you trust me to keep my word?"

Millie sets the tray on the end of the table and runs her fingertip around the rim of a dirty coffee cup. "Yessum. I trust you, Miss Anna. But Miss Adaire might run me off if I tell you about Miss Julia. Young Mr. Carl might fire me."

"He won't fire you, Millie, because I won't tell him. This will have to be a secret, you know, like your poems. It'll be something just between the two of us. Please tell me about this. Nobody is here this morning anyway. They've all gone somewhere, so we're completely alone. This is my home now, Millie. These are my people. Won't you please help me understand them? Why won't anyone talk about Julia?"

"Because she done something she won't supposed to." Mille removes a knife from the tray and begins to cut a piece of leftover toast into bits. "Miss Julia," she begins. "Miss Julia run off with my boy. My son, Joshua." Millie's lower lip trembles, and she turns and walks away from the table. For a moment, she faces the dirty dishes stacked on the sideboard. Then she pulls a handkerchief from her apron pocket and blows her nose. With her back to Anna, she finally begins to talk again. "When Miss Julia was a little girl, she lived here with Miss Adaire and the Colonel. After she was born, Miss Louisa was never well again, so Miss Julia come here when she was about four years old. I didn't think Miss Adaire could ever love any grandchild as much as she loved young Mr. Carl, but she sure dote on Miss Julia. She was the baby, and everybody gave her everything she wanted. Ponies and fancy dresses and dolls ordered all the way from New York. Miss Julia was real pretty. Kinda small and dainty like, with hair so straight and silvery. And she was real sweet. Quiet, you know, like a sweet little silver kitten. Cheeks so pink and big green-blue eyes and a smile to melt the devil's heart. Anyway, Miss Julia and my boy, Joshua, they played together all the time. They weren't no other children 'round. Just the two of them. And I read to them and fed them together everyday on a little table in the dogtrot or out in the cabin. And they run about in the woods and go fishing. And the Colonel taught 'em both to ride horses . . . taught 'em together. And one day I was working in a field down near the creek and I saw the two of them walking together at the edge of the woods, and they was holding hands. Both going on sixteen at the time. And I say, Lord, please don't let this happen. Then I corner Joshua and tell him I'll take the hide right off'n him if he does such a thing again.

"Well, that fall, Mr. Carl, Sr. and Miss Louisa sent Miss Julia off to boarding school up in Richmond, and I thought my prayers was answered. But Miss Julia hated it. And when she come home at Christmas, she beg 'em not to send her back. Just let her stay with her Granny and the Colonel until the next fall, and then she'd go to that Female Academy in Goldsboro. That way she could come home every weekend. So they let her stay here at the farm with Miss Adaire and the Colonel. Everything went along fine for a while, and I noticed that she and Joshua wasn't spending as much time together as they once had, and I thought maybe it was all just a fancy and it had passed. But Mr. Carl, Jr. come over for a visit sometime near the end of July and tells me he saw Julia and Joshua in the barn together. And he says to me, 'If that boy of yours value his life, he'll get the hell away from my sister 'fore I kill him.' Then he goes and tells Miss Adaire. Well, Miss Adaire real upset. She love Julia so, and she was always partial to Joshua. So she tells Mr. Carl, Sr. she thinks Miss Julia not getting what she needs at that academy in Goldsboro and that she should be sent back to that other school. That night, Mr. Carl, Sr. and Miss Louisa come over here to tell Miss Julia she going back to school in Richmond in the fall. But she tells them, no, she ain't. And they have a big fight right here in this dining room. And Miss Julia raise her voice at her daddy and call him a tyrant, and he get up from his chair and slap her 'cross the face." A shudder passes over Anna as Millie continues. "I know it to be the truth, Miss Anna. I was standing right behind the chair you sittin' in holding a jelly pie when he done it. Miss Julia run off to her room, and he set down at the table and put his head in his hands and sob like a baby. Miss Louisa gets up then and goes to Miss Julia's room, and I take the pie back out to the kitchen.

"Well, the next morning when I wake up, Joshua's already gone to the field. That ain't like him. That boy love his breakfast. But I don't think much about it. I come on over here to the big house and started slicing some bacon, and Miss Adaire come in the kitchen and say Miss Julia ain't in her room. She sent the Colonel over to Mr. Carl, Sr. and Miss Louisa's, but he come back and says Miss Julia ain't there neither. Mama and Daddy and me looked everywhere for Joshua, but it won't no use. Late that afternoon, I finally went and told Miz Adaire that I was afraid they had run off together.

"Well, Mr. Carl, Sr. come over here and throw a fit. I could hear him yelling from way out in the cabin. Then he rides into Goldsboro and tries to find out if anybody has seen 'em, but nobody has. About a week later, 'round the first of August, they get a note from a friend of Miss Julia's, a young lady at the school in Richmond, who says she's seen 'em and they are fine, but nothing about where they are. I always thought Miss Julia would at least write to her granny . . . they was so close. Anyway, a few weeks later, I got a letter from Joshua. It's out in the cabin. I'll go get it so you can read it." Millie crosses the room, passes through the door and closes it without a sound.

Isn't that strange, Anna thinks, twisting a napkin round and round in her fingers. Every board in this floor creaks when I walk across this room, but they're dead silent when Millie moves about. Strange. But not as strange as that story she just told. No wonder Carl won't talk about it. No wonder everybody is so hush-hush about Julia. And Millie trying to earn a living here. I guess that's why Carl was so reluctant about bringing her to Wilmington to help Mama with the wedding. That must have been a hard trip for both of them, but especially for Millie. She knows everything about Julia, and Carl knows she does, even though he and his family are pretending this never happened. Anna looks up as the door opens.

Millie tiptoes into the room and hands her an envelope addressed with a dull pencil. "Go on and open it, Miss Anna. It come here about two months after they run away."

Anna takes out the letter, unfolds the coarse heavy paper, and begins to read.

October 13, 1903

Dear Mama,

I want to write and tell you that Julia and I are married. I have a job making 60 cents a day in a factory. We have a little house and Julia is learning to cook and clean. We are very happy.

We will have a baby sometime in the spring. Please do not try to find us. We are in a safe place way up North. A friend is going to mail this letter for me from a city far away from where we live.

I will write to you. Please give Granma Ludie and Papa Tyner a hug for me. I miss you all.

Your son,

Joshua

Anna looks up at Millie, who says, "I took it to Miss Adaire as soon as I read it, and she cry something awful. Mr. Carl, Sr. and Miss Louisa come over here, and Miss Adaire show it to them. Mr. Carl so mad he struck Miss Julia's name outt'n the Bible. Miss Adaire beg him not to, but he did it so hard he tore a hole in the paper. I got two more letters from Joshua, Miss Anna. They're real short." Millie pulls a paper from her pocket and reads aloud:

"'Dear Mama, Julia and I have a son. We named him Fletcher. The baby is fine. Real pretty boy with yellow curls and green eyes. Looks like his mama. Julia is a bit poorly but I got her some tonic and she seems better today. I hope you and Granma and Papa are well. Your son, Joshua.' This one was written on April 28 . . . just a little over a year ago." Millie refolds the letter and opens another. "This is the last one." She passes the letter to Anna, who reads the brief message so splotched and stained that it is almost illegible.

August 2, 1904

Dear Mama,

Julia is dead. The doctor won't able to break the fever what killed her. All that is left is my son. I will try to look after him. Please pray for me Mama. Maybe one day I will know why Jesus had to take my Julia. I am sorry you have to be the one to tell her folk.

Your son,
Joshua

Anna tries to compose her face before she looks up at Millie. "And you haven't heard from him since?"

"No, ma'am. He must have found a woman to take care of Fletcher while he works. Bet that baby is pretty. My boy is real nice looking, Miss Anna." She hands Anna a photograph. In it, Ludie, Tyner, and Millie are standing with a tall, light-skinned boy who has wavy hair and a long, slender nose above his full, dark mouth. "He was fifteen when we had our picture took at the fair in Smithfield."

He certainly is handsome, Anna thinks, staring at the picture.

"He don't look like me, Miss Anna," Millie says. "His hair a nice brown color and his eyes the color of a fawn, all golden and sparkly. And he don't have no scars. Guess you can see his daddy was a white man."

A white man? Anna says to herself. Millie in love with a white man? I cannot imagine such a thing.

146

"Julia and Joshua loved each other, Miss Anna," Millie continues. "Even when they was just little things, they was always together, laughing and playing. Now Miss Julia's name ain't never mentioned here. After they run away and I got that letter about them being married, Mr. Carl, Sr. and Miss Louisa tell everybody 'round here that Miss Julia died of pneumonia, and they start wearing clothes like they was in mourning. Even told their girls that. Miss Amanda and Miss Florence never was told the truth." Millie puts the picture in her apron pocket and pulls out a small square of newsprint. "This is what Mr. Carl, Sr. put in the Goldsboro paper the day after I got Joshua's letter telling me they was married. Miss Louisa begged Mr. Carl not to write this. She kept saying, 'She'll come home, Carl. She'll come back to us before long.' But he said as far as he was concerned Miss Julia better not ever show her face here again and that she might as well be dead."

Anna's takes the paper from Millie. Oh, gosh, she thinks. No wonder Louisa cried at our wedding.

> Miss Julia Duncan Sanderson, 17, daughter of Mr. and Mrs. Carl Winfield Sanderson of Bentonville, died last Saturday following a brief illness. Miss Sanderson, a student at Merrywood School for Girls in Richmond, was class treasurer and a member of the school choir. She was buried in a private ceremony. The granddaughter of Mrs. Gladsden Hightower of Sand Hill Farm, she is survived by her parents, three brothers and two sisters.

"Millie, I don't understand this. It says she was buried in a private ceremony. Did they bury an empty box?"

"I don't know what they did in Richmond . . . or wherever they went, Miss Anna. After they knew Joshua and Julia was married, they come over here and had some kind of meeting with Miss Adaire. She told Mama and Daddy and me to stay in the cabin while they was here. Daddy drove them to the train station the next morning. Mr. Carl, Sr. and Miss Louisa and Robert and Mr. Carl, Jr. went somewhere for three or four days. Mr. Carl, Sr. threatened to run us off after that, but Miss Adaire wouldn't let him."

Millie walks to the end of the table and begins brushing crumbs from the white damask cloth. "Now you know, Miss Anna, why none of us is allowed to speak of Miss Julia. She died anyway, so Mr. Carl, Sr. got what he wanted. Just about killed Miss Louisa, and I thought Miss Adaire would never come out of her room again. She stayed right in there every day for weeks. Sat in that old rocker in her gown and wrapper, holding her sewing basket. Every day like that for nigh on to a month. Just about drove poor Colonel Hightower crazy. And when folk from the church started asking 'bout Joshua, I told 'em he was gone up north to get a job, which was pretty close to the truth. 'Course there was some whispering 'bout it just the same. Folk love a little piece of gossip, you know."

As she gathers the remaining dirty dishes, a sad melody reverberates low in Millie's throat. "Go on, honey," she says to Anna. "Daddy got the buggy hitched up so Mr. Carl can take you to see Dr. Cobb this morning. You forget about what I told you and put your mind on that baby you carrying."

* * * * *

"Watch your step, Miss Anna," Millie warns. "These roots and vines just seem to jump out the ground all along this path. Don't want you taking a fall. Seems like you done got bigger just this past week since you went to see Dr. Cobb."

Anna lifts the hem of her skirt and steps over a stout root, pausing to admire the tiny purple flowers growing beside it. "What are these, Millie?" she asks, bending to touch the delicate petals.

"Mama calls those spiders. All kinds of pretty flowers grow down in these woods, but you gotta be careful what you touch. Might get a rash."

Anna strolls the path with her companion, moving slowly, admiring the leaves and flowers of plants she has never seen. She stops abruptly as a thrush darts from a nearby shrub and takes flight. "That's the first bird I've noticed. I thought these woods were full of birds."

"They out scavenging for their breakfast, Miss Anna. Out in the fields. If you want to see lots of birds, you'll have to come down here in the spring. They're everywhere, carrying straw and building their nests."

"I'm afraid I'll be doing a little nesting of my own by then."

Millie giggles. "Well, you sure won't be out in the woods. You'll be setting up in that big house in Baker rocking your baby. Have you finished that pillow you making for its cradle?"

"Almost. Tyner says he'll have the cradle finished next week, so I've got to get busy. Before you know it, Christmas will be here."

"And your little one will come not long after that. The doctor said February, didn't he?"

"Yes, I'll be as big as a house by then. It's a good thing we let out my dresses because I can almost feel myself getting fatter every day. I wish I could wear these loose dresses from now on. They're so comfortable." Anna pulls at the front of her dress and watches as it billows around her waist. She giggles and pats it back in place as Millie pushes a large limb from their path. "Step right through here, Miss Anna. The creek over yonder."

Millie removes two flour sacks from a tin bucket and spreads them on the bank. "Here's your breakfast." She hands Anna a biscuit stuffed with a thick slice of glistening ham, and Anna sits down on one of the flour sacks and begins to eat. She accepts a tin cup of milk from Millie and wonders at the brown woman's ability to provide everything they need. This is perfect, she says to herself. A beautiful morning, a delicious breakfast, a lovely setting. She lifts her face toward the sun and recites a verse she learned in grade school.

> The lark's on the wing,
> The snail's on the thorn,
> God's in his Heaven—
> All's right with the world.

"See, you can make a poem, too, Miss Anna," Millie says. "That was mighty pretty. Prettier than any poem I ever wrote."

"But I didn't write that, Millie. Robert Browning wrote that. He's an Englishman."

"From across the water?"

"Yes, from England." Anna finishes the biscuit and the last of her milk. "You said we could find blackberries down here. Where are they?"

"Right yonder." Millie points to a place downstream where the creek makes a turn. "I'll show you." She picks up an empty bucket and leads Anna across the sandy bank to a massive bramble growing between two sycamore trees. Its sprawling green vines tower above the women's heads, wrapping around the tree trunks in intricate patterns that curl and twist like the tails of miniature dragons. Plump berries, black and gleaming, play hide and seek among feathery leaves and wicked thorns.

"Oh, Millie, that's quite a bush, isn't it?" Stepping up to the nearest bough, Anna picks a fat berry and pops it in her mouth, then another, and another.

"Been coming here since I was a little girl. My brothers, Sam and Amos, used to bring me down here when they come to fish or swim. We picked blackberries most every day this time of year," Millie explains. "And when Sam and Henrietta's boys was growing up, I brought them down here to play, too." She pulls a stem down and plucks a half-dozen berries from it. "By the way, Miss Anna, I guess I'll be going with you and Mr. Carl to your new house in Baker."

Anna grabs Millie's forearm, smearing it with berry juice. "Oh, Millie! Thank you. You don't know how I've prayed that you would come!"

"Yessum, I do, Miss Anna. Even heard you a few times when you got mad and slam the oven door on that woodstove. Most folks would cry for Jesus to rescue 'em, but you holler for me!"

Anna's laughter fills the warm air and Millie joins her, laughing so hard that water spills from her eyes. "You sure ain't lost no love on that woodstove, have you, honey?"

"Not just the woodstove, Millie, but everything in the kitchen. I fear I'm a hopeless failure in that domain." Anna clasps her hands together in a prayerful stance. "Thank you, Lord, for Millie."

"Guess you better thank Mr. Carl, too. He's the one what arranged everything. He told Justice last night that him and Zilphie could come and work on the farm all the time and live in the shed if I went to Baker. Mama ain't able to take care of everything for Miss Adaire like she did when she was younger. Mr. Carl told Justice that he'd hire Zilphie to keep house and cook for Miss Adaire and the Colonel, while Justice runs the farm in the summer and teaches at the school in the winter."

"Don't Justice and Zilphie have children?"

"Yessum. Two. Willie and Christmas."

"Where are they going to sleep? That shed has only one bed, and there's not enough room for another."

"The young'uns can sleep in the loft of the cabin, Miss Anna. That's where we slept." Millie drops another handful of berries in the bucket.

"You mean you and Asia and your brothers slept up there? Wasn't it cold in the winter?"

"Not too bad. We all huddle 'round the chimney and stay over where the heat from the fire come up. 'Course, when it snowed, it'd come in all the cracks. Thing I liked best, though, was lookin' out those cracks and seeing the stars shining overhead so glittery and beautiful and so far away. I just wanted to reach out and touch 'em . . . just feel the heat of 'em . . . all burnin' and burnin' . . . just like we are . . . 'til they burn themselves out." Millie raises a hand to shade her eyes and looks over at Anna. "Law, I sure didn't mean to go on like that. Sun gonna catch up with us iffen we don't stop dawdlin'. Gonna get hot."

"Yes, it is getting hot, isn't it?" Anna lifts the hem of her dress and wipes the sweat from her face. She peers into the bucket Millie is holding. "Won't be long before that's full. I guess we'll have enough for two pies, and we probably should make two because Mr. Carl and the Colonel can eat one by themselves. Do you think they'd like a hard sauce with it, Millie?"

"Sure would. Both them men will eat just about anything you set before 'em, and we got plenty of sugar and fresh butter. Mama told me that back during the war, they didn't have no sugar and no flour, neither, so they made this blackberry dessert with cornmeal and molasses."

"Blackberries are awfully pretty, aren't they?" Anna holds a particularly large one out for Millie to inspect. "Not only the ripe ones, but the red ones and the little ones that are still green. They look like jewels, don't they, Millie? Bright jewels shimmering here in the sun."

"Miss Anna, if you ain't careful, you'll get me started on a poem." Millie catches a thorny vine, ladened with a cluster of large, ripe berries. "Blackberry, blackberry, dancing in the sun," she begins, turning the bunch of berries to get a good look.

> Shining like a jewel,
> 'Til the day is done.
> Hanging from the vine,
> Sassy as can be,
> Laughing and a winking
> At a fool like me.

Anna claps her hands, smearing red stains along the sides of her fingers. "Those poems just come right out of you, don't they?"

Millie's face flushes with obvious delight. "Yessum. And I let 'em. They make the day go by quicker somehow. But that's enough poems for one day. Time for some fishing. Can't stay down here much longer because I gotta help Mama cook dinner."

They return to the flour sacks warming in the sun. Millie sets the bucket of berries on the ground, picks up the fishing poles, and hands them to Anna. "You hold these for a moment and I'll fix the bait," she says. From her pocket, she draws a piece of rough cotton fiber and a ball of damp biscuit dough. Anna watches, fascinated, as Millie rolls a pinch of dough into a small thread of the cotton, then pulls the lines away from the poles and threads each hook with a string of "bait."

"It's easier than digging worms, and the fish love it. We'll have us a nice mess for dinner in no time." Millie takes the poles from Anna and turns back to the creek bank.

"I think I'll have a little nap," Anna says, and Millie nods, remembering how often she napped when she was carrying Joshua. Anna sits down on one of the sacks and takes off her shoes, rolls down her stockings, and throws them aside. She moves Millie's sack to extend her resting place and lies down, taking the bonnet from her head and placing it over her face. "You go on, Millie," she mumbles from under the brim. "I'll join you in a few minutes."

Millie walks a short distance up the bank and thrusts the end of one pole into the sandy soil at her bare feet. Then she throws the line of the other into the creek as a muskrat peeks out from under a clump of sprawling, water-soaked roots and disappears without so much as a ripple. "Little rascal," Millie says out loud. "Think I'll catch you and make me a nice collar for my Sunday meeting coat." She glances over to where Anna is lying and watches the slight rise and fall of the younger woman's chest beneath the loose folds of the dress she let out just the week before. That baby is sure gonna make this family happy, she thinks. But the harsh cry of a bird grabs her attention. A blue jay bursts from the branches of the cypress tree above Anna's head. Millie looks down at the bonnet over Anna's face, at Anna's chest, across her stomach, and, finally, at her bare legs. That's when she sees the snake, its tongue darting from its flat, triangular head just inches from Anna's feet. Millie grips the bamboo pole and draws a quick breath as the snake, dark and wet with creek water, draws its long body up on the bank and disappears into the skirt of Anna's dress.

Without looking away, Millie bends to drop the fishing pole. She stands up slowly, pressing the palms of her hands against the sides of her skirt. "Oh, Jesus," she whispers. "Oh, Lord, Jesus." Be quiet, she says to herself. He'll hear you.

She moves quietly down the sandy bank, her eyes on Anna. When she reaches Anna's side, she kneels in the sand and whispers, "Don't speak. Don't move." She inches her way along the warm ground. "If you can hear me, Miss Anna, make a fist with your hand that's over here by me. Go slow now." Anna slowly draws her hand into a fist.

"Whatever you do, don't make a move. Don't even breath hard. Understand?"

Again, Anna draws her hand into a fist.

"A little snake done crawled up your skirt. I ain't sure what kind. But the best thing to do is be still. Real still." Millie takes a deep breath. Oh, Lord Jesus, help us, she silently prays. Save Miss Anna from this demon. "I'm gonna move your bonnet from off your face, Miss Anna, but you gotta be real still now."

Millie's hands tremble as she slides the hat away from Anna's damp face. "Snake's gonna go 'cross your belly," Millie whispers, watching as Anna's dress begins to ripple at her waist. "Can you see him, Miss Anna? Can you see where he is?"

Anna brings her chin down against her chest and looks across the dimity bodice where the material seems to be moving in small waves above her waist.

"Miss Anna, I want you to take both your hands and grab his head, grab through your dress," whispers Millie. "Grab it now!"

Anna's hands fly up, scattering sand in every direction, as she grabs at the snake. She can feel the outline of its head through the cloth and presses her fingers around it, just as the snake tries to wrap its long, thick body around her waist. Millie is beside her now, taking her by the arm, helping her up. "Don't let go," she warns. "He can't bite you if he can't get his mouth open. Just hold on now. Got to get you home. We're gonna take the shortcut. You just stay right with me and hold on to that snake's head. I'll do the rest."

She leads Anna away from the worn path and into a thick copse of pine trees. As they make their way through snarled brambles and limbs,

Millie moves just ahead of Anna, holding back intruding branches and tangled vines, and warning Anna of fallen tree trunks and thorny shrubs. Birds are darting overhead now, calling to one another, but Anna doesn't see or hear them. Briars grab at her skirt and bite her bare ankles, but she can't feel them. Her body stops at her waist. All she can feel is the snake.

"Won't be long now," Millie pants. "We'll be home in just a minute."

After what seems an eternity, they reach the hog pen at the edge of the woods behind Adaire's house and make their way around the mule lot and the barn. As soon as they are in hearing distance, Millie begins to call, "Mama! Mama! Bring a hoe! Gotta snake out here!"

She begins to unbutton the two-dozen pearl buttons down the back of Anna's dress as Ludie emerges from the kitchen door with Adaire behind. Be calm, she says to herself. No need to frighten everybody.

"Get me a hoe, Mama," she says to Ludie, who hurries as fast as her old legs will carry her to the side of the log cabin. She grabs a hoe and, with the know-how of a person who has had to deal with snakes before, takes up a long-handled planting spade.

"You're gonna have to step out this dress, Miss Anna," Millie says. "Gonna have to cut the shoulders to get you out of it." She looks over at Adaire. "Get me some scissors. Big ones."

Millie continues to unbutton Anna's dress, pausing briefly at the waist where she sees the dark brown splotches on the reptile's back that confirm her fears. As soon as she finishes with the buttons, she takes the scissors Adaire has brought and moves around in front of Anna.

"You're doing fine, Miss Anna." Millie manages a weak smile, but she is frightened at Anna's ashen pallor. Law, she thinks, she's whiter'n a hen's egg. Gonna faint on me any minute. "You just hold on a little longer and we'll get you out of this."

She slides the scissors along Anna's bare arm and into the lace-trimmed sleeve of the dress, cutting the flowery material and the petticoat strap beneath it. "Now, as soon as I cut this other sleeve, I'm gonna start moving your dress down to the ground. You hold on to the snake and move with me." Anna nods and closes her eyes, licking the top of her lip where beads of sweat have gathered. Her petticoat falls to her waist, exposing her naked breasts.

Millie throws the scissors to the ground and gathers the soft material in her hands as the body of the snake begins to squirm. "When I say so, you step away, Miss Anna. Don't do nothing 'til I tell you."

Slowly, the two women bring the dress, petticoat, and snake to the ground. "Keep holding on," Millie whispers, pushing the bunched up material away from Anna's bare legs and feet.

Suddenly, the snake's tail and part of its body emerge from inside the material and coils itself around Millie's arm. She looks up at Ludie. "I'm ready, Mama." Ludie takes a step and runs the long narrow blade of the planting spade against Millie's arm and into the middle of the snake's coiled body. "Now!" Millie cries. And Anna jumps away.

The snake's head shoots out like a bullet, its mouth wide with deadly fangs that attack the blade, sending a stream of clear liquid over the mud-caked metal. Ludie lifts the handle of the spade and hurls the snake against a nearby tree. It falls to the ground and, for an instant, is still. Then it begins to writhe and twist as it coils back on itself. Millie brings the hoe down and cuts off the cottonmouth's head. Blood spews from the wiggling, headless body, spreading along the lacey bodice of Anna's discarded dress, as the hideous mouth continues to hiss and bite.

Millie shudders, watching as the reptile squirms in its death agony. She hears the sound of retching and turns to see Anna bent over a puddle of slimy purple vomit. Adaire draws a handkerchief from her pocket and wipes Anna's mouth. Millie watches the old woman as she throws a shawl over Anna's naked shoulders and leads her toward the back door of the house.

Ludie picks up the planting spade and stares after Adaire and Anna. "Um, um, um," she mutters, shaking her head. "Mighty bad sign. Mighty bad."

"Hush, Mama. She might hear you." Millie grabs the hoe and begins to rake the soiled dress and bloody remains of the snake into a pile. "I'll clean up this mess. You go on in the house and get Miss Anna something to drink. Better get her some brandy."

CHAPTER 11:
FINGERS AND TOES

December 18, 1905

Anna presses the soles of her boots against the tin warming box in the floor of the buggy and leans forward to get a better view of the mud-filled streets of Baker. Since the war, it has grown from a crossroads stop to a thriving community of eight-hundred souls who make their living from the Sanderson and Son Cotton Mill and its warehouses. The red brick building that houses the Bank of Baker serves as the town's centerpiece. It is flanked by a general mercantile, a feed and grain store, two livery stables, a haberdashery, and a post office. Across the railroad tracks is a depot, a two-story hotel, and the sprawling yard of Baker Lumber and Coal. In keeping with the season, each building's doorway is decorated with garlands of cedar and pine, and display windows are filled with manger scenes and toys.

"Doesn't everything look pretty?" Anna says to Millie, pulling the buggy robe over her enormous belly and securing it under her arms. "And so many people are in town. Just look at all the buggies and wagons along the street here."

"Doing their Christmas shopping, I suppose. Folks come here from all 'round now that we've got these nice stores. Mr. Robert told me he had a time keeping watch fobs and handkerchiefs and ladies' hand mirrors in stock at Christmas time. Before you know it, this place will be big as Smithfield."

"I hope it will be, Millie. I'm looking forward to living in a town again. Aren't you?"

"Yessum, but you'll have to help me get to know it. In all my forty-four years, I ain't never lived nowhere but the farm." Millie pulls on the reins and brings the buggy around the corner to Carl and Anna's new house. "My, this is some place," she whispers, gently slapping the leather across Caesar's rump.

It's exactly what Carl wanted, Anna thinks, gazing at the imposing white structure that boasts four red brick chimneys. She watches as Tyner crosses the porch and starts down the brick walkway, his red russets edged with mud. "Careful, Miss Anna," he says, helping her out of the buggy and onto the stepping block.

She starts up the walkway where Ludie is waiting outside the double doors, her grizzled head wrapped in faded calico, a feather duster in one hand. The old couple has spent the last few days unpacking, cleaning, and storing Anna and Carl's wedding gifts, preparing the bedrooms and baths for habitation, and outfitting Millie's quarters behind the kitchen.

"I got your house slippers right here, Miss Anna," Ludie says as the younger women cross the porch. "You come on in here and get warm. Got a nice fire in every room so you won't get chilled. I know you're gonna walk about seeing if everything is to your liking. Don't want you catching your death."

Anna sits down on the bench of a fancy halltree in the foyer. Millie kneels to help her remove her boots and replace them with soft, low-heeled shoes. "Just smell that fresh paint," she says as she strains forward in an effort to get up again. Since early morning, she has had a nagging pain in her lower back, and the ride into town has made it worse. Last week, Dr. Cobb told her to stay away from the buggy. "I think I'll sit here for a few more minutes," she says, looking at Millie. "Don't let me interfere with your chores. You go on with Ludie. I'll be fine."

"You rest, honey." Ludie pats Anna's shoulder. "You carryin' around a lot of weight these days, and you need to take your time. Me and Millie going on out to her quarters and take care some things. We'll be back in a while. If you need us, just step to the back door and holler."

Anna watches as Millie slows her pace to match that of her mother and the two make their way down the wide polished floor. The Colonel has certainly done a grand job hanging my paintings, she thinks, surveying the collection she brought back from Florence. That cream-colored silk wallpaper and walnut wainscoting provide a handsome backdrop for my little collection.

With enough effort to produce an unladylike grunt, she rises from the bench and makes her way slowly to the mahogany table, where a crystal bowl holds fresh holly. I can hardly believe Carl and I are going to spend Christmas in our new house, she thinks. I wonder what it will be like to be alone with him in the evenings, without Granny and the Colonel? To sit in front of a fire after supper and rock our baby while the two of us talk about whatever married people talk about when there's no one else around?

The thought of such privacy, of her own home, her own yard, her baby, brings a smile to her lips that she carries into the drawing room. Its pale celadon walls set off a massive walnut mantle. Beneath it is a carved alabaster relief of Roman charioteers being welcomed home by women and children who bear laurel, fruits, and flowers. Anna sketched the mantle scene, and Carl hired a master stone-carver from Richmond to produce it. Before the fireplace are a pair of Sheraton sofas upholstered in cream, rose, and dark-green striped velvet.

Anna crosses to the dining room, where a large cherry table, a dozen chairs, and the sideboard she and Carl purchased in New York gleam in the weak, winter light. Soon, guests will sit around my table and I won't have to cook anymore to prove my worth. Thank goodness. Perhaps I can paint a mural on that far wall. Carl would like that, but it will have to wait, she thinks, until summer. Maybe then I'll be able to get to it. After the baby is a little older.

Behind the dining room, and connected to it by pocket doors, is Carl's library. It is one room Anna has neither planned nor purchased for. Carl's butternut sofa fills one wall, a brass smoking stand at one end, and a walnut and glass humidor on the other. Above it hangs a heavily framed painting of a snarling bear being attacked by hunting dogs. The back wall is covered with bookshelves filled with Carl and Anna's many volumes. Carl's desk, an elaborate affair of burled maple that was a gift from the Colonel, sits in front of the bookshelves.

Anna leaves the library and opens the door to the sitting room, where she hopes to spend most of her time, and where she and Carl will have informal meals. It's decorated in cherry wainscoting and a wallpaper of pink climbing roses. A dark green sofa and arm chair, their seats bulging with comfortable down, and a round pine table and four matching chairs that belonged to Anna's grandmother, give the room a lived-in look.

Pausing at the window to look out at the backyard, Anna collects her thoughts. In two months, my baby will be born and my back won't ache every minute, my feet won't be swollen, and I'll be able to sleep again. And soon the baby and I can sit out on the porch in the sunshine and watch the flowers come up. "Ah, spring," she whispers. "A new house. A new life."

Millie taps lightly on the open door. "Miss Anna, I can't wait for you to see my place," she says, coming into the room with Ludie. "Mama fixed me a nice chair by the hearth, and Daddy made a set of shelves for my books, and that picture you gave me, the daisy picture, is all framed now and hanging over my bed."

Anna turns from the window and takes Millie's hand. "Good. I want you to be happy here, Millie. After all, this is your home, too."

"Miss Anna, your hand's mighty cold. Just like ice. Bet your feet are, too."

"I'm all right. If only my back would quit hurting."

"Ain't gonna quit 'til you have that baby," observes Ludie. "Come on, honey. Let's get your boots on and get you home 'fore you gets a chill."

"But I haven't seen the baby's room yet." Anna sits down on the loveseat and tries to bend over enough to remove her slippers.

"Honey, you can see it when you move in tomorrow," Ludie replies. "It's mighty pretty with all those little bears and dogs and kittens on the wallpaper. And the cradle is just beautiful. I laid it all out with the blanket Miss Adaire crocheted and those pretty pillows you embroidered. The day bed is fixed up, and that fancy rocking horse Mr. Carl ordered is right where he wants it."

"What about our bedroom, Ludie? How does it look?"

"Draperies hung just so, and the walls look like they got a little flower garden planted all over 'em. That bed and dresser that belonged to your mama and daddy is so nice. Just think, your baby gonna be born in the bed you was born in. And those bathrooms is something to behold. All those brass fixtures so shiny, and the tubs nice and clean. Can't imagine just turning those taps and hot water flow out like manna from above."

Anna pushes against the back of the loveseat, lifting her oversized belly, in an effort to get her puffy feet back into the tight boots. "The first thing I'm going to do tomorrow, after we get settled in, is have a bath. I saved some bath salts from our honeymoon to christen those tubs."

Millie pulls a steel hook from her pocket and closes the dozen buttons that run from Anna's swollen ankles to her calves. "Let's go, honey. Got no business being out in this cold."

Tyner is waiting beside the buggy. "Y'all go on home now and set by the fire." He holds Caesar's bridle while Millie helps Anna get settled in the back of the buggy. "I'll stay here tonight and keep an eye on things."

Anna places her feet on the tin box that has been refilled with hot embers, draws the lap robe over herself, and spreads it to cover Ludie, who sits beside her. Millie takes the jump seat in front and grabs the reins. She turns to her father. "What about your supper?"

"Your mama done fix me a nice basket of vittles. I got some coffee and I'll be fine. Y'all better get on. Ain't long 'til dark." He waves as the buggy pulls away and the women begin the cold, muddy journey from Baker to Sand Hill.

Whey they arrive, Zilphie is at the woodstove frying sausage. Adaire is sitting at the kitchen table arranging a plate of green Christmas pickles and cinnamon apple rings.

Millie pulls the heavy cloak from Anna's shoulders. "You sit down," she says, "and I'll fix you some hot tea." Lifting a steaming kettle from the woodstove, she sneaks a look back at Anna, who is standing as still as rock beside the table. Her face's pale as a raw biscuit, Millie thinks, and she looks like she's caught in a vise. Stiff as a board. Millie sets the kettle back on the stove. "Miss Anna? You all right, honey?"

Grabbing one side of her belly, Anna slumps forward. A puddle of thin, yellowish liquid collects at her feet and begins spreading across the floor, leaving marble-sized clots of blood and ropy threads of bluish tissue. Millie grabs Anna around the waist, putting the younger woman's arm across her shoulder. She manages to move them both out of the kitchen and down the hall.

Adaire and Ludie exchange worried looks. "Zilphie," Adaire says, "go tell Justice to ride to Goldsboro and get Dr. Cobb. Tell him to take Caesar and not waste any time."

"I'll tell him to hurry, Miss Adaire." Zilphie slides the hot skillet away from the fire and hurries out the door.

"Never seen nothing like that in all my born days," Ludie whispers as soon as she and Adaire are alone. "Look like a rainbow, all that mess floatin' across the floor. Something gone wrong."

"Poor child," Adaire sighs. "It isn't time for that baby yet. You'd better get your catnip tea ready and anything else you can think of. I'll go dig out the birthing quilt. I just wish Carl was here. Of all days, why did he and Glad have to go to Raleigh today?"

* * * * *

In the soft light of a shaded gas lamp, Anna watches as Ludie removes the middle drawer from Carl's dresser and dumps his underwear, socks, and handkerchiefs in an armchair. The old woman takes the drawer to the hearth, stuffs it with a small pillow, and stands it on the floor in front of the fire.

"How you doing, honey?" she asks, resting the palm of her large hand on Anna's clammy forehead. "Your pains coming mighty fast for a first baby. Ain't been but two hours since your water broke. I'd better take a look at you."

She lifts the coverlet from Anna's bent knees and runs her rough fingers across the young woman's pelvis. "Yessum. That baby gonna soon be here. I can see it all ready and you beginning to open up wide."

Anna jerks forward as a band of searing embers dances along her lower spine. "Is it always this painful, Ludie?"

"It's pretty hard for most women. And first babies is always the worse." Ludie moves away from the bed as Millie comes in the room with a tray that holds a cake of soap, a ball of twine, scissors, balls of bleached cotton, and a steaming cup.

"You better drink this now, Miss Anna," she says, holding the cup in one hand and supporting the back of Anna's damp head with the other. Anna takes a sip of the bitter brew and pushes the cup away.

"It don't taste good, but you'll be glad you drunk it. Catnip tea the only thing that'll help ease the pain."

Anna jerks forward, cramming the end of the bed's coverlet in her mouth to stifle a scream. She can feel herself expanding like a menacing vapor, melting into the heat that surrounds her. Biting into the soft cotton, she savagely kicks at the birthing quilt. "It's too hot in here! I'm going to die from this heat."

"Now, Miss Anna." Millie's voice is as soft as a rose petal. "We gotta keep it warm in here for the baby. He's use to your warm body, and we don't want him to get too cold right when he's born." Pulling the cover over Anna once more, she puts a damp cloth on Anna's forehead. "I know this is hard, but you got to lie still and stay warm." She looks at Anna's sweat-covered face and sympathy fills her eyes. *I know what you going through,* she thinks. *I been there. We all have.*

Ludie comes to the bedside in a heavy white apron. Her long fingers, gnarled like the claws of an old eagle, are dripping with grease. "We better have another look, Miss Anna." She pushes the cover away, bends down, and runs the tips of her slick fingers along the birth opening. "Oh, no," she whispers. She straightens up and hurries to the hearth to wipe her hands. Millie follows and, with her back to Anna, mouths, "What is it?"

"The baby turned wrong." Ludie answers so softly that Millie can hardly hear her. "Cain't see nothin' but it's face. It's little nose is sticking out."

"Lord, Mama. What you gonna do?"

"Don't know. Never seen one like this. I recall one time I was helping with a baby and the shoulder come first. Had to push it back in. Took all night to get that baby out, and then it died. Henrietta's first girl. Look like this one might take all night, too."

Moans call them back to the bedside where Anna is rocking on her hips, her nightgown above her waist, her feet sprawled in front of her. "How much longer, Ludie?" she sobs. Her frightened eyes search the face of the old woman. "Answer me," she pleads. "Help me."

Millie takes Anna's hands and starts to rub them. "The baby turned wrong, Miss Anna. Mama and me don't know what to do."

"Turned wrong? How do you mean?"

Ludie moves closer to the bed. "The baby's face is at the opening, not the top of its head. I can see the nose and some of the mouth, but its little chin is stuck."

"Stuck? Stuck how, Ludie?"

"Stuck on the side, Miss Anna. The mouth is open and the bottom part . . . you know . . . the lip, is caught inside you."

Anna pulls herself up and looks toward the window. "I thought Dr. Cobb was coming. Where is he?"

"Justice says he's gone on a hunting trip to his cabin in Neuse Islands, Miss Anna. But he's on his way down there to try to find him."

"Oh, God," Anna sobs, falling back on the bed. *I'm going to die here,* she thinks. *All alone. Without Carl. Without my family. I'll never* see them again. Oh, Mama, why aren't you here to help me?

A knife rips at her lower back as the image of a baby's head pass-ing through a birth canal comes to her. A picture from a book. A book forbidden to little children, kept on the highest shelf of her father's of-fice. The same room where she and Bethany hid one day to spy through a crack as their father and his hired man delivered a colt. "It's turned wrong, Major," the black man had said as the laboring mare kicked and struggled on a bed of straw. Her father had rubbed his hand along the horse's belly, pressing his fingers deep into the outline of the unborn colt. Then he'd thrust his hand inside the mother, all the way up to his elbow. Anna and Bethany had watched in silence as sweat collected on their father's forehead and dripped onto the hind quarters of the mare. "I think I've turned it," he'd said as he withdrew his wet, slimy arm. Then he'd knelt beside the mare and pushed on her belly until the colt emerged in a pinkish blur.

"Get a mirror, Millie," Anna whispers. "Get my hand mirror and bring the lamp."

Millie hurries across the room and returns with the ivory mirror and oil lamp.

"Put them down in front of me so I can see the baby."

Millie holds the mirror and lamp close to Anna's bent knees, and Anna strains to make out the reflection before her. She sees a tiny red nose, covered in mucous, and the bluish rim of the baby's lip. Behind it, a bright pink tongue that seems to rise and fall with each movement of the baby's nostrils. It's breathing, Anna says to herself. Thank God, it's still alive. "Millie, you've got to help me. Put some lard on your hands."

Millie draws away. "But, Miss Anna," she stammers, backing to-ward the fireplace, "Mama's the one who brings the babies."

"Her hands are too big. Go on now, put some lard on yours. I'll tell you what to do. Hurry, Millie, or else I'll die here in this bed and my baby will die, too. You wouldn't want that on your conscience, would you?"

Millie hands the lamp and mirror to Ludie. She kneels and plung-es her hands into a crockery bowl of melted lard and hurries back to the bed with them dripping. "Don't worry," Anna says, her face contoured with pain. "The lard will come back out with the birth sac. Now, look at the baby again."

While Ludie holds the oil lamp near Anna's open legs, Millie bends to look. "I can see its face, Miss Anna. Like Mama says, the nose and part the mouth and some of one side the face."

Anna braces herself as a sledgehammer begins to pound on her hips. Her face tightens while her breath comes in short, shallow gasps. Like the baby, she thinks. I'm breathing just like my poor baby.

"Get a swab and clean the baby's nostrils," she orders. Ludie hands a swab to Millie, who carefully rubs it inside, and around, the baby's bloody nose.

"Now put your fingers inside me just under the baby's mouth and push it's chin back up."

A new fear haunts Millie's dark eyes. "No, Miss Anna. I might hurt you."

"Do what I tell you, Millie, or you'll be making a shroud for me. I can't have this baby unless you help me. Now, put your fingers up in me and try to close the baby's mouth."

A breath escapes Millie's dark lips, a long, loud breath. She closes her eyes and rubs her hands together, then is still.

She's praying, Anna thinks. Good, she can pray for both of us.

Several moments pass while the brown woman stands motionless, her face lifted toward the ceiling. Finally, she looks at Anna. "The Lord will guide my hands," she whispers.

Anna grits her teeth as Millie's fingers slide inside her. She bites her lower lip when they move just above her rectum, poking and scraping the walls of her vagina. Millie starts to cry, but after several tearful moments, she straightens up. "I got the baby's mouth closed," she says, gulping between sniffs.

"Now, put your fingers on either side of its head, Millie, and pull," Anna commands. "Pull gently, but hold on."

Millie's fingers stretch the birth opening wider as she grasps the baby's head. As she begins pulling, blood gushes around the face, filling the tiny nostrils. "Lord, Jesus," she cries. "Push, honey, push!"

Anna pushes with a force she does not know she has, a reserve so powerful it causes her bones to creak. It's the last sound she hears.

* * * * *

165

Anna feels Carl's hand pressing against hers, but her eyes won't open. The lids are so heavy, so tired and heavy.

"Here, let me put this under her nose, Mr. Carl," she hears Millie say as the sharp bite of camphor reaches her. She gasps, inhaling the peppery fumes, and her eyelids flutter.

"I'm all right, Carl." Anna's voice is barely audible.

"Dr. Cobb is here, honey. He wants to talk with us. Do you feel well enough?"

Anna gazes lazily at Carl, who is sitting in a chair beside the bed. She looks across the room to where Dr. Cobb is bent over a dresser drawer set across the seats of two straight chairs. Millie is standing near the hearth, dabbing at her eyes and blowing into a handkerchief.

"The doctor wants to examine you." Carl rises from his chair. The doctor, a short burley man, takes it. He throws open a bloodstained hunting jacket, sending dozens of bird feathers into the air, and puts his hairy hands into its pockets.

"Mrs. Sanderson," he begins, "I know you haven't had a chance to see your baby yet. It's a boy, by the way."

Anna's smile is weak. "Good. Carl wanted a boy so badly."

"Well, the baby's got some problems, Mrs. Sanderson. Not unusual in a baby that comes six weeks early."

Anna struggles to lift her head from the pillow. "What's wrong, Dr. Cobb? He's alive, isn't he?"

"Yessum, he is now. But he may not be for long. You see, early babies are prone to problems. They get sick quicker and have less to fight with. And this little fella . . . he hasn't any movement in his arms or legs. Evidently, he's suffered some type of spinal injury. Some kind of deformity. I can't see anything that might have caused it, so I expect its internal. I'm sorry, ma'am, but your baby has no use of his limbs."

A tightness swells in Anna's throat as tears well in her eyes. "Are you sure, doctor?"

"Yes, ma'am, I'm sure. I've gone over him pretty thoroughly. He seems fine otherwise, except for a couple of bruises under his chin and beneath his temporal lobes. Guess that happened during his birthing. Anyway, he weighs a little under five pounds, and his color is pretty good. His eyes are clear. Soon as I take a look at you, we'll get him over here so you can feed him. I want to be sure he can eat."

"What if he can't, doctor?" Carl asks, taking Anna's hand and sitting down on the bed beside her.

"Then we have a serious problem. Even more serious than the problem with his limbs. But let's wait and see about that in a minute." The doctor rocks back on the hind legs of the chair and grabs his knees with his hands. "I won't mince words, folks. Your boy may not live. If he can nurse, he might. But he'll probably never walk, or be able to use his arms or hands."

Carl winces. "What about his mind, doctor? Will he be able to talk? Will he be able to function like a normal child, otherwise?"

"It's hard to say at this point, son. He may not have much capacity in that area, either. The spinal stem that goes from the neck into the brain is a delicate and highly sensitive organ. The only thing we can do is wait and see."

Anna reaches for a handkerchief on the bedside table, and for a moment, the overwhelming shock of the doctor's remarks are dulled by the search for the small square of cotton. She dabs at her nose, then raises herself up on each elbow. "Bring the baby over here, Millie, and we'll see if he can nurse."

Carl stacks pillows behind Anna's back and shoulders. She unbuttons the top three buttons of her gown, pulls out a milk-swollen breast, and takes the baby from Millie.

His small face is red and wrinkled, and fuzzy dark hair lies damp against his elongated, small head. Anna opens the blanket to stroke his fingers and toes. They're as cool as stone. Small as a baby doll's, she thinks, bringing the baby's purplish mouth to her nipple. He nuzzles against it and begins to suck.

Dr. Cobb nods. "Thank God. He can eat. You go on and feed him, Mrs. Sanderson. Carl and I will step out of the room for a few minutes to give you some privacy, and then I'll come back and examine you. I expect you need a few stitches." He motions to Carl, who is staring at his little son, watching as he struggles to maintain a hold on Anna's breast. "Come on, Carl," the doctor says, "let's leave them alone for a few minutes." He puts his arm across the younger man's shoulder and guides him out of the room.

Millie retreats to a shadowy corner, waiting for the men to leave, her eyes fixed on Anna and the baby. As soon as the door closes, deep sobs overtake her and she covers her face with both hands. "Oh, Miss Anna," she whispers. "I didn't mean to hurt the baby." She backs as far into the corner as she can.

Anna strokes her son's smooth cheek. "It's not your fault, Millie. It isn't anybody's fault. The important thing is he's alive and, God willing, he'll live. We're both alive, and that's all that matters. Now, come and help me with these pillows."

* * * * *

Anna stares at the words on the cover of the purple booklet, a gift from the Borden Condensed Milk Company. "Baby Diary," she reads aloud as her finger traces the wreath of tiny pink rose buds surrounding the face of a blond, blue-eyed cherub. She opens the little book and removes a pen from the ink well. Beside "Name," she writes Warren McLean Sanderson. She had wanted to name the baby for her father but had never said so because Carl had seemed so intent on naming the baby after himself. But after he was born, her husband had told her, rather abruptly, to name the baby anything she liked. Date of Birth: December 18, 1905; Weight: 4 lbs, 13 oz; Height: 19 1/4"; Color of eyes: dark brown; Color of hair: black. Her pen scratches the delicate paper as she hurries to fill in the names of the parents, grandparents, and great grandparents.

She rises from the desk and goes to the cradle, where McLean is sleeping. For the past week, she has carefully bathed her son each day in warm soapy water, has rubbed his thin legs and arms until her fingers ached, has moved each toe and finger over and over, all the while praying. Please, God, let Dr. Cobb be wrong. Let my baby be normal. Please give him the use of his arms and legs. She has dried his little body with great care. McLean's skin, pale as parchment, looks as if the veins have been painted on. She has carefully dressed him in warm, soft garments and held him for hours. His appetite is good, his color has improved, but his arms and legs remain still.

Anna rests her head on the side of the cradle and begins her prayer once more. "Please God. . . ." She looks up as the door of the bedroom opens and Adaire enters, dressed in a gown of black taffeta that rustles with a sound like corn shucks in a breeze.

"Come in, Granny," Anna says, getting up.

"You're looking much better, my dear," Adaire remarks, sitting down in a chair near the fire. "And it was so good to see you enjoy the conversation at dinner today. You're eating again. Soon, you'll have your strength back."

"I feel much better, thank you. Who could resist that wonderful turkey and dressing Millie fixed? And those sweet-potato pies? I won't need to eat again for a week." Anna sinks into a chair opposite Adaire and pats her stomach.

"Yes, you will, honey. You're going to need to eat to keep your strength up. It takes a lot of energy to take care of a sick baby night and day. I know because I did it. But I lost my son anyway. He was such a tiny thing. Even smaller than McLean. And I nursed him night and day and prayed over him every hour. I just knew God wouldn't take my precious baby, but He did. And nothing I could do could change it. But I got over it when Janey was born. She was a healthy baby and hungry every minute. Kept me real busy."

Adaire reaches over to pat Anna's hand. "I know this is hard for you, honey, seeing that little baby struggle, and knowing he'll never walk or have any use of his arms. It's a terrible burden for a sweet, young woman like you to have to carry. And I know Carl's acting the way he is isn't making it any easier. He just doesn't know what to do, Anna. That's not unusual in a man, honey. We wait on 'em hand and foot all their lives, and feed 'em when they're hungry, and nurse 'em when they're sick, and pet 'em when they're blue. So you can't really blame Carl for the way he's acting. He's never had a disappointment in his entire life, and the only burden he knows is making sure the books balance at the bank.

"But what we women know . . . well, that's different. We know how hard it is to bring a baby into this world. That alone is enough . . . but to have to watch helplessly as that precious issue suffers. That's dreadful. And it's even harder when a baby lives and grows into child-hood before it's struck down." Adaire draws a handkerchief from her pocket and touches it to her eyes. "I can see my little Alice now, just as she was when they lowered her into that cold, icy grave. I can hear her sweet voice calling me. Alice was so special because I'd lost three babies before I had her. I never thought I'd be able to carry a baby again. But Ludie made me go to bed as soon as we knew. And she waited on me, like an angel, all those long hot months. I'll never forget that summer. John was with the Army in Tennessee, and I was here trying to look after a half-dozen field hands and all the children, and I was completely helpless. All swollen, and flat on my back in the bed I was born in. If it hadn't been for Ludie, this place would have gone to Hell. And I would have died delivering Alice. Janey was too young to know what to do, and I didn't want her to see it anyway. And Alice was like a gift from God. She was the finest, healthiest baby I ever had because Ludie took such good care of me. She stood by my bed morning, noon, and night, fanning me. And when Alice finally came, it was like a miracle. And then before I knew it, she was gone."

Adaire sits up in her chair, pushing against its arms. She takes her cane in one hand and slowly rises. "There's nothing you can do, honey," she says to Anna, "but love McLean and care for him and try to keep him from harm. And pray. I've known many a trial in my life, but the Lord has never sent anything I couldn't handle. We have to take what life brings and make the most of it. Even in the face of sickness and death and the life of a cripple, like this poor little boy." She's quiet for a moment, looking at the sleeping baby. Then she turns back to Anna. "When my first boy was born my husband, John, gave me this. I want you to have it." She holds out a delicate gold locket on a chain. "There'll be other babies, honey. And they'll bring you a world of joy." She drops the locket in Anna's hand, and carefully makes her way across the room to the door.

Anna gazes at the tiny piece of jewelry in her palm. She lifts the chain to unlock the clasp and fastens the locket around her neck. The diamonds and pearls sprayed across the gold heirloom flash as she runs her fingers across its warm surface. She imagines Adaire as a young woman burdened with the death of her first son. She can see Adaire's proud head, crowned with dark lustrous hair, bent with sorrow. She can almost hear the sobs that must have gripped the young mother's unlined throat, and filled her eyes with constant tears. Like mine, she thinks, filled with tears night and day. There's so much sadness in life. So much heartache.

From the yard, she hears muffled voices and tiptoes to the window to see a man, and a large woman, sitting on the bench of an approaching wagon, their faces obscured in swirling snow. As the wagon draws near, Anna recognizes Sam. Beside him, Henrietta holds a young child wearing a bright, red cap. Ralph Amos and his wife are huddled in the wagon bed with Cree. "Who is that child Henrietta's holding?" Anna asks aloud as the wagon draws close.

Ludie and Tyner's loved ones climb out of the wagon and dash into the warm cabin, while Anna continues to stand at the window. Her thoughts drift back to Christmas at the farm the year before. On Christmas Eve, it had snowed almost a foot. She and Carl had hung brass bells on Caesar's harness, bundled up, and laughed all the way to Baker to meet several of Carl's friends and business associates at a party. On the way home, Carl had stopped the sleigh in the middle of the deserted road and given her a silver box that held a cameo broach of the three Graces. They had kissed, softly at first, and then, after a few moments, with enough passion to make Anna uncomfortable. She had pulled away from Carl, had removed his hand from her breast. He had burst into laughter, told her she had too much starch in her corset, and said he could wait until they were married. She had put his arm back around her shoulder and nestled against his chest. We were so happy then, she says to herself, so very happy. Two carefree spirits falling in love. But that was another lifetime. Now, Carl hardly ever kisses me, and when he does, there's liquor on his breath. And he won't hold McLean. Won't look at him. Won't say his name.

She turns away from the window, tears in her eyes, to kneel once again at her son's cradle. "Mama loves you," she says, caressing the fringe of soft dark hair that rims the baby's narrow forehead. The back-door slams. McLean jerks, then snores softly again.

Millie enters the room carrying the child Anna saw a few minutes before in Henrietta's lap. "Miss Anna," she whispers, "this is Fletcher Sanders, my grandson." She pushes the red cap away from the child's forehead, releasing a fringe of thick blond curls. Fletcher thrusts his small hand toward Anna, his pink fingers working, his sea-green eyes inviting her to come closer.

"Fletcher?" Anna asks, caressing the tips of the little boy's fingers as Carl's words come back to her. What was it he had said? I want a boy. A boy with yellow hair and big green eyes like mine. Yes, that was it. Carl wanted a boy like this one.

"Yessum. Fletcher Sanders." Millie's scarred face is bright with joy. "Joshua brought him to Goldsboro yesterday on the train. Told Sam and Henrietta he wanted them to bring his boy out to the farm so I could look after him. Wants me to raise him as my own and teach him to call me 'Mama.' Ain't he beautiful?" she giggles, nuzzling her grandson under his chin.

"But, Millie . . . you're going to Baker to live with Mr. Carl and me, aren't you?"

"I aim to keep my promise to you, Miss Anna. Guess I'll be taking this pretty boy with me, if you don't mind." She pulls the little boy closer and rubs the end of her brown nose against his pale cheek.

What a beautiful child, Anna thinks. He surely does favor his mother. I expect Carl will be furious if he finds out that Julia's baby is here. "Does Mr. Carl know?"

"No'm." Millie pulls Fletcher's cap over his blond curls, and takes a step back. "I don't think so," she says as she moves toward the door.

"Well, you run along and enjoy your grandson, Millie. I'll talk to Mr. Carl about it later."

* * * * *

By nightfall, the house is quiet. Anna sits in her flannel gown and wrapper near the fireplace with McLean in her arms. Carl is dressing to go out.

"I've decided to stay over at the house in Baker tonight," he says, removing his striped shirt. "Some of the boys are coming over to play cards. The weather is so bad, we can't do anything else."

Anna wants to say, You could stay home and be with your wife and son. But she doesn't. Saying it won't make any difference. She presses McLean closer to her bosom.

"The baby's making progress, Carl. He's eating really well, and this afternoon when I finished feeding him, I wiped his little mouth and he smiled at me." She moves to the rim of the chair, holding the baby out to his father. "If you'd just pay some attention, Carl, you'd see how well he's doing."

Carl steps out of his suit pants and jerks on a pair of heavy wool trousers, slapping at the hem of his shirt tail as he hurries to finish dressing.

"Carl," Anna pleads, "he's your son. Can't you just spend a little time with him?"

Carl's hands shake as he buttons his sweater and pulls it down over his hips. He grabs an overcoat and thrusts a silver flask into one of its pockets. "What am I supposed to do? Teach him to ride? Take him hunting?"

Clutching McLean in her arms, Anna jumps to her feet. "What a hateful thing to say, Carl. You know he'll never ride and he'll never hunt with you." She puts the baby in his cradle and turns to face her husband. "He probably won't be able to sit in a chair, much less on a horse.

Carl turns from her and bends to fasten the brass snaps at the top of his boots. "Maybe it would be better if he had died."

"No!" Anna shrieks. "Don't ever say that again!" She rushes toward him, fists clenched tightly. "He's our son," she cries, pounding on her husband's broad back. "Our flesh and blood."

Carl grabs Anna, wrapping his strong arms around her. "Honey," he whispers, his mouth at her ear. "Calm down. I didn't mean to upset you." With one hand, he pulls the rocking chair across the floor and maneuvers Anna onto its seat. "Sit down, and be still. You'll work yourself into a state if you're not careful. I'm sorry, Anna. I shouldn't have said that. I was just . . . never mind, I shouldn't have said it."

Anna leans back in the rocker. There's no need to get upset, she thinks. No need to yell. It'll just frighten McLean. She pulls the wrapper smooth across her swollen breasts and closes her eyes while Carl puts on his coat. A draft sweeps her ankles as the door opens. There's a soft click as it closes.

Hours pass. Long, empty hours while Anna drifts in and out of sleep. Sometime after midnight, she gets up and begins to collect the clothes Carl left scattered on the floor. Beneath his striped shirt, she finds a pocket-sized photograph of Olivia Andrews. Anna stares at the picture, her lips parted as if she has been struck dumb, and Adaire's words ring in her ears. Never did love her. He just didn't. "Is that so?" Anna hisses. She rips the picture to pieces and throws them into the fire.

In the darkness, McLean whimpers, and Anna lifts the fretting baby to her breast. Patting his little back, she begins to sway from side to side, keeping time with the Tennyson lullaby she learned as a child.

> Sweet and low, sweet and low,
> Wind of the western sea.
> Low, low, breathe and blow,
> Wind of the western sea.
> Sleep and rest, sleep and rest,
> Father will come to thee soon. . . .

Her voice falters as a lump rises in her throat. She struggles to keep it down, but surrenders to the unforgiving knot that sucks at her insides, causing her eyes to burn. I should never have married Carl, she thinks, as she fingers the large square emerald ring on her left hand. I should have let Olivia have him, should have refused his advances, should have gone away. Oh, the things I should have done.

She looks down at the sleeping baby in her arms. It's too late, she sighs, too late to change all this. Now there's someone else to think about, and he's more important than Olivia. More important than Carl. More important than anyone. "Mama loves you," she whispers as her tears fall on McLean's dark head.

PART FOUR: 1917-18

Like A Good Little Wife

Chapter 12:
Jesus Has Nothing To Do With This

November 8, 1917

Millie wraps the last ham sandwich and adds it to the stack. "That makes two dozen, Miss Anna. One dozen chicken salad and one dozen ham." She begins packing the food in a large wicker basket.

"What about the cake?" Anna ties the strings of a long white apron over her blue-and-white striped uniform.

"It's in a box in the back of the wagon and everybody's waiting outside. All the young'uns is ready to go."

"I'll be ready as soon as I can get this darn thing on my head," Anna mutters, adjusting the stiff white cap with the big red cross in its center. "Whoever designed these things must think women are bald! What time does the troop train arrive?"

"Fletcher says it's due in at eleven-twenty-five. Left Camp Gordon before daybreak this morning. The parade starts at two o'clock."

"I don't like these parades. It's almost like drumming up business to kill people. All these boys coming here today so we can give them a big send-off to some God-forsaken place in France. Why, they're hardly old enough to shave." Removing a dishcloth from a peg on the side of the oak icebox, Anna spreads it across the broad, dark boards of the kitchen table. Millie hands her the cake knife, and Anna pauses to examine its sharp edge, holding it in front of her as if it were a rapier. "Now we're thrusting a bayonet in their hands and telling them to go kill somebody just as young and innocent as they are." Frowning, she wraps the knife in the cloth and slides it in the basket.

"Did you remember to put on your Red Cross pin?" Millie asks, opening the door to the yard where Fletcher and Anna's three children are waiting.

"Yes, yes. I remembered to put it on," Anna replies, her voice tight with impatience. "I know I've got to do my part and act like I agree with

177

all this stupidity. Otherwise, Mr. Sanderson will jump on me like a duck on a June bug." She goes to check on McLean, who is tied into a make-shift seat in the front of a wooden wagon Fletcher made so that he can pull the crippled boy around. "Are you ready, honey?" she asks, her eyes on the ragged stuffed animal McLean takes everywhere, a sock monkey Millie made for him years ago from which he has somehow managed to remove the arms and legs.

A crooked smile breaks his colorless face as he mumbles a reply that would be incoherent to a stranger, but is easily understood by his mother. "We'll get there on time, son. You'll see the train."

Anna smiles at her daughters, who are seated on the bench of a pony cart, their young faces filled with anticipation for the day's events. Claire, who was born a little more than a year after McLean, is the apple of her father's eye and, as a result, stubborn, self-centered, and spoiled. Beside her is auburn-haired Evelyn, a seven-year-old who makes up stories about fairies and dances to music no one else hears. Anna throws the girls a kiss, and Claire slaps the reins across Sinbad's shaggy rump. As the pony cart rumbles past her, Anna's eyes follow. I'm blessed to have my children, she says to herself. Thank God neither of you is on a troop train today. She motions to Fletcher, who takes the wagon's handle and follows.

"All my praying done paid off, Miss Anna." Millie closes the iron gate that leads to the dusty street. "It's a beautiful day. And the tall child and the baby child look beautiful, too, don't they?" she says, referring to Anna's daughters.

The women and their sons turn the corner and join the crowd filling Baker's Main Street. Anna recognizes several farm families who have accounts at the bank and come into town only on special occasions. They're dressed for an outing, the men in freshly laundered denim pants with suspenders over heavily starched shirts. Broad-brimmed straw hats shade the faces of the wives who are dressed in navy and brown frocks that reach their ankles. Young boys in knickers chase little girls in and out of the dozens of buggies and wagons parked up and down the street. Here and there, small crowds are gathered around a new flivver, listening to the proud owner boast about his machine.

"Look at that!" Millie points to a dark green Packard being driven by a woman in a large yellow hat. "Somebody new in town."

"That's Gertrude Weil," Anna explains, "from Goldsboro. She's come over to help us with our Red Cross booths today. You'll like her, Millie. I've never met a finer woman in my life than Miss Weil."

Anna waves to Gertrude and leads her family toward the depot where a large green army tent has been erected below the tracks. Inside are endless yards of waist-high chicken wire nailed in rows across the tops of dozens of sawhorses. The tent's entryway is decorated by a white poster with the word WELCOME in blue and NEWLAN COUNTY RED CROSS in red. Red-white-and-blue striped cotton drapes the top of the poster and the flap of the tent. Nearby, a smaller sign hangs over several library tables and chairs; SERVICE MEN: HAVE YOUR LETTERS WRITTEN HERE, it proclaims, and YOUR LETTERS MAILED HERE FREE OF CHARGE. In the front corner of the tent is an empty cotton basket adorned with a simple message: SAVE LIVES. PLACE YOUR PEACH PITS HERE. Below is a crude drawing of a soldier wearing a gas mask.

"The ladies have done a good job setting up. I can always depend on Emma Jenkins to get things done." Anna takes a tablecloth from her basket and spreads it over a section of chicken wire. Opening the cake box, she savors its chocolatey scent for a moment. "Wouldn't be surprised if cocoa isn't rationed at some point, would you?"

Millie nods. "I hear they're talking about asking folks to go without meat on certain days of the week. Justice said he heard that white flour and sugar might get scarce."

"It's that new food-control act. The one President Wilson appointed Herbert Hoover to run. We'll have to do without while farmers everywhere grow more food and the government runs up the prices. A little domestic arm-twisting in the name of freedom and democracy."

Anna cuts two slices from the chocolate layer cake, and Millie wraps them in a gingham napkin. "Fletcher," she calls, "here's some cake for you and McLean."

Millie's handsome grandson takes the treat as Anna pours two cups of water and holds them out to him. "You're going to stay close by, aren't you?" she asks, looking directly at the boy whose skin is as soft and light as saddle soap.

"Yessum. I know just where to take McLean so he'll be able to see everything, Miss Anna." Fletcher removes his cotton cap, places the wrapped pieces of cake on top of his golden curls, and pulls the cap down over them. He takes the cups of water from Anna and secures them between McLean's useless right leg and the side of the wagon. "Don't worry, Miss Anna. I won't let him get hurt."

"Thank you. Run along now. I hear the train whistle." Anna watches as the muscles in Fletcher's honey-colored arm bulge when he pulls at the wagon handle, and McLean's head bumps against the board behind it. My boy's always covered with bruises after excursions like this, she thinks, but it's worth it just to see him so happy.

She turns to greet Georgann Crumpler, secretary of her Red Cross Chapter. The two women begin to fill tin cups with water. They look up as the train rolls into the station, its open windows full of boys of every description. Blonds, brunettes, redheads in the first four cars; blacks in the last. All are shouting and waving to the crowd that surges toward the tracks. I won't look at their faces, Anna thinks. I won't look any of them in the eye. I'll just stay back here so I won't get to know some poor mother's son who's off to save the world in a rush of chicken salad and layer cake. All these boys having their last hoorah with a bunch of strangers. And some broken-hearted Iowa woman is staring out at a cornfield today, and wondering why she took such pains in raising her boy.

"Pardon me, Mrs. Sanderson." Anna turns to see Mayor Gordon behind her, his steel-gray hair parted in the middle and slicked down on either side, his morning coat shiny with age, a sprinkling of dandruff across its lapels. "Mrs. Sanderson, I was hoping you'd grace our platform today. We could surely use a pretty lady up there, and we want to hear from our Red Cross Chapter. I thought since you're the president, you might honor us by saying a few words. Nothin' fancy, just a little message of encouragement for these boys." He nods in the direction of the train and accepts the ham sandwich Anna offers him.

She looks over his shoulder to the group gathered around the depot. Scores of young women in tweed skirts and pastel shirtwaists are greeting the soldiers, their faces filled with adoration, their hands abloom with homegrown bouquets. "Are you sure you need me up on the platform?"

"Yes, indeedy. All of these fine boys deserve a big send-off, Mrs. Sanderson. You know we're the last stop before they get to Norfolk."

"Yes, I know, Mr. Mayor . . . I know we're the last stop. What time?"

"Program starts at one-forty-five. It'll be short. Just need a few words from you and Preacher Whitehurst before we start the parade."

"All right. I'll be there."

By one-thirty, more than two-hundred freshly trained white soldiers have been given the finest picnic food the ladies of Baker have to offer. Forty-three black soldiers have enjoyed the town's hospitality, too, but at a distance. The small tent erected for the black troops has been just as busy as that of the whites and, according to Millie, much more fun.

"Miss Anna," she says, coming into the big green tent with an empty water pail, "there's some mighty big courting going on over yonder. Those colored boys trying to make time with anything in skirts. Even a old woman like me. Lord, they sure doing some carrying on."

"Good for them. I expect their carrying-on will soon come to an end." Anna hands Millie the cake plate smeared with vestiges of chocolate icing and pulls a handkerchief from her pocket. "The mayor has asked me to say a few words on behalf of our Red Cross Chapter, so I'd better go on over to the platform and get a seat." She presses the thin cotton cloth against her forehead, dabs at her upper lip and chin, pockets the hanky, and adjusts the hairpins that are holding her cap. "Am I all right? Do I have chicken salad on my nose or anything?"

"No, ma'am. You look fine. Go on now and don't worry about this picnic stuff. I'll put it in the basket."

Anna climbs the steps of the platform and says hello to the Baptist preacher who is standing behind the mayor. The mayor nods to Anna and gives the signal for a drum roll. Dozens of people begin to assemble beneath the wooden platform. "Ladies and gentlemen, boys and girls, and members of the 141st Infantry Corps from Camp Gordon, Georgia," the mayor begins in his best ringmaster's voice, "I am here to welcome you today to Baker, North Carolina. We are so proud to be a part of this special day. So proud to have you soldiers here as our honored guests. So proud to offer our hospitality to this fine contingent of courageous young men and to wish you well as you prepare to embark upon one of life's most valiant missions—service to one's country in the name of liberty and justice." A roar from the crowd drowns the mayor's final words, giving him a moment to wipe his damp forehead. "I am pleased today to bring praise, in fact, to bring my highest accolades, to our own Newlan County Chapter of the American Red Cross." Hundreds of spectators applaud and a dozen cheers fill the warm autumn air as Anna gives a polite nod to the mayor.

"As you know, our chapter is headed by Mrs. Carl Sanderson, wife of our former mayor and the current chairman of the Newlan County Liberty Loan Committee." Anna continues to hold her smile as the crowd applauds again, but she is not smiling inside: Why can't they introduce women for who we are, not who our husbands are? she fumes. It's as if I wasn't a person before I married Carl. Almost as if I didn't exist before I was Mrs. So-and-So. "We'll be hearing from Mrs. Sanderson in just a few minutes," the mayor says. "But, first, I'd like to call on Reverend Thomas Whitehurst of Baker Baptist Church to bring the invocation."

Lanky Reverend Whitehurst steps to the front of the platform and removes his black felt hat. He holds a worn Bible in his hand, but does not open it. "Brothers and sisters," he begins, "I call your attention to the word of God as recorded in the Sixth Chapter of Ephesians, verses eleven and twelve." The reverend closes his eyes for a moment and lifts his thin face to the sun. "Put on the whole armour of God," he recites, his tone one of command as he turns to look at the soldiers gathered on the right side of the platform, "that ye may be able to stand against the wiles of the devil." His voice softens as he looks into the faces of the young men who are sitting as still as stones beneath him. "For we wrestle not against flesh and blood, but against principalities, against powers, against the rulers of darkness of this world, against wickedness in high places." He bows his head for a brief moment and says, "May God add his blessing to the reciting of His word. Let us pray."

His chin drops to his chest as he raises his open hand over the crowd. "Oh, Jesus, gird the loins of these brave young men and give them the courage to overcome the forces of evil in faraway lands. We ask, Lord Jesus, that you give these fine soldiers the strength, yea the power, to strike down the devil, to halt the destruction of the German despot. And, Lord, we ask you to guide them on this awesome journey, to love and protect them, so that their sacrifice may not be in vain. In Jesus' name, we pray. Amen."

Murmured *Amens* ripple through the audience as Mayor Gordon steps forward again. "Thank you, Reverend Whitehurst. As you know, the reverend here is a fine baritone, and I'd like to ask him if he would do us the honor of leading us in the first verse of 'America, the Beautiful.'"

The reverend steps forward once more and raises his right hand in the gesture of a choirmaster. "Everybody sing out now," he yells to the crowd. And the town folk and farm families comply, extolling spacious skies, amber grain, and mountain majesties. The song ends with another burst of applause.

"Now, ladies and gentlemen," the mayor says, "I wish to call your attention to the fine work being done on behalf of our brave young men in uniform by our own Newlan County Chapter of the American Red Cross. With the leadership of Mrs. Sanderson here," he says, nodding in Anna's direction, "our chapter has collected over five hundred quilts and blankets this summer and more than two hundred pounds of peach pits since July." Anna looks across the crowded street to where Carl is standing among some older men outside the bank's front doors. He sees her and waves as the mayor continues. "Our own Newlan County Chapter was cited just last week in the Raleigh newspaper for its contributions to North Carolina's support of our troops in the field. Before we begin our victory parade, I'd like to call on the president of our Red Cross Chapter, Mrs. Carl Sanderson, Jr., to say a few words." With a courtly bow, the mayor takes Anna's arm and ushers her to the front of the stand. There is a polite smattering of applause as she clears her throat.

"Good afternoon, ladies and gentlemen. I am Anna Sanderson of the Red Cross. It is with sincere gratitude that I stand before you today. Gratitude for your kindness and generosity on behalf of our chapter. Thank you for your tireless efforts in collecting blankets and quilts, and for gathering and saving the pits from this summer's peach crop. Because of your hard work and generosity, our young men will sleep warm and comfortably in their camps this winter and will be able to stave off great physical harm with the help of the filters in their gas masks. As you know, it takes seven pounds of peach pits to make one filter, so every single pit is important. Our chapter is currently collecting items for Christmas boxes to send our troops. We will appreciate your gifts of socks, gloves, hard candy, cookies, books, or any other items you think our soldiers might enjoy or need." She pauses for a moment and looks across the street to where Carl is standing. Her eyes meet his, and she licks her lower lip and raises her chin just slightly. "It is my hope that this war, this somber shadow thrown over our world by greed and lust for power, will soon be lifted.

"In the meantime, let us remember that the same spacious skies we are enjoying on this beautiful fall afternoon, the same sun that ripens our grain to gold, the same rain that falls on our majestic mountains, is the same sky, the same sun, the same rain 'over there.' For every American mother, for every American wife and sweetheart, who waits in Iowa, in Pennsylvania, in Oklahoma, in North Carolina, there is a mother, a sister, a loved one waiting in Belgium, in France, and, yes, even in the Black Forest of our foe. There is someone who is praying as we are here today, for the safety of a young man in uniform. And when this war is over, and I pray, as I know you do, that it will be over soon, let us not neglect our duty to democracy. May we, as Americans, stand as the purveyors of peace, not only in America, but around the world."

Amid the cheering and loud bravos, Anna mouths "thank you" and retreats once more to the back of the platform. The mayor steps forward and raises both hands to silence the crowd. "And now," he announces, "on to our victory parade. Sheriff Brown, will you do the honors?"

The sheriff moves to the railing, pauses to grin at the crowd, raises his pistol, and fires. From two blocks away, a roll of drums can be heard as the crowd hurries to line up along the plank sidewalks of Main Street. Wild cheering erupts as the Newlan County Fife and Drum Corps comes into view, its ranks swelled by the nearly one-hundred members of the local Army Reserve. With rifles cocked smartly against their shoulders, the men in khaki salute the people on the platform and the soldiers beneath it. The corps is followed by a large float draped with black bunting that features a life-sized dummy in a gray uniform, swaying from a hangman's noose. Beneath the dummy is a poster decorated with a skull and crossbones and the words, "We'll Hang the Kaiser." A dozen barefoot boys run along its sides, throwing apple cores and tomatoes at the effigy.

A pair of well-curried Morgans appears next pulling a double-bed wagon of denim-clad farmers and their straw-hatted wives. Red-white-and-blue bunting is snaked through the spokes of the wagon's wheels and draped across its rear panel. The farmers carry pitchforks, scythes, hoes, and signs that read "Food For Our Troops," "Conserve Now," "Keep America Strong: Grow Food."

Georgann Crumpler's two boys, Paul and Curtis, follow in a tiny goat-cart pulled by Ramses, their black-and-white ram. "We'll Get the Kaiser's Goat," proclaims a sign on the side of the cart. Now that's a good one, Anna says to herself, and she laughs with those around her. The Newlan County High School Band comes on at a brisk pace, horns blaring a noisy rendition of, "The Stars and Stripes Forever." Miniature American flags bloom in the lapels of the black-and-gold uniforms of the rosy-cheeked youngsters. Dozens of hats fill the air as the young musicians march by.

Anna and the other members of the Woman's Club of Baker prepared the next float, which features a live Statue of Liberty complete with lighted torch and spiked headpiece. On either side of "Miss Liberty" are placards proclaiming, "Liberty, Justice, Democracy." Anna's friends sit on the float, waving flags and throwing Mary Janes to the children.

A ragged line of veterans of the Civil War, their shabby gray uniforms hanging in loose folds on their thin, wrinkled bodies, staggers behind the women's club float. An arm is missing on one soldier, a leg on another. One veteran hobbles unsteadily on a wooden peg. Anna shields her eyes to make out the ranks of the chevrons in the group, and wonders how many were awarded just before the end of the war, a courtesy gesture on the part of some commanding officer to ensure the pride of future generations. Like my own father, she thinks. A major at age twenty.

Claire and Evelyn's pony cart appears with Sinbad's rump covered in navy bunting sprinkled with white stars, his harness and reins studded with tiny flags and miniature chrysanthemums. Evelyn stands at attention in the cart, her hand over her heart, her little body completely wrapped in an American flag. The crowd obviously approves of the tableaux for it sends up cheers, and several viewers throw kisses at the girls. Where in the world did Evie get that flag? Anna wonders as she waves to her daughters.

Members of Anna's Red Cross Chapter march past looking serious and intent on keeping time together, their striped uniforms wilted and streaked with food, their caps slightly askew. Behind them, a half-dozen veterans of the Spanish-American War kick up a cloud of dust as they spur their horses' bellies and slap their flanks with dusty cowboy hats. The town's barber, Zeb Troxler, and two of his cronies turn their ponies toward the crowd, shouting, "Remember the Maine! Remember the Maine!" Another rough-rider races ahead of the group firing his pistol in the air and shouting "Yee-hah!" as if he were auditioning for a Wild West show.

"Zeb and those boys must have had a nip or two this morning," Anna hears Mayor Gordon say to Sheriff Brown, who replies, "Won't hurt 'em none, I don't reckon. A man needs to get things out of his system every now and then."

Anna turns to see the Colored Benevolent Society, led by the pastor at Sanders Memorial AME Chapel, coming around the corner. Brown-skinned men, women, and children wave flags from behind a street-wide banner that reads, "Onward to Victory with Newlan's Negro Troops." Anna waves to Justice and Zilphie and their daughter, Christmas. How happy Ludie and Tyner would be, she thinks, to see their family marching along the streets of Baker, and how proud they would be to know that their great-grandson, Willie, is a private in the U.S. Army serving in France.

Shrieks, whistles, and thunderous applause greet the parade's last entry. Two black horses, their heads topped with inky plumes, pull a glass-enclosed hearse where the "kaiser" is resting on a catafalque draped in black satin. Heavily scrolled signs that read "Death to the Kaiser" hang between the broad-spaced wheels of the hearse. Its driver is dressed in a black top hat, coat, and trousers, as are the six "pall-bearers" who follow it. Sheriff Brown raises his fist and yells, "Kill the S.O.B! Kill the damned Krauts!"

Anna excuses herself and hurries down the platform. "Let's go home," she says to Millie.

* * * * *

Anna brings another chair to the drawing room and places it in the circle before the fireplace. She glances around at the group and realizes that not a single member of her woman's club is missing. So far, so good, she says to herself as she adjusts the oak music stand that will serve as a lectern for today's meeting. She smiles across the room at Millie, who is circulating among the guests, taking coats and pocketbooks, and continues to follow the brown woman with her eyes while her ears pick up the conversation on her right. Moon-faced Mrs. Sutton, wife of the school principal, is conversing with her neighbor, Mrs. Massey.

"I don't know why we have to send our precious boys overseas to fight for those no-good Frenchies," Mrs. Sutton announces. "They're just too lazy to look after their own affairs, drinking wine all day and visiting with their mistresses."

Mrs. Massey nods. "It is a shame, isn't it? I'm so glad Durwood is too old to go. But my boy, Blanco, will be sixteen this year, and he can't wait to enlist. I hope it will be all over before then."

"So do I!" hisses Mrs. Herring, a thin, horse-faced woman whose husband, Wylie, manages the Sanderson Cotton Exchange. "Why, just yesterday afternoon, Elizabeth told me she intends to enlist as soon as she finishes high school next spring. She's going to Washington to join the Navy, she said." Mrs. Herring gives her companions a *now top that one* look. "And I said to her, 'Young lady, you'd better go to your room and get a hold of yourself before your father gets home.' And she said, 'I've already told father I want to be a Yeomanette!' Whatever that is."

"You mean she really intends to join the Navy?" asks Mrs. Sutton. "Why, that's absurd."

"Well, I must admit I admire her spunk," replies Mrs. Massey. "All this war business must seem awfully exciting to young people."

"Even so," says Mrs. Herring, "I don't want my daughter going off to Washington to live under any circumstances. They say that city is a madhouse these days. Full of soldiers and foreigners."

"Speaking of foreigners," whispers Mrs. Sutton from behind her gloved hand, "I heard we were invited here today because Anna Sanderson promised that Weil woman from Goldsboro that she could come and talk to us about voting."

"Oh, so that's it," replies Mrs. Herring. "I thought we were going to pack books for the Christmas boxes we're sending to France."

"I don't think so. Miss Weil is sitting in the back of the room talking to Hephzibah Sanderson. Didn't you see her when you came in?" Mrs. Massey pulls a metal compact from her pocket, opens it, and studies her heavily powdered face. "You know Jews always seem to have some cause they're carryin' on about." She lifts a brassy curl from her forehead. "They say she has an office in her parents' home and runs all kinds of crusades out of it."

"Well, they're rich, you know," Mrs. Herring sniffs. "Got that big store downtown. That's how she gets by with all this stuff. If they didn't have money, we wouldn't even know who she is."

"Well, I, for one, wouldn't care." Mrs. Sutton's lips curl back from her long teeth. "My daddy always told me to be wary of Jews. He said they'd do you in if they got the chance."

"We'd better hush," warns Mrs. Herring. "It looks like Mrs. Sanderson is about to start the meeting."

Anna raps the music stand with the blunt end of a brass letter opener and pauses while Millie collects the last of the wraps and leaves the room. The women turn to face their hostess, their voices suddenly quiet, their gloved hands resting on laps. Anna looks around at the familiar group, smiles at Emma Jenkins, and begins.

"Thank you for taking time from your busy schedules to join me this afternoon, ladies. My purpose in inviting each of you here today is twofold. First of all, I'd like to present my sister-in-law, Hephzibah Sanderson, for membership. Most of you already know Hephzibah, who is a native of Wilson, and know that for the past year she has been very busy with her twin boys. Hepsi, won't you step up here so everyone can see you?" Anna pauses as the tall blond woman makes her way to the front of the room. "I would appreciate your consideration of Hephzibah for membership in our club," Anna says. "I'm sure you will find her creativity and energy an asset. Thank you, Hepsi, for coming today." Robert Sanderson's wife nods to the club members and takes the empty chair Anna has placed in the front row for her.

"And now for our other purpose," Anna continues. "Many of you have known Miss Gertrude Weil for years, and some of you met her for the first time when she came to assist us with our picnic for the soldiers last week. Miss Weil is from Goldsboro, where she is quite active in the Red Cross. She is also president of the Goldsboro Suffrage League. Miss Weil is here today to talk about a most important, and pressing, issue—an issue that will affect future generations of women across our state. The issue is voting. So without further comment, I present Miss Weil."

The club members turn to get a good look at the dark-haired woman in the yellow wool suit and matching hat as she walks quickly past them. They applaud, the sound of their gloved hands muffled and polite. Gertrude Weil steps behind the music stand, smiles, and says, "Good afternoon, club members." The women nod and smile. Several reply "Good afternoon."

"Ladies, I am here to talk with you today about an issue that is just as much our right as the air we breathe—the right to vote, the right to have a voice in choosing the best candidate for a particular public office, the right to voice an opinion on issues that affect our lives every day. I am speaking to you today not only as a woman, not only as a member of the North Carolina Federation of Woman's Clubs, but as a citizen." She pauses, and Anna notices that she has neither card nor paper before her.

"At this very moment, hundreds of our sisters are marching in Washington, marching on behalf of every woman in this room, on behalf of every woman in North Carolina, marching for a right that every woman in this country should have been guaranteed early on, way back when our Constitution was ratified.

"Just sixty years ago, our country was engaged in a war that pitted brother against brother, a war that tore our country apart. Many of you have heard stories of that conflict. Stories about your own family members. Stories of courage and valor on the battlefront and stories of sacrifice and deprivation on the homefront. And many of you know that our mothers and grandmothers took over businesses and farms when their men went off to fight. Those women raised children and crops, plowed and planted, tended the stock, kept ledgers, pruned orchards, and hunted game. And when their men came home from war, they found wives, mothers, and daughters who were knowledgeable about business and farming, who had ideas about production and economy, and who were politically astute.

"Now our country is in the middle of another conflict, and this war may work in our favor, as women, in a way the Civil War could not. For every banner, for every flag we wave, proclaiming justice, democracy, and freedom, has become a banner with a two-fold mission. How can we, in America, promote these rights when half our population is denied them?" The women interrupt Miss Weil with spontaneous applause, surprising Anna. Why, they're listening, she says to herself. They're paying attention.

"We have only to look at the freedoms of men in our society to know what we are missing," continues Miss Weil. "To have the simple freedom of dressing each morning and walking away from a household and all its cares to his chosen career is a freedom taken completely for granted by those men who practice it so blithely. And to return at the end of the day to an orderly household and sit down to a delicious meal prepared by women like us and to leave the dinner table, to leave the kitchen and its chores behind, and indulge in a nice cigar, or perhaps a nap, is a wonderful form of freedom. Yet men do not consider such things freedoms. They consider them God-given rights. The same right that allows men to own unencumbered property, and the same right that allows men to choose a profession and to enter it without fear of being paid less than the next man, nor fear of less opportunity for advancement if one works hard.

"Today, women are taking over jobs in this country as they did sixty years ago. They're taking over jobs that have traditionally been held by men. In cities across this vast nation, women are entering the workforce in offices, factories, and mills. But they are being paid significantly less than the men who held, or still hold, these jobs. In fact, women are making, on the average, less than half of what men in similar jobs are making." A murmur rises from the audience. Miss Weil pauses.

"We are proud in this country to stand up and tout a heritage built on liberty and justice for all. But the reality is that liberty and justice are not for all; they are only for some. And, as long as women are not directly involved in the issues that affect their lives, their lives will be controlled by that segment of our population that has the right to vote. Only by obtaining that right will we be able to move on to the larger challenges of our lives as women. The right to hold a job and make the same salary as a man makes in that job. The right to participate, without criticism, in the democratic process right here at home, and, yes, even in Washington. Who knows the real needs of this town, of Baker, North Carolina, better than the women in this room? Name one man who knows more about the need for good education for our children, for good hospitals and health care, for recreation and sanitation? But none of this will be possible until we women have the right to vote.

"Think, if you will, for just a moment. Imagine what you would be doing today, right this very minute, if you were not married, if you were not a wife and mother. Try to envision yourself as the bright and talented woman that you are, but single and childless. Where would you be? What would you be doing? Suppose you had just finished school and could be anything you wanted. Where would your dream lead you?

"It isn't just the vote. No, it's much more than that. It's casting aside the old notions, the old traditions and expectations of what women are supposed to do and be. Our vision is a world where a woman is free to choose a career, a life, without being punished by being told that she cannot marry as long as she holds a job. Why should women teachers who are married, who are mothers, not be the same excellent

teachers as when they were single? Why do we allow society to perpetu-
ate the idea that women are incapable of thinking beyond the words 'I
do'? Why should women be constrained in their lives, as men are not,
by child-rearing? Why shouldn't a woman have the right to choose if,
and when, she will have children?"

Anna hears the scrape of a chair on the floor and turns to see
Reverend Whitehurst's wife coming toward the front of the room. The
older woman stops beside the chair where Anna is sitting. "I'm surprised at you, Mrs. Sanderson," she says, while a bunch of black cherries
dances above the brim of her gray felt hat. "How could you allow such
blasphemy right here in your own house?"

Anna's clasped hands tighten around one another. "I beg your
pardon, Mrs. Whitehurst."

"And beg it you shall," the older woman huffs. "Children are a gift
from God, and only He decides when we will have them. That decision
is out of our hands, and it would be a sin for it to be any other way."

Anna is aware of a low hum of voices as club members put their
heads together throughout the room, the same low hum, the same
hushed murmurings that floated around the bed she was born in when
she almost died in it three years before. I wonder how many women in
this room today have suffered as I did during that horrible miscarriage?
How many have faced the never-ending blood of that slow, life-draining
brush with death? She clears her throat and slowly stands. "But, Mrs.
Whitehurst, why should women suffer unnecessarily when there are
ways . . . ways to prevent such suffering?"

"Because the Bible says we must suffer in order to gain salvation.
We must adhere to the word of God, to the teachings of Jesus." Mrs.
Whitehurst starts toward the archway, where Millie is waiting with her
coat.

"Jesus has nothing to do with this," Anna blurts, looking quickly
at Gertrude. "He never married, never had children, never even had a
menstrual cycle."

Mrs. Whitehurst turns, her black eyes blazing. "Mrs. Sanderson,
really!" she shouts above the clatter that ensues. "I fear your soul is in
danger of Hellfire and Damnation."

"Then I'm afraid I'll take my chances." Anna lifts her right
hand as if to swear on her words, but brings it down quickly. Oh, my
God, she thinks, what have I done? She'll tell everybody in town how

I'm going to Hell and why. Carl will be even more furious with me. She sinks into her chair as Mrs. Whitehurst snatches her coat from Millie and walks toward the front door, her heavy shoes striking a cadence on the polished floor.

As soon as the front door slams, the women fall silent and Gertrude takes the opportunity to get their attention. "Ladies," she says, looking nervously at Anna, "let's not forget why we are here. We have a right to voice our opinions, to make choices, and to be heard. The North Carolina General Assembly has managed to stall every effort, every bill, that has been presented on behalf of women seeking the vote, even though abundant support for such a bill has been in evidence in this state for the past several years. Like criminals, lunatics, and idiots, we have been denied a basic human right. We have committed no crime, nor are we mentally incapacitated in any way. This is the strongest indication of our second-class status, and a more demeaning message I cannot imagine.

"Won't you, as intelligent, public-minded citizens join your sisters in this effort? Won't you help us write this page in history by giving your time and energy to this most serious need?"

Mrs. Herring waves her hand. "Just tell me what I need to do, Miss Weil." Others in the group are nodding and talking among themselves as a shaky Anna rises from her seat to join Gertrude Weil at the lectern. "Please raise your hands if you are willing to work for the right to vote," she says, struggling to keep her voice steady. A dozen hands go up among the eighteen women present.

"The General Assembly will be presented with another bill early in the new year," Miss Weil continues. "Won't you come to Raleigh and join me and thousands of other North Carolina women in support of that bill? Please stand if you. . . ."

Mrs. Massey and Hephzibah Sanderson stand up at the same time. "I'll be happy to make posters for us to carry," Hepsi says to Miss Weil. "And I could drive and take several other members with me," suggests Mrs. Herring, and then she turns and whispers to her friend, Mrs. Massey, who is standing behind her. "Elizabeth is going to think I've lost my mind!"

Gertrude Weil raises her hands, signaling for silence. "Let's all wear yellow, ladies, as often as possible. It's the color adopted by the pioneers of this movement." She looks up to see Millie standing in the doorway, a tray of cookies in her hands. "I invite you to enjoy some refreshments while we talk about our plan of action. Please step across the hall to the dining room, ladies."

The women leave the drawing room, busily conversing with one another and bombarding Gertrude Weil with questions. Anna is left alone with Mrs. Sutton. "I'm sorry, but I have to go now, Mrs. Sanderson," she says. "Thank you for inviting me. I'm afraid I can't join your cause. Mr. Sutton wouldn't. . . . " Her fingers nervously work the braid on the flounce of her jacket. "He wouldn't like it. You understand, don't you, Mrs. Sanderson?"

Anna stares at the pattern on the rug beneath her feet as Carl's words of the night before ring in her head. Stay away from that Socialist Gertrude Weil, he had shouted. Keep her away from here, Anna. You and your women friends need to be doing what you're supposed to do for the boys . . . knitting socks and packing books. You leave this war business to the men. Don't you realize the farmers are getting more for their crops than they ever have? We've got more business at the bank than we can handle, and the mill is going night and day. And we're going to do what's good for business . . . what's good for morale . . . what's good for this country. And you're going to keep your opinions to yourself from now on. Do I make myself clear?

Anna takes Mrs. Sutton's hand. "I understand very well," she says. "Thank you for coming anyway."

CHAPTER 13:
A LETTER FROM ANNA
TO HER SISTER

Baker, North Carolina
January 15, 1918

Dearest Bethany,

Happy New Year! I trust this letter finds you and Bryson well and rested after a busy holiday season. Thank you for the lovely gifts. McLean has to hear a chapter from his *Swiss Family Robinson* every night, and the girls enjoy it, too. They have worn the darling bracelets you sent them almost every day since Christmas. Did you get their thank-you notes? Carl and I love the beautiful compote; it is sitting in the center of our dining room table on one of Mama's exquisite doilies and has been there since Christmas day. Carl's parents were here, along with his sister, Amanda, and Robert and his wife, Hephzibah, and their four children. We had a grand time and a magnificent feast, even though Millie and I had to hoard sugar for weeks to make our candy, cookies, and cakes. Much of our work went into comfort boxes for the boys in France. I am proud to report that our Red Cross Chapter shipped 184 boxes out in November. You know Christmas for our soldiers must have been hard, but it was probably harder for their families. Baker has sent fourteen of its young men for service, including Justice and Zilphie's oldest son, Willie. We see every one of his letters, and it makes me sick to read them. He complains about the weather and the food, of course, and living in the field, but he seems to be doing fairly well, otherwise. Thank God Graham is at the university now, and may he remain there until this horrible slaughter is over.

Did I mention in my card that Carl and I were invited for New Year's at the Grover's in Richmond? We had a lovely trip. Mr. Grover sent his private train car down for us on the 30ᵗʰ, and we stayed three days. Their home is quite large and very luxurious, with baths in every suite of rooms. There were thirty for dinner on New Year's Eve, and a small ensemble played until one in the morning. I like Mrs. Grover, who is courtesy personified, but I fear I have little in common with her and her friends. Their lives appear to be so dictated by the status of each of their husbands. The men played golf almost every afternoon, and I am sure Carl took care of as much business as possible. You know Carl. He never misses an opportunity to make another dollar, and Mr. Grover has been one of his best clients through the years. We had a nice time, but I was glad to get home to my children and my own bed.

Since I have told you of our soiree, I must mention another. Claire has been invited to a birthday party for a friend from Goldsboro who will be thirteen next Friday. It's to be a sit-down dinner with ten of the young lady's friends invited, and the invitation was for "seven in the evening." I was flabbergasted! She asked me if Fletcher could "chauffeur" her to Goldsboro in the Cadillac, and when I said "no," she went straight to her father, who told her he would arrange something suitable. I am afraid she is terribly indulged by Carl and, as a result, is much too self absorbed and spoiled. But her grades are excellent and she plays the piano beautifully.

Evelyn continues to blossom. She's full of laughter and has an odd sense of humor that is awfully dry for one so young. The other children in our neighborhood love to play with her because she makes up wonderful stories, and they all join her in acting them out. She tells her friends that she is going to be an actress. I didn't know she knew what an actress was until she was chosen to be Mary in the church Christmas pageant. She has loved taking dance lessons this year and is quite good, if I may say so. Millie is working on her costume for an upcoming recital. It's a red-spangled affair with fringe . . . a bit too showy if you ask me, but Evelyn thinks it's wonderful.

McLean continues to do well with his studies. He loves poetry, especially long epics like *Lochinvar* and *The Lady of the Lake*. I have been teaching him algebra equations this fall the same way I taught him elementary mathematics. I explain the process, give him a few examples on my slate, and then offer four answers. He shakes his head when I get to the correct one. We are reading *Romeo and Juliet*, which he loves.

Bless his heart, he is so bright; he smiles at the funny parts and frowns at all the right places just like any normal person would. I hope we'll get to *Julius Caesar* this spring. Oh, Bethany, what a joy it is to see how well his mind works. If only his body would! Millie and I have been taking turns nursing him because he has had a nasty cough since Carl and I returned from our trip. He seems to be weaker than usual and has little appetite. He even refused Millie's chicken-and-rice soup yesterday, and he loves it. Dr. Baucom has given him an expectorant, but I haven't noticed much of a change. He is resting in bed now, propped up on several pillows because he fills up with congestion the minute he lies down, so our studies are on hold. Winters are so hard on my boy. The girls have been taking tidbits in to him and reading to him when they get home from school. Fletcher has kept the fire going in McLean's room night and day and sits at his bedside every evening until McLean falls asleep.

We learned just this morning that Millie's son, Joshua, was killed in action in France before Christmas. This has been quite a blow after all these years of not knowing where or how he was. She got a letter from her brother, Hector, who has lived in Pennsylvania for about 30 years. I suppose Hector has always known where Joshua was, but neither Millie nor any of us knew he did. I wonder if Millie will finally tell Fletcher about who his real mother and father were now that Joshua is dead.

Millie and I went out to the farm last Thursday to clean the cemetery and put greenery in the urns on Granny Adaire's headstone. Big Carl and Louisa (and Amanda, who is not married) have moved into Granny's old house at Sand Hill and sold their home to Warren and Patsy and their five children. I miss Colonel Hightower terribly, even though he is faithful in his correspondence. He seems to be adjusting well to life with his brother and sister-in-law in Ohio and mentioned that he is happy to be sleeping in his boyhood room once again. Carl was distraught that he did not want to remain here and be buried beside Granny, but the Colonel told us that, at the time of their marriage, he and Adaire agreed that he would be buried with his first wife and she (Adaire) at Sand Hill. All of Granny's farm holdings were left, free and clear to Carl, Sr. and Louisa, while Aunt Janey and Uncle Phillip received bank stock and cash. Carl, Sr. has divided the farm into two sections: Warren and Robert will run the northern half; my Carl and his father will operate the south section. Each is a bit over six-hundred acres. Of course, Justice is the one who really runs Sand Hill. The Carls, Warren, and Robert are too busy with the bank, the cotton mill, and the store. Granny left a considerable amount of stocks and bonds to my Carl, the only grandchild to receive an outright gift of "money" from her. I thought this was blatantly unfair, but everybody knows Carl was her "eyeball."

While Millie and I were busy in the cemetery, a young colored girl rode by on an old white mule and went straight to the back of Granny's house. After a few minutes, Zilphie came out and told us that the girl's mother was sick and that she had come to her for help. Wouldn't we please go with her over to the Everette plantation? So we climbed into my car (all four of us) and the girl (who is about fourteen) told us that her mother couldn't get up and wouldn't eat and that her father had been injured the week before in a logging accident. Old Mr. and Mrs. Everette have been gone for years, but their son still runs the place with the help of several Negroes. They live in what were the slave quarters behind the homeplace. The girl, whose name is Peach, took us inside her family's cabin, and although there was little light, I could tell immediately that her mother was dead. She was lying on a stack of ragged quilts, and there was blood all over her skirt. When Millie and I took her clothes off to bathe her, we found a shoe hook covered with dried blood and a bloody mass of tissue rolled up in newspaper under the bed. Despair is a vicious motivator, isn't it? I have seen despair in my sister-in-law's eyes, my own dear, sweet Hepsi, who announced at Christmas that she will have another baby this summer, her fifth in a little more than five years. She smiled as she told Carl, Sr. and Louisa before dinner, but she broke down and cried later when the two of us were alone. She has the hollow-eyed look of a waif, and I doubt she has the strength to deliver another baby. I have called on her at least two afternoons a week since we got home, and have taken her twin boys and little Pamela and Nora Ellen home with me as often as she will let me have them. I fear that she needs more rest than she will ever be able to get. But that poor colored woman out in the country . . . who was there to help her? I saw six children in the cabin younger than Peach. What will happen to them now that their mother is gone? They have food (I saw jars of vegetables and molasses and a bag of meal), but who will prepare it? I suppose Peach will grow up fast. I told the father I would try to find a job for the oldest boy, who is twelve, but he will have to come into town and live in a barn or stable somewhere. The father told us that the boy has no clothes or shoes, so Millie and I collected some things from friends—enough for all of the children to have at least one pair of shoes and some warm clothing—and took it out there yesterday. The father seemed genuinely grateful. Mr. Atkins, at the livery, thinks he can use the oldest boy and will let me know when to have him come into town. Millie says there are many Negro families out in the country, hidden on the old farms, with only seasonal work to sustain them. She says they manage to get by on the fish they catch and small game, a few chickens, and a garden patch. The children don't go to school because it's too far to walk, and besides, they haven't any clothes. There are many white children in the same desperate circumstances. The next time you and Bryson are at a dinner party with the Governor, I hope you will talk with him about these people . . . especially the children.

I fear this is more than poverty of the body, Bethany; it's a poverty of the soul. The kind of poverty that makes desperate women (brown and white) slip into dark alleys, clutching their last five-dollar bill and begging some butcher to help them start their cycle again. (You will have to burn this letter. "Ladies" are not supposed to know such things.) Just think of all the money that is being spent on uniforms and shirts and boots so our young men can wade in ankle deep mud in France or, worse, lie dying in their own blood while our arsenals turn out expensive guns and ammunition, and children, right in our own backyards, shiver in the cold and go hungry. This is madness.

I have written before that Carl is chairman of the Newlan County Liberty Loan Committee and is very busy making calls at night to solicit from business associates around the county. We are hosting a liberty party here this weekend, and Millie and I are up to our elbows (literally) in sugar and flour, preparing for it. (We always seem to be able to get enough white flour and sugar to entertain for the Liberty Loan drives.) I find these events so difficult . . . parading through the "guests" in one of my expensive frocks and looking pretty, but saying nothing of any consequence because I might offend one of the bank's customers. It's the same old routine . . . smile at the old boys, fill them up with good food, flatter their endless egos, and stay in the background when they get down to "serious business." In other words, retreat to the kitchen like a good little wife. I am trying to teach my girls that they must stand up for what they believe, and that there are other roles for women besides housewife and mother. I tell them "the world's your oyster" as often as possible and hope that one day they will understand.

Your loving sister,
Anna

P.S.—Here's an update on our voting campaign: We have decided to call ourselves the Baker Balloteers and now have 23 registered members. We're holding Suffrage Teas at each other's houses each month, trying to recruit more members, and writing dozens of letters to our representatives in Raleigh and in Washington. Emma and Birdie Jenkins had a fight because he told her she couldn't join the Balloteers, so she has taken to staying with her sister every weekend as a protest. She stays at home with Birdie during the week cooking, cleaning, washing . . . but not talking. And every Friday night for the past month, she has gone over to her sister's to stay. It's the talk of the town.

Do you remember Caroline Dudley from Peace? She graduated about three years before I did. Told me she sat in the pew behind you at First Presbyterian. Anyway, she married a lawyer, Walton Pruitt, who is a judge here. She will host our tea this month.

Millie is organizing a group at her church and has recruited eleven members from two other colored churches near Goldsboro. She's asked Gertrude and me to come to their meeting tomorrow night. We're hoping to pull all these groups together for the big rally at Capitol Square next month. I'll look for you there. OXOXOX

CHAPTER 14:
WHAT I REALLY HAD IN MIND

May 15, 1918

Anna and Millie move around the bed of peonies, bending and clipping the long-stemmed blossoms, carefully selecting the brightest pinks, the creamiest whites, and those with double blooms. Shaking the dew from the velvety petals, they inspect each cutting for the busy black ants that ravage such flowers. Anna places the last stem among the colorful bounty in their basket.

"Nothing makes a lovelier bouquet than peonies. Except possibly roses. What do you think, Millie?" Anna holds a large white beauty aloft.

"'Bout the prettiest flower there is, Miss Anna. Miss Hepsi sure will enjoy these."

"Poor thing. She may not even be able to see them, she's cried so much. And I've been negligent. I should have paid her a visit sooner."

"No need for you to feel guilty, Miss Anna. The funeralizing just yesterday." Millie's voice softens. "That poor baby. . . ." She looks at the flower in her hand, touches the petals with her fingertips, and brings the bloom to her nose. "Never known of a baby that was already dead when it was born," she whispers. "Least not one some woman carried the whole time."

Anna holds the flower basket out to Millie. "Yes, it's sad, isn't it? To carry a baby for nine months and have it die inside you without your knowing it." She removes gardening gloves, stuffing them into the pocket of her smock. "How many babies are at Sand Hill now?" she asks as she and Millie walk back toward the house.

Millie shields her eyes from the bright May sun and prepares to recite the names of the babies buried in the family cemetery. "Let's see," she begins, "Miss Adaire's first baby, John Sanderson, Jr., and her girl, Alice . . . who was a year or so younger than me . . . and Mama's boy,

Clancy, and Henrietta's two baby girls, and Zilphie's baby boy what died when Christmas was a little thing. Then you add Miss Hepsi's baby, that makes eight. Eight little coffins out there, no longer than my arm."

Anna opens the door to the screen porch and puts the peonies on the counter beside a large crystal vase. Throwing her hat into a chair, she wipes the sweat from her forehead on the back of her hand. "I'll arrange these now so they'll be ready because I want to go on over to Hepsi's before dinner." Picking up the vase, she watches a rainbow play among its crevices.

"Mr. Robert gave us this vase when we married." Putting the vase in the tin sink beneath the mouth of the pump, she fills it with water and adds several flowers. "I'll eat a sandwich or something after I get back, Millie. Don't worry about me. I expect Mr. Sanderson will be home for dinner today at his usual time. His train leaves at two-fifteen."

"Going to Richmond again, Miss Anna?"

"No. He told me he has business in Baltimore and left the name of the hotel where he'll be. He won't be back until Monday night."

"You mean he's going to be working on Sunday?"

"I expect so. The war's changed everything, hasn't it? Even Sundays are workdays. Nothing's sacred anymore." Anna adds the last pink flower to the vase.

Millie nods. "Seems strange, don't it, the way some folks act 'cause of the war. It's like they done forgot their upbringing." Millie starts toward the kitchen. "You go on and bathe and dress, Miss Anna. I'll see to dinner and McLean's nap. And I'll help Mr. Carl get his satchel ready. You go on to Miss Hepsi's. She needs you more than we do."

* * * * *

As Anna approaches the yellow bungalow where Robert Sanderson's family lives, she pauses for a moment to study the fancy cutwork brackets along the top of the porch. Robert is so proud of his home, and he should be, she thinks. It's warm and comfortable. So unpretentious. I wish Carl liked simpler things. She hurries up the wide plank steps to what remains of a wake. A dying rose, once white, fades to gold on a windowsill near a wicker table that holds several scummy glasses and an ashtray filled with cigar butts. Black bunting drapes the top of the window frames and double front doors. Several rocking chairs, their arms wide and inviting, sit motionless in the still, warm air. This is one of the nicest porches in town, Anna thinks, remembering many late afternoons and evenings she and her children have come to hear Robert play his mandolin and join in the singing, laughing, and talking that make for a happy occasion. I wonder if this porch will ever hear laughter again, she asks herself, cradling the vase of peonies in her arm while she knocks. The door opens and Anna says hello to Christmas, Millie's great niece, the daughter of Justice and Zilphie.

"Morning, Miss Sanderson," the young woman answers with a slight bow of her head. "Miss Hepsi resting, but she ain't asleep. You can go on in."

"I thought the children would be here to greet me. Where are they, Christmas?" Anna steps into the shadowy hallway.

"Miss Louisa and Mama come and got 'em yesterday evening. Miss Hepsi can't seem to get no rest. They took the young'uns out to the farm for a few days."

"Good. The last thing Miss Hepsi needs is a houseful of little children to look after." Anna pauses outside the door to Hepsi and Robert's bedroom before pushing it open.

She finds her sister-in-law in bed. Hepsi's uncombed hair is carelessly arrayed against a stack of pillows; a stained satin bed jacket covers her bony shoulders. She looks up as Anna enters the room and forces a weak smile. "Dear Anna," she says, her voice as bland as oatmeal. "Thank you for coming. I'm awfully lonely."

Anna takes Hepsi's hand and gazes down at the spidery lines that have spread around the younger woman's eyes. Why, she looks ten years older, Anna thinks, as she presents her gift. "Robert gave us this lovely vase when we married. And these are my first peonies." She places the vase on a table nearby.

"They're beautiful, Anna. Thank you," Hepsi manages before she bursts into tears. "Oh, Anna," she cries. "This is all so horrible! I don't know what's gotten into me! I've been waiting for you to come so I could tell you . . . because you are the only one I can tell."

Anna sits down on the side of the bed and squeezes Hepsi's hand. "It's all right, honey. You can tell me anything. I know you're upset. Losing a baby is hard."

"It's more than losing the baby," Hepsi mumbles. "Much more."

Anna leaves the bed to close the door. "I know this has been an awful experience for you, Hepsi. Every woman feels this way when they lose a baby. I know I did."

"No, they don't," Hepsi whispers, her red-rimmed eyes blazing like twin pools of fire. "I hated that baby. Hated her!" As she pounds her pale white fists into the coverlet, heavy tears start down her thin cheeks. "I tried my best to get rid of her, Anna. You don't know how hard I tried! I sat in baths so hot I thought my toenails would melt. I ate red pepper until I vomited. I threw myself against the side of the shed until I was black and blue from my shoulders to my hips. And when all those things failed, I became Machiavelli's finest pupil."

Anna pulls away, alarmed at her sister-in-law's revelations. "Oh, Hepsi, hush. You couldn't have done such things."

"Oh, yes, I could," Hepsi vows as her lips form a thin, hard line. "I was so tired, Anna," she sighs, her slender fingers busy on the counterpane. "I thought I would die if I had to deliver another baby. I never want to nurse another baby as long as I live! I hate it." She slaps viciously at one swollen breast. "And Robert was so nice about it, of course. He hired Christmas to help out full-time instead of just two days a week and he bathed the children every night and put them to bed. But it didn't help much. I was exhausted, and I knew I couldn't bear to look after another baby. That's why I came up with a plan to get rid of it right after the holidays. When you and Carl went to visit that bank client over New Year's, I told Robert I wanted to go to Wilson and spend a day with my parents. Of course, he didn't want me to . . . it was so cold and all. But I begged, and finally, he gave in. You see, I knew this doctor in Wilson who would. . . ." She pauses and her finger traces the outline of the curved pattern on the heavy cloth beneath it. "There's this doctor there, Anna. I heard he had helped a girl. She wasn't married at the time. He helped her when we were in college. And I thought that I would tell Robert I was going to visit my folks for the day, but what I really had in mind was that doctor." Hepsi's chin falls and she begins to sob. After a few moments, she wipes the dripping mucus from her nose and gulps a breath of air. She begins to talk once more, hiccupping as she tries to get the words out. "And there was poor Robert, poor sweet innocent Robert, stacking and arranging everything so neatly along the shelves at the store and greeting customers with that dear smile of his, going about his business without the slightest idea that his wife was up to murder."

"Hepsi darling, you couldn't really do that sort of thing," Anna says, as much to reassure herself as her sister-in-law. "You were just frightened."

Hepsi's head falls back against the pillows. "Yes, Anna, I could have," she states in a voice as cool as ice water. "The problem was, I didn't know how to cover it up. But I got that figured out, too. I planned to leave the doctor's office and start back home and have an accident."

Anna gasps. "An accident?"

"That was my plan, Anna. I'd drive the automobile into a tree or a bridge railing or something." Hepsi recites her plan as if it were a well-used recipe. "I even had the spot picked out. You know that big grove of trees on Old Man Gaskill's farm just north of town? The ones that almost sit on the road? Well, that's where I thought I would wreck Robert's Ford. And that way, everyone would think I'd lost the baby because of the accident."

Anna is surprised at Hepsi's capacity for deceit, at her clever but deadly plan. How could I have been so blind? she thinks. Not to have known how really desperate she was. And what about Robert? How could he have lived here with her all these months, lived as man and wife, and not seen the despair in her eyes as I see it now? How could she have hidden it from him? "You might have gotten away with it," Anna remarks and is instantly sorry that the words slipped from her mouth. "Why didn't you go on with it?"

"I couldn't do it to Robert. He would have never gotten over it if he had found out the truth, Anna. That his wife murdered his child. The more I thought about it, the weaker I got. By the time I reached the outskirts of Wilson, I was sweating like a mule in August, and it was thirty-five degrees outside. I just broke down and cried right there on the side of the road. And this old farmer came along on a wagon and asked if he could do anything for me. But I shook my head and went on out to my folks' place. They wanted to know why my face was so red, and I told them it was because of the cold. Mama looked at me real hard, but she didn't say anything. I stayed for dinner and came back early just like I promised Robert I would. Never even went downtown. Never went near that doctor's office. But I got what I wanted anyway," she whispers. "A dead baby. A precious baby girl with a headful of golden hair and ten perfect little fingers and toes. An angel, Anna, as cold as the marble Mr. Price has ordered for her headstone."

Anna stands up and pulls the coverlet over her sister-in-law's trembling shoulders. "That's enough now, Hepsi. You should eat something, honey."

"Not hungry . . . ," Hepsi mumbles. Her swollen eyelids begin to drop toward the purple circles beneath them. "I'm just tired, Anna . . . so tired."

Anna watches as the younger woman drifts off to sleep. "Poor thing," she whispers. "Poor girl, so sad and alone with her guilt."

She picks up a dark blue bottle on the bedside table and sniffs the chalky residue under its cap. "No wonder she's so tired," she whispers. "She'll never get her strength back as long as she's got this. Damn that doctor." Anna slips the bottle of laudanum into her pocket and tiptoes out of the room.

* * * * *

Anna and McLean sit on the side porch and watch as Evie and Claire play croquet in the late afternoon sunshine. Afterwards, they have supper at the round table in the sitting room. As soon as Millie clears the dishes, Claire scrawls an X on the wall calendar, where she and Evelyn are marking off the few days left until school is out. Anna winds the curved brass handle on her Victrola and the stirring sounds of "The Blue Danube" fill the room. McLean grins.

"Come on, girls," Anna calls, turning to her daughters with her arms open. "Time to work on your waltzing." Evelyn rushes to her mother, burying her face in Anna's soft voile skirt. "One, two, three, one, two, three," Anna begins. "Here we go!" She guides her little girl across the floor, taking steps that are half the size she would take if Carl were her partner. "That's it," she says. "You've got it." She turns to look at Claire, who is waiting patiently beside McLean's wheelchair. "You come take my place, honey. You waltz well enough to be the boy." She slides away from Evie, counting aloud as she goes, and sits down in a rocker near the window. Evie and Claire giggle at each other and smile at their mother as she continues to count one, two, three. McLean moves his small head from side to side in time to the music. "Gah, Gah," he mouths, his version of "good, good."

Anna stands up and pulls the long skirt of her dress away from her legs. "Hold your skirt out, Evie," she calls, and her youngest grabs at the gingham apron she's wearing. "Oh, Mama," Claire begins, "that's old fashioned. Nobody does that anymore. Skirts are straight now, and there's nothing to hold on to."

Oh, dear, I must be getting old, Anna thinks. I've got a daughter telling me how to dance and what to wear. "I suppose you're right," she says aloud. "How foolish of me to forget how the styles have changed since I was a girl way back in the Dark Ages." She lifts her chin in a mock gesture of defiance and laughs deep down in her throat. I never thought I'd see the day, she muses. She glances at McLean and winks, but the look on his face tells her that he is upset, and the odor rising in the room tells her why. Evelyn and Claire retreat to the loveseat, their noses wrinkled in mutual disgust. Anna steps to the Victrola and lifts its arm before crossing the room to call Millie. "You'd better ask Fletcher to come, too," she says. "McLean has had an accident."

Millie rushes into the back hallway and enters the room, a dish-cloth in her hand. "Fletcher ain't here, Miss Anna," she reports. "You and me will have to get McLean upstairs by ourselves. Go run some warm water in the tub, honey," she says to Claire, who hops up from the sofa and sprints out of the room. Anna looks at Evelyn. "Run up to McLean's room and get his pajamas and some clean underwear and put them on the end of his bed, sweetheart. We'll be up in just a few minutes."

As soon as Evie leaves the room, Anna tousles McLean's hair and begins pushing his chair toward the hall. "It's all right, son," she says softly, securing the brake as they reach the edge of the staircase. She removes the stuffed monkey from McLean's lap and runs her hands under his armpits, then clasps them together over his bony ribcage. Millie puts a hand under each of his small thighs. "One, two, three," Anna says, and the two women lift him out of the chair. They mount the stairs in tandem, moving carefully along the wall. As they pause to catch their breaths on the landing, Anna calls to Claire once more. "Did you put down some newspapers, honey?" She and Millie can hear Claire's footsteps as she hurries to spread newspapers on the bathroom floor.

They reach the upstairs hallway and round the corner into the bathroom, where they lower McLean onto the front page of the paper. Anna removes the boy's shoes and socks as Millie unbuttons his shirt.

McLean's bright, water-filled eyes stare at the ceiling. "It's all right, honey," Anna says, unbuttoning his knickers. "We know you couldn't help it." She looks at Millie. "I guess it was those strawberries. Sometimes his system can't handle fresh fruit."

Anna removes her son's pants and pulls down his cotton shorts. Millie helps her roll him over, and the two women remove his soiled underwear. "One, two, three," Anna counts again, and they lift McLean over the rim of the tub and into the warm water. Anna begins to wash the feces from his body as Millie rolls his dirty clothes into the newspaper.

By nine o'clock, the children are in bed and Anna and Millie have retreated to the sitting room as they sometimes do when Carl is out of town overnight. Anna sits in her gown and robe by the window darning one of Carl's socks, while Millie hems a dresser scarf. They share a small circle of lamp light and a pair of embroidery scissors.

"Poor McLean." Anna carefully clips the end of her darning thread using the small, sharp scissors. "I know these accidents are becoming harder and harder for him now that he's older, Millie."

"Bless his heart. You know that kinda thing just mortify a person."

"Especially someone as sensitive as he is. And at his age, it's got to be worse. He'll be thirteen at Christmas."

Anna throws the finished sock into her darning basket and begins to remove the wavy black pins that hold the chignon on the back of her head. "I never dreamed McLean would live to be a teenager. With every year that goes by, I'm more amazed." She picks up a brush and begins working on her long, thick hair. "And thankful. Thankful that he's alive and still with us. But more than anything, thankful that he has a good mind. If only his father would pay some attention." With nimble fingers, she quickly weaves a plait. "It helps sometimes to know that he's smart, Millie, that he understands things and appreciates the beauty in this world." Her voice fades as she leans against the slats of the rocker and sets it in motion.

Millie looks at the grandfather clock. Almost nine-fifteen. The screen door opens on the back porch. A moment later, there's a tap on the outside door. It opens slowly and Fletcher steps into the room. He looks over at Anna and nods. "Evening, Miss Anna."

"Evening, Fletcher. Won't you come in?"

Fletcher crosses to where Millie is sitting and goes down on one knee beside her chair. "Mama, they got this machine downtown, and they showing these things they call flickers on the backside of Mr. Robert's store," he says, his breath coming in short, excited spurts. "I just seen one called *Fatty's Faithful Fido*, where this big man named Fatty has this dog and it climbs a ladder!"

Millie cuts her eyes at Fletcher. "Ain't no dog can climb a ladder, son."

"Well, this one sure did. These two men got in a fight in a mud hole and the dog chased the bad man up the ladder. I swear it, Mama."

"Don't swear, honey. It ain't Christian."

"Mama, there's a big crowd down there, and they gonna show another flicker in just a few minutes. Can I go back and watch it, Mama? It don't cost nothing, and everybody's in the alley looking at 'em."

Millie glances at the clock once more. "It's almost nine-thirty. You be home by ten o'clock."

Fletcher jumps up and starts across the floor. "Yessum," he says, putting on his cap and opening the door. "I'll be back by ten."

As soon as the door closes, Millie turns to Anna. "That boy is good, but, sometimes, he sure does vex a person. Always wanting to go somewhere."

"That's pretty normal for a teenager, Millie. They want to be where their friends are and have fun."

"I sure wish he'd spend as much time thinking about his schoolwork as he does running around the neighborhood getting into mischief."

"Fletcher's a good student. You should be proud of him, Millie. You've done such a good job of raising him."

"Oh, I'm proud, Miss Anna. Real proud. I just wish he'd think about his future more than he does. I want him to go to college. In just two more years, he'll finish high school, and he's real good with numbers, you know. Just like Mama. She could figure out stuff faster'n you could say *jack rabbit*, and it'd be right every time. Even percents." Millie folds the dresser scarf she's working on and puts it on the table. "Miss Anna," she says, "I been meaning to ask you a big favor."

Anna looks up. "Well?"

"I got something I want you to take care of." Millie pulls a thick envelope from her pocket. "Remember those letters I read to you way back before McLean was born . . . the ones that was written by my boy Joshua about him and Miss Julia?"

"Of course I remember, Millie. You still have them, don't you?"

"Yessum. They're right here in this envelope, along with that picture we had made at the fair in Smithfield. You know, the one with Mama and Daddy and me and Joshua?"

"I remember, Millie. You said it was the only picture you ever had of Joshua."

"I want you to hold on to that picture and these letters," Millie says, thrusting the envelope toward Anna, "in case something happens."

"Nothing's going to happen, Millie. What are you talking about?" Anna asks.

A lump rises in Millie's throat as the image of a filthy yellow beard knotted beneath a hateful mouth of rotted teeth fills her mind. She lowers her head and swallows in an effort to clear her throat. "I know I need to tell Fletcher about his mama and daddy, but I just don't think I can tell him yet. His daddy being killed in France . . . and all this other stuff, too. It's just too much for a boy his age. I guess what I'm saying is, I'd feel a whole lot better knowing these letters and this picture was safe with you. Always been worried that something might happen to them. Won't you keep these things for me, Miss Anna, here in the house where they'll be safe?"

I wonder why she's doing this, Anna thinks, as she takes the envelope. Why doesn't she give them to Justice and Zilphie?

"Now that Mama and Daddy are gone, you're the only one who knows the truth that I can trust," Millie says. "And I'd feel better if you knew where these things are because you understand. Some folks that know about this . . . they ain't like you, Miss Anna, and they might tear this stuff up, or burn it."

Anna nods, recalling the argument she and Carl had when he learned that Henrietta and Sam had brought Fletcher to the farm the Christmas McLean was born. "You keep that little bastard away from me. I don't want to know one thing about him," Carl had said when Anna suggested that Millie might bring her grandson to live with them in the new house in Baker. Anna had protested. "But Carl," she'd said. "He's just an innocent baby. And besides, he's your nephew." Carl had grabbed her by the arm then, had flung her toward the bed and shouted, "You keep that nigger bastard away from me. He's no kin of mine."

Anna opens the drawer to her desk, pulls out a stack of writing paper, and puts Millie's envelope in the back, rearranging papers to cover it. "All right, Millie. But you come get these things as soon as you think the time is right for you to tell Fletcher." She closes the drawer as the clock begins to chime.

Millie smiles. "Thank you, Miss Anna. That sure take a burden off'n my shoulders. I know they'll be safe here, and I'll get 'em when Fletcher is older. I wonder where that boy is? Not like him to be late."

"Oh, he isn't late, Millie. It's just now ten. Give him a minute or two. He'll be here."

Millie picks up the dresser scarf and prepares to sew again. "Wish my mama could have seen you in that wedding dress we made."

"So do I. Oh, Millie, that was one beautiful gown. I hope Claire will want to wear it someday."

"She will." Millie giggles. "I remember the day you came to live at Sand Hill after your honeymoon, with them trunks of pretty frocks, and you had all those fancy hats with the bird feathers stuck all around on 'em. And I was just like a young'un at the circus watching you get all done up. I'd sneak out in the yard to look at you while you were painting and forget all about my work!" Millie slaps the scarf across one knee.

"Oh, we were so young and innocent then, weren't we?"

"I don't know about innocent, Miss Anna, but we sure were a lot younger." The clock chimes the quarter hour, and Millie picks up the embroidery scissors and clips a thread from the scarf. "It's ten-fifteen. That boy should have been home by now."

"Maybe the flicker isn't over and he wants to see the end of it."

"He said he'd be here by ten, and he always comes home when he says he will." Millie rises from her chair, slips the scissors in her pocket, and drops the scarf into the darning basket. "I think I'll walk downtown and see can I find him, Miss Anna."

"You'll probably meet him on the way. Sure you don't want me to take you on the Dodge?"

"No'm. I'll walk." Millie starts toward the door, pausing to tuck stray pieces of gray hair into the calico scarf wrapped around her head. "Ain't far to Mr. Robert's," she says, closing the door behind her.

Anna picks up a *Collier's* and leafs through its pages. An article entitled "Women Wage Their Own Battles at Home" catches her eye, and she begins to read. The chiming of the clock at eleven startles her. Leaving the magazine on a table, she tiptoes across the back hall and down the steps that lead out to the kitchen.

She stops beside the window of Millie's room and calls. There is no answer. So she walks up the drive and stands, listening for footsteps or voices that might assure her that Fletcher and Millie are nearby. All she hears is a dog barking and the *chug, chug* of a Model T. Under the porte cochere, she bends in front of the Dodge to make sure its crank is in place and pauses again to listen to the night sounds that float on the velvety air. After straightening and retying the sash of her robe, she steps into the cool, dark shadows and cranks the car.

* * * * *

Anna makes her way along the dark, dusty street toward Robert's mercantile. She sees a group of teenage boys, the sons of mill workers, outside the livery stable, where a lone woman waits on the seat of a wagon. A bunch of farmers, hands thrust deep in the pockets of their bib overalls, take turns spitting tobacco juice outside Robert's store. Anna turns the wheels of the Dodge into the alley behind the building and is surprised to find it empty and dark. She glances at her watch, puts the car in reverse, and backs out.

Across the tracks, she notices several men sprawled on the platform at the depot. A naked bulb blazes from inside the Railroad Hotel lobby, throwing light into the adjoining barbershop. She sees the town bully, Zeb Troxler, and his rowdy friends, the Grissom brothers, inside. With them is another troublemaker, John Tharrington, who works in the cotton mill. She can't hear what they're saying, but she notices a bandage wrapped around Tharrington's right hand when he hoists a crockery jug. Probably got in a fight, Anna thinks.

She puts the Dodge in reverse, backs out into the street, and continues around the corner. Where in the world can they be? she wonders as her eyes search several darkened doorways. Perhaps they went to visit a friend. She turns the car toward a grass-lined path that leads to "Brown Town," a settlement on the east side of town where a dozen Negro families live. She finds the houses there closed and dark. It must be close to midnight, she frets, and the children are alone. I'd better go home.

She drives slowly through the streets of the downtown area again, but sees no one but Troxler and his friends, who are still in the barbershop. After pulling into her driveway, she goes to Millie's room behind the kitchen and calls once more, but there is no answer. She sees nothing in the blackness but the glowing beams of lightening bugs that hover around shrubs in the backyard. The lonesome chirp of a frog in the chinaberry tree is the only sound she hears. She continues to stand for several moments, listening, on the top step at the back screen door. Finally, she opens it and goes inside. Dragging a rocker from a corner, she sits down to wait.

CHAPTER 15:
MY POOR HEART IS ABOUT TO BUST

December 16, 1918

A cold morning wind chills Anna's ankles as she crosses the walk from the back of the house to the kitchen. Opening the heavy plank door, she is surprised to see Fletcher hugging Willie Sanders. A bit leaner, a bit straighter, Anna thinks, as she quietly observes the young war hero whose uniform jacket is decorated with bright ribbons and a purple heart. "It's wonderful to see you again, Willie." She offers her hand to Justice and Zilphie's son.

Willie removes his cap. "It sure is nice to be home, Miss Anna," he replies, his long brown face broken by a smile. " 'Specially right here at Christmas time. You're looking well. How are the children?"

"They're fine, Willie. Just fine. Growing like weeds and eating us out of house and home. Isn't that right, Millie?" Anna turns to the stove, where Millie is removing a loaf of fresh bread.

"Yessum, they sure can eat," the brown woman agrees as she places a basin of carrots and potatoes on the table.

"Please don't let me keep you from your visit." Anna takes a chair at the table and starts to peel the vegetables. "I just came in to help Millie with dinner. You all sit down here where it's warm and talk. I'd love to hear about your life in the Army, Willie. Your letters were so interesting, but I know there must have been some things you couldn't write home about. Won't you tell us more?"

"I ain't sure what's fitt'n for a lady to hear, Miss Anna," Willie begins. "Lots of things happen in a war that nobody should never speak of again. And lots of things happen a person don't even want to think of again, much less talk about. Going to war ain't like going on a picnic, you know."

Anna nods as Fletcher nudges his cousin on the knee. "Tell us about it, Willie," he says.

"Well, thing I remember most is mud." Willie smoothes a wrinkle across the sleeve of his spotless uniform. "Seem like it rain all the time, and everywhere was mud. All over your clothes, in your hair, even in your underwear and on your food. Won't nothing for miles but mud, and more mud. No man's land. That's what they call it. Ain't no houses, no trees, nothing but rats and lizards, and poor boys lying around with their guts hanging out." He cuts his eyes toward Anna, but she doesn't look up, so he continues. "Seem like hurt boys is everywhere, crying and screaming from their wounds, thrashing 'cause they're in so much pain. You hear 'em calling all night long for their mamas and daddies. Some crying for Jesus. And them poor fellas what was gassed. They was a sorry sight to behold. Bodies all covered with blisters and the skin falling off just like leaves off'n a maple. And them Red Cross women rushing everywhere trying to take care of everybody. Hadn't been for them nurses that came from Paris, Old Willie wouldn't even be here. I'd be a dead man," he says, rubbing his left shoulder.

Fletcher leans toward his cousin. "You mean it was the French Red Cross that came to help you, not the Americans?"

"That's right," Willie nods. "Bless their sweet souls. After I got hit in the shoulder, I had all grades of pretty French ladies buzzing 'round me in the hospital tent. Those Frenchies are all right."

Fletcher takes a mug from the kitchen table, fills it with coffee, and hands it to Willie. "You told us in one of your early letters that you were on a special assignment. What was it?"

Willie sips the hot coffee for a moment, his brow furrowed. "Oh, yeah," he says, "I remember now. When we first got to France, I was in the reg'lar infantry. You know, just a foot soldier. That was the hardest part. Them Germans coming at you with a big old bayonet pointed right at your middle. And they got the hardest look on their faces. Their eyes cold as ice, and they teeth clinched tight enough to crack a hick'ry nut. Just scare you so bad you know you gotta do something or you gonna die." Willie pauses to drink his coffee. "You don't need to know too much about that, though. Where was I? Oh, yeah. One day, we was out scoutin' along the edge of some woods and we spotted a dead pigeon in the brush. Well, I told the sergeant about how I use to raise partridges on the farm for old Mr. Carl, so they put me on this detail . . . that's what they call it, a detail. Anyway, they tell me to work with the pigeons." He takes a big gulp of coffee and sets the mug on the table before he spreads his hands on the worn planks. "See, they got these pigeons in cages," he explains, "and us soldiers fastens messages to their legs about what we're gonna do next on the battlefield, and then we send the pigeon on over to another brigade across the way so they'll know what to do. I worked for this high-up colonel who's in charge of the pigeons, and he treated me real good and kept me right with him 'til the end of the war. Got me right to the hospital tent when I got hit. Colonel Rollins his name, and he was from Arkansas. Me and him travel together right on down to Marseilles when the war's over. I rode with him and all these other high-ups in a truck. You never seen such a mess as we seen on that trip. All the villages and little towns burnt to the ground. Won't a barn, or shed, not even a chicken coop to be seen nowhere. And everywhere you go, women and children crying for food. *Monsoir, pain, s'il vous plait.* That's French for please give me some bread, mister. 'Course, I didn't have no bread to give 'em. At one place we stopped, I saw a bunch of old men kneelin' round a dead mule, picking off its flesh and eating it right there. Raw." Willie shakes his head and looks at Millie, who is stirring a pot of beef stew. She scowls, drawing the spoon out of the pot and putting on a lid. Willie looks down at his hands. "I saw many a woman holding a baby to one breast while another one her children sucked on the other and another one stood behind waiting his turn." He looks up at Fletcher and reaches across to pat him on the arm. "I hope you never see such as that as long as you live. All those men dyin' and all them women and children starvin' and freezin' in the cold. It ain't worth it, boy. Ain't nothing worth what I saw. When we got off the ship in Norfolk, I got down on my knees and kissed the ground. I say, thank you, Lord Jesus, a hundred times before I even got down the plank. And I won't the only one done that. Ain't never gonna leave here again to go fight in no war. I'd go hide out in Neuse Islands first, and take you with me," he says.

Anna rises from her chair, dumps the peeled potatoes and carrots into the stew pot, and glances over at Willie. You may be laughing, she thinks, but there's no humor in your eyes, and I don't blame you. I'd run away, too, before I'd go to war. "We're mighty happy to have you back, Willie." She puts a vinegar pie on the table and cuts two slices. "You boys sample this pie I made. I need to know if it's fit to eat."

Willie and Fletcher hang back for a moment, nervous about having a white lady wait on them, but when Anna motions once more for them to begin eating, they do.

"Miss Anna, you ain't changed a bit." Willie cuts into the golden triangle on the saucer before him. "Always make a person feel good. Just like those ladies in France."

"Thank you, Willie. You know you're always welcome here."

"Did you get to Paris, Willie?" Fletcher asks. "I hear there's lots of things to do in Paris. All kinds of music and entertainments."

"Yeah, I was there for a couple of weeks. Kinda quiet," Willie replies, winking across the table at Fletcher. "I'll tell you about that later," he whispers. "Mighty fine pie, Miss Anna. Sure is good to have some home cooking again. Rations the army gave us sorta like eating something somebody already ate." He pushes the empty plate away and leans back in his chair.

"Glad you enjoyed it. What are you going to do now, Willie? Work at the farm?"

"No'm. Gonna go to a place call High Point. Man on the train coming home offered me a job with the railroad. Said he could use a nice colored boy like me to work in the dining car. Pays good, and you don't need no clothes much. He says I'll be wearing a white jacket and the railroad folks keeps 'em clean for the boys what serve in the car."

"How soon will you go?"

"Right after Christmas. He gave me a ticket and wrote down an address and told me to report at eight o'clock on the second of January."

"Well, Willie, that sounds fine. I hope you'll like working for the railroad," Anna says as Millie taps her on the shoulder, points to the window, and says, "Mr. Carl's machine just turned in the driveway. Wonder why he's home so early? Ain't even noon yet."

Anna watches Carl get out of the car and sees his flushed face, shiny with sweat. "I'll find out," she says, wiping her hands on her apron. "He complained last night about a sore throat and coughed so much he kept us all awake 'til way in the morning." She opens the door to a whoosh of cold air and hurries out.

"Sure hope Mr. Carl ain't sick," Millie says to Willie and Fletcher. "Miss Anna gets mighty upset any time somebody gets sick 'round here 'cause she's so afraid the boy child will get sick, too."

"You still pulling him 'round town in that wagon you made?" Willie asks.

"Yeah. Least, I try to when the weather's good. Too cold now. Pulled him out to the farm a couple times last summer. He'd rather go out there than stay here in town."

Willie nods. "What you gonna do when you finish school, Fletcher?"

"Go to college," Millie blurts before Fletcher can answer. "He's going to college and make something of hisself."

"Naw, I ain't, Mama," Fletcher contradicts. "And there ain't no need to talk about it no more. Done and had this conversation a dozen times."

"Why not?" Willie asks. "You smart, Fletcher. Always make high marks in school. You'd do good in college. I know you would."

"Why should I?" demands Fletcher. "So I can get me a job sweeping streets in Raleigh or Wilmington or maybe work on the railroad like you? I don't need no college to teach me how to do that stuff. I'd rather stay on the farm and help Uncle Justice."

"Fletcher, there's a whole big world out there, boy," Willie argues. "Lots of places to go and things to do. You could go up north and make a good living. Somebody like you who is so . . . so light. Why, a person light-skinned as you can get in about anywhere."

"Ain't interested in going up north, Willie. Wouldn't change nothing. I'm always gonna be a nigger no matter how light I am. Ain't nothing gonna change that."

"Lots of folk has done real well in the North," Millie says. "My brother, your Uncle Hector," she looks at the boys, "made a good living in Bethlehem, Pennsylvania, and sent both his sons to college. The principal at school told me he thinks he can get a scholarship for Fletcher. He knows somebody up at Shaw University in Raleigh."

"You're living in a dream world, Mama. I ain't going to Shaw University or no other college and that's final."

Millie moves the stew pot to the back of the stove and covers the remains of the pie with a dishcloth. "I'd better go see about Miss Anna. She might need me. I hope you stay for dinner, Willie. Maybe you can talk some sense into this boy. Ain't every day a person like us gets a chance to go to college." She pats the top of Fletcher's curly head.

As soon as Millie closes the door, Willie goes to the stove and picks up the coffee pot. He pours himself and Fletcher another cup. "Now she's gone, we can have us a talk."

"You mean you gonna tell me all about them womens in Paris? About them shows they do when they dance and kick their draws off?"

"Where you hear sucha thing, boy?" Willie says, laughing. "Naw. That ain't what I had in mind. In one your letters last summer, you told me there was some trouble downtown one night and some men tried to hurt you and your mama. Who was it?'

"Harley Grissom and his brother, Zeb Troxler, and John Tharrington. You remember him, don't you?" Fletcher takes the dish-cloth from the pie and cuts two large slices. "They grabbed me one night last May behind Mr. Robert's store and drug me down to the barbershop. They was gonna cut off all my hair, but Troxler decided it would be more fun to try to make me drink a bottle of castor oil."

"Castor oil?" Willie takes another bite of pie.

"Troxler said I wasn't brown enough." Fletcher raises his right hand and slowly spreads his fingers. They expand like a golden leaf. He turns back to Willie. "Then Troxler grabbed me by the back of my neck and told them cracker friends of his'n that I was a uppity nigger and he was gonna bring me down a notch. He said if I drunk that whole bottle of Castor oil, I'd be shit brown all over like I oughta be."

"Them boys is meaner than rattlers. What'd you do?"

"I didn't do nothing. Mama jumped on Tharrington's back and stuck him with some scissors."

Willie's fork hits his plate with a clatter. "She what?"

Fletcher gets up from the table and goes to a cupboard on the far side of the kitchen. He opens the cabinet door and takes out a book. "This is where she hides little things she wants to keep," he says, handing the book to Willie. "Something from the newspaper about it in here somewhere."

Willie reads the title, *Treasure Island*, and hands the book back to Fletcher. "You open it," he says. "I ain't messin' in none her private stuff."

Fletcher leafs through the pages and pulls out a newspaper article, which he hands to Willie. "Here's the way it was reported in the *Baker News and Record*."

Millie Sanders, a local Negro woman age 54, was found guilty yesterday in Newlan District Court of aggravated assault on a white man, John Mabry Tharrington of this city. Witnesses reported that the woman attacked Tharrington with a pair of scissors, viciously striking him in his right hand. The attack occurred behind the Railroad Hotel at approximately 10:45 P.M. Tuesday night. The woman told the presiding judge, Honorable Walton F. Pruitt, that she was trying to protect her 15-year-old son from Tharrington. This was denied by several male witnesses, and the woman was sentenced to 30 days in jail and fined $100.

"Lord," Willie exclaims. "Did Aunt Millie go to jail?"

"Well, both of us stayed in a cell the rest of the night. Miss Anna come and got us about six the next morning. She said Christmas had come to see her and told her that she had heard Mr. Robert tell Miss Hespsi that we'd been arrested. I'd been helping Mr. Robert some in his store at night, and I guess the sheriff went and told him. Anyway, Miss Anna was some upset that morning at the hearing. She tried to speak to Judge Pruitt, but he wouldn't listen to her. Left that courtroom with fire on her heels and asked me to drive her over to the judge's house right then. So I did. She went on in the front door, and I went 'round the back to see Betsy. Remember old man Claxton's girl what run off with your mama's cousin? Real pretty gal? Anyways, she give me some ice tea and a plate of tea cakes, and then she took some on a tray out to the parlor where Miss Anna and Mrs. Judge Pruitt was visitin'. Then Betsy tiptoed over to the door that went to the hall, and she told me they was talkin' about when Judge Pruitt appointed Mr. Carl to head the Liberty Loan Committee for Newlan County last fall. I ain't sure what the trade-off was, but not long after that, Mrs. Judge Pruitt's brother from Kinston come to Baker and went to work in the bank. Clarence Thompson, what cleans at night in the bank, told Uncle Justice and me that Mrs. Judge Pruitt's brother just come in one morning and move into a office right beside Mr. Carl's and that he don't do nothin' all day but study these long sheets that say Army Supply Ordnance on 'em. They lists all these things the soldiers need like underwear, sheets, towels, and such. You know. And Clarence say Mrs. Judge Pruitt's brother puts little checks beside some of the stuff on the lists. Then he give the lists to Mr. Carl, and Mr. Carl takes 'em on over to Wylie Herring at the mill."

Willie nods. "And you think Miss Anna knew about that and lets Mrs. Judge Pruitt know she knows?"

"Betsy told me Miss Anna say something about privileged information and that Mr. Carl and Mrs. Judge Pruitt's brother was breaking the law and that Judge Pruitt knew what they was doin'. The judge is one them . . . them shareholders at the mill, see?" Fletcher cuts his eyes at Willie. "The judge gave Mama a suspended sentence that afternoon. He released her into Miss Anna's . . . custody . . . and told her to stay at home. That she didn't have no business hanging around the hotel at night."

Willie pushes the pie plate to the center of the table and covers the last portion with the dishcloth. "Just can't give it up, can they?"

"Naw. Don't seem like they can. Mama didn't say one word to Miss Anna 'bout it, but I know Mama was wondering what happened and why she got to come home."

Willie moves closer to his cousin, his head cocked to one side. "Did she really stab that bastard Tharrington with scissors?"

"Sure did. Got him good, too. His hand a' bleedin' like a stuck hog."

Willie grins. "Too bad it won't his throat."

* * * * *

By late afternoon, Carl is burning with fever and complaining every few minutes about how cold he is. Anna calls Dr. Baucom, who arrives at dusk, stethoscope in hand, anxiety plain on his face, dark circles under his eyes.

"I've seen too much of this for the last couple of days, Mrs. Sanderson," he says in a weary voice as the two start up the stairs to the bedroom. "This stuff is mean, and there's no cure for it."

They find Carl buried beneath a mound of quilts, his face covered with sweat, his breathing irregular.

"He's been like this all afternoon, doctor." Anna pulls the cover away from her husband's chin. "He keeps complaining about how cold he is, but we've kept a fire going since he came home, and you can see how many quilts he's pulled over himself."

"That's probably good. Sometimes folks can sweat a fever out. All that cover won't hurt him none."

"What else should we do?"

"Not much you can do, I'm afraid. Quinine won't touch it. Try to get a little broth in him now and then. Be sure to strain it. He won't be able to have any solid foods for a while."

"What about buttermilk? My mother always gave us buttermilk when we had a fever."

"Try it. Can't hurt." Doctor Baucom unbuttons Carl's pajama top and sticks the ends of the stethoscope in his ears.

Anna stands quietly by the bed while the doctor examines her husband. She nods to Millie, who comes into the room bringing a small basin of water and some clean towels. The doctor pulls the heavy cover back over his patient and places the palm of his hand on Carl's glistening forehead. "Mighty warm. You'll need to keep an eye on him most of the night."

"What about an icebath?" Anna asks.

"I wouldn't just yet." The doctor crams the stethoscope into his black bag and starts toward the door. "I'll come again in the morning," he assures her as he steps into the hallway. Anna follows him down the stairs and across the foyer to the front door, where he turns to speak to her once more. "Whatever you do, keep your children away from that sickroom. Keep the doors closed upstairs. Influenza's a mighty dangerous infection, and it's highly contagious."

For the next five days, Anna and Millie nurse Carl. The house is ignored while they spoon fresh buttermilk and broth between his feverish lips, and hold his sweating head while he vomits it back up. With Fletcher's help, they move the daybed from McLean's room into Anna and Carl's bedroom so that Anna can catch a few hours sleep each night.

When the Christmas holidays begin, Claire and Evelyn are confined, along with McLean, to the sitting room during the daytime, where they make paper chains for the Christmas tree they hope to decorate, and sing Christmas carols for their brother. They celebrate his thirteenth birthday with a small cake, but there's no party. Anna's friend, Emma Jenkins, comes by with a tissue-wrapped book for McLean and a jar of pine needle tea for Carl. "My mama swore by it," she tells the girls when she sets it on the table. "You tell your mama to try to get a little in your daddy morning, noon, and night. It'll do the trick. You'll see," she promises them on her way out.

Two days later, Carl rises early, takes a bath, and dresses before Anna awakens. She is startled to find him sitting at his desk in a gray suit, reading the *Wall Street Journal*. "What on Earth?" she says, rushing into the room to put her hand to his forehead.

"Oh, Anna, cut it out!" Carl brushes her hand away. "I'm fine."

"Surely you're not thinking of going to the bank today."

"I intend to do just that. As a matter of fact, I feel great. Slept like a baby."

"But your fever. . . ."

"Broke about midnight. I got up and changed pajamas. You were snoring on the daybed and never even moved." Carl folds the paper and opens his leather briefcase. "By the way, Anna, you look a bit peaked. There are circles under your eyes. You'd better rest up a bit for the holidays. We've been invited to several parties."

Anna wants to say that he's the reason she's so tired, but she's so relieved to see him well again that she doesn't. "The children will be so happy to know you're well. The girls have been making ornaments for the tree and baking cookies. Shall I tell them you'll take them out to the farm tomorrow to get a tree?"

"No. I won't be able to do that until Christmas Eve. I'm going to Richmond this afternoon."

"Carl, you can't be serious. Right here at Christmas? And besides, you've been so sick. A trip in this cold might cause a relapse."

"Well, Christmas or not, I have to go. Now that the war is over, my clients are becoming a bit skittish about their investments, and I need to make some transfers before the end of the year." He rearranges a stack of papers from a portfolio stamped Bank of Richmond. "I'll be home day after tomorrow on the five o'clock train."

"But, Carl," Anna begins. She stops when Millie enters the room with a tray of breakfast.

"Morning, Miss Anna." Millie sets a plate of poached eggs and link sausage on the desk. "What can I fix you this morning?"

Anna watches as Carl cuts into one of the eggs, sending a spurt of bright yellow over his plate. "Nothing, Millie. Thank you," she murmurs as she watches her husband bolt down his food.

Carl gulps the last of his coffee, wipes his mouth, and rises from the desk. He picks up the briefcase and closes its clasps. "My train leaves at two o'clock. I won't be home for dinner today. I'll eat on the train. If you need to reach me, I'll be at the John Marshall," he rattles off as if he were dictating to his secretary. "Tell the girls we'll go to the farm on Friday afternoon and get a tree. I promise I'll close the bank by three o'clock."

Anna follows him across the hall and helps him put on his overcoat. "Try to stay inside, Carl. You don't realize how sick you've been."

"Oh, Anna. You're such a mother hen. I can take care of myself." Carl bends to peck Anna's cheek as he opens the wide walnut door. "I'll see you on Thursday at five." Popping a felt homburg on his head, he hurries down the steps, leaving Anna shivering in the cold.

I've a million things to do, she thinks, closing the door. All the presents to buy and wrap, and the cooking that will have to be done. I'll send the girls to Robert's store for oranges and dates, and Fletcher will have to go to the farm to get mistletoe and cedar. There simply isn't enough time to prepare everything, but we'll have to get the tree decorated as soon as Carl gets back. I'd better get the ornaments from the attic.

She crosses the foyer and starts up the stairs, but stops at the landing where Millie is standing. "The girls are up, Miss Anna," she says, "but the boy child ain't doing so good this morning. You better come."

Anna finds her son still and pale. His lips are dry and cracked, his thin face bathed in sweat. "Oh, no," she moans, bending to touch his hot cheek. "Call Dr. Baucom, Millie, and tell Claire to bring a cool bath cloth. He's burning up." She sits down on McLean's bed and takes his hand in hers. "Muh, muh," he whispers, rubbing his cheek against the monkey doll he loves.

Millie returns to tell her that the doctor isn't in. He's out in the country tending a houseful of sick children, and after he leaves there, he's going to see his brother, who is down with the same thing. "Mrs. Baucom told me there's twenty-three cases of influenza in town," Millie reports. "She says to tell you that she'll get the doctor over here just as soon as she can."

Anna frowns at the news. "Get me some buttermilk, Millie," she instructs, "and call Mrs. Jenkins and ask her to bring some more of that tea she made for Carl."

The afternoon drags as Anna and Millie tend to McLean. A cold rain taps against the window and brings the dreaded darkness. Dr. Baucom finally arrives a little before six. His tired eyes widen when Anna answers the door in her robe and slippers, but he says nothing. Sickness disrupts the simplest routines, he thinks as he stands beside the bed, his hand on McLean's hot forehead. He opens the young boy's eyes, peers closely at each, and shakes his head.

"This is such a powerful disease, Mrs. Sanderson," he begins before Anna interrupts him. "But, doctor, Carl recovered," she argues, making him think that she knew what he was about to say.

"I'm sorry," he continues while his fingers probe McLean's chest. "Your boy has never been healthy, and his condition will probably complicate this situation." He turns from the bed to look at Anna. "Your husband is a big, healthy man, and a stubborn one to boot, but your boy here, well. . . ." He strokes the stubble on his chin. "I'm afraid your boy hasn't the strength."

A lump rises in Anna's throat. What do you know, she says to herself, of my son's strength? Of his passion for life? How could you ever comprehend what it's like to live in a world where every hour is a struggle, every passing day a victory? She follows the doctor into the hallway, but does not accompany him down the stairs.

"Thank you for coming," she says as he reties a thick, wool scarf around his neck.

"This weather hasn't helped any," he comments. "It's nasty. Try to stay inside, Mrs. Sanderson. I'm sorry I can't do anything for McLean. We'll just have to wait and see."

And pray, Anna thinks as she returns to her son's bedside. Sometimes it helps to pray.

Millie comes in with a tray of vegetable soup and fresh cornbread, but Anna refuses it. "But, Miss Anna, you haven't eaten a thing all day. You've got to eat to keep up your strength."

"I don't want anything, Millie. Did you bring some of Emma's tea for McLean?"

"Yessum. Nice and warm." Millie hands the cup of tea to Anna and watches as she puts a spoonful in the boy's mouth. He begins to cough so violently that Anna throws the cup to the floor and grabs her son, hauling him up into her arms. She presses his weak body against hers until the gurgling sounds subside, and after a moment, she begins to rock him just as she did when he was a baby. A lullaby plays on her lips, softly, incoherently, as she pats his damp hair, rocking and rocking, her mind suddenly empty, her eyes blank, her hair tumbled about her shoulders.

An hour later, Millie comes to tell her that the girls are in bed. She waits for Anna to respond, and when she doesn't, Millie tiptoes out of the room. She returns just as the clock strikes midnight to find Anna lying beside her son, her arms wrapped around his thin body. Millie hears a faint rattle coming from McLean's tiny chest. She steps back and clasps her hands. "Oh, Lord, not that," she whispers. "Not the chains of death, Lord."

After a moment, Millie moves to the bed and touches Anna's shoulder. "Miss Anna," she says, "you go on over to the daybed and try to get a little sleep. I'll sit here with the boy child." She takes Anna's hand and tries to pull her away. "Come on, honey," she insists, "or you ain't gonna have nothing to fall back on tomorrow. You got to get some rest."

Anna removes her arm from beneath McLean's shoulder and slowly sits up on the bed. "I feel as if I'm ninety," she murmurs.

"Go on," Millie says, and Anna crosses to the narrow, footless couch and lies down, curling her tired body into an S atop the musty brown upholstery.

Soft gray light wakes her at dawn. Turning toward McLean's bed, she is surprised to see Millie asleep on the rug beside it. She pushes the blanket away and tiptoes to the bedside to touch her son's forehead. "Thank God, the fever's broken," she whispers. Taking a cloth from the washstand, she dips it in a basin of water and begins to bathe McLean's face. He'll awaken any moment and give me a big smile like he does every morning, she thinks, gently touching each of the boy's eyelids. But McLean remains still. Anna squeezes the bath cloth, then lets it drop, and climbs up on the bed. Taking the boy into her arms, she wraps herself around his wasted frame, drawing him like a lover into her breasts, her belly, her thighs. The muscles in her young face sag, giving her a look of the ancient.

"Eyes, look your last," she whispers. "Arms, take your last embrace, and lips, O you the doors of breath, seal with a righteous kiss. . . ." She presses her trembling mouth to McLean's dry cheek. Thirteen years, my darling, you were ours for thirteen years. Now you belong with God.

She places McLean's head back on the pillow and turns to find Millie standing beside the bed. "You'd better call Mr. Sanderson. Our boy is gone, Millie." Her fingers caress the tips of McLeans's small, oval fingernails. "Our beautiful boy is gone."

Tears start down Millie's face as she bends over the body. "All these years we been so careful, Miss Anna. Now it's happened, and it's just as hard as we knew it would be. Life ain't nothin' but a vale of tears . . . a vale of tears. My heart . . . ," she sobs, "my poor heart is about to bust."

Resting her palms against the bed for support, she sinks to her knees. "Oh, Lord Jesus, take this precious boy child into your care. A fine angel, Lord, is on his way to you. And, Jesus, if you see fit, we sure would appreciate it if our boy could walk the streets of Heaven and lift his hands to Glory now that he's done with the awful burdens he had in this life. In Jesus' name, we pray. Amen."

Anna covers Millie's hand with her own. "Thank you. Go on now and call Mr. Sanderson. The number is on my dresser. I'll stay here with McLean until you get back."

Millie leaves the room and is gone long enough for Anna to pull down the shades and light a lamp. She hurries back in and begins to stammer, clutching the hem of her apron as she tries to talk. "I'm sorry, Miss Anna, but. . . ."

"What is it, Millie? Isn't he at that hotel?"

"Yessum. He's there, but. . . ." Millie looks down at her hands. "The man what answer, he say Mr. and Mrs. Sanderson say they're not to be disturbed."

Anna sighs. "It isn't the first time that's happened, Millie. I'll call later and leave a message. You'd better get Mr. Price on the line. Tell him he can come and get McLean this morning, and I'll go down and discuss the funeral arrangements with him before noon." She gathers the bath cloths and the basin of water from the bedside table.

"Do you want me to put some camphor on a handkerchief and put it over McLean's face, Miss Anna? He's gonna turn dark if we don't."

"No. There'll be no viewing of the body, Millie, and no wake either. Just a brief service out at Sand Hill. I'll send a notice to our friends this afternoon. The burial will be tomorrow at eleven o'clock."

"Tomorrow?" Millie asks. "We gonna bury the boy child on Christmas Eve?"

"Yes," Anna replies. "Christmas Eve."

* * * * *

Anna stands at the upstairs window in McLean's room, watching as family and friends congregate in front of the house, the arms of their overcoats dressed in wide black bands. Hepsi and Robert, and Warren and Patsy, are huddled together beside Robert's Ford. Carl's parents and Amanda are talking with Bethany and Bryson. Emma and Birdie Jenkins, and Mr. and Mrs. Herring, are on benches in the side yard with Georgann Crumpler, Gertrude Weil, Evelyn, and Claire. Millie and Fletcher wait beside the Cadillac. Anna sees Carl emerge with the preacher from under the eave of the porch. He turns and looks up at her, motioning with his gloved hand for her to come down.

Anna nods. She turns to caress the carved head of the handsome rocking horse Carl had ordered for his unborn son. A son who would never ride a rocking horse, never sit on a seesaw, never jump a ditch. From the corner of her eye, she sees Mr. Price rein in the matched black horses pulling the glass-enclosed hearse that bears the mahogany coffin. Those are the last horses my son will ever know, she says to herself. The last horses, the last ride, the last of life on this earth. All of this is over now, she thinks, looking about the room. She picks up the stuffed monkey McLean loved and holds it to her bosom while waves of hurt squeeze her aching heart. Pulling on a pair of black leather gloves, she crosses the room to the hallway. Her hand is on the doorknob, but she turns to take one last look at the shaft of sunlight falling on McLean's wheelchair.

PART FIVE: 1932-33

The Girl
At The Back Door

CHAPTER 16:
EVERY LOST SOUL

July 29, 1932

Maddie Gaston rubs her son's naked belly. "Hush now," she whispers, caressing the boy's damp skin. "I know you're hungry. So am I. Your daddy's gonna bring us something to eat." No, he ain't, she thinks. He's been gone since daybreak, and he ain't coming back.

Crouching beneath a fragrant magnolia, she scans the empty street looking for her husband. She crawls across the cool ground beneath the tree and looks back at the railroad platform where he left her at dawn. The door to the ticket office opens, and the stationmaster pokes his head out.

Why don't you go away, old man? Maddie says to herself. Been coming out that door every half-hour since we been here. We ain't doing nothin'. She pulls at her dirty skirt, wrapping it around long, muscular thighs, and sets the baby on her lap. Oh, Daniel, how could you leave us like this? You know we ain't got nothin' to eat. Ain't got no money, neither.

She looks up to see the heavyset railroad man coming toward her, fists crammed deep into the pockets of his striped overalls. "Listen here," he says, squatting to get a look at her. "You can't stay out here all day. I got other trains pullin' in, and folks don't want to be greeted by no ragged darky settin' under a tree with a cryin' young'un. Who you waitin' for, anyhow? You got folks here?"

Taking the fussy baby in her arms, Maddie begins to crawl out. She glances at the man's dusty brogans, says a little prayer, and slowly stands. "No, sir," she answers, shifting the baby to her hip. "My husband told me to wait here with our boy. He's coming back. Please, mister. Can't I stay just a little longer?" She reaches down to pick up her only possession, a water-stained cardboard box tied with string.

"How long you been here, gal?"

233

"Got here 'bout daybreak. The clock in the station say 6:20."

Pulling a watch from his pocket, the stationmaster opens it and squints. "Well, it's 10:35 now. You're gonna have to find somewheres else to wait. You gotta get that young'un away from here. Can't you make him hush?"

Maddie pulls at the dingy diaper around her baby's bottom. "He's hungry, mister."

The man removes a greasy cap and smoothes back the stringy hair that falls on his forehead. "Lord have mercy on a bunch of no-good, helpless niggers," he mutters, drawing a nickel from his pocket. "Here, take this and go over yonder to that store on the corner there." He points to a run-down building. "Get you some vittles. And don't come back here, you understand?"

Maddie reaches in the rough yellowish palm and takes the coin. "Yes, sir, I understand. Thank you, sir." She turns toward the hot, dusty street.

Although there are few people around, Maddie approaches Baker Grocery Company with care. She knows no one in this place, and no one knows her. She has heard stories of women traveling in search of work who have disappeared, and never been heard from again. Her stomach churns as her bare feet cross the worn planks of the store's porch. Clutching the baby close to her breast, she stares at the *Merita* sign in the center of the rusty screen door. As she opens it, the hinges whine. In the dim, cool interior, several men are sitting around a cold, pot-bellied stove. Maddie glances at them and quickly looks away. After a moment, one of the men stands. "What you want, gal?"

Looking down the counter that runs along the wall, Maddie sees a wooden cheese box topped by a penciled sign, RAT CHEESE 12 Cent Lb. She runs a calculation in her head. "Three cents worth of that cheese, please."

The man slaps his hands against his knees, raises his arms in a slow exaggerated stretch over his head, and saunters to the counter to remove the oily, orange wheel. While he cuts a thin slice, Maddie's eyes wander to dust-covered shelves that are filled with canned peaches and pears, spools of thread, cakes of soap, tins of flour and cane syrup, cartons of lye, and snuff. She puts the stationmaster's nickel on the counter, swallows hard, and clears her throat. "I need some crackers, too."

The clerk looks at the nickel, frowns, and stomps to a wooden barrel by the door where he grabs a stained paper sack. He fills it with crackers and tosses it across the counter toward Maddie. "Take that cheese and get on out of here. You can't stay around here nasty as you are with that crying young'un."

* * * * *

Just beyond the brick facade of the Bank of Baker, Maddie pauses to read the crudely written menu that hangs on the front door of a small cafe. Stew Beef 15 cents, 2 Eggs and Sausage 15 cents, Vegetable Soup and Crackers 15 cents, Fried Chicken Plate 20 cents. Her mouth waters as she pictures a glistening ham hock resting on a mound of fresh turnip greens.

At the corner of the building, she stops to peer into an alleyway. Stepping carefully to avoid a scattering of broken glass, she makes her way along the wall and sits down on a wooden box. She peels paper from the cheese and breaks off a small piece for the baby boy on her lap. "This will make us thirsty," she says, peering into the bag of broken crackers, "and there's nowhere to get water." She nibbles at the crackers and cheese, her mind busy. Lordy, what a mess. Ain't got nothin' else to feed my baby. No way to get nothin'. Didn't ever think we'd end up like this when we started up the road. Daniel said he'd take care of us. That we'd be all right 'cause we was together. That he would find a job, find somewhere for us to stay. He said it would be better than the river. Well, it ain't. At least we had something to eat there. Maddie finishes the last cracker and leans against the warm brick wall. Soon, she's asleep. An hour later, the sound of a train whistle wakes her. The cheese is gone, and only tiny crumbs remain in the cracker bag. Maddie lifts the baby to her hip, picks up the worn cardboard box, and slowly returns to the street.

Two blocks away, Anna sits on the side porch in a rocking chair, the morning paper across her lap. "Vets Driven From Homes," the headline reads. Beneath it is a picture showing General Douglas McArthur and Major Dwight Eisenhower leading a group of armed foot soldiers who are demolishing a "nest of squatters" camped in cardboard shanties along the Potomac River. Veterans of the Great War, the squatters had gone to Washington earlier in the month to protest the cancellation of their long-promised pensions. Many took wives and children with them. Their makeshift houses, containing their few worldly goods, are being burned by the soldiers.

Anna stares at the photograph. Where will this end? she wonders. How could a thing like this happen right under the dome of the Capitol? This is the richest country in the world, and people can't even feed their children anymore.

She rises from her rocker and starts to the kitchen, where the breakfast dishes are waiting. Now that Millie is suffering so from arthritis, I'll have to find someone else to help me with the housework, she thinks. But that shouldn't be hard now. So many people are out of work.

Anna fills the dishpan with hot, soapy water and collects the egg-stained plates and coffee cups from a tray on the table. Glancing at the clock, she is surprised to see that it is almost noon. Carl has been gone more than three hours, and she doesn't expect him to return until suppertime. She's looking forward to a quiet afternoon on the side porch where she has set up easel and paints. After turning on the radio, she plunges her hands in the dishpan and listens closely as the announcer reports the latest stock-market averages. The market remains high. "And here, ladies and gentlemen," the announcer says, "is our most requested tune." A happy-sounding voice delivers the song's lyrics.

> It's only a shanty in old shanty town
> The roof is so slanty, it touches the ground.
> But my tumbled down shack, By an . . . .

Anna snaps off the radio as the *slap slap* of the back screen door draws her from the Potomac. I need to ask Fletcher to tighten those hinges, she thinks, hurrying across the kitchen to the side porch, where she finds a thin colored girl holding a baby. Homeless white men come often these days to Anna's back door, their soiled oversized clothing reeking of campfires and sweat, their weary faces etched with the shame of begging. But this is the first time she has found a colored girl there. She's dressed in a dirty frock made of flour sacks and wears a faded yellow scarf around her head. Anna silently admires her bronze skin and large, almond-shaped eyes. Not from around here, she thinks.

"Yes?" Anna asks, watching as the girl looks down the moment she speaks to her. "Can I help you, child?"

"Yessum. I was wondering if maybe you had some work I could do. My boy and me been traveling, and we ain't had much to eat. I'm a good cook, and I know how to clean real good. We don't eat much, ma'am."

Anna is mystified by the girl's speech as one-syllable words flow from her dark mouth stretched into two, or even three, syllables in a steady rhythm.

"Well, now," Anna says with a smile. "Where are you from?"

"South Carolina, ma'am. Place on the Waccamaw River, belong to old Colonel Lyles."

"And what's your name?"

"Maddie Gaston, ma'am." The girl looks up at Anna.

"Are you alone? Is your husband with you?"

"I don't rightly know where he is," the girl whispers. "He told me to wait at the train platform. He was going to look 'round for something to eat. I waited a long time, but he never come back. The man at the station, he run me off."

Anna nods. "So you're not sure of your husband's whereabouts," she says. Maddie shakes her head.

"You see that bench over there?" Anna points toward a white high-backed bench near her rose garden. "You go on over there, Maddie, and sit down. I'll bring you something to eat in just a minute. By the way, how old is your baby? What's his name?"

"Albert. He's gonna be sixteen months next week." The girl turns quickly to hide her smile, and starts down the steps toward the bench.

Anna returns to the kitchen, opens the icebox, and removes three brown eggs. The frying pan she used at breakfast still sits on the stove. After a few minutes, she returns to the yard and hands Maddie a plate of food and a glass of milk. Sitting down on the bench, she smiles at the curly-haired Albert. "How did you get to Baker, Maddie?"

"On the train. Rode in a boxcar with some other folk who was traveling."

Oh, my God, Anna thinks, a boxcar. "How long have you been on the road?"

Maddie's thick brows knit. "'Bout three days, I reckon, ma'am."

"Why did you leave . . . what did you call it . . . Colonel Lyle's place?"

Maddie wipes Albert's chin with a torn handkerchief. "Last March, our house in the street burnt down, and young Mr. Lyles, that's old Colonel Lyles's son, he said it was our fault. We wasn't home at the time, but he still blamed us. So we had to leave. My husband, Daniel, he's been talking about going north to find work for the longest. So we struck out down the road."

"Weren't you frightened, Maddie? I mean, weren't you worried about being out on the road with your baby?"

Lord Jesus, yes, Maddie thinks. About the scaredest I ever been in my life. All them white men chasing us at the train yards. "Yessum," she says, "I was scared, but I know Daniel gonna look after us. But he ain't here now and . . . and I don't know what I'm gonna do."

Anna looks at the girl, at her filthy dress and bare feet, at the baby sitting beside her. She thinks about Claire and her two grandsons. It's hard to imagine that they might ever be in such a fix as this, she says to herself, but if they were. . . . "You said you need some work, Maddie. I'm Mrs. Sanderson, and I have some work for you if you want it." Maddie helps Anna gather the dirty dishes, and they return to the house.

"I have a highchair right here in the pantry," Maddie hears Anna say as they enter the kitchen. "I get it out when my grandsons come to visit. Come on in and take a look so you can get acquainted with the house."

Maddie sticks her head inside the pantry, where shelves are filled with commercial and home-canned goods. Large sacks of flour, corn-meal, and sugar stand in each corner. Three sugar-cured hams hang from the ceiling, giving off a sweet aroma that mingles with the sharp scent of onions and green peppers beneath them. Nearby, a tin bowl of fresh peaches glows in the sunlight.

Anna drags the spindled highchair out of the pantry to the middle of the kitchen floor. She motions for Maddie to put Albert in the chair and runs a soft dishcloth across his tummy, tying him in. "There!" she says, wrinkling her nose at the little boy. "Now, Maddie, why don't you start by washing the dishes and sweeping the kitchen floor?"

Anna turns from the highchair to find Maddie staring, open-mouthed, at the gleaming appliances and porcelain sink. Sensing the young woman's dismay, she steps to the sink to run her hand along its smooth, white rim. "We added this kitchen a few years ago and put in these modern things. Our old kitchen caught fire, so we tore it down. Here, let me show you how to work these faucets."

Maddie can hardly believe hot water is so easily gotten. She stands at the sink while it flows over her hands and listens as the tall white woman gives her instructions. "The sweeper and cleaning supplies are there in the pantry. Just go over the carpets and floors and dust everything, if you will. The house hasn't been cleaned in more than a week." Anna opens the door to the front hall. "Just these rooms down here today," she says, as Maddie takes in the double staircase and sun-drenched foyer. Anna points to the sitting room nearby. "I'll be in there if you need me."

Left alone with a dust cloth and carpet sweeper, Maddie stares at the leather-bound volumes in Carl's library, the ornate crystal chandeliers, the Persian carpets, and striped velvet sofas. Old Colonel Lyles's house on the Waccamaw River once held such splendors, but Maddie never saw them. The Civil War left the Lyles family poor, and the house fell on hard times. Many of the enslaved families, including Maddie's ancestors, remained on the plantation throughout the war and for generations after. It meant a roof over their heads, hand-me-down clothes, and a meager, inadequate diet, but for them it had been better than life in the streets of some strange city.

Young Mr. Lyles, the son of the Confederate colonel, allowed the children of his sharecroppers to use an old pack house as a schoolroom in winter. Maddie and her classmates huddled around a small stove, taking turns adding and subtracting, multiplying and dividing, with bits of charcoal on a big flat board. What few books they had were the dilapidated castoffs of the white family. Like their teacher, they left school behind in March when they returned to the fields.

Maddie never worked in the fields. At ten, she was taken to the big house to be trained as a cook's helper. She spent her days hauling buckets of water, scrubbing iron skillets with corn shucks and sand, and watching "Cookie" prepare the dishes that gave low-country cooking a worldwide reputation. After three years of training, Maddie perfected the art of the roux, and held her own when it came to shrimp gumbo and scalloped oysters. Unfortunately, her time in the big house kitchen was short-lived.

One cold January day, as she pounded the dough for beaten biscuits, Maddie heard her younger brother call to her. She did not answer immediately, as her brothers and sisters came to the kitchen door almost daily to beg for scraps. Her brother called again, his tone more insistent. Since she had not been down to the family cabin for several days, Maddie was unaware that her mother was sick. The white doctor who came to look at the dying woman called it consumption, but Maddie knew that the real killers were starvation and neglect.

After her mother died in the bed she was born in, Maddie was forced to return to the shack in the quarters to care for her younger brothers and sisters. At thirteen, she became housekeeper, cook, gardener, nurse, and mother-figure to a brood of hungry, ill-clothed children. Since she could no longer work in the kitchen at the big house, she was told that she would do laundry for the white family. Winter and summer, Maddie spent Mondays outside stirring a cauldron of boiling laundry, rinsing the heavy pieces in buckets of cold water, and hanging them on bushes and along the fence to dry. For the next two days, she ironed for the Lyles. In between, she changed diapers, hauled water, and cooked black-eyed peas and cornbread for her own family in the same fireplace her mother, grandmother, and great-grandmother had used. Because she had never left the plantation, Maddie has never seen a washing machine, an electric iron, or even a telephone.

She returns to the gleaming kitchen, where she is surprised to see Anna standing at the sink bathing Albert. She watches silently as the white lady, with the crown of silvery hair, gently lifts her son's stout arm, rinsing it with dripping water squeezed from a blue washcloth. Albert laughs as he tries to catch the bubbles with his little brown hand. He sees Maddie and begins to call, "Ma-Ma, Ma-Ma."

"Oh, Maddie, I hope you don't mind," Anna says. "We're having lots of fun. I found some of my grandson's clothes. He's about two-and-a-half. I know these playsuits are much too small for him now. Do you mind if Albert wears them?" She nods to a pile of colorful material on a chair nearby.

"Thank you, ma'am. All his stuff is in that cardboard box, and Lord knows there ain't much." Maddie caresses the soft cotton of one of the four playsuits. Like other clothing worn by young children, it is faded and stained. "I like this one." She hands it to Anna.

"Would you like to have a bath, Maddie? I know it must have been hard to stay clean on the train. I'll bring you fresh towels and a washcloth in just a minute. You can bathe right here at the sink."

Maddie looks at her bare, dusty feet and runs her fingertips over the end of the grimy sash knotted at her waist, while she searches for an answer.

"It's all right, Maddie," Anna reassures her. "There's no one here but us. You can have the kitchen all to yourself."

"That's mighty kind, ma'am," Maddie finally says, "but . . . well, you see, I ain't got no more clothes. My husband took 'em along with him in our satchel." She wiggles the toes of her dirty left foot. "Ain't got no shoes, neither. Left 'em in a boxcar night before last. Some men waitin' at the train yard had guns and sticks, and they run us off. I was sleeping, and plumb forgot about them shoes 'til it was too late."

"You dress Albert. I'll be back in a minute," Anna says, handing the boy to his mother.

Maddie empties the big washbasin, rinses it, and runs her hand around the bright red rim. She opens the cardboard box and takes out a fresh diaper. After fastening the pins, she picks up her baby, shaking him gently. "Ain't you something?" she laughs, watching Albert's bright eyes dance. "Ain't you a beautiful boy?" She puts the clean playsuit on her son.

Anna returns to the kitchen with two fresh towels and a washcloth, which she places on the side of the sink. Over her arm are several cotton housedresses. "I haven't been able to wear these for years," she explains, hanging them on the pantry door. "We're about the same height, aren't we?" She turns to check Maddie's height. "I seem to be gaining around my middle. Middle-age spread, I guess. You wear these, Maddie. They are just wasted hanging in a closet upstairs." A pair of flat black shoes appears on the table. "Come on, Albert, let's go see the kittens out by the garage." She takes the child's hand, matches her step to his, and slowly guides him across the porch. "We'll be back in a little while, Maddie. Enjoy your bath."

Turning to the sink, Maddie pulls the miraculous tap and fills the red-rimmed basin with hot water. After removing her dusty dress and underwear, she begins to bathe with the fragrant blue soap. Her thoughts turn to Daniel. He'd be glad that we're safe, that we got something to eat, but he wouldn't like that white-haired lady who fed us. And he wouldn't want me to have no nice dresses from her, either. Charity, he'd say. White folk doin' a good deed to try to ease they conscience. "Oh, Daniel," she whispers aloud. "You ain't here. Maybe that be for the best."

Maddie dries herself, empties the gray water from the basin, fills it again, and unties the yellow sash that's wrapped around her head.

Dozens of tiny braids are pinned like little black flowers above each of her ears and along the back of her neck. She removes the pins and piles them on the edge of the kitchen table. Using the sweet-smelling soap, Maddie works up a rich lather and rinses her hair with fresh water, before wrapping it in the towel Anna used on Albert.

In the cardboard box, she finds a yellowed slip and her only pair of cotton drawers. She slips these on and walks over to the pantry door to remove a striped frock from its hanger. As she dresses, she hears a truck pull into the backyard. Maddie runs her fingers through her hair, grabs a couple of hairpins from the table, and thrusts them into the wavy knot she has twisted on the back of her head. She hears the screen door open and a man's voice saying, "Yessum, we sure have had some hot weather lately, Miss Anna."

There is a tap on the door, and Anna steps in. "A perfect fit!" she exclaims when she sees Maddie in the dress. "Feel better?"

"Yessum. Thank you, ma'am."

Anna motions for Maddie to follow her. "Come on out here. I want you to meet someone." As Maddie steps onto the porch, Anna says, "This is Fletcher. Fletcher Sanders. He runs our farm. Fletcher, this is Maddie Gaston from South Carolina."

Fletcher carries a bushel basket filled with fresh vegetables. "How do, miss," he says, smiling at Maddie.

Maddie nods, but says nothing. She looks at the man in the blue plaid shirt and gray work pants. Passin', she thinks, staring at Fletcher's golden hair, pale skin, and soft green eyes.

Anna hands Albert to Maddie and says to Fletcher, "Just put those vegetables right in the kitchen, Fletch. Maddie can fix some for supper tonight. She's going to be helping me here for the next few days, aren't you, Maddie?"

"Yessum," Maddie answers, her eyes on Fletcher.

"The squash be mighty good this year," he says. "Had just the right amount of rain. I best be going now. Mama wants me to drive her to Goldsboro this evening. Says she wants some lace to put on a dress she got, but I don't see how she's gonna do it, her hands is so swoll."

"You tell Millie to pick out what she wants, and you bring it to me with the dress and I'll put it on for her."

"I'll do that, Miss Anna." Fletcher tips his hat to Maddie. "Hope to see you again, Miss Gaston."

Anna opens the screen door. "I'll be looking for you in the morning, Fletch. Give Millie my regards and tell her I'll be out to see her this week."

The women stand on the porch watching Fletcher back an old Ford truck out of the driveway. "I don't know what we'd do without him," Anna says. "He keeps everything going out at the farm, and looks after his mother and all of the crops, and has a big garden every year. Let's see what he brought this time."

Deep red tomatoes, tiny okra, yellow squash, cucumbers, and a dozen ears of corn fill the basket. Anna removes the cucumbers and tomatoes and says, "Do you know how to fix squash and onions, Maddie?"

"Yessum."

"Well, there are some leftover pork chops in the ice box. You'll need to make some biscuits. Mr. Sanderson always wants rolls with supper, but there isn't enough time to make them tonight. Oh, and slice these tomatoes and put some cucumbers in a bowl of vinegar water. I'll fix some peaches later for dessert. Now, be sure to fix enough for you and Albert, too. You can eat right in the kitchen. We'll eat at the round table in the sitting room. The one with the lace tablecloth, remember?"

Maddie nods.

"I'll show you where I keep the silver and napkins. There will be only the two of us. Our daughters are grown and gone. Evelyn lives in New York City. She's a model and a dancer. And my oldest daughter, Claire, is married and lives here in Baker. She's the mother of my two little grandsons. They live just down the street and around the corner. Now, let me show you where to find everything. The paring knives are right here," Anna says, pointing to the top drawer of the Hoosier cabinet, "and there are several skillets hanging in the pantry," she continues. "I'll be out on the side porch, right outside the sitting room, if you need me."

* * * * *

Maddie hustles about the kitchen peeling and slicing, paring and chopping, while Albert sits in the fancy highchair and plays with a sock doll Anna gave him. When Maddie goes out to the sitting room to set the table, he sets up a howl that brings Anna running. "Is he all right? Is he hurt?"

"No'm, he's fine," says Maddie. "I guess he's a little scared because he can't see me. We been in so many strange places lately." She puts the last napkin in place and returns to the kitchen with Anna, who says, "I wish you'd tell me what it was like on the road, Maddie. Hardly a day goes by that some poor man doesn't come to my back door and ask for food. I've always wondered where they come from and how they get here. I know they're living in these hobo camps and sleeping in barns and all, but I've never known anyone I could ask about it. Were there other people in the boxcar with you and your husband?"

She sure ask a lot of questions, Maddie thinks. I'd better say something 'cause she's gonna feed me and Albert. "Yessum, other folk was with us. Some we know, and some we don't. Two white men and a white woman with a boy rode with us from Columbia. She was nice. Ask me all about Albert. When we get to Columbia, weren't no one with us but two of my husband's friends. They been planning to go north for some time and wanted Daniel, that's my husband, to go with 'em, but I begged him not to."

Anna sits down at the table and begins to peel a peach. "Were they bachelors?"

"No'm, they're married. Have seven young'uns between 'em. Ain't no work for colored folks where we live. You just stay on them farms and raise a crop or two and try to earn enough to keep food on the table."

"What did your husband plan to do up north?" Anna asks as fuzzy spirals of peach skin coil beneath her hands.

"Well'm, he's real good with tractors and trucks. Had Detroit on his mind, I reckon. Anyways, he said Detroit a few times. We didn't know we won't headed that way 'til last night. We thought we were on a train to Tennessee, but a man told us we were headed to Richmond. Guess that's why my husband left me. He had to go try to find the right train, I reckon, so he could go on to Detroit."

"Did you want to go to Detroit, Maddie?"

"Didn't have no other idea in mind, Miz Sanderson. Won't my place to decide. Need to stay with my husband, feed my baby."

"Why did you come to my house, Maddie?"

"'Cause of the sign."

Anna's hands are still for a moment. "What sign? There's no sign here."

"Yessum. Sign be right out front on the gate post. There's a little cross scratched."

"A cross? On our gatepost?"

"Yessum. When we were in Columbia hiding in the woods back behind the train yard, some white folk told us to always look for the cross. When you find it, you know somebody at that place gonna give you something to eat. They say all the folk what be on the road know right where to stop. They just walk 'round in a town until they see the cross at somebody's house. That's how I know to stop here."

"So that's it. No wonder I get so many visitors. I wonder who put it there?"

"Some man who be hungry. He come here and you give him something to eat and then he scratch it on the gatepost, I reckon."

"Well, I'll just have to see for myself." Anna puts a half-peeled peach in the bowl and rises from the table, leaving Maddie with her hands in the biscuit dough.

* * * * *

Maddie moves quietly around the sitting room table serving supper, trying not to disturb Carl's on-going narrative about his busy day. As he finishes a bowl of peaches and fresh cream, he says, "You're a good cook, Maddie. Do you need a job?"

"Yes, sir." Maddie does not meet his eye as she removes his dessert dish.

"Well, you and Mrs. Sanderson work out the details. I'm looking forward to some of your fried chicken." Carl drains his coffee cup. "Might you join me in the library for a moment?" he says to Anna.

She follows him out of the sitting room and across the hall. Carl closes the pocket doors, removes his suit jacket to reveal an expanse of middle-aged girth, and motions for his wife to sit down. "Have you ever seen this girl before, Anna?"

"I don't think so."

"Is she from around here?"

"No, Carl."

"Has she got folks down on the line?"

"No, Carl. She's from South Carolina."

"South Carolina!" Carl's voice booms across the high-ceilinged room. "You don't know a thing about her, do you?"

"She seems to be a nice girl. Sweet and friendly. And she's a good cook. Her husband's gone up north to try to find work. And he left her here with the baby."

"Baby!" Carl shouts. "You mean that little yellow gal has a baby here, here in this house? Anna, what in Hell is wrong with you? We can't keep a baby here." He slams the palm of his hand across the back of Anna's chair. "You'll have to find them another place."

"I'm working on it, Carl."

"Why don't you just send them on out to the farm? They can stay with Fletcher and Millie in that shed beside the cabin."

"I can't send a married woman with a baby out to stay in the same house with a single man."

"What difference does it make? Coloreds do that kind of thing all the time."

"I thought maybe Maddie and her baby could sleep out on the screen porch tonight, and we'll find somewhere for them to live tomorrow."

"Anna, you never cease to amaze me. How many bums have you fed today? I'll bet a half dozen have stopped here this week. I can't figure it out. Every lost soul who passes through this town ends up on our doorstep. And now you want to let a complete stranger, and a darky to boot, sleep on our back porch."

"I think it's the least we can do, Carl. Anyway, Maddie is not a complete stranger. She's been here helping me most of the day, and she's told me about her family and home. She needs a job, and I need some help."

"And you think you can just take some gal off the street and make her into an acceptable maid and housekeeper."

"I think she has a lot of potential. She's a good cook, Carl. You have to admit that."

"All right, Anna. I'll never be able to keep you from trying to save every helpless simpleton who comes along. But remember, if there's a problem," Carl raises his hand to point a finger at Anna, "just one, and out she goes. Understand? We're really taking a risk here."

"You take risks everyday at the bank, Carl. Maddie will be a good risk. Wait and see."

"I will. I don't know what's gotten into you these days. It must be that stuff women go through at your age."

"Do you mean the change, Carl?"

"Oh, for God's sake, Anna. I don't need to hear anything about that. Please close the door on your way out." Carl crosses the room to his desk and sits down in the big leather chair behind it. "And, Anna, let's have rolls at supper tomorrow night." He lights a slender cigar. "The Moseley's will be here."

"I'll see to it, Carl. And we'll have a nice meal. Don't worry." Anna closes the door, leaving her husband to his smokey room. She returns to the kitchen, where she finds Maddie finishing up the dishes. "Did you have some supper, Maddie?"

"Yessum."

"Do you have somewhere to stay tonight? Somewhere to sleep?"

"If you don't mind, me and Albert could sleep out in your back-yard."

"You can sleep out on the side porch if you want to. I'll bring down a couple of quilts. Do you think you'd like to stay here and work for us, Maddie?"

"Yessum. I sure would."

"Good. Now you finish up in here, and I'll get those quilts." Anna turns to leave the room, but stops midway. "Oh, Maddie, Mr. Sanderson has his breakfast every morning at seven-thirty sharp. He'll want two eggs over easy, two pieces of sausage, a bowl of grits, two biscuits, and black coffee. Has the same thing every morning. You'll need to take it to him in the library right at seven-thirty. He'll be in there reading the paper. Just put it on that wooden tray hanging on the wall by the stove. I'll just have coffee later, but you be sure to make enough biscuits for you and Albert." She steps across the threshold toward the hall. "I'll get those quilts."

* * * * *

After long nights huddled in the corners of jolting boxcars that smelled of manure, urine, and unwashed bodies, Maddie finally relaxes on Anna's back porch. Dressed in her slip, she stretches out to rub toes, elbows, and knees along the soft, cool nap of an old quilt. The roar of passing trains and the constant clacking of metal wheels have been replaced by the chirp of a cricket and the call of cicadas. Maddie breathes deeply, inhaling the sweet smell of fresh earth turned up around Anna's rose bushes and the fruity aroma of the pear trees just outside the screen door. She nuzzles against Albert, says a prayer for Daniel, and drifts off to sleep.

As early morning sunlight creeps across the backyard, Maddie draws water from the porch pump and washes her face. She changes Albert's diaper and takes him into the kitchen. An old hymn plays in her head as she moves about the gleaming appliances, preparing breakfast.

Maddie, who loves the smell of fresh buttermilk and the smooth powdery feel of bleached flour, pinches and pats eight biscuits, and puts them on Anna's baking tin. She spreads the wooden serving tray with a fresh napkin and sets it with gold-banded china. Then she cracks two large eggs into a sizzling frying pan, scoops up a bowl of grits, and butters two biscuits. If he still likes my cooking, he'll want me to stay, she thinks as she picks up the tray and starts down the hall.

After Carl leaves for the bank, Anna appears downstairs wearing a faded housedress and her gardening shoes. "Well, how did you sleep?" she asks as Maddie comes into the sitting room.

"Just fine, ma'am. Albert and me slept just fine, thank you. Can I get you a cup of coffee, Miz Sanderson?"

"No, thank you. I'll have some later. Maddie, I've been thinking. There's an old washhouse out back. We haven't used it for years. It's pretty solid. Has a tin roof and a window. It might be just the place for you and Albert to stay until we could arrange for a more permanent place. I thought we'd have a look at it, and when Fletcher gets here, we can clean it out and fix it up for you."

Oh, Lord, Maddie thinks. Gonna live in a washhouse. "Yessum, sound fine to me."

"Well, that settles that, unless we find some big gaping hole in the roof or something. By the way, Maddie, do you know how to make aspic?"

"No'm."

"We're having company for dinner, and Mr. Sanderson will want aspic. He just loves it. Let's go in the kitchen, and I'll show you what to do. Fletcher is bringing two hens from the farm. We'll boil them and make some chicken salad and deviled eggs. And rolls, of course. Maybe we could have peach cobbler for dessert. How does that sound?"

"Mighty nice. I know how to make a good cobbler, ma'am."

"Maddie, why don't you call me Miss Anna?"

"Yessum," Maddie says. "Yessum, Miss Anna. I sure will."

The washhouse is full of rusty cast-offs. A baby buggy, two narrow iron bed frames, bird nests, cobwebs, plowlines, and boxes of old kitchen utensils fill the small structure. Near the back is the huge black wash pot Millie used during the early years of Anna and Carl's marriage.

Anna and Maddie, with Fletcher's help, move the dusty items into the yard. Fletcher ties a plowline to one leg of the caldron and the other to the rear of his truck. "Here goes," he shouts as he lets out the clutch and drags the heavy pot through the doorway. This leaves a deep hole in the rear of the shed that's more than a yard wide and filled with broken bricks and ashes.

"Run down to the barn and get a shovel, Fletcher. We'll have to fill in this hole. I can do that while you go up to the attic and get that old oak washstand and those two featherbeds. They'll fit in the back of the truck, won't they? Maddie and I can clean up these bedsteads for her and Albert to use."

She motions for Maddie to follow her to the empty washhouse. "We'll have to do something about this floor, Maddie," she says staring at the hard-packed earth. "I've got an old hooked rug rolled up on the side porch that I use when I serve refreshments out there. We could put down some pine straw and then cover it with that rug. You sweep this place out, and I'll see about the rug." She steps out into the sunlight to see Claire and her two little boys coming up the back drive.

"Hello, Mama," Claire calls. "Isn't this a glorious morning?"

Taking out a handkerchief, Anna quickly wipes her sweaty forehead and smiles. "How lovely," she says as the boys hug her around the legs. "This is a nice surprise."

"What are you doing, Mama?" Claire laughs. "Your dress is all dirty."

"Having fun! Come and meet the newest member of the household. Maddie," Anna calls, "come on out and meet my daughter."

Maddie emerges from the washhouse with Albert on her hip and a broom in her hand.

"Maddie, this is my daughter, Mrs. Charles Kirby. And these are her boys, Wallace, we call him Wally, and Clifton. Wally just turned four, and Cliff is two-and-a-half. Claire, this is Maddie Gaston and her son, Albert. Maddie is going to be working for us. She's a wonderful cook."

"It's nice to meet you, Maddie," Claire says. "Mama can surely use some help. What are you two doing? Why is my old baby buggy out here?"

"We're cleaning out the washhouse so Maddie and Albert will have somewhere to stay until we can make better arrangements. Maddie is washing down the walls, and Fletcher is bringing down some old furniture from the attic. But we don't have to stay here and talk, honey. Maddie can take care of this. Let's go sit on the porch. You boys run and play," she says to her grandsons. Anna puts her arm around Claire's shoulder as they walk across the yard. "How is Charles? Is he working today?"

"He's fine . . . and working, but it may not last much longer. Mr. Hardy told him yesterday that at least one man is being laid off every week now. I may have to find a job myself."

"Oh, no, honey. Not while your boys are so young. You can't just leave them."

"I may not have a choice. I'm so glad I got my teaching certificate. And I'm a good typist. I don't think it would be too bad."

Anna tugs on her daughter's arm. "Claire, I would hate to see you go to work while your boys are so little. You know your daddy and I will lend you whatever you and Charles need."

"I know, Mama. But Charles would never take money from Daddy, and you know it. It's a miracle they even speak to each other. And Charles is too proud to accept a handout. Everybody is feeling the pinch these days, Mama. All my girlfriends are doing their own housework, and nobody has had a steak or new clothes in ages."

"Do you have enough money for groceries? Do the boys need anything?"

"Oh, they're fine. Nothing in their world has changed. I'm sure Christmas won't be too big this year, but they're still too young to realize it."

"Claire, you'll tell me if there's a problem, won't you?" Anna squeezes her daughter's hand. "You wouldn't hide anything from me, would you?"

"No, Mama. I wouldn't hide anything from you. We're okay. Honestly. Now, I'd better go. We're on our way to the drugstore. You're having company for dinner, aren't you?"

"Yes. The Moseleys are coming."

"I don't envy you an evening with them. He's such an arrogant boor, and she's a mouse. I hope they're bringing their girls to brighten up the group. Why are you having them over?"

"Mr. Moseley's a good bank customer. Your father wants to let him know how much he appreciates his business. Their girls aren't coming."

"And will Maddie be able to help you prepare everything?"

"Claire, she's a Godsend. You know Millie's hands and knees are so full of arthritis now. I miss having her here, but she needs to rest. She can hardly get around."

"Does Maddie live here in town? I've never seen her before."

"No. She's not from here. Her husband has gone up north to find work."

"Well, Mama, I hope she'll be everything you need." Claire turns toward the yard and calls to Wally and Cliff. "I'll call you later this week, Mama. And we'll all be here for Sunday dinner."

"All right, honey. Have a good time with your boys. Children grow up so fast. One minute you're changing their diapers, and the next minute you're packing them off to college. Enjoy them while you can."

"I will. Bye, Mama." Claire waves, then takes each son by the hand. "Please give Daddy a hug for us."

Anna tries to wave back, but her gesture comes off a bit short. She knows Claire is struggling. "Doing without," as most folks call it. Charles has lost two jobs in the last six months due to layoffs. He is a fine craftsman, but there is little demand these days for furniture makers because no one can afford to buy new furniture.

By eleven o'clock, the washhouse has been converted into a snug, but pleasant cottage. Two small beds have been pushed together on the rug that covers the hole where the cauldron was. An oak washstand sits beneath the window on the left wall. A cushioned wicker chair from Anna's porch fills one corner. The old rug gives the interior a homey touch, but Anna really caps it off when she brings in a lusterware chamber pot, a wooden comb-and-brush set, and a red-and-gold quilt in the wedding ring design.

"Fletcher's grandmother, Ludie, and his mother, Millie, made this for us when we got married." She spreads the colorful quilt across the tops of the two joined beds. "Isn't it lovely? Just what this place needs to give it a little life."

Maddie watches a moment as Anna smoothes the beautiful bed-cover. She turns away and nervously fingers the comb-and-brush set on the washstand. "Thank you, Miss Anna," she whispers.

* * * * *

Maddie waits while Anna places a porcelain basket full of fresh roses in the center of the dining-room table. Then she circles the table checking for spots on the silverware and examining the folds of each napkin. "The table is perfect, Maddie," Anna says. "You did a grand job. The Moseleys will be here any minute, so you'd better cut the aspic and put it on lettuce. I'll let you know when to bring the food in."

Maddie returns to the kitchen and begins final preparations for the meal. As she feeds Albert, she listens to the muffled voices of the guests rise and fall on the warm, evening air. The sound of a tinkling bell calls her to the dining room.

She enters, and Anna gets up. "Maddie, would you please collect the plates now, and I'll freshen everyone's glasses." Maddie begins to move around the table. With care, she lifts Mr. Moseley's empty plate as he continues his conversation with Carl.

"I don't care what you say, my friend. If Roosevelt's elected, we're going to be in for a helluva mess. He's gonna turn the banking industry upside down. You know how these Jews operate."

Carl takes a sip of iced tea and fingers the raised border at the end of his dessert spoon. "He'll never touch the Bank of Baker."

Anna, who is standing at the other end of the table, fills Mrs. Moseley's water glass. "Mr. Roosevelt's not Jewish," she says.

"He may not be now, but his folks sure were. With a name like Roosevelt, you can be sure he's a kike." Mr. Moseley rears back in his chair and rests his arms across his ample paunch. "And that ain't the only thing worryin' me, Carl. Why, just last week, I heard they're gonna build a new school for the niggers over in Pineville. The city and the county are gonna build it. If we're not careful, the Jews and the damn niggers'll be running this country."

Maddie sees the salad fork leave her hand. She hears it land with a loud thunk on the plate beneath it. "Excuse me, sir." She looks quickly at Carl, then picks up the fork and puts it on a tray piled with dirty dishes. She heaves the heavy tray and leaves the room.

The kitchen door swings closed behind her, and Anna pushes it open again. "Oh, Maddie. I'm sorry," she says.

Maddie's hands shake as she removes a pan of peach cobbler from the top of the stove. "That kinda thing gonna happen, Miss Anna. It ain't your fault."

"Why don't you stay in here, Maddie, and wash the dishes? I'll serve the cobbler."

"No'm," Maddie says, spooning the dessert into the pink crystal bowls she has arranged on a silver tray. "It's my job, and I'll take care of it." She smoothes her apron and picks up the gleaming tray.

CHAPTER 17:
LONG GRAY LINES

August 12, 1932

Claire sits on her great-grandmother's loveseat and stares at the wall above Anna's desk and tells her mother that Charles has lost his job, that they are two months behind in rent, and that she has sold the living-room furniture to keep from being evicted. Charles has taken their second-hand Chevy and gone to Chicago to look for work.

"We have no car insurance because we haven't been able to keep up the payments," she tells her mother. "If Charles is in an accident, he'll probably die in some place up north and we won't have enough money to bring his body home. Oh, Mama, how did this happen? When Cliff was born, we had everything. A nice house, a good car, plenty to eat, a savings account, and two healthy boys. We were able to set aside a little money each month for their college. Now, all I have are my boys." She begins to cry.

Anna leaves the rocker and sits down on the loveseat beside her daughter. "Claire, your father and I will give you whatever you need. Let me write you a check."

"No, Mama. We won't take charity," Claire sniffs.

"We'll call it a loan, then. Is two hundred dollars enough?"

"We can't accept a loan, either. You have to pay those back, Mama." Claire removes a handkerchief from her pocket and dabs at each red-rimmed eye. "I didn't come around here to burden you with my troubles, but I do want to ask for a favor. Could you keep Wally and Cliff for a while this afternoon?"

"Of course, honey. Is that all you wanted? You know I love having them here."

"No, that's not all. May I borrow your car?"

"Where are you going? Do you want me to come with you?"

"No, ma'am. I'm going to Raleigh. Betty Covington told me yesterday that her cousin, who teaches fifth grade in Raleigh, had to give up her teaching position. She's expecting. Betty just found out over the weekend. I called the school this morning. It's Hargett Street Elementary, and I made an appointment to see the principal at three o'clock today." Claire bends over the loveseat to look for her pocketbook. "I've got to get a job, Mama. We're flat broke." She drags her bag from under the sofa. "I'm ready to go. I just need to freshen my face. And don't worry, Mama. I'll be back before dark."

"Oh, Claire. Are you sure you have to do this? Why don't you get a job in Smithfield?"

"I've called. There aren't any available. Everybody is holding on like a snapping turtle in a thunderstorm. People are scared."

"Well, the key is in the car, Claire. And the tank's almost full. Please be careful."

"I will. Don't worry. There isn't too much traffic on the highway these days. Nobody can afford gas. Wish me luck." She pats the crown of her straw hat as she hurries from the room. "And, Mama," she calls, "thanks for looking after Wally and Cliff."

Anna folds her hands, closes her eyes, and leans back against the sofa. Oh, no. Something else for Carl to yell about. *I told you so. I told you Charles was no good.* When Claire went off to college, I prayed she would marry one of those nice young men who buzzed around her when she made her debut. Two law-school students. And another who was studying to be a doctor. But she went away with Charles's high-school ring on a chain around her neck, and she never even looked at another young man. None that I know of, anyway. Came home almost every weekend to be with him . . . cook for him, iron his shirts. And when she got pregnant, I thought Carl would kill us all. Threatened Charles with a shotgun until I managed to get it away from him, yelling at the top of his lungs at Charles and Claire, calling them terrible names and threatening to cut off her inheritance. It made no difference. They simply ran away. Didn't need permission since they were both of legal age. Legal age? What difference did that make? They were nineteen. Just babies themselves, with another on the way. And the next seven months were pure Hell while Charles and Claire lived in that cold water flat in Smithfield. And Carl stormed around the house every night carrying on about how his rotten, unappreciative daughter had ruined his social standing. Then Wally was born, a tiny replica of his blond, green-eyed grandfather, and everything changed. Carl could not do enough for that baby or for Claire. Visited them once a week while Charles was at work. Gave little Wallace a twenty-five dollar savings bond. But the friction between Carl and Charles has never abated, even if they are decent to each other in my presence. I know Carl hates Charles' guts, hates having him here, even when Claire and Wally and Cliff are present. But I have to try to keep the peace. If I didn't invite Claire and Charles to dinner occasionally, and try to keep that little thread of civility between Carl and Charles from breaking, we'd hardly have a family.

It will be harder now, Anna thinks on her way to the kitchen. Charles' leaving will be another shortcoming for Carl to gloat about. And he'll be furious if Claire goes to Raleigh and gets a job without his permission. I just won't tell him.

* * * * *

Friday September 9, 1932
Raleigh, NC

Dear Mama,

How are Wally and Cliff? Please give each of them a big hug for me. I miss them so much, Mama, but I know they are happy and content because they love being with you. I know you must be thanking our Lord every day for Maddie. What a wonderful blessing she was—just out of the blue and right when you, and I, needed her so much.

I am sharing a room in a boarding house with another teacher. Her name is Louise Evans, and she's from Wendell. She teaches sixth grade at my school, so we walk to work together every day. Our room is upstairs over the kitchen. Mrs. Hodges, our landlady, said it would stay warmer than the other rooms in winter. It's a nice sunny room with high windows, blue flowered wallpaper, and a little pot-bellied stove. Each of us has a bed, and there is another single bed in one corner, so we may have a visitor now and then. The bathroom is down the hall and shared by six other full-time boarders. This has been an adjustment for me, but I think I've got the hang of it. To get a bath, I have to be up by 6:15. So I am at school by 7:30 each morning.

The dining room here at the boarding house seats twenty-four at several tables, and they are usually full. We have oatmeal and biscuits for breakfast, with coffee, of course. Mrs. Hodges has two seatings at lunch because so many men walk the two blocks over from the business district. She fixes sandwiches and cake or cookies for Louise and me to take to school (10 cents a day, peanut butter and jelly, sometimes leftover meatloaf). Eating lunch at school is hard, Mama, because so many of my children have so little to eat. I usually give away half my sandwich. There's always a child who has nothing, and often more than one. Occasionally, a problem arises in my room that calls for discipline. I stop and ask myself, "What has this child had for breakfast?" So many of their fathers are out of work. The school is only six years old, and I have a nice, big room and most of the supplies I need. I am enjoying my job and the children. They are so sweet and eager to learn. They love to touch my hair and clothes. Thank you for the twenty. (Sneaky, you shouldn't have.) I went to the dime store yesterday and bought enough ribbon for each little girl in my class (12) to have a bow for her hair, and I bought each boy (17) a 10-cent penknife. Tomorrow, I plan to teach a class on grooming and cleanliness. Many of my children live in homes with no indoor plumbing, so I know it is difficult for their mothers to keep them clean. I count my blessings every day and thank my Maker for the lovely home in which I was reared and for my parents who taught me to stand on my own two feet.

Louise and I often go "home" in the afternoon by way of a nearby city park, where we sit and talk, mostly about school and our students. We grade papers and prepare lessons from 4:30-6:30, and then we have dinner. It's modest and filling. The best thing is dessert—wonderful berry cobblers and pies just like Millie used to make for us. Mrs. Hodges has two colored women who help her clean and cook, and they do a good job. One is a Bridges from Smithfield. Her father delivers coal in Baker, and I think you might remember him. He lost a leg in France.

I rec'd a letter from Charles this week forwarded from the Baker P.O. He is in Chicago with his friends and has a part-time job as a short order cook. He is living at the YMCA, six to a room. They sleep in old army bunks. He says everyone there is talking about the upcoming election and most of the men who live at the Y like Roosevelt. The men whom he meets have only part-time jobs that come and go, and most have families out in the rural areas of Wisconsin and Illinois. I am so glad he was able to find work; his days as an army cook have paid off. Every night when he goes out to dump the garbage, a crowd of people (children, too) are waiting so they can pick through it. He has talked with lots of unemployed men who have come to the restaurant to beg for leftovers. Charles sees these same men standing in long lines outside the soup kitchens. (Charles said he thinks there are about a dozen such places in the city, sponsored mostly by churches.) He has seen hundreds of these poor men huddled against the sides of buildings like a long gray dragon's tail (his words) waiting for hours to get a bowl of soup and some bread and, if they're lucky, to have shelter for the night. Charles says they spend their days in the city parks and public libraries. They're living in cardboard shanties they've put up on vacant lots. Charles says they live on day-old bread the bakery gives away and rotting vegetables thrown out by the street vendors. He fears the Windy City will be a hard place for them come winter.

Mama, surely it won't get that bad here. I pray there won't be any long gray lines of people begging in the streets of Raleigh. I am so thankful that Charles was able to find work. Maybe we can get back on our feet and he'll be able to come home and find a job in Baker before too long. I miss my house, my own kitchen and little bathroom, and especially my three boys.

It's ten—my usual bedtime, so I'll close for now. Please hug and kiss Wally & Cliff for me and tell them I'll come home on the train next Friday and we'll got out to the farm on Saturday and go fishing in the creek. Tell Millie I'll come to the cabin and visit with her then.

How is Daddy? How are things at the bank? Mrs. Hodges says that all the bankers who eat lunch here at the boarding house are pretty somber these days. I miss all of you so much. Take care of yourselves and say a little prayer for Charles. I hope he never becomes one of those poor men in the soup kitchen line in that big hateful city.

OXOX Claire

Anna had received Claire's letter on a Wednesday morning. That evening, as she and Carl prepare for bed, she reads it to him and, for the second time, finds it distressing.

"Oh, Carl, those poor men and their families worrying about where their next meal is going to come from. Surely, it won't get that bad here."

Carl removes his silk socks and trots across the room in his bare feet to place a pair of gold cuff links on his dresser.

"Anna, you worry too much. That's just Charles talking. What does he know? The stock market was on a steady up-hill climb all summer."

"But, Carl, if things are not so bad, and the stock market is doing well, why are people hungry?"

"Because they haven't got jobs."

"I don't understand. Why haven't they got jobs, Carl?"

"Because nobody can afford to hire any more workers."

Anna persists. "Why, Carl?"

"Because nobody's buying anything. Businesses can't sell their products."

Anna rises from her dressing table, brush in hand. She walks back and forth across the room, brushing her long silver hair. Finally, she sits back down, all the while rubbing the smooth back of the brush against her palm. "Well, it seems to me that companies ought to hire people and pay them a decent wage so they'd be able to buy what those companies manufacture. If the workers made more money, they could buy more products. Then everyone would benefit, the workers and the companies."

Carl props his foot on Anna's needlepoint stool and takes out a cigar. "You've been talking to your friend, Gertrude Weil, haven't you?"

"She called yesterday to ask if I would serve on the Governor's Committee on Interracial Cooperation."

"What an absurd notion. There's no such thing as interracial cooperation, Anna. It's just a matter of haggling. Like haggling with the niggers about barning tobacco every year. If you go to talk to them about it, to see if you can hire them, you never get a yes or no. They either show up on the first day, or they don't."

"Well, you have to admire Governor Gardner's efforts, Carl. It is a start."

"Mr. Beau Geste, himself. The best thing old Max can do is keep the coloreds off the streets, keep a hoe in their hands, keep them busy." Carl settles back in his chair and opens the latest edition of *The Baker News & Record*. "Anna, you worry too much. Why don't you just relax and let me read the paper in peace."

Anna shrugs. "All right," she says, removing her robe and slipping into bed. Snuggling down against her pillow, she begins to plan the foods she'll take to homecoming at her church.

* * * * *

The next day, Anna and Maddie spend several hours preparing for Anna's church picnic. While Albert sleeps on a pallet on the back porch, Anna sits at the kitchen table icing a seven-layer chocolate cake and Maddie prepares the unmixed contents of a large bowl of potato salad. "Who taught you to cook, Maddie?" Anna asks, dipping a knife in the icing bowl.

"The cook at the big house."

"Was she your mother?"

"No'm. They come and told my mama they needed a new cook, and she sent me to be trained by the old one."

"Did they pay you?"

"No'm, but they give my daddy fifty cents a week because I was learning so good. My daddy used it to buy my mama's tonic. My mama didn't try to teach me to cook, but she did teach me to sew. Nothing too fancy. I helped her make quilts and the clothes for the children and shirts for my daddy. My mama was a good seamstress. She sewed for Mrs. Lyles and other ladies."

"Where exactly is the old place, Maddie?"

"On the river. The Waccamaw River. House set high up on a bluff that looks down on the river. Real hot there. Lots of birds in the marsh, tall grass 'round the riverbank, and all these big old oak trees bowing down to the ground. Mighty pretty place."

Anna nods. "How do people make a living there?"

"In the old times before I was born, they grow all this rice. Made them white folks rich."

"I've read that those rice plantations were really big." Anna turns the plate checking to be sure the cake is covered with icing.

"I heard my daddy say Colonel Lyles's place close to twenty-thousand acres 'fore the war."

"Was your grandmother there then?"

"Yessum. She and my granddaddy set up housekeeping about a month before the old colonel rode off to Charleston to join in the fighting. She said her people run off after that. Run and hid out in some caves up the river. Some of our folks still there now. After all the folk run off, won't nobody to plant that rice and chop it."

"But your grandparents stayed. Why?"

"Don't know, Miss Anna. They had a passle of young'uns, fourteen lived. My mama was the baby. They had to feed 'em, I guess. My mama said. . . ."

Maddie's comments are interrupted by the ringing of the doorbell. She leaves the potato salad to rinse and dry her hands. "I'll go see about the door."

She returns to tell Anna that a Mrs. Jenkins is in the sitting room, and from Maddie's description, Anna knows her friend is upset. "Her eyes are red and her voice is trembling," Maddie says.

Anna is surprised to see her friend, Emma Jenkins, on a Saturday afternoon. They hug each other and sit down together on the loveseat. Anna asks Maddie to bring in some of the fresh lemon tarts and iced tea. Then she takes Emma's hand. "Now, Emma, what in the world is the matter? You look like you've lost your best friend."

As Emma clutches Anna's hand, she begins to talk in jumbled spurts. "Carl called on me yesterday afternoon. He said we were behind in our payments at the farm and he was going to have to take drastic measures to correct the situation." Suddenly, she grabs Anna's arm just below the elbow. "And," she cries, "he's going to foreclose on my farm!"

Disbelief fills Anna's face. "Oh, Emma, surely you're not serious. Carl wouldn't do a thing like that."

"Oh, yes, he would." Emma assures her with a nod. "He already has. He told me that the bank couldn't keep carrying the farm, and that he had presented our case to the Board of Directors and they had instructed him to foreclose on my property. It's the only thing my daddy left me. Anna, you know it's all we have. What with Birdie so sick and the boys still young, we don't have any other income. And last year just about wiped us out. You can't raise a crop if there's no rain to keep it growing. Everything dried up on us, Anna. Lots of farmers are in the same boat, but the bank hasn't closed them down."

"I'll speak to Carl about it as soon as he gets home, Emma," Anna replies. "Now, let's have some tea. You just sit here and relax for a few minutes. We'll work this out. I'm sure Carl has no intention of taking away your farm." She smiles at Emma and offers her the plate of lemon tarts, but Emma turns away.

* * * * *

Carl has every intention of foreclosing on Emma Jenkins's farm and makes his plans clear to Anna when she brings up the subject that evening. "Anna, you have no business meddling in my bank affairs!" he shouts. "I don't hang around here everyday and tell you how to run this house, do I?"

"But, Carl. It's Emma Jenkins," Anna argues. "She's my closest friend in Baker."

"Anna, I've known Emma and Birdie Jenkins all my life. They're nice people. I'll admit that. But they're not good risks. When Birdie had those heart attacks, things changed."

"Birdie can't help that."

"And I can't help it if his debts aren't paid. They haven't paid one red cent on their loan for the last two years. What am I supposed to do? Pay the mortgage for him?"

"Well, you could make him a loan from your personal account, Carl."

"Don't be ridiculous, Anna. That's a good farm. Somebody can make it pay, and I'm going to find somebody to do it. I'll get Fletcher to help me find a good colored willing to work on shares and we'll turn that place around in a couple of years."

Anna's mouth drops. "You mean you bought Emma's farm? You foreclosed on it and bought it yourself, Carl?"

"It'll be a good investment."

"Carl, surely you don't intend to take someone's livelihood away from them and make it your gain. How can you be so vile?"

"Vile? What I did is well within the law. Happens every day."

"It may be within the law, but it certainly isn't within the bounds of decency. It seems that it's becoming fashionable these days to make money off other people's problems." Anna sets her coffee cup on a tray and reaches for Carl's. "That's one of the things Mr. Roosevelt has been talking about in his campaign. How the rich are getting richer and the poor are getting poorer. He says he's going to do something about it."

"That fool Roosevelt will never be elected. And even if he is, it won't change a thing. It's always been fashionable to be successful."

"Leaving people to starve is not exactly what I'd call success, Carl. It certainly isn't something people consider admirable."

"Admirable? I don't care if it's admirable or not, Anna. It works, and that's all that matters to me or any good businessman. You have to let go of all that foolish, sentimental trash that people mistake for brotherly love or some other charity. I got rid of that burden long ago." Carl starts toward his desk. "Are there any other of my shortcomings you wish to discuss tonight?"

Anna looks over at the portrait of Carl's father above the marble mantle. She thinks about the maroon Packard he drove the last few years of his life, a touring car with rich leather upholstery and tiny crystal vases that were filled with fresh pink rosebuds every day. She thinks about the last time she saw Carl, Sr. alive, here in their library, handing out five-dollar bills to his two young granddaughters.

"I thought I'd go to Raleigh Saturday and take the boys to have lunch with Claire," she says. "I want to do a little shopping. I'm sure Claire could use some things, and I need a hat to go with my wine-colored suit."

Carl rises from the desk. "How much do you need, Anna?" he asks, removing a wallet from his suit pocket. "Is this enough?" He hands Anna a fifty-dollar bill. "And take this, too. Claire probably needs a new dress," he says, handing her a twenty.

"Thank you, Carl. This will be plenty. I'll be sure to tell Claire you sent this to her."

Anna puts the bills in her pocket, picks up the tray of dirty cups, and goes across the hall to the sitting room, where she removes a cream-colored envelope from her desk drawer. She puts the folded fifty in the envelope, gives the inside flap a quick lick, and addresses it to Mrs. Emma Jenkins. "Oh, Maddie," she calls. "Could you run an errand for me?"

CHAPTER 18:
THE VOICE EVERY
MOTHER DREADS

October 6, 1932

Warm fall afternoons, Anna and Maddie sit on the screen porch, where they can enjoy the gentle breezes. Anna sometimes paints while Maddie polishes off a whole chapter from *My Antonia, Ethan Frome,* or some other work from Anna's collection. In between, they darn socks, crochet, and shell shucky beans. Sometimes Fletcher brings his mother to town, and Millie spends the day at Anna's, helping the two younger women with their chores.

During the summer, Anna cleaned out a trunk of old evening gowns and draperies, and decided to make a crazy quilt for Evelyn's Manhattan walk-up. The combination of velvets, laces, and taffetas will make a gorgeous conversation piece, she had told Maddie. The two women have reserved an hour each afternoon to work on the quilt so they can finish it by Christmas.

Not a day passes that Maddie does not think of Daniel and wonder where he is. She hopes to hear from him soon, hopes to hear that he is safe, that he has a job, and something to eat, and a place to sleep each night. Every time she sees a beggar on the back stoop, she thinks of Daniel. She wonders if he is begging at some white woman's door, if he thinks of her as often as she thinks of him, if he misses his son. With every bounteous meal, she says a silent prayer thanking Jesus for her good fortune, and imploring Him to look out for her husband.

Now that the immediate danger of destitution has passed, Maddie has relaxed enough to allow herself the luxury of having a future. Anna pays her two dollars and fifty cents a week. Part of this she puts in a baking powder tin she calls her "dream box." Her dream is that she and Daniel and Albert will be reunited and that they will be able to rent a house and make a living in a place like Baker. She takes pride in her work, cooks good food, cleans to perfection, and looks after Anna's grandsons and her own precious boy. And every Saturday, she carefully folds a dollar and puts it in her dream box.

Maddie is up before dawn each day because Wally and Cliff are usually out of bed by six-thirty. They play quietly in their pajamas until she comes upstairs to dress them. She feeds Albert and Claire's two boys Wheateena, and biscuits with jam, while Carl has his breakfast in the library. As soon as he leaves for the bank, Anna comes down. She takes all three boys in the sitting room, where they scoot around on the rug with their trucks while she reads the paper. By mid-morning, they're in the backyard whooping and shrieking on make-believe steeds, chasing each other, and rolling in the damp grass.

One morning, Maddie is standing in the pantry when she hears the shrill yap of a dog followed by Albert's startled cry. Then Wally calls, "Grandmother! Grandmother!" in a voice every mother dreads. As Maddie runs across the back porch, she sees Anna coming across the yard. Albert sits on the ground, howling and kicking.

Wally intercepts Anna and grabs her hand. "You better hurry, Granny. Judge Pruitt's dog bit Albert." Maddie kneels beside Albert and twists his leg around so that she can see the bite.

Anna stoops down beside her and looks at Wally. "What happened, honey? Buster's never bitten anyone before. Did you aggravate him?"

Wally shakes his head. "No, ma'am. We didn't do nothin'. He run in here through the hedge and showed his teeth and snarled, and Albert got scared and started crying. When he tried to run away, Buster bit him. Cliff and me were real still. He just snarled at us, and then he run off."

Anna touches Albert's wet cheek. "Come on to the house. We'll have to dress it, Maddie. Doesn't look too bad."

Maddie washes Albert's leg with soap and water and holds his arms down while Anna pours turpentine over the bite. Albert wails and kicks as the liquid seeps into the raw punctures. "No! No!" he cries, trying to escape from Maddie's arms. Wally and Cliff stand beside the kitchen table, their eyes big, quietly watching the ministrations of the women.

Maddie puts Albert on the table and wipes excess turpentine from the wound. "Hush, baby," she whispers. "Hush, now. We have to clean it up so it won't hurt. Be still for Mama. Be still like a good boy." She spreads carbolic salve over the bite and wraps clean strips of bandage around Albert's sturdy leg.

"I better rock him to sleep now," she says, lifting Albert to her hip. "I'll go out to the front porch if you don't mind."

Anna puts the medicines away and cleans up the table. She goes to the big cookie jar on top of the Hoosier and takes out a handful of Maddie's oatmeal cookies. "Wally, you and Cliff go play on the screen porch. Don't go back out in the yard today. One dog bite is enough."

An hour later, Anna hears the doorbell and hurries to the front of the house to find a sheriff's deputy on the porch.

"Afternoon, Miz Sanderson," he says, touching the brim of his hat.

"Good afternoon, deputy. What can I do for you?"

"There've been several reports of a dog gone wild hereabouts, ma'am, and I wanted to warn you about it. I know Mrs. Kirby's little boys are living with you now, and I don't want them to get bit. It's Judge Pruitt's dog. You know, that little brown fice. He plays with all the young'uns around and never bit one before that we know of. But he bit several this morning, and Dr. Baucom is saying that everybody who got bit has to come to the hotel. They think that dog may have rabies."

"Oh, no." Anna looks beyond the deputy to the rocker where Maddie is holding her sleeping son. "We did have a child bitten. Maddie's little boy." She nods toward the side of the porch as the deputy looks at Maddie. "You say all the children who were bitten are supposed to go to the hotel. Why?"

"Well, ma'am, if that dog has rabies, every one of 'em could die. So Dr. Baucom has sent one of our men to the hospital in Raleigh to get some vaccine. The young'uns have to get shots."

Anna looks back at Maddie. "Well, we'd better get down there. Albert will need a shot."

The deputy takes off his hat and runs it around in his fingers. "I don't know about that, Miz Sanderson. They ain't gonna let no colored children go in there. That hotel's for white folks."

"But Albert's been bitten. He'll have to be treated."

"Well, you can take him to the hospital in Goldsboro, Miz Sanderson. They got a ward for the nigras."

Anna calls to Wally and Cliff. When they reach the door, she takes them by the hand and walks past the deputy to where Maddie is standing. "Come on, Maddie," she says, leading the group down the walk and into the street.

The porch of the hotel is full of curious townsfolk and the relatives of dog-bite victims who can hardly believe the much-loved Buster could have done such a deed. Anna pushes her way through the crowd and opens one of the hotel's double screen doors. A rough-looking sign is tacked to the center post in the lobby, DOG BITES UPSTAIRS. As she and Maddie and the boys pass the barbershop, Zeb Troxler emerges, his dingy barber's apron covered with fine black hairs, a pair of long scissors in his right hand. Zeb is older now, heavy of jowl and belly, but time has not mellowed him.

"Jest a minute," he says, looking at Maddie. "You can't go up there. Ain't no nigras allowed in my hotel." Stretching out a well-muscled arm, he motions toward the front door. "You and that young'un better get on out of here, gal."

Anna leads Cliff and Wally to a dusty sofa and sits them down. Then she steps in front of Zeb. "Maddie's boy's been bitten. He needs attention."

"Well, he ain't gonna get it here," Troxler spits. "They's a passle of white young'uns upstairs, and you know ain't no coloreds allowed in here, Miz Sanderson."

"I know you don't take in colored guests, Mr. Troxler. This is a baby. And he's been bitten by Judge Pruitt's dog."

"Don't matter." Troxler turns and points the scissors at Maddie. "You ain't taking no nigger baby upstairs." He raises the scissors to eye level. "You hear me, don't you?"

Anna takes Albert from Maddie's arms. Resting him securely on her hip, she walks toward the steps, turning back to look at Zeb. "I believe my husband and I own this building, don't we, Mr. Troxler? And I believe you're behind on your lease payment. Isn't that right?" She mounts the stairs and turns to Maddie. "You take Wally and Cliff home now. I'll let you know if I need anything."

The dark hallway at the top of the landing smells of stale urine, cheap hair tonic, and dead mouse. Anna stands in the doorway of the railroad worker's dormitory-like room with Albert in her arms and looks at the dozen mothers who sit on cots holding their crying children. Dr.

Baucom is making his way among them. He stands over a tow-headed lad with ragged overalls whose bare pigeon-toed foot is wrapped in a ragged dishtowel. The little boy looks up and his pale eyes meet hers. "Look," he says, pointing a grimy finger. "A tar baby."

All eyes turn toward Anna as she comes across the room with Albert in her arms. Dr. Baucom leaves his patient. "Mrs. Sanderson, what are you doing here?"

"This little boy's been bitten by Judge Pruitt's dog. The sheriff's deputy told us that the children who were bitten were to come here, Dr. Baucom." Several of the mothers rise from their cots, huddling nearby, eager to hear the conversation.

The doctor takes Anna's arm and leads her to the far end of the room. "You know you can't bring that colored child in here with these white children, Mrs. Sanderson."

Anna holds Albert out from her body and raises his leg toward the doctor. "You can take a look at him right here, right now. We cleaned the wound and dressed it. Isn't that enough?"

The doctor scratches his head. "It don't look like it. These young'uns say Buster was acting funny, kinda skittish and snarly. That scares me 'cause he may be rabid. All these young'uns," he raises his arm and sweeps the room, "all these young'uns are going to have to be quarantined for the next three weeks."

"You mean isolated, doctor?"

"Yessum. And the only place to do it is right here. It's the only place in town that's big enough. You see, I'll have to come every day and give each child a shot, a vaccine to ward off the rabies."

Anna has seen rabid animals before and remembers the effects of hydrophobia—the nausea, swelling, and ravings of its victims. "These children will have to stay here in this room for the next three weeks," Dr. Baucom continues, "and someone, an adult, will have to be with each one of them night and day. You can't stay here, Mrs. Sanderson. Not with that boy."

"We pay taxes in this town just like everyone else," Anna reminds the doctor. "And my husband and I own this building. I intend to stay here with this child, and you'll have to treat him just as you treat all the others." She turns to the front of the room where a half-dozen windows are lined in lop-sided symmetry. "I'll sit down up there away from the crowd and wait for you."

"You'll be sorry, Mrs. Sanderson. Folks ain't gonna like that boy being here one bit. But I know I ain't gonna get you to change your mind, am I?" The doctor shakes his head before he shuffles back toward the group in the middle of the room.

Anna puts Albert on a cot, where he curls up in a ball and goes to sleep. She sits down on a chair near the windows and looks back at the room's occupants. She knows many of the women and recognizes several children who play with Wally and Cliff. There is a mother and daughter who go to her church, and another mother whom Anna met at a school play. Several went to school with Evelyn and Claire. They stare openly at her and steal glances at Albert.

Dr. Baucom makes his way down the row of narrow cots and finally gets to Albert's. Unwrapping the bandage, he takes a look at the bruised punctures left by Buster's sharp teeth.

"Carbolic salve, eh? Well, you did the right thing." He redresses the wound and covers it with a thin patch of snowy gauze. "If you're determined to stay up here, Mrs. Sanderson, you stay as far away from these other people as possible. They're upset, and they don't want you and that boy up here. I hope he don't cry much."

"Don't worry, doctor. We'll keep to ourselves. Why don't you hang a sheet or a blanket up here beside the bed? That way, they won't have to look at us." Anna says this in a voice loud enough to be heard by the curious onlookers at the other end of the room.

"Not a bad idea." Dr. Baucom removes a rolled-up blanket from the foot of the cot and hangs it across a low beam that runs the width of the room. "The sheriff should be back by now with the vaccine. I'm going down to check."

Anna settles into a chair beside Albert's cot. Spreading her hands across her knees, she looks at the pattern of blue veins stretched across each one. She takes a moment to study her delicate fingernails, now brittle and thin, and thinks about the hours she spent as a girl buffing and filing them, and the care she always took to see that her hands were soft and unlined. I wonder why we spend so much time grooming ourselves, she thinks, as if all that care makes any difference. The only thing that matters now is that both of my hands are intact, they're still working. Thank God I'm not plagued with arthritis or some horrible skin disease like so many women my age. I've been luckier than most, she thinks. I've had three healthy children and a husband who's been a good provider, for all his other faults. And I've got my health.

She hears heavy footsteps in the hallway. Two sets. They continue down the aisle between the cots, coming toward her at a rapid pace. Dr. Baucom slings the blanket back, and Anna sees Sheriff Brown behind him.

"We've got the vaccine," he announces. "I've told the sheriff that you're determined to stay up here with this boy." He turns to look back at his companion. When the sheriff says nothing, he continues. "I'm going to start with you, Mrs. Sanderson, so the other young'uns won't see this and start yelling. Pull up his shirt and clean his little belly with this swab." He hands Anna a large wad of cotton that smells of alcohol.

"Clean his belly, doctor?"

"Yes. I have to give the vaccine just below the navel."

Anna rolls Albert onto his back. He stares sleepily at her as she rubs the damp cotton across his stomach. The doctor takes several bottles from the sheriff and puts them in his bag. He sets the bag on a nearby table and takes out the longest needle Anna has ever seen. She winces as he turns toward her, the needle poised in the air. "You'll have to hold him really still. It takes a minute or so for the vaccine to go in 'cause the needle's so long. It has to go in real deep, you see." He moves toward the bed. "Sheriff, you hold his legs, and Mrs. Sanderson, you take his arms." Anna moves to the head of the bed and holds Albert's arms, while the sheriff puts his hands over the little boy's fat knees. Albert begins to whimper. "Here we go," says the doctor.

It is the same for each of the other children. For all of Dr. Baucom's precautions, many scream at the sight of the large needle and continue to howl until they finally wear themselves out and fall asleep. Afterwards, Anna holds Albert in her arms, singing softly to him until he dozes off. Then she lies down across one end of the cot and sleeps for a couple of hours.

She is awakened at dusk by a Negro woman who cleans at the hotel. "Your girl," she whispers to Anna, "she say for you to come down and get the supper she done fix for you. You run on now. I stay here and sit by this little one."

Anna finds that she is stiff from sleeping on the hard cot. She rises slowly, puts on her shoes, and pats the sides of her hair. She wants to wash her face, but she has nothing to wash with. Might as well get used to it, she thinks. You're going to be here for a while.

Maddie stands on the sandy sidewalk in front of the hotel with a brown paper sack in each hand. As soon as Anna steps out onto the porch, Maddie hurries toward her. "Oh, Miss Anna, I'm so sorry. So sorry you had to stay up there with my baby. Is he all right?"

"He's fine. He's sleeping now."

"The doctor come by this afternoon. Told me you're gonna have to stay at the hotel tonight. I brought you some supper and some stuff you might need to spend the night."

"How thoughtful. Yes, I'll have to stay up there with Albert, and not just for tonight. The doctor says it will be quite a while before any of the children can go home. He thinks the dog may have had rabies."

"Oh, law," Maddie cries. "Rabies!"

"Do you know about rabies, Maddie?"

"Yessum. My daddy had to kill one his possum hounds one time. Got bit by a coon. Next day, started acting funny. Got real foamy 'round the mouth and showing his teeth. My daddy, he had to shoot him."

"The doctor says all the children will have to stay here for the next three weeks. They're quarantined."

Maddie eyes fill with tears. "You mean I'm not gonna see my baby for three weeks, Miss Anna?"

"Yes, Maddie, that's what it means." Anna puts her hand on the brown girl's shoulder. "You look after Cliff and Wally and Mr. Sanderson. Please bring us something to eat each day. Albert's fine. All of the children and their mothers are in a big room upstairs. We have a nice bed to sleep on. The doctor will come every day, and," she hesitates, "and give Albert some medicine."

"He's not getting foamy 'round the mouth, is he, Miss Anna?"

"No, he's just fine. Now you go back home and feed that crowd of hungry boys. I'll let you know if I need anything." Maddie stands rooted to the sidewalk. "Don't worry now," Anna says. "Albert's going to be fine. You take care of my boys, and I'll take care of yours."

Anna takes the bags from Maddie and goes into the lobby, where she opens them. One contains several pieces of fried chicken, biscuits and jelly, a pint jar of milk, and a thermos of coffee. The other holds her nightclothes, a comb and a brush, a washcloth, a toothbrush and a small can of tooth powder, clean underwear, a *Ladies Home Companion*, and diapers and clean undershirts for Albert.

She returns to the blanket-enclosed area and thanks the woman who kept an eye on Albert. She feeds him fried chicken and milk while she picks at the same. Later, she tells him a story, and before long, he drifts off to sleep and so does she.

During the night, he cries, off and on, for his mother and rubs the bandage on his lower leg. Anna rocks him back to sleep each time. She supposes it is the same for the mothers on the other side of the blanket. Even though she cannot see them, she hears children whimpering throughout the night. At dawn, she goes to the bathroom down the hall and takes a "birdbath" at the sink and puts on fresh underclothes. After taking down her long white hair, she brushes it until her scalp tingles. She pulls it tight against her temple and twists it into a ball on the back of her head. Thank the Lord no one will see me up here, she thinks, cramming her used underthings into a bag.

For breakfast, she feeds Albert a biscuit and some milk. She sips the last of the stale coffee from her thermos and listens to the conversations of the other women in the room. Someone brings in fresh doughnuts and passes them around. She hears the delighted shrieks of the white children and wonders at Albert's contentment. He obviously smells the doughnuts and he knows the other children are having them, but he never asks for one. When he finishes his biscuit and milk, Anna washes his face and hands. He climbs onto her lap and she reads to him from her magazine, pointing out pictures of people, cars, and animals in an effort to keep his attention.

Dr. Baucom arrives at nine and comes straight to Albert's cot. "We'll start here again," he announces without a *good morning* or *by your leave.* His nurse follows him into the blanketed enclosure, and Albert begins to whimper. He clings to Anna's neck, crying, "Mama, Mama." Anna puts him down on the cot, holds his arms, while the nurse holds his legs, and Dr. Baucom administers the vaccine with the horrible needle. Albert begins to wail. She knows the vaccine must be painful, and just the sight of the huge needle is terrifying, but the vaccine obviously contains a sedative, for soon all the children are asleep. Their exhausted mothers relax.

On the second night of the confinement, the women at Anna's church send pots of steaming chicken pastry, baked sweet potatoes, and gallons of iced tea to the dormitory. Soon, other churchwomen send toys, games, and books. Relatives of the victims bring cakes and pies, and other goodies, that make the constraints of quarantine less hateful. Maddie sends cookies by the dozens, and Claire contributes a dollar's worth of penny candy for all the shut-ins.

Late one afternoon near the end of the first week, Anna stretches out on the cot beside Albert and falls asleep. She awakens to find Emma Jenkins sitting in the chair beside her.

"Emma," she says, sitting up. "What are you doing here?"

"I came to relieve you," Emma replies.

"You can't come in here, Emma," Anna insists. "It's dangerous."

"Not for me, it isn't. I used to be a nurse. Remember? And I helped Dr. Baucom with lots of cases at the hospital. We had several patients who had been bitten by rabid animals. All of 'em lived through it."

Emma sets her pocketbook on the floor and takes the pins from her black straw hat. "Anyway, I went by Dr. Baucom's before I came here and told him I was going to come up here and relieve you."

"But, Emma, you can't do that. You've got your own children to look after."

"Birdie can look after 'em, Anna. He's able to cook and make the beds. He just can't plow anymore. So you go on home now and get yourself some supper and a good night's sleep. I'll stay here and watch out for this boy. Maddie told me his name's Albert. Same as my daddy's name." She stands up and takes Anna by the arm. "Run along now, honey. I'll be here when you get back in the morning."

"But, Emma. . . ."

"Never mind now," Emma says in her high, thin voice. "You leave this to me, Anna. Run along and get some rest. How else will you stand this for three weeks?"

* * * * *

Anna keeps her sanity in the stuffy dormitory room by writing long letters to Evelyn and Claire. She knits an afghan for Emma and works on the fancy quilt she intends to give Evelyn at Christmas. She reads all the books and magazines she can lay her hands on, and she nurses Albert, day and night. She totes a basin of water from the bathroom each morning and bathes him before the doctor arrives with the big needle. She reads to him, rocks him, and sits by the window with him on her lap, making up stories about life in the street below.

She sings to him and plays games with him. She holds him in her arms each night, and thinks about McLean and Millie, and the untold hours the small brown woman devoted to her helpless son during his thirteen years. Three weeks does not seem too much in comparison.

The quarantine comes to an end on Halloween. Dr. Baucom arrives a bit earlier than usual and, after administering the final shot to each patient, tells them they can go home. As Anna and Albert step off the hotel porch into the blazing sunlight of the late autumn morning, Maddie comes up the sidewalk, a broad grin spread across her face. "My baby, my sweet baby boy," she cries as Anna hands Albert to her.

Chapter 19:
My Thoughts And Feelings
December 25, 1932

Dear Diary,

Christmas is over and Albert and me had a good time. Miss Anna made what she calls a Lane Cake and fix ambrosia while I stuffed the biggest gobbler. I made oyster stew and Mr. Carl really liked it. Miss Millie come yesterday and we decorated this holly tree Fletcher brought from the farm. We put red ribbons and long strings of popcorn all over it and tiny paperdolls of the baby Jesus and Joseph and Mary and lambs and kings. Then Miss Anna clipped little candles to the branches and everybody sang "O Little Town of Bethlehem" and "Silent Night." Miss Evelyn is home from New York. She so pretty it take your breath away. She brought all these fancy presents for everybody and she wears these shiny pajamaz right in front of the whole family and company to. She just loved the quilt me and Miss Anna made for her and she come to the kitchen when she opened it and give me a big hug. Miss Claire got a blue sweater and some nice underwear. Mr. Carl give her boys a little toy train on a track. He give Miss Anna a fancy pin with a diamond and blue stones. She told me it was a broach and she spelled it for me. Miss Anna knit a sweater for Albert and give him a old sock full of candy canes and oranges. She give me a pair of gloves. First pair I ever had. And a new black coat. Miss Evelyn gave Mr. Carl and Miss Anna a picture of her that was in a magazine. She's holding up this glass ball, and has on this real short dress. Her hair is all curled round her face and she got roses in it. Down at her feet is this bottle with a moon on it and the word ETERNITY. It's perfume. She give me a little sample for Christmas and I like it. Miss Anna told me Miss Evelyn is a model in New York and that she makes a living letting people take her picture to sell stuff. She talks a lot but she real nice.

277

Miss Anna give me this book that says Diary on the front. She said I should write down things that happen and my thoughts and feelings. It will help me with my grammar cause I want to do better so I can teach Albert when he gets bigger.

The main thing I'm thinking about is Daniel. I wonder where he is on Christmas and if he has turkey to eat and warm gloves to wear. Does he miss me like I miss him? Does he miss his boy? Albert's gone to sleep in his own little bed. Me and him are staying in the big house now in what Miss Anna calls her dressing room. He got a youth bed and I got a day bed and Miss Anna put a nice old chest in here for us and the rug and quilt out the washhouse. I got to go to bed now. We had a happy day but I'm tired.

* * * * *

January 1, 1933

Dear Diary,

Happy New Year. I hope 1933 is better than 1932 for Albert and me. Maybe Daniel will come back and find us this year. Mr. Carl give a big party last night and folks come from all around the county. Miss Anna dressed up in this lace evening gown and her new pin and Miss Evelyn wore some of those pajamaz and smoked this long black thing that look like a pencil. Me and Miss Anna got out the silver and I made lots of little sandwiches and ham biskits. Fletcher came to help us. He wore this white jacket and Miss Anna put a flower on the collar. Some handsome. He took out big trays of champagne. Miss Anna spelled that for me. I saw some men point at him and laff. But he just smiled and kept on passing. Miss Millie came to help us to but she stayed in the kitchen on account of them scars on her face, I reckon. Miss Claire played the piano and Miss Evelyn sang all these sad songs about the man she love. Made me think of Daniel. Then Miss Claire played that happy days song they play on the radio for Mr. Roosevelt and Mr. Carl got real mad and told her to stop. Every body went home after that.

* * * * *

January 18, 1933

Dear Diary,

Today is Albert's birthday and he's 2. We had a party this afternoon in the kitchen with a nice cake Miss Anna made. Miss Millie and Fletcher came and we sang the birthday song before we ate it. Miss Anna gave Albert a set of blocks with letters on them. She said they belonged to her boy McLean who died. Wally and Cliff gave Albert a book with dogs, cats and horses in it. I gave him a little truck. Red with yellow wheels. Miss Millie brought Albert this little bird made out of wood she said her daddy carved. Its real pretty and I don't want Albert to play with it. We got a snow last night so I took Albert, Wally, and Cliff out to play. We made a little snowman and they named it Daddy Charles. Guess they miss their pa the same way I miss Daniel. I hope where he is there is not to much snow and he has warm clothes like Albert and me. Wish he could see his boy on his birthday, growing so fast.

Me and Miss Anna made soup this morning. Two big pots from beans and corn and tomatoes we canned last summer and we put in lots of ham for strength Miss Anna said. We took it to Miss Anna's church at dinner time. Lots other ladies was there. Some brought soup and some brought cornbread and pots of boiled taters and pinto beans. Folk was already lined up at the back door holding big jars and empty buckets like sirup comes in. They looked sad out in the snow with them skinny children hanging onto their legs so hungry their eyes looks weak. Most all the folk who came was women and I sure feel sorry for them standing in the yard shaking cause its so cold. I thank the Lord every day that I found this house and got a job and Albert and me ain't out in the cold. Wonder if Daniel is at some church house begging for his dinner?

* * * * *

February 14, 1933

Dear Diary,

Miss Anna and me went out to the farm to see Miss Millie cause she sick. Fletcher don't know what to do. Miss Anna took a big pot of chicken soup and heated it over the fire. Then she fed Millie who say she got mizery in her chest and she coffed a lot. She told Miss Anna she can't stand up on count of she swimmy-headed. Miss Anna gave her a bath which was hard since Miss Millie can't get up. Then she rubbed her chest with salve and wrapped it in old rags she heated over the fire. We put a clean nightgown on Miss Millie and Miss Anna rubbed her feet and legs with this cream that smelled like roses. Miss Millie said she was so clean and smelled so good that she might as well go on to her maker and that she was ready. She asked Miss Anna to pray for her and Miss Anna tried but she was crying so hard she won't able to get a word out. She just kept saying hush Millie don't talk like that. And then Miss Millie took both Miss Anna's hands and held them and she said if you won't pray for me, honey, I'll pray for you. And she closed her eyes and her lips moved for the longest but I couldn't hear what she said. Miss Anna and me went home after that and she had a hard time steering because she was crying so much she couldn't hardly see the road. We had a lot to do because Mr. Carl had a party tonight for this man from Richmond called Mr. Grover. He come down here today on his own train and Mr. Carl invited some other folk for dinner. Miss Anna had this lady in Goldsboro make these little candies in the shape of hearts. I served red punch when they got here and Fletcher passed the heart shaped sandwiches me and Miss Anna made. We had ham because Miss Anna said we needed something pink. Mr. Carl and the men stayed a long time in the library after dinner and I had lots of empty glasses to wash from the likker they drank. They were talking business Fletcher said and he said they all hate Mr. Roosevelt. Mr. Grover asked Mr. Carl to bring me and Fletcher out from the kitchen after I served dessert and he gave each of us $5.00. I need the money but I don't see why he had to give it to us in front of every body.

* * * * *

February 26, 1933

Dear Diary,

Miss Millie is real sick. Miss Anna and me went out to the farm today cause Miss Louisa call and tell Miss Anna she's afraid Millie is going to die. Miss Anna said Millie has the influenza. She felt Miss Millie's head and set to sponge her off with some of Miss Louisa's alcohol. She told Fletcher to go to the house and tell Miss Louisa to call Doc Baucom. Then she sent him and me back to town to get buttermilk. She said that was what saved Mr. Carl when he was so sick back in the war time. I don't remember no war but I went with Fletcher cause I know where Miss Anna keeps the buttermilk. When we get back to the farm Miss Anna told us to lift Miss Millie out the bed while she changed the covers. Then she put them sheets in a big pot in the yard and told Fletcher to boil them and stir them with a stick. She told him to keep the place as clean as he can and give Millie all the buttermilk he can get in her. When the doc got there he gave Miss Millie a shot and a bottle of big yellow pills. He said she got a bad case. Might have to put her in the hospital. Millie cry like a baby when he said that. She beg Miss Anna not to take her to the hospital. That sure scared me. Never been in no hospital. After the doctor left Miss Anna and me went up to Miss Louisa's house and Miss Anna called on the telephone and talked to a man about putting electricity in the cabin. She spelled it for me. The man coming out to do that tomorrow. Tonite when Miss Anna told Mr. Carl he got real mad and said nigger ain't worth it. She say if he don't pay for it she will sell some her jewelry and pay for it herself. She said it was so cole in that cabin at the farm it was a miracul Millie and Fletcher won't froze to death. Mr. Carl said folks stay warm when they working stead of sitting. Miss Anna go up to bed then.

* * * * *

March 4, 1933

Dear Diary,

Miss Anna and me listen to Mr. Roosevelt today on the radio. Miss Anna said it was his inauguration. She spelled it for me. Now he's president and he's going to make it easier for people. He said he would get jobs for people. You could hear folks clap real loud when he said that. He said we got to trade stuff with other folks and share. And he asked God to help him. Miss Anna's real happy about Mr. Roosevelt being president. She says we'll be able to tell a change now. Mr. Carl is mad because his man lost. Fletcher says most the folk he knows round town like Mr. Roosevelt. Fletcher asked me to go with him to church last Sunday and I did. The church is out at the farm. Its called Sanders AME Chapel for his grandmama and granddaddy Ludie and Tyner. It's white and has pretty wood floors. The benches is hard. Not much heat. The preacher said a prayer for Mr. Roosevelt and all the folk join in with him at the end. The preacher said the church needs teachers to teach folk how to read and write. He said lessons will be held at the church on Monday nights. Won't folk help their brothers and sisters rise above ignorance? Fletcher raised his hand and then he smiled at me. He asked me to come to but I'm to scared. He said you can do it. You write and read good. So I went with him tonite. Lots of folks come. Seven men and five women. First a man stood up and said he don't see how learning to read is going to help him with his crops. He said the land all wore out and he ain't got no money for no fertilizer. Then this other man who is real dark stood up and said he wanted to learn how to write so he can write a letter to the white men what runs the schools. He said it ain't fare for the white young'uns to get to go to school so long each year and the colored get to go only a little while in winter cause they got to work in the fields. He's tired of bowing and taking off his hat every time he sees a white person on the street and then his chilren don't have enuff clothes and no learning. Then this woman said Mr. Roosevelt going to change that. He's going to help colored folks get on their feet. But that man said he don't believe it. He said ain't no white man ever done nothing for no colored man and he ain't specting much. Then the preacher gave everybody a piece of paper that already had writing on one side and tells them to turn it over. He gave them a pencil to. Then he started to draw big letters on a board. Everybody drew the letters he drew. Then he asked me to tell them a word that starts with the letter he wrote. We go thru all the letters like that. Then everybody sang Gonna Have A Little Talk With Jesus and went on home.

* * * * *

March 12, 1933

Dear Diary,

Mr. Carl locked himself in the library today and won't let no body in. Miss Anna is real nervous. She told me to take the boys down to the drugstore for ice cream and for a long walk. We stayed out the house most of the afternoon because Miss Anna is real worried about what Mr. Carl might do. Some men from Raleigh done come down here and close up the bank. Run Mr. Carl and the men that works for him right out. Fletcher said Mr. Carl is in trouble cause he done lots of things that ain't right like when he close down on Miz Jenkins and widows and poor folks. Fletcher said Mr. Carl asked him to find some colored men to work his farms but Fletcher couldn't find none because they all scared of Mr. Carl. Say he got the devil in him. Wild look in his eyes. Don't tell folks the truth and can't never be found if you need him. Sound like old colonel Lyles boy what run us off the place on the river. Guess that kind is all over. I fix Mr. Carl a tray of fried eggs and ham this evening because he loves that. But he don't touch it. I know he's drinking in the library. Miss Anna in her rocker in the setting room darning his socks. She tried to talk to him through the door tonight but he don't answer her. She came up to bed and I heard her walking the floor for the longest.

* * * * *

April 3, 1933

Dear Diary,

Miss Anna and me work in the flower garden today where her tulips are so pretty. Purple, pink, yellow and red. Miss Anna got about a hundred. Fletcher came and helped us trim the rose bushes. He brought Miss Millie with him because the weather was so nice and she is better. He told Miss Anna what a fine job I was doing helping folks at the church read and write. I said I can do it because Miss Anna is helping me learn. She is teaching me to spell hard words. Miss Emma Jenkins come to call on Miss Anna this afternoon. They go sit on the side porch and Miss Anna asked me to bring them some tea. Then I stayed in the kitchen and work on supper. Miss Emma told Miss Anna those men from Raleigh came to see her and asked her about Mr. Carl closing down her farm. She said those men said Mr. Carl did a bad thing and that she is going to get her farm back. She said everybody in town is talking about how all the money they had in the bank is gone now and that everybody thinks Mr. Carl took it. Miss Anna said Mr. Carl don't have it. Then Miss Emma sipped her tea. She said I have something unpleazant to tell you, my dear. I hope you won't hold it against me. I saw Carl at the hotel in Goldsboro last week having dinner with a woman in the dining room. A redhead. They were drinking champagne. Birdie and I went by to see his old maid aunt who lives there. I'm so sorry I have to be the one to tell you, my dear. Miss Anna got up then. She just opened the screen door and I heard her go on down the steps. Miss Emma just set on the porch. I went on out there and asked if she needed anything. She got up and went on out the door but Miss Anna won't nowhere in site. Tonite she stayed in her room. I took a tray up to her but she won't eat a thing. How come everybody got to mind Miss Anna's private business? How come her old friend got to take it on herself to bring the bad news? I wish Miss Emma would stay home.

* * * * *

April 11, 1933

Dear Diary,

Miss Anna's yard is something to see. All the dogwoods and azaleas so pretty. Look like a fairy land. Miss Anna made this big bouquet for Miss Millie's church for Easter. A big silver vase like thing full of dogwood blossoms she put in it for our Lord's suffering on the cross and his ascent into heaven. She spelled that for me and told me why dogwoods are so special. I went to church on Easter with Miss Millie and Fletcher and took Albert. We had dinner with them in the cabin and then Fletcher played with Albert in the yard. Albert is crazy about Fletcher and runs to meet him every time he sees him and grabs him around the legs. Fletcher is real nice but I wish Albert could be with his own daddy. Miss Anna told me about her boy who died. His name was McLean and he was a cripple. Miss Anna showed me some pictures of him and Miss Claire and Miss Evelyn when they was little. He was sitting in this funny chair with big wheels on it. She got out a box that had this pretty white baby dress in it and told me Miss Millie had made it for her son to wear in church. He never did wear it she said because he was to sick but Miss Claire and Miss Evelyn did. It is so beautiful with tiny tucks all up and down the front and lace on every one. It has little flowers sewed at the tops of the sleeves with ribbons hanging down each arm. Looks like something for a girl baby instead of a boy. Miss Millie sure can sew. Even better than Mama.

Mr. Carl is at the bank now. He is quiet but he's still mad. Lots of men come by of a evening to see him. Miss Anna calls them directors. They go in the library and talk. Miss Anna asked me to see if they want coffee but they don't. They're drinking hard stuff. Too many folk drinking these days. Miss Anna and me went to Smithfield last week and I saw a white man trade bottles of whiskey with some colored men who gave him their ration stamps for food. All kinds of things be given away now. Miss Anna and Miss Claire went to the movies last night and they were selling dishes there. Miss Claire got a salad plate for 25 cent. White with pink flowers. Miss Anna got one like it and she gave it to Miss Claire because Miss Claire wants a whole set. Miss Claire said they call it dish night at the movies. Fletcher told me his was going to take me and his mama to a movie next week.

* * * * *

May 21, 1933

Dear Diary,

Trouble live in this house these days. Mr. Carl got a visit from some men Miss Anna called a banking commission. She spelled it. They came here three days last week and put Mr. Carl on the hot seat. Fletcher said he thinks they might close the bank and maybe even sell it. He says Mr. Carl stole farms from poor folks like Miss Emma and sold them and kept the money for hisself. Sound kind of stupid to me. Mr. Carl had a accident after the bank men left and run his car off the road into a ditch. He cracked his head open pretty bad above his right eye. Some boys brought him home and his face was all covered with blood when he got here. You could smell the likker all over him to. He wouldn't go to the hospital and when Miss Anna tried to wash his cut eye, he pushed her into the wall and told her to leave him alone. Miss Anna sent me for Doc Baucom and he came and sewed up the cut above Mr. Carl's eye. As soon as he left, Mr. Carl went in the library and slammed the door and didn't come out all night. I sure will be happy when Miss Claire comes home so she can help out with her boys. All this is a big mess and we got our hands full.

* * * * *

June 5, 1933

Dear Diary,

Miss Anna and me went out to the farm today to help Miss Millie pick peas and dig potatoes. We had to take Miss Millie back to the cabin not long after we got there because she didn't feel good. Those scars on her face get real shiny when she gets hot. I know they must hurt her something awful. Miss Anna made Miss Millie lie down and she fanned her for a while and then rubbed her legs and arms with alcohol.

Miss Claire come and got her boys last week. They went up to a place called Black Mountain with Miss Bethany and Mr. Bryson and their family. They are on vacation Miss Anna said for a month. She spelled it for me but I don't know what it is. Miss Claire got a letter from Mr. Charles telling her he joined this thing called the CCC. He left on a train with all these other men and went out west to this place called Idaho to work for the government. The men in the CCC live in a camp and they get three free meals a day. He told Miss Claire that he will send his paycheck home to her each month. She cried all day and Miss Anna patted her and patted her and said hush now Claire it could be a lot worse at least he has a job again. I wonder if Daniel is in a CCC camp. Miss Claire is going back to teach again next year in Raleigh and me and Miss Anna will keep Wally and Cliff again. Mr. Carl went to Raleigh real early this morning. Fletcher told me he had to answer some questions for that banking commission. He's mighty quiet these days in and out of this house but never staying very long. Long enough to eat and sleep is all. Him and Miss Anna don't talk much. She lets him go his way and don't say nothing. She said he has never had any dissapointments Maddie and he doesn't know what to do. I think its more than that and I know she knows just what happened but he is her husband so what can she do. I wonder how I would feel if Daniel stole money from people. The bank has been closed for two weeks now and Fletcher says it might not be open again for a long time and that they might send Mr. Carl to prison.

CHAPTER 20:
HARVEST

October 8, 1933

"That was Fletcher on the phone," Anna says as Maddie enters the kitchen carrying a bowl of raw chicken. "He asks if we could come out to Sand Hill this afternoon and clean the cemetery. He was going to do it, but the preacher needs him at the church. Millie is afraid people will come by the cemetery to see Ludie and Tyner's graves after they leave homecoming tomorrow."

"Why would they do that, Miss Anna?" Maddie removes a large black skillet from the wall beside the stove and spoons lard into it.

"Oh, there's always somebody from the homecoming service at Sanders AME who goes by the cemetery to pay their respects to the founders. Sort of a tradition, I suppose. I told Fletcher we would go out there about two, and he said he would come by the cemetery and get Albert so he could play with the other children at the church. I sure do hope it's cooler tomorrow."

Maddie rolls a chicken leg in flour. "I can't wait to see Miss Millie's face when the preacher makes that announcement about it being Millie Sanders Day and gives her that fancy plaque. She sure is going to be surprised, isn't she?"

"Yes. And embarrassed, I'm afraid. Millie doesn't like to be singled out. Those scars . . . But she is the oldest member of the church, and I'm glad I'll be there to see it happen."

"Think we can get those pies baked before we go?"

"I don't see why not. I'll roll out the crusts as soon as I put the sweet potatoes in the oven. Don't let me forget to put that new lace collar on Millie's dress. I promised I would press it and take it out to her before bedtime. Did I tell you she bought a new hat?"

"She showed it to me yesterday. Put it right on her head and paraded around the room like a peacock." Maddie giggles and pauses to take a sip of water. "Don't tell her I said so, but my mama always said pride was a sin. Miss Millie can't be having no sin, especially when she's the one the church is gonna say is perfect in the eyes of the Lord."

* * * * *

Anna and Maddie find Fletcher and Millie waiting in his truck when they arrive at the cemetery. Maddie helps Millie out and hands Albert to Fletcher, who tells her, "Don't you worry now. I'll keep an eye on him. See you all in about an hour." He puts the truck into gear and starts off again, with a grinning Albert standing on the seat beside him.

"Law, he's gonna spoil my boy to death," Maddie says, shaking her head. "Next thing you know, Albert'll be driving that truck." After taking Millie's arm, she walks her through the cemetery's wrought-iron gate to one of the benches Anna added after Adaire died. "You sit here, Miss Millie," she says, "and keep us company. I'll help Miss Anna get some things from the car."

Anna brings two of the half-dozen bronze and yellow chrysanthemums she and Maddie dug up from her yard and puts them beside the front gate. Maddie follows with another that she places in front of Ludie and Tyner's double headstone. Anna takes one over to the large cedar tree where a carved lamb marks the cemetery's oldest grave, that of John Sanderson, Jr., born and buried in August, 1845. Just beyond it, she sets another flower at the foot of McLean's grave.

The last bloom she puts between the graves of her father-in-law and the new mound of fresh dirt that is the resting place of her mother-in-law. Louisa, who has been dead a little more than a month, had succumbed in the blazing heat of late August to a massive heart attack. Following his mother's funeral, Carl drank himself into a stupor, and the next day had gone on a binge and not come home for two weeks. When he returned from God knew where, for Carl remembered nothing, Anna enlisted Robert's help, and the two of them finally convinced Carl that he needed serious treatment. After a meeting with Doc Baucom, Carl admitted himself to a hospital in Asheville. He has written Anna only once in the three weeks since he left.

Robert, who served as executor of Louisa's estate, had divided the remaining assets among the five children, and Anna has come to the hard realization that Carl's small share of the farm is all they will have to live on the rest of their lives. The Bank of Baker is closed permanently with her inheritance lost in the debacle, and the Sanderson Cotton Mill is in receivership. Water over the dam, she thinks. We're all in the same boat now. She stares at the new shoots of grass that have begun to take hold in the black dirt atop Louisa's grave. From life to death, she muses. From death to life. That's how it is. Glancing at the two undisturbed plots that adjoin her in-laws, she sighs. One of these days, I'll be here, too.

Millie appears at Anna's side and puts a shaky hand on her arm. "Bless you for bringing those beautiful mums, honey. I was so worried that everything in this place would be bleak as winter this time of year, and I didn't have nothing at home I could bring to brighten it up. Now those folk who come here tomorrow will know we ain't ignoring our kin. They'll see for sure that we care about those that's gone before. Thank you." She turns toward Anna's car. "Got a rake with you? Maybe I could get up a few of these dead leaves."

"Why don't you just rest, Millie? You're going to have a busy day tomorrow, and we want you to be in tip-top shape. Did you get your pound cake made?"

Millie hesitates. "Yessum," she says after a moment. "Made it this morning. Got my ham sliced for the biscuits, too." She hobbles back to the bench and sits down.

"Gosh, this place is a mess," Anna fusses, grabbing at vines that have invaded the fence. She pulls furiously, extracting the tough shoots from along the front section. "And filthy," she adds, glancing at the lacy spider webs in each corner. "The leaves are beautiful this time of the year, and the sky is so blue, but things somehow get dirtier in the fall."

Maddie begins collecting broken tree branches that lie scattered over the graves. "I always liked the fall when I was growing up," she says. "After the crops were in, we'd have this big corn shucking, and the folk would get together and make that shucking go so fast. Then we'd have a laying-out kind of supper with all this food. Somebody always had a fiddle and a banjo, and they would play while us young'uns whooped around doing the buck. Old Mrs. Lyles would let us gather all the pumpkins, and she'd give us one or two, and my mama would make pies." Maddie straightens up, a bundle of branches in her arms.

"Some good times," she says, staring out across the surrounding fields of billowing cotton.

"Millie wrote a poem about fall one time," Anna says. "That was a few years back, long before you were even born. Do you remember that poem, Millie?"

Millie nods. "I remember it, but I'm not sure exactly what I wrote." She dabs at her sweaty forehead with a handkerchief. "Been too long, Miss Anna."

"It's one of the best poems you ever wrote, Millie. You called it 'Harvest,' if I remember correctly," Anna prods. "Give us a few lines. It'll come back."

"I'll try," Millie says. She closes her eyes and, in a moment, begins to speak.

> The plow is resting 'neath the shed,
> Its blade is clean and sharp.
> The cornfield's empty, the cribs are full,
> The hay lies stacked beneath the tarp.
> Crocks of fruit, and jars of jam,
> Golden syrup and hominy corn,
> Are lined upon the cellar's shelves
> To warm us on a frosty morn.
> At harvest, you have blessed us, Lord,
> With food to fill our bowls,
> We bow our heads to say our thanks,
> And your spirit fills our souls.

Anna starts to clap, and Maddie joins her as Millie takes a little bow. "My pleasure," she says, smiling. "We've got so much to be thankful for. That's why we're gonna have a homecoming tomorrow."

"Ain't that the truth," Maddie adds. "We do have so much to be thankful for . . . all of us." She turns to look at Millie. "Tell me about the church. Do you remember when it was built?"

"Lord, child, I sure do. Finished it in 1870. I was about ten years old, I reckon. Daddy and my Uncle Ben had just finished making the pews for the new church Miss Adaire and her congregation had built. It was over near Bentonville, where her old church had been before the Yankees burned it down. Miss Adaire had this little piece of hilly ground that was covered in pine trees. Every time Daddy said something to her about clearing it and planting there, she told him no, they didn't have no need to plant that piece. Well, Mama got to thinking. If Miss Adaire didn't want to plant it, maybe she could talk her into giving it to them for the church. Well, Miss Adaire was one them people you don't never let know they got something you want. She would give you the shirt off'n her back as long as you didn't ask for it. So Mama waited. And every year when it was time to cut timber, she'd mention that stand of pines to Miss Adaire. Finally one day, Miss Adaire told Daddy she had decided to sell that timber and that he could have that piece of ground if he'd clear it. Mama said it took her five years to get Miss Adaire where she wanted her. So Daddy and Uncle Ben and my two brothers, Sam and Amos, started clearing it. Then Daddy bought some them pine trees he cut for Miss Adaire, and he sawed and planed them and started building." Millie pauses to wipe her sweaty face again. "Mighty hot, ain't it? You got any water with you, Miss Anna?"

Anna hurries over to the bench while Maddie pours some of the water they brought from home into a coffee cup. Anna holds it to Millie's dry lips. "We'd better get her to the car," she says to Maddie. "It's too warm for her out here."

Anna puts an arm around Millie's shoulder and tries to get her up, but Millie doesn't move. Her head lolls back onto Anna's arm, and her right hand moves toward Anna's face. It drops suddenly to her lap and lies trembling for a moment. Millie's eyes cloud as she looks up at Anna. "Is this my funeral?" she asks.

"No, honey," Anna says, shaking her head. "Why in the world would you ask that?"

" 'Cause it feels like it," Millie mumbles.

Anna looks over at Maddie. "Let's get her up to the cabin."

Maddie moves in front of Anna. "Let me," she says as she puts one arm under Millie's legs and the other behind her back. With little effort, she lifts the small woman and carries her to the back seat of the car. Anna jumps in front, puts the Cord in gear, and, in her haste to start, throws an arc of dirt along the cemetery's path. "Miss Millie's eyes is rolling back," Maddie whispers as Anna turns into the yard.

Maddie takes Millie into the cabin and puts her on the bed while Anna hurries to dip a cloth into a bucket of water. She wrings it out and folds it across Millie's forehead. "This is the bed she was born in," she says, looking down at the still figure lying beneath the walnut head-board Tyner made almost a hundred years before. "Millie," she calls. "Can you hear me?"

Millie's eyes open for a moment. "Yes, honey," she says. But her voice is small and weak.

Anna takes Millie's wrist and is frightened to find her pulse rac-ing. "Could you run get Fletcher, Maddie? There's a path through the woods to the church. It's right behind the cemetery beside that big pop-lar. You know where I mean?"

"Yessum," Maddie says as she hurries out the door.

Millie's eyes open again, and she tries to sit up, but Anna encour-ages her to lie back down, saying, "Be still, Millie. And rest." Millie's fingers pull at the neck of the dress she's wearing, and Anna unbuttons it. Then she goes to the end of the bed and carefully removes Millie's dusty shoes. Oh, God, it's so hot in here, she fusses. Her eyes scan the room until she sees a battered cardboard fan hanging on the opposite wall. A pastoral scene advertising a local funeral home holds her atten-tion for a brief moment before she grabs it and frantically begins mov-ing the warm air around Millie.

Millie stirs, mumbling something Anna cannot understand. Suddenly, she sits up. "Sam," she calls in a voice that sounds as if her mouth is filled with marbles. "You better come on, Sam."

"Hush, honey," Anna whispers. She takes Millie's hand and is alarmed to find it puffy and discolored by a blue tinge from wrist to fingers. "Oh, no," she mouths as she climbs onto the bed and takes Millie into her arms.

Without warning, Millie thrusts her head into Anna's chest cry-ing, "Mama? Is that you, Mama?" Raising her arm as if to wave, she calls "Mama" once more and slumps against Anna. A thin rush of air escapes her lips, and she is still.

Anna blinks. She puts a hand under Millie's chin and finds it cool to the touch and as flacid as putty. Her fingers caress Millie's swollen hand, and she brings it to her lips and kisses it.

Tears start down Anna's face. She tries to swallow the moisture that fills her mouth. "The Lord is my shepherd, I shall not want . . . ," she begins. Her throat continues to swell as waves of sobs force her into silence. She sits quietly in the still, close room, listening to the tick, tick, tick of Ludie's mantle clock. After a moment, she pulls a handkerchief from Millie's pocket and blows her nose. Her voice cracks as she stumbles over the opening line of "What A Friend We Have In Jesus," the first hymn the congregation would have sung on Sunday to honor Millie Sanders. But there will be no celebration tomorrow, Anna thinks. It will be a very sad day . . . and an even harder one will follow at Sanders AME on Monday. I suppose I'll have to put that new lace collar on her dress tonight so she can be buried in it. Oh, God. . . .

Anna looks down at Millie. "I love you," she whispers. "And I'll miss you very much." She lowers Millie's body to the bed and bends to press her mouth against the shiny blue scars that cover Millie's right cheek. "Take good care of her, Lord," she sighs.

A sackcloth curtain flutters at the small window above the bed, and Anna watches sunlight filter through, casting rays on the old plank table in the center of the room. I learned to make biscuits there, she thinks. That's where she taught me to make biscuits. And that pie plate hanging on the hearth is the one she used to teach me how to flute a crust. I hated cooking, but I loved watching Millie turn an ordinary thing into art. My lovely wedding dress, the debutant gown she made for Claire, all the dance costumes she created for Evelyn . . . each one so beautiful. And not once did she ever use a pattern. She thought I was the artist, but I had no talent compared to hers. Mine was simply the acquired lessons of a young woman of means. But hers was natural, heartfelt. . . . The plow is resting 'neath the shed . . . Its blade is clean and sharp. . . .

Anna stares at the picture hanging above the bed, the daisy picture she had painted and given to Millie so many years before. A smile plays on her lips as her mind goes back to a warm summer day so many years before when she had stood in the yard outside the cabin door with this unlettered and guileless woman. This shy, loving woman who bloomed into beauty when she said, "Don't tell nobody, but I write poems."

THE END

Epilogue

Thanksgiving Day, 1941

Dear Diary,

    I have not written for a long time now because I have been so busy. This has been about the best Thanksgiving I can remember and one of the best years of my life. I still cannot believe that Fletcher and I are married and that we have a beautiful baby girl. If Miss Anna hadn't gone over to see Judge Pruitt last May, and told him I was a grass widow, I don't think they would have let us have a license to get married. She told me because I had not seen Daniel for over 7 years, I was a grass widow and the law said I was now free to marry again. That sure was some good news. Never did feel right sneaking around behind the washhouse with Fletcher. But I sure liked his kisses and all the presents he brought me. I guess I've been in love with him for a long time, but I just couldn't bring myself to believe that I would never see Daniel again. But I don't feel guilty, dear diary, and I am about as happy as any woman can be. Got this precious baby girl we named Millie Ann for Miss Millie and Miss Anna. We are going to have her christened in the church here at Sand Hill Sunday after next, December 7th. She will be three months old that day. Miss Anna and I have been working on her christening dress, and it is so pretty with lots of tucks and ribbons. Miss Anna is making all these tiny pink satin roses to sew round the hem. Fletcher is real excited, and so is Albert, because we are having all the folk from the church over for sandwiches, punch, and cake afterwards. Fletcher and I have just about killed ourselves trying to get ready for the party. Now that we are living in Miss Adaire's old house, we have had so much to do. No one has lived here since Miss Louisa died in 1933. We had to scrub everything and put some new tin on the roof and new floorboards where there were leaks. We painted the living room and dining room a cream color, and our bedroom is pale yellow. Fletcher moved the old bed his Grand Pa Tyner made for Grand Ma Ludie into our bedroom. It is almost 100 years old and is this real pretty walnut.

And Miss Anna gave us the beds Albert and I slept on at her house for his room and Millie Ann's. She also gave us an old rocker that had been in the attic since Miss Adaire died a long time ago. We still have to paint the kitchen, and the floor of the front porch, and I hope we can get those things done before December 7th.

All this is coming right on the heels of Mr. Carl dying. He's been sick for years and I didn't expect him to just up and die so fast, but he had a stroke right after breakfast Tuesday before last and was dead before dinnertime. Young Dr. Baucom came, but he told Miss Anna there wasn't nothing he could do. I felt kind of sorry for Miss Anna because hardly any people came to the funeral. The ones that did were mostly her friends. She is living by herself now, and everybody is so worried about her rambling around alone in that big house. She told me that she has lost everything because Mr. Carl mortgaged all they had and then lost it. Even the house is mortgaged. But she has borrowed some money from her sister and brother-in-law in Raleigh, and has sold some of her jewelry, so she can pay it off. She told me last week that young Dr. Baucom had hired a new nurse and she didn't have anywhere to live, so Miss Anna is going to rent one of her bedrooms to this nurse. That way, she will have a little money coming in to help with expenses.

Miss Anna came out to have Thanksgiving dinner with us today. I was so afraid she wouldn't because Miss Evelyn called from New York yesterday morning to tell her that she had let go of her apartment and was sailing to England on a ship this Saturday. Miss Anna was very upset and begged Miss Evelyn not to go, but Miss Evelyn is determined to join the Red Cross and do something worthwhile, she said. When she was home for Mr. Carl's funeral, I heard her telling Miss Anna about how she had aged out of the modeling business, and that she was thinking about doing something really different. She talked about the war and Hitler, and all those poor people being bombed in England, and how she thought she would go there to try to help. I think Miss Anna thought she was just joking, but she must not have been. That really has upset Miss Anna. Upset her more than Mr. Carl's passing, if you ask me. She hasn't ever gotten over the fact that Miss Claire and Mr. Charles took their boys and moved to California four years ago. She says she is going out to see them on the train this spring. Things are so bad in Europe these days that I don't think she will be able to visit Miss Evelyn.

I fixed a hen today and some dressing and a sweet potato pie and got out some of Miss Anna's pickled peaches. It was cool, but sunny. Miss Anna is pleased because we are living at the farm, and she brought us some curtains she made for Millie Ann's room. White with pink and green flowers. Real nice. We talked a lot during dinner about the christening, and I tried not to say anything about Miss Evelyn cause I didn't want to upset her. After we had our pie and coffee, she told us that she had something important she wanted to show us. We cleared the table and she took this brown envelope out of her purse and spread out some papers and photographs. She looked over at Fletcher and took a deep breath and told him that she had some pictures and letters for him. The first picture was of Miss Millie with Grand Pa Tyner, Grand Ma Ludie, and this tall boy with light skin and curly hair. Then she told Fletcher that that boy was his father. She said his name was Joshua, and that Miss Millie was really his grandmother, and Joshua was her son. Fletcher did not say a word. He just kept looking at the boy in the picture and back at Miss Anna. Then Miss Anna took out another photograph. I knew right away who all the people in it were. Miss Adaire and the Colonel, and Mr. Carl and his mother and daddy, and all his brothers and sisters. I recognized all of them except this real pretty girl with white-looking hair. Miss Anna showed the picture to Fletcher and pointed to that girl and told him that she was his mother and that her name was Julia. Well, Fletcher got up from the table then and went over to the sink and got a glass of water. He didn't turn around for the longest time. Just stood at the sink drinking that water and looking out the window. Then he sat down again and asked Miss Anna how that could be. Then she told us that Julia was Mr. Carl's baby sister and that she and Joshua had grown up at Sand Hill together and had run away to Pennsylvania and gotten married in 1903. She showed us 3 letters that Joshua had written his mama, Miss Millie. In one, he told her that they had had a baby boy they named Fletcher and that Julia had died after the baby was born. Then Miss Anna told us that she was living at the farm with Miss Adaire and the Colonel after she and Mr. Carl were married, and that she saw Fletcher's Uncle Sam and Aunt Henrietta when they brought Fletcher to Miss Millie that Christmas. She said that

Joshua had brought him to Goldsboro on the train and had gone back to Pennsylvania and left him with Millie so she could raise him. Then Fletcher asked Miss Anna why Joshua did that, and Miss Anna said she wasn't sure, but she thought that he probably thought he couldn't raise Fletcher alone and he knew that Millie would raise him right. Then she told us that Joshua had been killed in the war in France in 1918. Fletcher kept wringing his hands and chewing on his lip. Then he slammed his fists down on the table and tears come in his eyes. He said Why didn't she tell me, Miss Anna? Why didn't Mama tell me this when I was growing up? Miss Anna shook her head and said she didn't know. Some things are just too painful, she told him. But you know Millie loved you more than anything on this Earth. She got up then, picked up her coat, and started for the door. Fletcher ran after her, took her hand, and told her how much he appreciated her telling him what she knew and how happy he was to have a picture of his parents. He watched her drive away and came back over to the table and sat down. He didn't get up the whole time I was washing and drying the dishes. Just kept staring at those old pictures and reading those letters over and over. And he didn't say a word until we were in bed. I went into Millie Ann's room and got her out of the cradle and took her into our room and told him to look at her. She looks like you, I told him. Got that same beautiful light hair and eyes as green as yours. Miss Anna said your mama had green eyes. Can't you see the resemblance, I said. She sure don't look like me, Fletcher. Guess you know that this means that Mr. Carl was your uncle and Miss Anna is your aunt. And Mr. Robert and Miss Hepsi are your folks, too. You been thinking all these years that you ain't got no kin but your cousins Willie and Christmas and their young'uns. Now you know you got all this other kin. He just looked at me like I was crazy. I took Millie Ann back to her cradle and went and got in the bed with Fletcher. You found out what you've been wanting to know, I said. And now you're living in the house where your mama grew up. We got so much to be thankful for, Fletcher. A fine son and a sweet baby girl. I reached out and touched his cheek. We got our own place now and we can go in and out the front door any time we like. Yeah, he answered finally. Ain't like messing around behind the washhouse, is it? I kind of miss that. Then he put his arm around me and turned out the light.

SOURCES

Bronson, Eve. *Companion Guide to Florence*. Harper and Row, 1966.

Fox-Genovese, Elizabeth. *Within the Plantation Household: Black and White Women of the Old South.* University of North Carolina, Chapel Hill, 1988.

Genovese, Eugene D. *Roll, Jordan, Roll: The World the Slaves Made.* Vintage Books, 1976.

Heritage of Wayne County, The. The Wayne County Historical Association, Inc. and Old Dobbs County Genealogical Society. Hunter Publishing, 1982.

Holy Bible, The. Revised Standard Version. Thomas Nelson & Sons. New York, 1952.

Hopkins, J.G.E., Ed. *Album of American History. Volume V.* Charles Scribner and Sons, 1960.

Jekel, Pamela. *Deepwater: a Novel of the Carolinas.* Kensington Books, 1944.

Joyner, Charles. *Down By the Riverside.* University of Illinois Press, 1984.

Lash, Joseph P. *Eleanor and Franklin.* Signet New American Library, 1971.

Lefler, Hugh T. *A History of North Carolina. Volume II.* Lewis Historical Publishing, 1956.

Luvaas, Jay. "Johnston's Last Stand--Bentonville." *The Battle of Bentonville.* State Department of Archives and History. Raleigh, N.C.

Peterson, Houston, Ed. *A Treasury of The World's Great Speeches.* Simon and Schuster, 1954.

Editors of Time-Life Books. *This Fabulous Century.* Volumes I - VI. Time-Life Books, 1970.

Williams, Ben Ames. *Time of Peace.* Houghton-Mifflin, 1942.

Wright, W. Aldis, Ed. *The Complete Works of William Shakespeare.* Volume I. Doubleday, Inc., 1970.